AN OCEAN LIFE

A Novel

T.R. Cotwell

Cover design: T.R. Cotwell
Cover photo by: Jedd Wasson

First Printing: May 2024
Benthic Press

ISBN: 979-8-9905837-1-9 (paperback)
ISBN: 979-8-9905837-0-2 (hardcover)
ISBN: 979-8-9905837-2-6 (e-book)

Printed in the United States of America
10 9 8 7 6 5 4 3 2 1

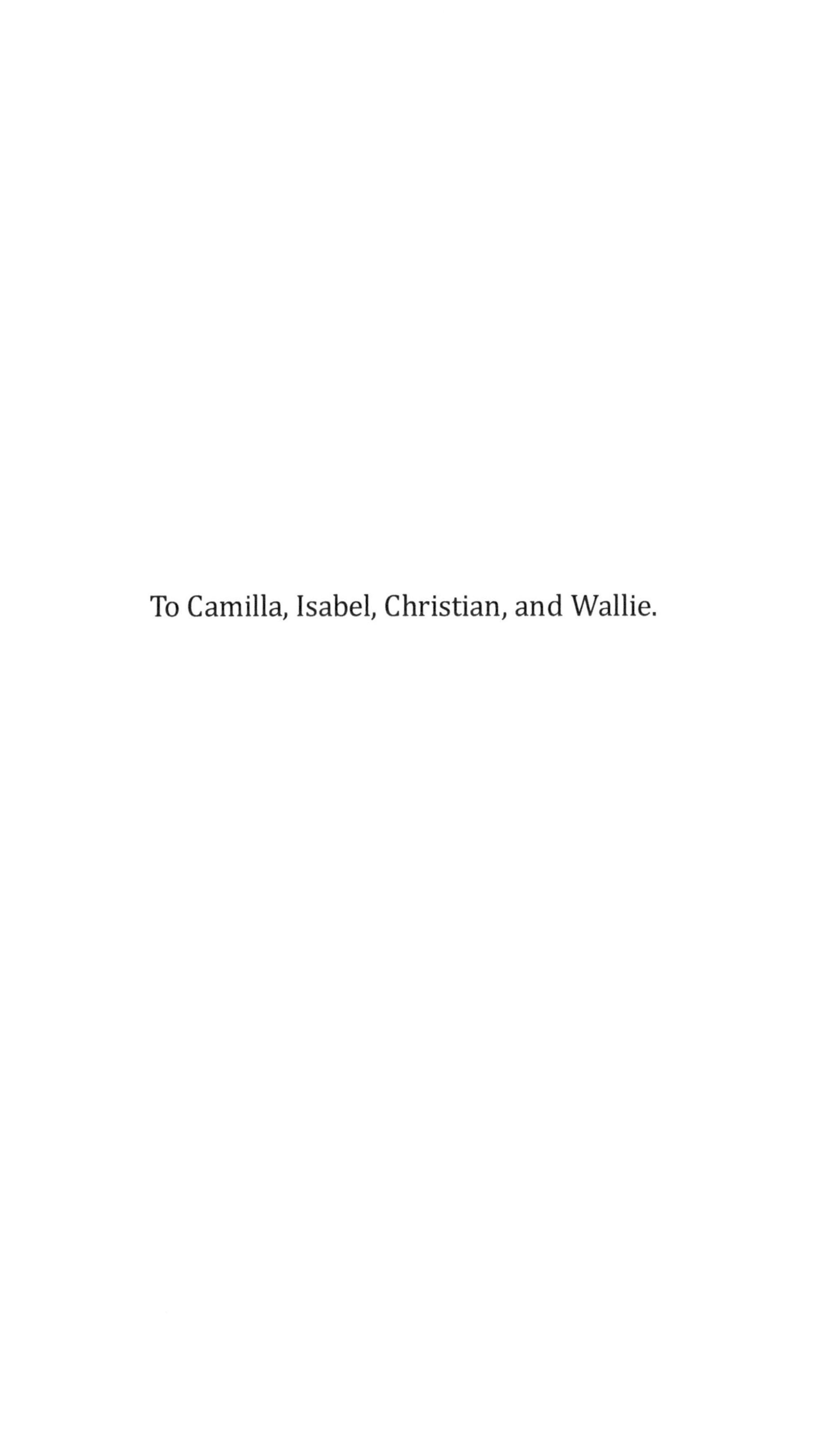

To Camilla, Isabel, Christian, and Wallie.

Prelude

The museum was eerily quiet today. Sarah was standing over a hundred feet from me, crouching at the base of one of the large parabolic "whisper" dishes designed to send and receive sounds over a distance. I stood at the other end of the long hallway, next to my dish. There were no fancy electronics such as microphones, amplifiers, or transmitters to help the signal along. It was unadulterated acoustics. This configuration was quite a step up from the methods from my childhood, where a string linked two empty soup cans. These dishes improved upon that method a thousandfold and only used the air between them as a transmitting medium.

From this distance, it was difficult to establish Sarah's intentions. She covered her mouth and whispered childish nonsense into the reflector, knowing full well I couldn't read her lips at this distance. I also crouched, leaning on one knee with my ear inches away from the focus point of the nearly eight-foot-diameter dish just behind me. To listen, I had to place my ear near the small ring defining the point where the captured sound waves converged, squeezing my nose and applying pressure to my eardrum to improve my hearing. Years of live concerts and a few bad scuba ascents had reduced my hearing range, with noticeable dropouts at those frequencies that nearly matched my spouse's voice when excited. I could clearly recall years ago when my ear doctor, upon examining my eardrum after I had punctured it for the third time, remarked how the surface of the thin membrane resembled an Austrian tapestry. Even at this distance, the dishes were quite effective in transmitting sound, despite my handicap.

I could clearly make out her whispers. "Daddy is giving me a laptop for Christmas," or "Papa is buying pizza tonight or else..." I could also hear Sarah's muffled giggling through the ether. There was also a barely audible tap-tap sound, some long and some short, followed by the requisite pauses, entering our communication. She was softly tapping on the disk. The evening discussions about oceans and the men who sailed them had sunk in. I began teaching Morse to Sarah a year ago. In the beginning, we treated it as a game, a form of secret communication between the two of us. Little did I expect her young mind to take to it with such fervor. Her command of Morse code had certainly improved, both in speed and accuracy of her tapping.

I replied to her with both voice and Morse. Despite her young age of thirteen, my daughter possessed a mischievous spirit. I tapped: *I want you to clean up your room and then we can talk about pizza.* Composing that snippet took great concentration and effort.

Sarah jumped up and feigned indignation, but a smirk quickly appeared on her face. I walked across the long, empty concrete space between us and requested her hand.

"What's that?" Sarah asked, pointing at a big floor model ahead of us.

"This, my sweet, is a three-dimensional model of our planet's largest ocean. Can you name it?"

"The Pacific," she replied with confidence.

Nearly fifty feet on each side and almost two feet deep, the three-dimensional scale reconstruction of the Pacific Ocean was impressive. From the looks of it, they had modeled the ocean floor after available bathymetric data. My guess was that it was constructed out of plaster and then painted different shades of blue along vertical surfaces according to depth. A thick piece of transparent polycarbonate represented the surface of the ocean, allowing one to walk over any part of it. The modeling of the Pacific seafloor was something to behold; Islands, atolls, trenches, and seamounts were carefully detailed. The Mariana Trench appeared, even at this scale, like an unforgivable place. I was also impressed by the reconstruction of the deep waters beneath the Golden Gate Bridge.

"Look at all the islands, rising like dimples to the surface. Amazing to see it in this perspective, wouldn't you agree?" I asked, to which Sarah responded by nodding. She walked over to the middle and pointed down toward the Hawaiian Islands.

"We're landing here on Maui, right?" she asked.

"Yes. Can you see the town of Kahului, situated between the volcano and the mountain? That's where we will land in a few days," I said.

"What are those small mountains beneath the water?" she asked.

"Those are seamounts," I answered. "Imagine an island that starts its life as a volcano deep underwater. It rises until it breaks the surface, like Hawaii, and then after some time the volcano dies, and the island sinks slowly back into the sea. Sometimes the volcanos never reach the ocean surface."

"There's a bunch of them near the big island," Sarah noted.

"If you look eastward, you can see a trail of them all the way to Baja, Mexico," I added.

"Like breadcrumbs."

"Funny you should say that. There are scientists who say that these ancient islands act as beacons for migratory fish and mammals, like sharks and whales," I said.

"How?" Sarah asked.

"These mountains might contain special metals or minerals

that sea life can detect and use for navigation. And memory might be involved. Do you ever wonder how birds can find their nests after flying some distance away? Kind of the same thing," I said, explaining as best I could to a young but curious mind. The explanation was slightly more complex, but the comparison made sense.

After we were done with the map, we walked beneath the wings of a large retired Caravelle, a recent addition to the museum's aircraft collection. With its unique teardrop-shaped windows and characteristic tail, the aircraft was a sweet remnant of a bygone era. Suspended on massive stilts, which left a clearance of several feet beneath the landing gear and the floor, the aircraft appeared as though still in flight. We walked past a loud compressor that pushed clean air into the aircraft's musty interior.

Cecilia and Amelia were just emerging from an adjacent exhibit, giddy smiles on both their faces. My wife discreetly pointed her finger at her youngest daughter, then pinched her nose with her fingers. Amelia laughed at her mother. The two sisters then ran off to the gift shop near the museum entrance, giving my wife and me a much-needed reprieve. Cecilia grabbed my arm and held me close.

"Your daughter has been crop-dusting for the past half hour. What did you feed her this morning?" she asked, looking mournfully at me.

I raised my gaze to the ceiling and rolled my eyes in fake surprise. "The usual weekend fare: omelet with peppers and onions, and some hash browns with onions and… Did I do something wrong?" I asked innocently.

Cecilia gave me a long look and said, "You realize she reacts quite odiously to onions. Much like a sweet person I know."

"I had no idea the repercussions would be so severe."

"You are such a liar, Mark," she scolded me half-heartedly.

We both blurted out, laughing, startling an older couple

passing by. "Let's get some coffee," Cecilia insisted.

We sat in the cafe for an hour, watching the girls run around in the museum's lobby, clearly annoying the lone museum guard on duty. The technical museum lay on the outskirts of one of the many industrial quarters that lined San Francisco. Retirees gathered here on weekends to fix old airplanes and build large train sets. It was a dusty old place, existing on the limited contributions from the public. Looking around, I saw only a few visitors, and it was midday Saturday. The thought that the museum's days were numbered saddened me. The girls loved coming here and exploring the museum's vast archive of little-known and desperately outdated mechanical things. The museum was becoming a living embodiment of ennui. Still, the museum and my outings with the family were a lovely distraction from the toil my work had become.

"You look relieved. A penny for your thoughts," Cecilia said to me.

I turned to face her.

"Yeah, I actually am. It's the first time in years," I replied. I was relieved, but in a partially committed way. Old habits die hard. I was still wrestling with work-related problems from the previous week. As my mind replayed the previous week's turmoil at the office, I could sense Cecilia's intense gaze weighing on me. I had promised her I would focus on family, and only family, as we were preparing for some time off.

"I'm a little worried that you won't be able to let go once we're off," she added. "Looking forward to leaving this place and traveling with all of you. God, I miss the ocean. A warm one."

"Me too. I can't wait. This vacation has been on my mind for weeks," I said.

"Along with everything else, Mark, I so want to have some time alone with you. And this need of yours to do some diving, is that really necessary? This is our first trip in years."

Here we go again.

"Honey, we already talked about this. Diving is one of my great passions. It feels like an eternity since I last did it. It's just two mornings. I mean, you can sleep late and then I'm back for lunch. Is that so bad?" I asked, trying to get her to see my side of the matter.

Cecilia shrugged her shoulders. I could sense her disappointment with my decision, but to my mind, we had two full weeks to spend time together. Why the big deal over two mornings?

The years of financial stress and a substantial workload had taken their toll on both of us. We both cherished the idea of traveling for pleasure, aware that the happiness it brought would be short-lived. The expectation of leaving, however, even weeks before we did so, was wonderful. For five years, my partner Ben and I had been hard at work getting our startup in a state that gave us some confidence that it would survive. I had promised Cecilia this would be my last startup. If this failed, then it was back to some stable outfit, which usually meant a mid-sized or large corporate entity.

This was my fifth startup. My fifth attempt at floating an idea that I hoped would generate a steady revenue stream and the potential of a lucrative sale. I often wondered why I was so willing to repeat the misery of starting a company again and again. There was the challenge of building a company, being your own boss, all of which was an absolute illusion. When you signed off on funding, from that point onward, your illusion of ownership was complete. I supposed the risk and the potential reward drove me and many of my fellow co-conspirators to think irrationally and run off the fiscal cliff like lemmings, with someone else's money. *It's all about leveraged risk.*

This was not the complete story, however. A long time ago, I'd sold the idea to Cecilia that one day, one startup would eventually succeed. We would then be free from worrying about our future. The idea of working into my retirement years and then surviving on a modest pension seemed like defeatism. We were both caught up in the idea of having the means to determine our destiny. Even if I was preparing for a short-term solution to my life, I was always looking at the long game. After Ben and I dumped our last startup, Cecilia began to worry about whether we were just chasing a pipe dream. The hard reality was this: one in nine startups succeed, or more accurately, survive. I was determined to believe that the odds were in my favor this time around.

A stern voice popped up in my brain from time to time, reminding me that the clock was running. Monthly reports, burn-rate fluctuations, performance reviews, inevitable board meetings, long discussions with banks, and just about everything related to running a small outfit consumed most of my attention. I much preferred the banter between engineers trying to solve a problem over bean counting. I honestly couldn't recall much that had happened these past five years. With work and life intermixed, it was hard to tell where one started and the other ended.

I'd promised Cecilia that I would totally shut down on this trip. No phones or laptops. Maybe just the phone. From the moment we landed to the moment we left, my undivided attention would be with family. That was, at the very least, my plan.

Two days passed with little fanfare. Today would be my last day in the office until I returned. Hopefully, no fires to put out at the office. A smidgen of contentment had replaced Ben's familiar dour expression of late, and perhaps a little jealousy. We had twenty-five employees, and we had just completed our latest round of funding. The money did not line our coffers yet, but there was enough cash in the till and a relatively comfortable number of customers waiting in the queue for our products and services. If we needed a bridge loan, it was available, but I was certain it could wait, or perhaps we could avoid it altogether. Logistics were in order, and we reduced our backlog to something manageable. I felt some pride in what we accomplished. No more caustic comments from our investors. They were noticeably quiet.

I looked at my phone, scrolling up and down old messages. No bold lines save for one message from Ben, wishing us a pleasant vacation. I responded with a kiss emoji, followed by something more scatological. As for the rest of the staff, I'd made it clear to everyone I was not to be disturbed for the next two weeks. One could always dream.

I walked through the front door of the office expecting chaos, but the halls hummed with orderly activity. Software development teams went about their scrum meetings, machinists carried thick tubes of carbonized steel over their shoulders, and office assistants carted boxes of deliveries down to the other end of the building. A few of the staff waved.

In the lab, I found Max and his team aligning the optics of one of the submersible probes we were prototyping. It was a thing of beauty. Torpedo-shaped and almost fourteen feet long, with a silvery cone dotted with quartz portals for cameras and sensors, and a set of beautifully tapered control fins near the rear. The unmanned submersible was designed with a flexible tail section, one that could articulate in any direction to provide thrust vectoring. It was truly one of a kind. A toroidal propeller machined from a single block of steel provided quiet thrust. Small dimples punctuated the surface along the entire length for flow stabilization. The control surfaces could flex for optimum maneuverability. I was so proud of this design I had a miniature model of the probe 3D-printed for my desk. Our team had designed the probe for non-tethered use in deep water over an extended time. We were not the first kids on the block, but our system had unique speed and maneuverability features. As such, it had a lot of intelligence built into the guidance system.

The team had placed the probe on a crane and was lowering it into the water tunnel for testing. Primarily developed for deep underwater research, the probe received most of its funding from the U.S. Navy, something Cecilia was not very happy with. I reminded Cecilia that it could never be used for sniffing out submarines, though ultimately it was at the customer's discretion. Its primary purpose was to capture detailed topography of the ocean floor.

Max focused a pair of lasers intersecting a few inches in front of the cone. His gaze was firmly on the Doppler signal displayed on the screen. I watched the mean velocity of the testing tunnel rise until it nearly matched the maximum specified speed of the probe. The noise from the water pumps filled the room.

"All good?" I asked from the doorway.

Even over the din of the pumps, Max could hear me. Max maintained his gaze on the display as he replied, "We're dealing with some low-level resonance, but it's nothing we can't compensate for."

"Separation anxiety?" I asked in a teasing tone. This was an inside joke amongst fluids specialists.

He took his gaze away from the instrument panel and glared back at me. Typical Max response.

"Are you satisfied with the control surface response?" I asked him.

Max gave a slight shake of his head, his features softening into a semblance of modest satisfaction—a rare departure from his usual stoic demeanor. Max was ultimately a pragmatic engineer. It was nearly impossible to get him to smile about anything, and he usually irritated the other staff with his smugness. But no one denied his abilities. He was the man for the job.

"We have no issues at low and moderate speeds, but at maximum speeds we're picking up a lot of slip. In a tight turn, separation occurs along the length of the probe. Mark, as much as it hurts me to say this, we may need to redesign the control surfaces at some point."

"We're already twice as fast as the competition. Let's just bring down the max speed, if that helps," I said.

"In this, I am in agreement. My confidence at thirty knots is a little shaken. The safe limit in my book is somewhere between twenty-two, maybe twenty-four knots. Redesigning the fins later might buy us some more speed," Max explained, with his usual mechanical delivery.

I wasn't thrilled about the speed reduction, but we were still far ahead of the next guy. The team throttled up the propeller and activated a strobe light, triggering it to match the rate of spin. With the strobe lights synchronized, the narrow stream of cavitation bubbles emanating off the propeller tips became nearly still, resembling melted glass pulled into a helical form and stretching several feet behind the probe. To the uninitiated, the vision looked like magic. To us nerds, it was just plain cool. Max then manipulated the tail section, twisting the helical pattern of the cavitation bubbles. Both satisfied and mildly disappointed, I left the team to continue their work.

The watering hole was unusually quiet today. I entered the kitchen, hoping someone had made a fresh pot of coffee. My nose searched for that familiar yet enticing aroma of freshly brewed java. I searched the cabinets and storage rooms for a spare bag of beans, but there was none to be found.

"Are you in need of some beans?" a familiar voice said. I turned around to see Ben entering the room with a crate full of bags filled with coffee beans and place them on the table. Staff members passed by the door with smiles on their faces.

"You can't run a company without coffee, Mark," Ben said.

"Yeah, thanks for picking it up, Ben," I replied.

"I told Kyle to dock it from your pay," he said half-jokingly.

"You realize I actually don't receive a proper salary," I countered. "You've seen my house."

"That's right," he conceded. "Well then, stock boy," he added, throwing a bag at me.

I opened the bag of roasted beans and dumped its contents into a plastic container while sniffing its divine contents. My nose detected accents of chocolate, almonds, a hint of strawberry, and nutmeg, if I wasn't mistaken. There was no company identification on the glossy black bag itself. Another boutique roastery from Ben's secret list. Most of the beans ended up in the espresso machine, others were ground up and placed into drip coffee machines, the mainstay of most companies. Despite the option for cheaper ground coffee, Ben was adamant about using only whole beans.

Abruptly, Jenny entered the room with documents in hand, her long green dress making a swishing sound. As operating officer at our fledgling outfit, Jenny was the engine and the grease that made our world function.

"Mark, these just came in from the bank. Also, Kyle from finance says there's some irregularity in the ledgers. Here's the monthly balance sheet from last month." Jenny said, pointing to rows on the datasheet, "He underlined rows ten and fourteen. Those are problematic. He would very much like this resolved before you leave."

Ben looked up and must have seen the resignation on my face. He turned to face Jenny. "Jen, can't you just park that on my desk? By the way, Kyle should be able to handle this."

Jenny was adamant. "Kyle wants this pronto. He thinks this could create near-term difficulties for us."

I reached out and gently pulled the documents from her hands and studied them.

"Fine," I said. "I'll have a look at these now and clear the rest up by the end of the day. Would that be satisfactory?"

Jenny's stern expression subsided after a few seconds. I wondered if she was looking forward to my absence. At times, I found myself questioning the true authority within this outfit.

"Mark, I wish you and Cecilia a glorious trip. We're all a tad jealous here," she said with a soft smile.

It was time for me to speak up.

"Look everyone, I'm only away for two weeks. If something serious pops up, I have my phone. But we are past the worst." Possibly the cycles of meeting investors, banks, and other lenders over the past few months while cash was burning had unnerved the staff. Inevitably, some members of the staff had bailed, but most had stayed on. Such was life in a startup.

Soon the room emptied, and it was just Ben and me sitting by the lone lunch table. I studied my partner's face while he drank his coffee. The past five years had aged him: his once dark locks had turned gray, and he was thinning. He was also still single. His wife had left him years ago, unwilling to wade through the many challenges he faced creating a business. It wasn't for everybody. I was constantly haunted by the fear that Cecilia would eventually do the same.

"Do you remember the times we were going to bury the hatchet in this place and dump everything?" I asked.

Ben looked up and nodded. "I wanted to burn the place to the ground," he said with a sigh. "I'm amazed we still talk to each other."

"By the way, sorry about the other day," I said.

"No worries." He breathed in the glorious fumes of his freshly made espresso.

"We should have gone into the coffee growing business," Ben lamented. "If our business model didn't float, we could, at the very least, sit around and roast the stuff till our day's end."

"Hear, hear." We tapped our coffee cups together.

"I'll be back before you know it," I muttered.

"You better," he replied firmly.

As we were packing our luggage into the car, Cecilia looked back at the house, drew a deep breath, and smiled at me. "I'm so looking forward to this. Really hope nothing burns down while we are away."

I nodded in agreement. Our poor, decrepit house in West Alameda was crying out for some love and had seen better days. Cecilia and I had made a long list of things to repair or replace, from the wiring on the second floor to the water leakage in the basement. We had our work cut out for us. The house was over a hundred years old and had withstood two large earthquakes. It was hardy and stubborn, like us. Cedar shingles, burnt from decades of harsh sun and neglect, called out to me. I enjoyed doing repair work on the house myself, but it seemed I never had the time or energy to do it. If this trip of ours reinvigorated me and if I found time, I would attempt to start again.

Sarah and Amelia brought their backpacks down from their rooms, which I assumed were filled with drawing supplies, a few books, and small electronic pads, when all else failed and boredom was inevitable. Somehow, I didn't think that would happen. The girls were old enough now to busy themselves in the car and plane. They were currently reminding each other of the necessities of travel, from a kids' perspective. The girls were close in age, separated by a little over a year. Irish twins. Cecilia was absolutely livid when she found out she was pregnant again, a few months after delivering Sarah. She'd wanted me neutered. In hindsight, we both saw it was a gift. Not exactly something one can plan.

Earlier this morning, I parked my laptop and placed it in the safe, along with several external drives. I figured my phone would have to do if an office emergency arose. I checked my diving gear twice last night. I had gotten pretty good at disassembling my regulator and cleaning all the vital parts. Typically, I would scan the hoses for signs of wear, but not having dived for several years, I was more concerned with the state of the connectors. O-rings could get hard and brittle with age. Out of caution, I replaced them with spares from my toolbox. I'd also dipped them in silicon grease.

Despite not being activated for some time, my dive computer, which was quite old, worked fine. Hopefully, the battery wouldn't suddenly die on me mid-dive. That would be a drag. I connected the device to my laptop and checked its memory status and battery state. With the few dives I had planned, the battery should hold. So far, so good. I flexed my fins to check for cracks. They were probably the oldest part of my kit. Satisfied, I put them aside. Packing my goggles, I noticed they were based on an older prescription. My eyesight had improved a notch since then, but I figured the discomfort would be limited with the few dives I had planned.

My buoyancy compensator vest, or BCD, was quite old, bearing scuffs and tears from years of diving. It was designed to hold weights internally, as opposed to carrying them on a weight belt, so I had to decide whether to bring the integrated weights as well. Given all the stuff we were packing, and weight considerations, I figured it was best to leave the vest at home and rent one on the boat.

Years ago, before we had the girls, Cecilia had dived with me. She was my super enthusiastic partner and my inseparable dive buddy. Diving was our escape from the predictability and stress of modern life. We spent years covering remote spots in Indonesia, places like Raja Ampat, Sulawesi, and Borneo. Back in those days, there weren't as many resorts as there are now, just simple huts by the water. Diving campsites, we used to call them. Divemasters would need to get permission from the local islanders to use their land and dive in their waters. This often required an agreement of sorts.

Despite the advanced gear we carried with us, we often slept in a simple hut or lean-to, and, occasionally, under a mucky tarp. It didn't faze us to live in the wild like that. The ocean served as the great cleanser, removing the dirt and detritus from the terrestrial world above the waves. The soul emerged from the sea refreshed and cleansed.

As we got older, our responsibilities and interests shifted. We loved each other dearly, but we moved on in different ways. Diving became an infrequent and very much solo activity for me. Cecilia stopped altogether.

We arrived early at the airport in the hope of avoiding the peak season traffic. Long queues could be seen everywhere we looked. Our driver helped us with our baggage and said goodbye. Fortunately, the check-in process was reasonably smooth. It's a wonderful feeling once you hand off the luggage, like a great weight lifted, especially where dive gear is concerned. Even better once the security screening is complete. As the luggage disappeared down the belt, I wondered if we forgot anything. Worrying about it now was pointless.

With lightness in our steps, we made our way to the gate. Sarah and Amelia chatted the whole way, discussing activities and meals, not realizing yet that fish would make up an important part of their daily diet on this trip. Cecilia was unusually quiet, yet occasionally, a gentle tug in my hands would draw my attention. At those moments, she would cast a wistful glance in my direction. It reminded us of our early years, the prospect of adventure with the occasional intrusion of the unknown.

I planned to make four dives on this trip, spread out over two mornings, and I expected on those days to be back at the resort by noon. It was clear to me that Cecilia was not fully on board with me disappearing for those mornings, but had made her peace with it. I promised her I would not ask for more dives. I looked forward to frolicking in the sand and water with the girls. It would take a few days to settle into island mode, so I made a concerted effort to shut off the outside world once we boarded.

The flight itself was uneventful. I dare say I even dozed off for an hour. I sensed someone tapping on my shoulder, followed by that familiar request: "Please place your seat trays up and bring your seat into the upright position."

I woke up to two smiling faces gazing at me: Cecilia's, and the flight attendant's.

"We're about to arrive, so you might want to straighten yourself up," Cecilia said in a mindful tone. I grinned at her, fully aware that she was teasing me. Evidently, I had been snoring and my mouth had become entirely dry. Cecilia took a half-consumed water bottle from her bag and gave it to me.

I turned to look out the window and saw the Maui coastline. It is likely that we were only a few thousand feet up and on approach, so the deep blue ocean filled the view. We were flying in from the south of the island. The volcano, Haleakalā, stood prominently to our right. Below us, the white beaches contrasted with the semi-translucent ocean and the reefs lying just below the waves.

As I emerged from the aircraft, the cold and dry air of the cabin instantaneously gave way to the warm and humid tropical air of the tropics. It was delicious and brought back so many memories of our visits from many years ago. By midday, we had arrived at our hotel in Kaanapali and settled in. Cecilia appeared satisfied with the room and started unpacking. The girls rushed to find their swimsuits and snorkels. I was in my shorts and intended to stay that way until dinner. By the time Cecilia finished unpacking the first suitcase, the two girls were waiting next to the door with flippers and masks in hand. We looked at each other and laughed. That was quick. Their engagement encouraged me.

"Why don't you all head to the pool while I unpack the last suitcase," Cecilia said, smiling.

"Are you sure? We can wait," I replied.

"Nah, those two haven't been in a pool in some time. I'll be along soon. Let me settle in."

I nodded and walked to the door, grabbing a towel on the way. "A pina colada then?" I asked. In my peripheral vision I registered a thumbs up.

The girls were unable to control their excitement. Walking down the hotel corridor with their flippers on resulted in some funny glances from the other children, but they didn't care. They were determined to have their fun.

Most resorts on Maui fall into one of two categories: large corporate enclaves with hundreds of rooms, plus the requisite giant pool with waterfalls, and the other a collection of apartments with kitchens, barbeques, and some basic amenities. I preferred the latter because of the spaciousness of the apartments, but since we had not traveled in years, we'd splurged this time around to get a good one. The unfortunate aspect of all this was that I waited too long to book and ended up with a suite that had two rooms, but without a door between them, thus depriving us adults of the privacy we had desired.

As expected, the pool was a mob scene of screaming children, out-of-control teenagers and exhausted parents. The girls came to an abrupt stop as a small boy exited the shallow side of the pool and dropped his shorts, exposing himself for all to see. The boy's mother was running from the opposite end of the pool, navigating between the crowds of people lining the pool's edge. Sarah looked at me and motioned to the adult pool through the gates. I didn't resist at first, but then, looking over to the beach on my left, I pointed to an unpopulated area in the sand. To this, I got two smiles.

The sea appeared quite calm, and it seemed likely to remain

so with the low winds, so I felt confident enough that the girls were capable of swimming within their abilities. We set ourselves down midway between the wooden walkway and the water. I motioned for Amelia to take a float with her for safety, and they sprinted towards the water's perimeter. Amelia wasn't happy being told to use the float and promptly discarded it once she got to the water's edge. Briefly, the girls stood together, pondering what to do next.

I laid down a towel and parked myself in the middle of it. The surroundings were peaceful and calm. Surveying the beach, I noticed that most parents with young children clung to the security of the pool. To travel all this way just to spend your days by the pool seemed such a waste to me. Sarah and Amelia started horsing around in the shallows, dragging bucketfuls of sand back to a small dune they had built.

Cecilia came down an hour later and parked herself next to me. She took off her tee-shirt, revealing a new colorful bikini. Despite its minimalist function as clothing, this bikini left something to the imagination. From dark azure to bright turquoise, I found the myriad shades of blue in her outfit captivating. She eyed me coyly. I peeked from beneath my hat and gave her my stamp of approval.

"That's nice. Is it new?" I asked.

"Yes. The others have faded and, well, my rump hasn't shrunk," she replied with a smidgen of regret.

"Looks good to me," I said. I didn't know what she was talking about. The woman had remained unchanged for a decade, as far as I could tell. She was as lovely today as the day I met her. Her skin emitted a radiant glow in the sunlight, and her bikini toyed with my thoughts. I was unable to resist admiring her lying there. *Can we just leave the kids here and run back to the suite?*

She caught my attention. "You're incorrigible, Mark. We just got here," she said, grinning.

"I seriously must take you to the beach more often. Can't I just sit here and fantasize a little?" I asked innocently.

"So, me wearing jeans and crocs at home doesn't turn you on anymore?" she teased.

"Funny thing about crocs." I replied.

"By the way, the mirror does not lie." Cecilia laughed.

"Yes, it does. All the time." I rebuked. "You know, when I look at myself in pictures and in the mirror, it's as if I see two different people."

"That's because you're always posing," she countered.

"Do you really think I'm a closet narcissist?" I asked.

"Nah, just insecure." She said with a smile.

She knew my buttons and pressed them with abandon. I would not win this battle.

"Are you thirsty?" I asked. She nodded. I rose and ambled to the mob by the pool and the conga line outside the bar. It took a good twenty minutes to order drinks. For good measure, I also ordered shakes for the girls, since I had no intention of joining the line again. As I lay down next to Cecilia, she asked, "Did you put sunscreen on the kids?"

"Fuck, nope."

She gazed at me with disapproving eyes. I got up.

"What kind of father are you?" she teased me.

"The most self-absorbed kind," I replied sarcastically as I retrieved the sunscreen from her bag.

I walked over to the girls and caked them in lotion. Amelia had already started to turn red around the neckline. Sarah was designing some kind of structure in the sand while Amelia looked on. Digging deeply with their hands, they fought the incoming tide to maintain their fortress. Unfortunately, the sea always wins. I looked up and scanned the horizon. *Still can't believe I'm actually here.* A warm and fragrant aroma filled the air. The delicate scent of plumeria and hibiscus flowers drifted down from the hotel, mixed in with perfume and sun lotion. *I guessed this was a paradise of sorts. We talked about this trip for months and now we're here.*

Cecilia lay down, eyes closed, basking in the sun. It would take a few days for us to settle into our new rhythm. The sea appeared relatively calm, with nary a cloud in the sky. I walked a short distance down the beach from the girls, gazing out at the clear blue water. The small head of a green sea turtle popped up not fifty feet from me. It gave the impression of looking at the swarm of people on the beach, but its behavior lacked any sense of urgency. A young couple was swimming toward it. By the time they got within fifteen feet of it, the turtle submerged and went on its merry way.

I eagerly anticipated diving, but I would have to wait until the day after tomorrow. The upcoming day's schedule was still up in the air, but I had a strong desire to go snorkeling with the family.

Towards the end of the afternoon, after we felt sufficiently baked, we headed back to the room to shower and change for dinner. While waiting for the girls to finish, I sat out on the terrace, admiring the setting sun. Cecilia came out in a light blue sarong, fully prepared for a night out in the town. The little sunshine she'd got today did wonders for her. I was still as white as a sheet.

"You mean you actually have plans for tonight? Are you sure you want to be seen with me?" I asked her with one eyebrow raised.

Cecilia sat down beside me. "I'm famished. The girls are starving as well. Any ideas?"

"I'm open to anything, as long as I can get some fish."

"Should we reserve a table down at Duke's? It's usually a good idea. There are so many people here. Literally throngs." There was a Duke's just down the street at one of the neighboring resorts. I thought about it, but I was feeling lazy. "Let's just wing it. I'm sure we will find a place that accepts walk-ins."

Shortly after, I ate those words. We spent the next two hours searching hopelessly for a table, walking from restaurant to restaurant and being summarily dismissed by the waiters. We saw crowds of people everywhere. Cecilia was furious with me, but most of all, she was starving out of her mind. We'd barely eaten anything the whole day. I heard her swear under her breath every time we were shown the door.

The girls were unusually patient. I guess they figured with their mother pissed off, there was no need to contribute to Dad's suffering. Eventually, we lucked out with a small venue that had a last-minute cancellation. It meant sitting outside and putting up with the noise generated by crowds of people walking by, but we didn't care. In rapid succession, we surveyed the menu and then ordered. They'd run out of fish, but I had no reason to complain. I ordered some teriyaki chicken, Cecilia chose a Thai salad, and the girls went with a satay. An hour later, we'd finished eating and sat back in our chairs, somewhat satiated and no longer at the edge of our sanity.

"I'm sorry for being so cross with you. I was so hungry," Cecilia said apologetically.

I certainly regretted my decision, but at least we'd got food. Perish the thought of ending up back in the hotel without so much as a morsel. I reluctantly admitted my mistake,

"My bad, honey."

After paying the bill, we strolled back to our room, taking in the lovely night air. Amelia and Sarah walked ahead of us, softly tapping the flowers along the path.

"Mark, I don't want to jinx our holiday from day one." Cecilia pressed against me. "We waited so long for this and now we're finally here. I'm thrilled we made it in one piece."

I placed my arm around her waist. "How about we drop off the girls and head to the beach for some old-fashioned stargazing, and maybe I can get some forgiveness, hm?" I suggested.

She smiled mischievously. "After your performance tonight, don't you think you're pushing your luck?"

"I can show off some of my new parlor tricks. Ben has been teaching me," I said, grinning like a schoolboy.

"Really. Card tricks? That's what it's come to, after a decade of marriage?"

"Oh, yes," I replied. The girls glanced back at us, curious about the cause of all the laughter.

We dropped off the girls at the room and requested that they brush their teeth and go to bed, at least within the hour. Amelia found a remote and selected some children's programming. Sarah was clearly tired from the day's events, and with little ado took her toothbrush from the toiletry bag. I grabbed a towel on our way out.

We sauntered out to the beach and looked around for a secluded spot. The footpath ahead of us featured lamps that extended in an arc. At this hour, most of the beach was empty, so we settled for a secluded spot near the rocks. We lay down on the towels, side by side, gazing at the moonless sky filled with stars. I pointed out the constellation Pisces and the star Sirius, which was directly overhead. In the darkness, the small waves of a placid sea had a calming effect.

"This reminds me of when we were young, lying out here without a care in the world. No worries and no kids," Cecilia said.

"Is our life really that bad?" I asked. In the absence of light, I observed her furrowing her brow. She turned toward me.

"I hardly see you anymore. You come home every night looking so drained. We argue constantly. I feel guilty just asking you to spend a little time with me. The weekends with the kids fly by. When you are at home, the four of us are always together. It feels like we've been at this for years.

Something has to give."

I thought carefully about how to answer.

"How about we get a babysitter one night, or maybe for a whole day while we are here?" I asked.

Cecilia looked down toward the beach, but I could see a slight smile forming.

"Really? You'd do that?" she asked.

"Don't write us off yet, dear."

Out of the blue, Cecilia rolled on top of me, straddling me, and gazed deep into my soul. I could see stars around the silhouette of her head. In the darkness, she kissed me softly. I could smell her perfume, the ocean, and our dinner, all at once. As if driven by my subconscious, my hands were already climbing up her thighs, until they reached her bottom. It was all lovely and perfect until I heard a chorus of young men whispering. Cecilia raised her head to look around. I also looked around but saw nothing. In the darkness it was difficult to make out anything. It became quiet again. Satisfied, we continued kissing.

There it was again. It almost sounded like they were trying to keep quiet but were too drunk to do so. I recognized an Australian accent, and I was sure there was a Brit in there as well. As our eyes acclimated to the darkness, we eventually located the culprits. Above us on the rocks, four young men had sequestered, or rather stolen, some of the hotel chairs and nestled them in the rocks.

They were clearly drinking hard liquor and smoking something that smelled awful. Wafts of horribly smelling weed came down from above. They were having a grand old time, and then we'd showed up as a bonus to their soiree. A few of them had their smartphones out. If they were trying to be subtle, it was not working out for them. What had started out as low-level snickering gradually grew to a full-on gabfest. Someone tossed a chair, and it landed in the rocks with a thud.

We both got up and faced the music. Overcoming our embarrassment, we walked back towards the hotel room with our heads held low.

"You know," I said sarcastically, "if they had just remained quiet, they would have gotten the experience of a lifetime, but sadly…"

"At my age, I don't know if I could get over the shame of seeing myself getting shagged on the beach, and then spread over the internet for eternity." She swore under her breath. With her eyebrows lowered and her lips curled inwards, I could see frustration growing on her face. This was not how she saw her vacation playing out. Maybe we were expecting too much on our first day.

I tried humoring her. "It would have been glorious. Just think of all the likes you would have gotten. In the darkness no one would have recognized you."

She punched me in the shoulder. I scowled with fake pain. Having failed at rekindling our romance, we returned to the resort a little disillusioned. I tried to lift her spirits, "Look, this is day one. We just got here."

I could see she was still brooding. Who was I kidding? I had my work cut out.

"Do you want to talk about it?" I asked.

"For fuck's sake, Mark!" she yelled. "You make light of everything. You couldn't get your ass together for dinner. To come all this way and go from place to place. It was humiliating. I mean, all it took was to make a simple reservation. And now this. It's like this with you all the time."

That last one hurt.

"Look, Cecilia, I promised my attention would be with family."

"I need you to be here for me, not just the girls."

We walked silently back to the hotel.

She grabbed my hand. "You know, if you were more

present, the shit with those idiots back there would not have meant anything to me."

Ouch.

Upon returning to the room, we found that the girls had fallen asleep. Sarah's leg was dangling off her bed. Amelia was snoring at full blast. The room air had a pungent quality which I traced to a poorly functioning air conditioner. I shut it off and opened the windows. The breeze coming in was lovely.

"Who designs a two-room suite with no door?" Cecilia asked irritably. I shrugged my shoulders. Truth be told, I was too tired to discuss the matter. It had been a long and eventful day, a day of transition, in more ways than I could count. No need to push it so early on. I laid my head on the pillow and quickly fell asleep.

An hour later, I woke to someone tapping on my arm. Cecilia was lying on her side. She was staring at me. I turned onto my side to face her. Her eyes were red and puffy. She wiped her nose. It was obvious to me she was not happy.

"Are you having trouble sleeping?" I asked.

"I haven't, can't."

She extended her hand and touched my chest, near the sternum. I reached out to embrace her, but she pushed back, which worried me.

"I know you're angry with me. What can I do?" I asked.

"I've been angry for a long time. And frustrated. And I hate being angry. Ever since Charlotte left Ben, I didn't want to be that wife. The one who gives up. Both of you will stop at nothing to succeed. The rest of us are just left to follow along. I so miss our time together, like the way we had it before all of this. Now you spend whatever time you have left with the girls. I just feel left out."

I tried reassuring her. "You know I care about this family more than anything."

"There you go again—the family. What about me? Do you still even care how I feel? Sometimes I feel like enough is enough."

I was stunned by her statement. I'd assumed we would always be together. I'd never doubted it for a moment.

"I have always loved you, and I have never doubted you loved me," I said, adding, "Am I wrong?"

I brought her hand up to my face, studying the ring on her finger. The same ring I'd put on her finger over ten years ago. I thought about the day of our wedding, how happy she was. What an amazing day that was. The scent of after-sun lotion and sweat filled the room. It was still quite warm. I kissed her hand and placed it up against my cheek. For a while we lay there, gazing at each other. Eventually, her gaze softened, and she rolled away. I reached up behind her and put my arms around her waist, holding her close.

An hour later, I woke up with a shudder. Cecilia was fast asleep. I watched her chest rise and fall with each breath. She looked peaceful and lovely. My mind was at an impasse: trying in vain to find a way to make everyone happy. *Correction, make my wife happy.* A part of me would simply not back down from diving. It was a calling that was simply ingrained in me. I wanted Cecilia to be happy, and I wanted us to spend time together like we did so many years ago. I believed that both things were possible. It was just two mornings.

I lay there for an hour, my mind unable to find peace. In frustration, I stood up and walked out onto the terrace to breathe in the refreshing ocean air. I could hear the soft crashing of waves in the distance. The horizon was barely visible in the distance. I was about to go back inside again when I heard the familiar sound of a bottle and some glasses clinking.

"Feel like a nightcap, neighbor?" a voice said.

Startled, I looked to my left and saw an older gentleman enjoying a whiskey on his own terrace. It must have been, what, two or three o'clock in the morning.

"Sure, why not" I replied. *I could use a drink.*

The older gent filled another glass halfway. "Ice? No ice?"

"I'll take it straight. Thank you."

He reached over and gave me the glass. We raised our glasses to each other and then looked out at the ocean. *Single malt*, I thought. *At least something good came out of this day.*

"Having a nice day?" he asked.

"I've had better," I replied. "Actually, I feel like I've made a mess of things. And we just got here."

"Tomorrow will be better," the man said. "I'm sure of it."

"Not sure if I share your optimism. I work too much, my wife feels ignored, and whatever time we have left goes to our children."

"My late wife used to say, 'Harry, if you must work late, when you come home bring a dry martini to the bedside and take off all your clothes. We'll make up in the morning.'"

That elicited a chuckle out of me.

"She sounds like a reasonable woman," I said.

"That she was," he replied.

"You're not worried about getting a chill?" he asked with a smile.

"No, why?"

"You have yourself a good night, then. I believe you have already taken my advice," he replied with a wink before going inside and closing his door behind him.

I thought it was an odd reaction from the old fellow until I had gone back into our suite and closed the terrace door and realized that I was in the buff. *That was interesting. I guess I deserved that.*

Something About Barry

I woke around seven, bleary-eyed and a little tired from the events of the previous night. Try as I may, I could not fall asleep again, but then I remembered why I wanted to get up in the first place. Cecilia lay sprawled next to me. She was muttering to herself in her sleep.

I had a weird taste in my mouth, which upon closer inspection turned out to be drool. An empty whiskey glass stood on a dresser. From the sounds of snoring coming from the next room, it was plain that the girls were still asleep. I could see the sun had risen over the horizon through the curtains. A soft yellow glow filled the room, and it felt quite warm since we hadn't been able to run the air-conditioner during the night. I thought about last night and the drunk Australian voyeurs on the rocks who spotted us making out on the beach. My joy of starting a new day fresh was tempered by memories of my conversation with Cecilia last night.

My phone buzzed a few times. Lines of text messages filled up the display. *We just got here. This is my second day away, for fuck's sake.* Some messages had urgent flags. *Really?* Irritated, I flipped the phone display downwards.

A plan was forming in my head. I'd get up early and head due north along the coast to Honolua Bay. Years ago, Cecilia and I frequented the bay for snorkeling and scuba diving. While locals and tourists were familiar with the bay, it was always possible to show up early before the crowds and enjoy the place on your own terms. From experience I also knew that fish life would be more active and interesting early in the morning. An old tradition of ours was to snorkel early in the morning and then, after several hours of this activity, head to the farmer's market and load up on acai bowls and fresh Kona coffee. It was my idea of nirvana. I simply could not wait to get started.

As for my family, island time had evidently taken over, or perhaps it was the three-hour time difference with the west coast. Despite my urging, no one wanted to get out of bed. Cecilia murmured, "We're on vacation. What's the rush?"

I replied, "Remember our time there years ago, how important it was to get there early, before the crowds."

She grunted in response. Amelia had gotten up and sat up next to her mother. Gently, she reached over and started pulling on her mother's thong, giving her a wedgie.

"Get your hands out of there!" Cecilia yelled. She pushed Amelia away with her hands.

I sat on the chair opposite the bed and grinned heartily at them. Sarah stood up to see what the commotion was all about. I could see Amelia was clearly enjoying taunting her mother.

I barked orders: "Now that we're up, let's pack our gear and go. Amelia, please pack your snorkel and mask together with your sister. We'll grab breakfast afterward. Your mom and I used to visit this place a lot when we were young."

They looked at me sheepishly but slowly got themselves ready.

Cecilia looked at me with disapproving eyes. "Today, I'll let you get away with this. I mean, we just arrived."

"You know it'll be fun. I'm really excited about doing this together with you and the girls. And it'll be like old times for you and me."

She shrugged her shoulders and gave me a hug. I could see she was still tired and could have easily slept another two hours. But I was going diving tomorrow, early in the morning, so she would have plenty of opportunity to catch up on her sleep.

"I'm still a little peeved with you, dear," she murmured.

I nodded.

"What's with the whiskey glass?" Cecilia asked, looking at the dresser.

"Oh." I smiled.

"Care to explain…"

"I was getting marital advice from the widower next door, on the terrace last night." *That came out so weird.*

"So, speaking about our personal problems to strange old men late at night is a new thing with you?"

"I couldn't sleep. He was just there on his own deck, and we started chatting. He offered some very good whiskey," I explained somewhat unsuccessfully.

"Anything else I should know?"

"I didn't realize it at the time, but I had no clothes on," I added bashfully.

"You are indeed hopeless, Mark," she said, shaking her head and laughing. Seeing her laugh made my morning. *Perhaps I can salvage this day.*

I pulled the dive bag out from the closet and emptied it of scuba gear to make space for snorkels and fins. Cecilia filled several water bottles and placed them in her pack. It took about twenty minutes to get everyone out of the hotel room and into the car, but that was fine. We were on the road by eight. The drive time up the coast was around fifteen minutes, so we were reasonably early, but I had no way of knowing how big the crowds were going to be, after so many years away.

The drive toward Honolua had not changed. There were a few new houses here and there, and a grocery store had popped up where there used to be a gas station, but mostly the area appeared unchanged. I pulled down the window to let the morning breeze pass through the car. In the rear-view mirror I could see the girls were excited. Cecilia was wide awake now and smiling, her gaze fixed on the ocean. Honolua Bay had always been a special place for me. It was a place where I could truly relax and escape from the world.

Honolua Bay is not a typical marine park, since technically much of the land is an orchard of sorts. A trailhead marks the start of a path that takes one through nearly a half-mile grove of papaya and mango trees. After parking the car, we unpacked our gear, which meant I slung the lone dive bag with everything in it over my shoulders. We entered the trailhead from the road.

"Where's the water?" Amelia asked.

"It's just at the end of this path," Cecilia replied.

A mob of feral chickens greeted the girls as they skipped their way down the path. Papaya and mango trees lined the trail. Further in, monkey pod trees and java plum trees made up the brunt of the canopy. A thick cover of vines, native and non-native, draped both the trees and the ground.

We arrived at the end of the trail to be greeted with a vista over the entire bay. It was just as pretty as I remembered it. The bay extended more than half a mile out on both sides. The shoreline was quite rocky, making the entry challenging. We walked over to the side of the path, and each sat on large stones to take in the view.

Cecilia was the first to speak. "It's been so long. I was afraid my memories had betrayed me and the whole thing would underwhelm." I watched her soak in the scene, hoping that she could reconnect with the place after so many years away.

"It feels good to be back," she said, "but it's not quite the same, looking at it with older eyes. I've changed."

"Do you recall all the fun we had back then, romping

around out there?" I asked.

Cecilia's smile barely touched the corners of her mouth. The glimmer in her eyes held a trace of melancholy. *Why? I thought.*

Sarah was sitting next to Cecilia, clearly looking forward to the prospect of snorkeling with her mom and dad. Amelia was already putting her fins on and spitting into her mask. Apparently, she had been listening to me earlier when I was explaining the dos and don'ts of snorkeling. Both girls were quite small when compared to the enormity of the ocean. Despite my exuberance, a part of me was reluctant to throw them into the wild. It wasn't so much fear of the unknown, but more related to simple things, like exhaustion, exposure, and getting injured on coral. Cecilia didn't seem to share these concerns, or she was good at hiding them. She spat into her goggles and walked over to Amelia, who was already launching herself into the water.

"Sure doesn't look like it's changed much," I said.

Cecilia surveyed the scene, clearly assembling memories in her mind from our previous visits here. The water in the bay was very calm, and there was only a light breeze. The tourist boats had not arrived yet, so the bay belonged to us and a few others, for a time.

A small cluster of rocks and some broken concrete, a remnant of an old boat launch, lay at the end of the path. I picked up my fins and mask and headed to the water's edge. I stepped carefully forward and sat down on a submerged rock. In the shallows near the boat launch were rocks infested with algae, which continued at least a hundred feet out. It made it slippery to get in and out of the water. I could see the coral reef some two hundred feet further out in the shallows. The underwater visibility near the launch was quite dismal, hampered by the runoff from a nearby stream, but I knew it would improve as we approached the reef.

We all swam slowly out, adjusting to our new environment. I looked at Amelia and Sarah and got the OK hand sign from both of them. I swam on the outside of the group, ensuring that the girls were never too far from shore should they have problems. A few scattered reef fish darted back and forth as we passed over the algae-covered stones. My idea was to swim along the northern side of the bay and make our way to a falloff where I recalled seeing large schools of fish during earlier visits. The stone bottom eventually became sand, and the clarity of the water improved so much that I could see the reef some fifty feet away. A pair of iridescent blue jacks swam below us, unperturbed by our presence. A small group of perhaps a dozen yellow snappers hid under the first coral bommie. As we passed over the first coral structure, I tried to recall my impressions from my last trip here, nearly a decade ago.

Fields of coral lined the two sides of the cove, and a deep channel of sand ran between them. At its widest, before it emptied into the ocean, the channel was perhaps five hundred feet. However, the northern edge of the bay was longer than the southern shore.

As we moved slowly further out into the bay, we passed a few snorkelers. An older lady, apparently swimming alone, passed by, clutching her camera. She appeared caught up viewing the images on its screen.

A juvenile sea turtle rose slowly from the coral below us. The girls gave it a wide berth as it ascended to the surface to breathe. Sarah and Amelia held each other's hands and watched the turtle take a few breaths on the surface. It was clear from their crimped cheeks that the girls were smiling behind their snorkels. From its slow motion on the surface, the turtle had a relaxed, unhurried look to it. I was pretty certain that the turtle was accustomed to the flocks of tourists that invaded the bay daily. By the afternoon, it would become inundated with people. It had been a wise decision to come early.

I extended my camera pole and took a few pictures of the girls next to the turtle. It eventually lost interest and descended back into its little cove in the coral.

The coral looked reasonably healthy, despite the many daily visitors to the bay. There was nothing worse than seeing snorkelers standing on living coral or breaking chunks of it off for personal gain. Thankfully, the snorkeling season ended with the close of summer, and the coming of the winds of winter would make snorkeling difficult, if not dangerous. A welcome respite for the coral.

Today, swimming was leisurely, and it didn't stress the girls. About halfway up the bay, I asked if they wanted to turn back, but the vote to stay was unanimous. It filled me with pride to see the girls so confident in the water. This was still a novel experience for them, so I watched them at regular intervals.

We encountered several juvenile moray eels lurking in the coral. They were no more than a foot long. At this size they were harmless. One of them had a black-and-white dot pattern, and another was a mottled brown. Because of their size, these morays hid within the relative safety of the coral. Further afield, reef and clown triggerfish intermittently swam into view, along with Moorish idols and a school of goatfish. In the distance I saw the faint outline of a small school of trevally.

I had an odd sense I was being watched, and I wasn't sure by what. It was uncanny. Whatever was watching me, it was good at hiding.

The coral structure directly in my view was a mix of live and dead coral, with several small sponges growing from it. I lay as still as possible on the surface, and after a moment, the small head of an octopus emerged from the hollow of the sponge. It was dark purple to match the sponge, but I knew it could change color. I'd located my stalker. We stared at each other for a moment before the octopus scampered from the safety of its sponge and descended into the coral below. I glanced to my left and saw that the girls were watching me and giggling.

As we swam further out, we neared the falloff of the coral reef to the sandy bottom on our left. The depth was probably only twenty-five feet, but it continued to increase slowly as we swam further out. To the right of us, the coral shelf was probably five or six feet deep and extended all the way to the shore. As I glanced over at Cecilia, the furrow in her brow and the tight press of her lips signaled to me she was concerned, that perhaps we had gone too far with the girls. Any further would be risky, and we still had a long swim back waiting for us. The shallows of the bay were nearby, so we could always swim in and rest on the rocks if necessary. I motioned for us to just relax and float for a short while before starting back. Sarah and Amelia each gave the OK signal.

Floating over the drop-off, I watched schools of fish enter and exit from view. Years ago, I'd dived in this area, though much further out. Back then, an occasional manta ray or reef shark would show up out here on the fringes of the reef. I scanned the deep blue and decided that it wasn't necessary to alarm anyone.

After resting for several minutes, we started our return trip and followed the boundary of the coral field. Here, the coral was a little deeper, the falloff more dramatic, and we saw more sea life. More sea turtles, a larger moray came into view, and even a small reef shark that got spooked and sprinted off into the blue when it registered our presence.

And then it happened. First there were only a few fish, but then an entire school enclosed us and slipped by us like an endless parade. These were bigeye scad, common in these waters. They were slightly over a foot in length, silvery metallic in appearance, with oversized eyes. In large schools the fish pack tightly together, making it hard to view individuals.

A massive school of fish swimming rapidly makes a characteristic sound underwater. I glanced behind me to see both kids nestled behind me, with Cecilia taking up the rear guard. My adrenaline rose from the excitement. We just needed to relax while the fish swam by. It was nearly impossible to see anything other than fish.

The mass of fish was moving rapidly, as if chased, which concerned me. I looked left and right, but all that I could see was a wall of fish. Sometimes the school would pass below us or just to one side. I motioned for the girls to follow me. Slowly, I moved forward, making my way deeper into the school. The darting motion of the fish was disorienting. They often moved en masse in one direction and then shifted direction instantly.

I came to a halt. Ahead of me, no more than fifteen feet away, a large lone barracuda came into view. A long silvery, torpedo-shaped body with a mouth lined with rows of large, needlelike teeth. It was looking straight at me.

I had seen many barracudas in my time as a diver, but never one this large. The girth of its body was nearly ten inches in diameter. It was over six feet in length. No exaggeration. Its body twitched aggressively, which made me very concerned for the safety of the kids. I signaled to Cecilia to take the girls to the shore behind us. She nodded and swam slowly towards the nearby rocks with the girls. It was imperative that we did not make any sudden moves or splashes on the surface. Gradually, I expanded my camera pole until it was fully extended, nearly five feet long, and backed away slowly to widen the gulf between me and this massive fish.

For a few minutes I drifted while observing it. The barracuda darted suddenly to the right and followed the terrain of the coral, but it did not leave the area. It weaved back and forth between the grooves of coral, occasionally darting back, testing my resolve, perhaps looking for a weakness or acting territorial. The vast shoal of fish enveloped us again, which made watching the barracuda difficult. I kicked my fins a few times to push myself out of the school.

Cecilia and the girls were no longer in sight. I only hoped they were on their way back. Even inside this passing shoal, I sensed the barracuda watching me. Then, as suddenly as it had appeared, the massive school evaporated, and the barracuda, too, was gone. I turned, and in the distance, recognized the kicking fins of my family. I sighed with relief.

And then it occurred to me. *I am such an idiot*, I told myself. Many years ago, Cecilia and I had seen the same barracuda, albeit much smaller. It had doubled in size over the years, eating its fill of the massive school it swam in. It traveled with its own personal food supply. I recognized the scar on its left lip, made by a fishhook, which was there the first time I'd seen him. I was certain it was him.

I peered above the surface to see that the girls were following the coastline in the shallows back to the boat launch. I caught up with them and asked if they were alright. Sarah and Amelia gave a thumbs up. From the worried look on her face I gathered that Cecilia was not happy but relieved I was back. I pulled the snorkel out of my mouth and chatted with her as we made our way back to the entry point.

"Do you recall the barracuda we saw way back, all those years ago?" I asked.

She paused for a moment, apparently searching through her memories. Her brows rose suddenly in surprise. "No way! Was that Barry?"

"That thing has grown so much," I said. "I have never in all my years of diving have seen such a large barracuda anywhere. It must be him. I recognized the scar."

Sarah asked, "Daddy, are barracudas dangerous?"

I wanted to give a thoughtful answer. "They're territorial, but more often than not they are scavengers. They like to follow people around, thinking that we'll catch something, like a fellow predator. Lazy fish if you ask me. With all the smaller fish swimming around us, it was difficult to see where it was. It kinda came out of nowhere."

Cecilia interjected, "What your father is trying to say is that normally, no, barracudas usually stay away from people. But they have large, sharp teeth, so it's not a good idea to bother them."

Sarah nodded. "I'd like to go to the pool now."

Amelia nodded in agreement. I didn't know whether to laugh or cry. It had been my goal to introduce my daughters to the ocean and the awesome creatures that inhabit it. I did not wish for them to be fearful of it from an early age. Maybe I was trying too hard.

Cecilia was really giving it to me with that cheeky grin of hers. "Oh, come on. We can sit by the pool, slap on some lotion and get served drinks all afternoon. If you play your cards right, mister, you just might get lucky."

I thought about those Australians (and Brits). The girls were oblivious to our banter.

I replied, "You realize there are children here."

Cecilia shrugged her shoulders. "They never listen to us, anyway."

After placing our gear back in the car, we drove back into town and stopped by the farmer's market. Cecilia uttered those most important of words: "It's time for coffee!" Sarah and I took care of ordering the acai bowls while Cecilia and Amelia bought coffee. Despite the midday heat, several hours in the ocean cools you down, so the girls asked for hot cocoa. Having never ordered an acai bowl before, Sarah studied the pictures on the wall. Did she prefer pineapples over strawberries, or kiwi over papaya and mango? I already knew what Cecilia wanted and ordered ours. Sarah squirmed from the choices, visibly frustrated, unable to decide.

"Are you up for trying your mom's bowl?" I asked.

Sarah looked up and nodded in resignation. I ordered two more bowls like Cecilia's and we both watched as the young woman prepared them. Sarah was beside herself watching the woman slice ripe strawberries, pineapples, kiwis, and papaya, decorating the bowl with the color fruit. The scent of fresh fruit was everywhere. There was something about eating fruits in a tropical environment. It was never the same experience back home, even when they were in season. It just tasted better here. The guava was riper, more nuanced in flavor, and the papaya actually had a distinct flavor. It was the same with the fish.

We sat at a park table and bench just outside the market. It was a blissful morning, and not even Barry's entrance could tarnish it. Staring down at an ocean predator had definitely perked up my outlook. Not a single thought of work passed my mind while we were out, and that made me happy. I was beginning to unwind from all the pressure from work. I thought of poor Ben, hunched over his desk, tasked with ensuring we remained liquid and keeping the staff happy, which was no easy feat. He had enough office assistants to help him get through the worst of it. I dismissed all thoughts of home and returned to the present even as I felt my phone vibrate again, knowing full well my message queue was enlarging by the hour. At some point I would have to deal with it.

It was already noon, and the morning traffic had increased, throngs of beachgoers making their way to their favorite beach spots. I was thrilled we had got out as early as we did. That poor bay was probably overrun by now.

"Do you know what we're going to have for dinner tonight?" I queried the troops.

"Burgers and fries!" Amelia answered loudly.

"Nope," I replied. "Poke."

Amelia glanced up at me with a hurt expression. "Pookie?"

Cecilia laughed and grabbed the little girl in a mock tackle. "No silly. Poke. It's raw marinated fish on rice."

Sarah and Amelia both pouted.

"Girls, trust me, you're going love it," Cecilia said. "Your dad wasn't a great fan of it back when we first came. Now he can't get enough of it. It's a Hawaiian delicacy."

I nodded in agreement, but they remained unconvinced.

Sarah was the first to finish her breakfast. She fiddled with her spoon, looking for scraps of acai puree and fruit in her bowl that she might have missed. I glimpsed the telltale signs of hunger, a silent plea for more sustenance. Unsatiated, Sarah reached over and took a long slurp from Cecilia's iced latte.

Cecilia turned and confronted the thief. "So now you choose to like coffee?"

Not missing a beat, Sarah replied, "It's not the first time I took a sip from your coffee. This is good. I like it when it's iced." She attempted to get another sip, but Cecilia took her cup back.

Cecilia stared at me, cocking her head. "Did you know anything about this, mister?"

"News to me," I replied.

Our kids were growing up. Even though Cecilia spent a lot more time with the girls, there were aspects to their growth that not even she was privy to. Sarah was imitating her mother, rebelling against her, taking advantage and taking stock of adult situations. Amelia was the smaller one, but she kept a keen eye on her older sister, awaiting her own turn. It all felt too fast.

I watched the way Cecilia handled the girls. She had an easier time handling one daughter at a time. The girls were so different in temperament that it required considerable effort on her part to manage them both. Sarah was very much like me:

blonde hair, tall and stringy in form, and quite nerdy in her interests. We could sit for hours together and play with Legos, or practice Morse code or whatever took our interest. She'd even come to the office a few times and showed interest in what we were building.

Amelia was a miniature of her mother, dark-haired and brown-skinned, with elfin features. She loved spending time in the kitchen with her mother. I would often find the two of them sitting together on the sofa and reading.

The two girls were very close in age but could not be more different.

Cecilia caught me gazing at the girls and smiled.

"Nice, isn't it?" she said. "The girls have really missed you."

"Yeah, I know," I replied. "I've really been looking forward to today, spending time with all of you."

My phone vibrated in my pocket. I could feel the heat of Cecilia's glare.

She swore under her breath. "Really? It's been what, two days?"

"I made the mistake of letting them know that I was available by phone, but only for critical matters."

"And when did the messages start?" she asked in an irritated tone.

"I've been getting messages since we arrived."

Cecilia's eyes narrowed, her lips tightening into a thin line as my phone buzzed again with notifications.

"I have not looked or answered any of my messages," I said, trying hard to downplay my involvement. "I'm as annoyed as you are."

"That company of yours has been like a wrecking ball on our happiness, my happiness," Cecilia said angrily.

"Look, when we get back to the hotel, I'll call the company from the suite and put an end to this." I said to her.

Cecilia nodded, but it was clear to me that she did not

believe that the company would leave us alone.

Back at the resort, I took a quick shower and sat on the terrace to relax. Cecilia and the girls had already gone down to the pool. I called the office and ran through the most urgent messages. To me it was extraordinary that I could spend days or weeks going to the office and nobody would even give me the time of day. I could work undisturbed, attend meetings, deal with phone calls and meet people occasionally in the dining room. Leave for two weeks and panic ensued, and my phone became inundated with calls for help. It almost seemed deliberate.

I spoke with Kyle and Jenny on a conference call. One of our investors was not happy with the market value of our company. The estimate had come out on the low side, and he was demanding more equity to compensate. The thing with valuations, especially in a startup, is that they bear no relation to the company's true or potential value.

I called the investor and talked him out of an equity upgrade. Afterward, I called Ben and asked how he was holding up.

"Sorry for disturbing you guys," he said. "I imagine Cecilia is seriously pissed with me."

"Ben, she's pissed at the entire company," I replied. When Ben laughed, I said, "It's not funny. You of all people should know this."

"That's low, Mark, even by your standards," he said.

Realizing my over-treading, I said, "Sorry, that's not what I meant. It's just that we haven't been on a vacation for years, and my fear is Cecilia has reached her limit with this stuff."

"I'll chat with the staff, and any calls or messages with your name on them will go by me first. Would that be OK?"

"Thanks, Ben. I think Cecilia would really appreciate that. Try to keep communications to a minimum."

We ended our call and then I disabled the vibration mode on my phone. No more interruptions. *The company can wait ten fucking days.*

I looked over the railing and watched the mass of tourists lying by the pool like beached seals, and others still hunting for the few remaining chairs to lie on. The tenacity of guests at the resort at reserving or, better yet, occupying or stealing deck chairs was, from my perspective, revelatory. As I saw it, there was a distinct strategy in place. Some guests circled and watched their prey like vultures, waiting for a moment to jump and abscond with a chair. While a few guests actually resorted to politeness, most acted with impunity.

Cecilia found a lone chair at the edge of the pool area, near the grass that afforded some shade from a small banyan tree. An older woman was rising up from her chair to get lunch and called out to Cecilia as she was passing by. She would not always be this lucky at this time of the day.

The girls were already in the pool, splashing each other. I wondered if our morning snorkel run had left any impressions on them, or was it already a distant memory? Sarah was wearing her snorkel gear and traversing the width of the pool underwater. Maybe she was dreaming about the turtles and the fish and the world beneath the sea that we'd experienced in Honolua Bay. Amelia, despite her smaller size, attempted to do the same, only to bob up in the middle of the pool.

For me, the memory of the day was running in a continuous loop. What was Barry thinking when he saw me? Prey or competitor?

Cecilia waved to me, pointing at her watch. After making a few inquiries with a local dive operator over the phone and checking my gear once more, I made my way down to the pool. Since there were no more chairs to be had, I parked myself under the banyan tree and lay on a towel on the grass in the shade. Cecilia was deeply engrossed in the crime novel in her hands. Casually, I gazed over at the pool and saw the girls were still at their horseplay. Feeling relaxed, I rolled over onto my stomach and stared out at the ocean.

By early afternoon, I could hear my stomach grumble from hunger. Cecilia looked over at me and smiled. "I can hear your stomach from here. Shall we go up and change?"

I replied sarcastically, "Yeah, I'm starving after all this heavy activity."

We gathered our things and signaled to the girls that it was time to go up. Reluctantly, the peanut gallery left the pool and dragged their feet all the way back to the room. Cecilia chatted with the girls while I fussed with the hotel key. Having worked with technology for so many years, it frustrated me no end that I could not open a simple hotel door. I ran the plastic key through the lock mechanism several times, only to be rebuffed with a small, irritating red light. My wife reached over, took the key from my hand and opened it on the first try.

"I figured it out last night," she said reassuringly. "You have to slip the card quickly. It doesn't let you in if you're too slow sliding the card, see."

Sarah was snickering behind us. "Adults..." she said, using the sarcasm she had apparently genetically inherited from her father.

Having learned my lesson the night before, I promptly sat down with my phone and searched for places with poke on the menu, which was pretty much every place, even the imported ethnic restaurants and food trucks. It was still a challenge, but I found a local family-run takeout restaurant that specialized in preparing poke and other seafood dishes. It wasn't fancy, but customers appeared to be happy with it. Lots of high marks. We could order and then go down to the waterfront and sit on park benches.

After showering, we all walked down to the restaurant, where a line had already formed. We were early, so it was not a long wait. The restaurant appeared to be split in two: on the left was the takeout desk and on the right was a fishmonger where rows and rows of fresh fish were on display. It looked absolutely divine. Ordering poke required dealing with both sides of the shop, which made for some interesting exchanges between the young woman at the cash register and the fishmonger, who appeared as though they were shouting at each other.

Amelia looked dubiously at the raw tuna blocks on display, which were deep red. Sarah and Cecilia studied the large menu board behind the cashier. A couple in front of us ordered coconut shrimp and, upon seeing the dish delivered with the food container open, Amelia's eyes lit up, as did Sarah's. No surprises here. We ordered our food and then headed down to the beach.

The setting sun gave the beach a lovely soft orange glow. We found a serviceable table with benches and ate in silence as we watched the sun set.

After we were done, Cecilia leaned into me and said, "You know, if the kids really like the coconut shrimp from this place, you and I could go out alone tomorrow night. Eat some serious food." *What a cunning woman*, I thought.

"If it pleases the lady, your wish is my command," I responded quietly.

Sarah, never to be outdone, had the last word.

"It will cost you a movie, at the resort—our choice. And lots of candy." Amelia nodded in agreement. Deviousness runs in the family.

Lovemaking is challenging when there is an open doorway and children are sleeping soundly a few feet away on the other side. We waited as long as we could before trying. Cecilia moved slowly above me, her eyes intermittently darting to the children, trying to keep quiet while she rose and fell in rhythm.

I couldn't help but smile at all her efforts to maintain composure. She caught me looking at her and gave me a hard, icy look, which for obvious reasons didn't last very long. We heard Amelia turn in her bed and paused to make sure she was asleep. Relieved to hear our youngest resume her snoring once more, we continued. *This is genuine desperation*, I thought to myself.

Afterward, we lay on the bed in an embrace, still sweating.

"Are you alright?" I asked.

"I am now, but who knows what tomorrow will bring," she answered seriously. "I hope Ben keeps his word."

"Yeah." I slid her hair away from her eyes.

"Look," I said, "As soon as I'm back tomorrow I'll drop by the hotel office and get them to install a barrier of some kind or a curtain. This situation is unacceptable."

"Yes please," she said with a growing smile. "Mark, please be careful tomorrow. It's been years since you last dived," she said with concern in her voice.

"I've been diving for thirty years," I reminded her. "It's literally in my DNA."

"Still, the ocean can be a tricky place. I remember some of those times." She poked me in the chest. "Remember?"

"I miss you out there with me," I expressed with as much sincerity as I could. "Any chance?"

"I think my diving days are done, Mark, but I can live with snorkeling."

The finality of her reply troubled me. I really did miss having her with me, but I wasn't going to make an issue of it—we had enough to deal with already.

The brief period of quiet was suddenly interrupted by Amelia's snoring.

"She really snores, doesn't she?" Cecilia said.

"She's a miniature of you," I said, grinning. Cecilia slapped me hard on my chest. "Ouch!", I said as I defended myself from my wife's assault.

"Quiet, Mark, you'll wake the kids," she scolded me with a twisted smile.

The Dive

I rose quietly from the bed and put on my shorts and a tee. To avoid disturbing the girls, who were still soundly sleeping at this ungodly hour, I'd packed my gear the night before and placed it by the door. I gave Cecilia a soft kiss on the cheek.

It was five in the morning and still dark out, but the first rays of the sun were slowly creeping up the horizon. I retrieved a few energy bars and my water bottle from the kitchenette, together with my gear bag, and slipped quietly into the hallway. The door closed with a soft thud.

The entire resort was dead quiet. Walking over to the open-air garage, I felt some guilt for slipping out like a thief, but I was confident it would subside once I entered the water. I looked back at the resort and our room up on the second floor. The entire building was dark—even the rooms of those who had partied through the night were now quiet. I would be back in six hours, fully refreshed from a morning dive. That idea alone filled me with anticipation. Backing out the car from its spot, I took a last look at the building and then drove off on my next adventure.

After an uneventful two-hour sail in semi-darkness, the *M/V Ray Chaser* pulled into the bay just off Lanai's southwestern shore, near Manele Harbor. The captain reduced speed and carefully piloted the boat toward one of several mooring buoys that lay ahead. A few tugs in reverse from the pair of diesel motors brought the craft to a stop. A young deckhand took off his shirt and jumped into the water from the bow to secure the boat to the buoy. Other deckhands were busy preparing the rear of the boat for the divers. Suddenly, the boat was alive with activity. Surface conditions in the bay were calm, with moderate currents. The sun, still perched low in the sky, made it easy for us to look down through the transparent blue and see the coral structures below us in clear detail. The urge to just jump in was palpable.

I walked over to my gear and began running through a mental checklist. Like many recreational divers who traveled with families, I rented most of my equipment except for my regulator, dive computer, fins, and mask. Normally I would also have my three-millimeter suit with me, but I'd simply lacked the space in my luggage. I wasn't particularly fond of renting neoprene suits. Dive companies did not appreciate having their customers relieve themselves in their suit and reminded you constantly about this little detail. The irony was that you were also told to drink lots of water to prevent dehydration. The reality, to my mind, was that some, if not most, patrons regularly relieved themselves at depth when they needed to. Spend an hour at depth and you will inevitably begin to feel cold, and that will trigger the need to pee. I slowly pulled on the suit given to me, trying not to think of all the poor souls who'd worn it before me.

Jeff, the dive guide, called all the guest divers together on the back deck and pulled out a chart that described the underwater topography both inside and outside the harbor. Drawn on it in magic marker was a dashed line that outlined the route we would take. Jeff had drawn symbols describing things to look out for. From the chart, I could see that the slope of the terrain near the southwestern corner of Lanai was quite steep.

"Hi everyone, nice to see you all," he greeted us. "As you can see, the weather this morning is perfect. We've got flat seas and not a lot of current today. It should stay like this for the next few hours. The wind typically picks up in the afternoon. I'm going to run through the dive plan and point out the kinds of wildlife we might see."

The plan was to descend to thirty feet from the boat and then proceed to the terraced reef just below us. Jeff described some of the fish and coral species we were likely to see and where to look. Beyond the terraced portions of the reef the terrain dropped precipitously, giving us a ringside seat to incoming pelagic life. Once at the wall, we would descend to approximately ninety feet and then, depending on time and air left, we could drop a further twenty feet. Thereafter we would steadily ascend to fifty feet and follow the east side of the reef towards a site called the Cathedrals, and then back to the harbor to carry out a safety stop at fifteen feet. Jeff was adamant that we stick together and not wander too far from each other. This would be a drift dive, even though the currents were perfectly manageable.

"I'd like to add that it is October, so there is the likelihood of seeing a tiger shark out here. But I've been diving in these waters for several years almost daily and have yet to see one," Jeff explained, with a hint with regret.

It was definitely high on my list to see one. I had been diving for over three decades, and the largest shark I'd seen was a six foot white-tip reef shark at Mala pier over on Maui. Nothing to get all misty about.

There were five paying divers on the boat, and from where I was standing, they were quite the motley collection. George was tall and lean, most likely in his early sixties. Probably started diving late in his life, and desperate to get as many dives in as possible. From what I could see from his dive log, he'd completed a total of eighteen dives. I preferred more seasoned divers as dive buddies and looked further afield. There was Jason, a smallish, round man with thick spectacles who sported a tattoo of Neptune on his right shoulder. He struggled to zipper his suit shut about his stomach and chest. His face became rather plump and rosy as he hopped on his toes to get the suit closed. The scene reminded me of Cecilia after she'd left her jeans in the dryer a tad longer than they should have been.

Marco, a young but experienced diver from Italy, sat down beside Jason with a scooter between his legs. From the lack of branding information, I surmised it was a home build. Two sets of large propellers protruded from the back of the long cylinder-like body. It was a poor man's version of the submersibles we built in my company. By volume, most of it was probably batteries. Marco was already kitted up and appeared ready to dive in. Underwater scooters annoyed me for several reasons. For one, they were noisy and scared away all the wildlife, and they made it difficult for the divers to communicate with each other. It rather surprised me that Jeff permitted this.

This left me with Janet, a semi-retired professor who was on sabbatical, and clearly the most experienced of the bunch. Despite her small size, she worked well with the dive team, moving heavy dive tanks, weights, and camera gear seemingly effortlessly. Her camera rig comprised multiple arms and strobes extending from the central camera case and was literally larger than herself. I was looking forward to seeing her handle all this hardware during our dive. I watched her clean the seal of her camera housing, meticulously applying grease and using her tee-shirt to remove the excess.

She turned and looked at me. "I could use a spotter."

"Sure. Anything specific you'd like me to look for?" I asked.

She studied her lens for a moment. "You know, I'm always on the lookout for critters. Much easier to stage. But with this location I might be better off with a wide-angle. What do you think?"

I pondered her question. "I'm not sure myself. I haven't dived this site before, but I figure we might see both. On the big island I saw ghost shrimp and a few rare nudibranchs on an earlier dive, besides rays and sharks."

She looked at me. "By the airport?"

"Yeah."

"I know that area well. Fun place to dive, both day and night."

She tied back her hair into a ponytail and pulled her mask partly over her head. We both sat down and pulled the tanks and BCDs over our shoulders. I looked down at the computer to check my tank, then pushed the release valve to clear the regulator. The tank gauge stood at nearly 3,000 psi. Sometimes dive companies don't properly fill the tanks, and you have to make the best of it, or complain and get another tank, or dive shallow to extend the down time.

Jeff came over and asked for tank pressures. He reminded everyone to clock in their pressures every fifteen minutes. I checked my dive computer one last time and then looked out over the railing.

The sea was relatively calm, with hardly a ripple disturbing its surface. One at a time, we walked to the rear edge of the boat, like ungainly penguins on land, checked the seals of our masks for the last time, and then, each with one hand on our mask and another on the regulator, we took that one long step into the ocean realm.

It took a few minutes for everyone to meet at the reef below the boat. I adjusted my BCD, inflating it with small bursts of pressurized air from my tank, and leveled off at thirty feet, just above the sandy bottom. The integrated weights in my BCD shifted as I adjusted my profile. George was having difficulties equalizing and signaled that he would return to the surface. Jeff swam over and convinced George to wait and let his ears adjust. I watched him as he equalized, squeezing his nose and trying desperately to release the pressure difference between his inner and outer ear passage. He shook his head a few times and gave Jeff the OK signal.

Regardless of the number of years you dive, the first dive of the season is always a little awkward. For me, it was always about reminding myself to breathe and to relax. I absolutely love diving, and despite that, I can't wait to get over the first dive. By the second dive of the day, you more or less have figured out your buoyancy and you settle into a routine.

The mouthpiece of my regulator felt a bit too supple. I was a little annoyed with myself for not having caught this sooner, preferring stiffer mouthpieces for better control. My concern was that it would slip out of my mouth at any moment. I adjusted my bite to ensure that it didn't.

After George successfully cleared his ears, he descended to our depth. Jeff used hand signals to tell the group to stay together and pointed to the reef shelves in front of us. Hawaiian reefs differ from Indonesian or Australian reefs, with most of the coral being of the hard variety. A few dominant coral types dictate the topology of the Hawaiian reef, like the smooth mounding coral and rice coral which was literally everywhere. I missed the liveliness and multicolor character of soft coral that I'd found so breathtaking in Papua New Guinea. This did not diminish the experience for me. What the Hawaiian reefs lacked in variety, they more than made up with in pelagic fish life.

Large bommies of rice coral stood in front of and below us. Looking around, it was easy to see how volcanic activity had shaped the seafloor terrain. Lava tubes and other structures formed from ancient eruptions were everywhere. As we swam out to the first set of bommies, I could hear Marco revving up the scooter. And off he went. Thankfully, it wasn't a terribly loud scooter, and he wasn't moving particularly fast. I probably could have snorkeled or swum above him without falling too far behind. Long and phallic, with a pair of beastly propellers, the scooter looked far larger and more overpowered than the variants I was familiar with. I shook my head and turned my attention to the others.

The reef here appeared healthy. As we moved steadily away from the harbor, the scenery improved. A clear sign of a worn reef is the overabundance of broken or dead coral. Satisfied, I turned on my strobe and started looking for life in the reef. Janet and her large rig were just behind me. Moray eels are standard features in most reefs, and it didn't take long to find one. Most are resident eels that move from one hiding place to another, like most of the creatures here. A large school of snapper passed us as we approached the second reef terrace. The school opened and split into two streams. Because of the massive numbers of fish, the sound they generated was impressive, reminding me of a passing train. The shoal occasionally changed directions, generating a familiar whip-like sound. I moved away from the school and closer to the reef.

The reef below teemed with the usual suspects. The charismatic yet common parrot fish with its luminous blue and yellow colors poked its head out of its den and surveyed its surroundings. Below it, a Hawaiian hogfish, with its mix of bright orange and red and white bands, was rearranging rocks with its jaws, pushing them into small piles. Damselfishes, another common fish in these parts, were everywhere. But I was more interested in finding something unique, like a rarely seen nudibranch or shrimp. Sometimes it is staring you in the face. A yellow boxfish swam a few feet in front of me and just hovered. It only took me a couple of seconds to recognize its brilliant, orange-colored carapace and blue dotted pattern. I shined my strobe on it to get the full effect. It gave me great pleasure to come across such a specimen. Very rarely seen in

Hawaii, its presence perked up my mood. *This is going to be a good dive*, I told myself. I looked around for Janet and the others, but sadly no one was nearby to witness my special find. Janet was fully engrossed in her own find just a short distance away. You can't exactly shout underwater.

We were at fifty feet and descending slowly. The falloff was close by, and I had a clear view of the expanse of blue emptiness in front of us. Jeff pointed out a few ghost shrimps hiding in the small cracks of the reef. A white-tipped reef shark coasted along nearby, undeterred by our presence. A small reef octopus was making decent progress along the seafloor, jetting between clumps of coral and rock, and studying us discreetly. I wouldn't have noticed if not for the slow bobbing of its head. Like its cousin we'd encountered in Honolua Bay, it exhibited curiosity at our passage. Janet approached from another direction, slowly swam over it with her gear, and took some photos of it. I could see she was pleased. The octopus was changing its color scheme as we approached it, from nearly translucent white to colors matching the coral behind it. Its arms folded continuously in a slow ballet of motion.

Above us, a large green sea turtle swam slowly downward from the surface. Jeff tapped a small steel rod on his tank to get our attention. He was studying an oddly large frogfish nestled between clumps of dead coral. I couldn't recall ever seeing one this large. Nearly a foot long, Commerson's frogfish, or giant frogfish, overshadowed its more diminutive cousins in southeast Asia. We all took our turn gazing at this oddly shaped creature as it lumbered slowly between the arms of some cauliflower coral, using its adapted fins to crawl. It was pale green, with numerous bright orange warts and scabs along its body and did not seem alarmed by our presence. With its enormous mouth and formidable jaws, a frogfish can swallow prey as large as itself, so we kept our hands to ourselves. Janet was having an absolute field day. The entire scene was lit up by the flashing of her strobes.

We approached the reef drop-off and gazed over the edge. The falloff was not particularly deep, but in some places the bottom was not visible. There is a sense of the infinite when looking off into the blue, this massive column of water occasionally punctuated by the presence of some great pelagic. A large solitary yellowtail tuna passed beneath me. Jeff looked curiously at it. From my experience, tuna tend to stay in schools or small groups, and are rarely seen swimming solo. A massive school of juvenile barracuda approached from our left and formed a large bait ball. The school moved slowly toward me and for several seconds hung still in the current. These juveniles were each less than fifteen inches long, and there were probably a few hundred in the group. In those few seconds, I got a superb closeup of individuals in the school.

The current picked up and Jeff banged his rod to get our attention. He motioned for us to follow closely along the wall and not to wander off. There were large pockets of coral growing out of the vertical surface. Deep in the coral fissures lurked lots of critters which piqued my curiosity. As I slowly descended, I poked my strobe inside some of these cracks in the reef wall. Nearby, a small juvenile spotted moray eyed me. Its gaping maw resembled that of the adults, but far less menacing. In another hole, a lone Moorish idol was consuming tunicates near some dead stag coral. A small collection of yellow snappers passed below me. Butterflyfish, familiar at most reefs, darted in and out of lava tubes.

I could hear the dim rumbling of Marco's scooter in the distance. As long as he stayed far away, I would tolerate him. I heard Jeff's rod banging against his tank but didn't turn to see what he was looking at. I was far too occupied with a small goby that was building its nest in the sand. The poor goby was fighting a losing battle with the sand and current. With each attempt to move sand away from a small opening, the current brought new sand and plugged it up.

The banging was much louder now, so when I turned around, I received the shock of my life. A large shark, most probably a tiger shark, was slowly making its way up the reef wall toward us. I reckoned it was more than a hundred feet away, near the edge of visibility. It was enormous, and it moved slowly, its tail undulating from side-to-side behind its massive girth. *I'll bet Jeff is happy now.* Impressive how something so large can approach without warning. It was clearly aware of our presence and was coming in for a closer look. I estimated the shark was fourteen, maybe fifteen feet in length, and probably well over a thousand pounds at a conservative estimate. I nestled slowly behind some flimsy, hard coral and held my breath.

As it approached, Jeff stood up from his perch as if to receive our uninvited guest. It had become fairly common practice for professional divers to approach a curious tiger shark and guide them away by placing a hand on their snouts and redirecting them. In mid-motion Jeff paused and then dipped down again. It was then that I realized from the shape of this beast that this was in fact not a tiger shark but a great white, a rare sight this close to the coast in these waters. Tiger sharks are easily identified by their characteristic flat-edged snout and vertical stripes. Up close, there was no mistaking the great white's conical head and white underbelly, the mottled pattern of gray and white running across its midline.

I could feel the hairs on the back of my neck stand on end. This was a surprise. I tried to imagine how I would explain this to Cecilia. As it approached us, it slowed and appeared to hang languorously in the water above us, swimming slowly against the current, taunting us with its massive form. Below it, several remoras clung to its belly, waiting for scraps to be passed down. Jeff and Jason had, like me, reflexively nestled behind some hard coral. Personally, I would have preferred a narrow lava tube, but there were none nearby. Despite all the hiding places a reef supposedly supplies, there really wasn't anywhere we could conceal ourselves. All we could do was stay low and hope it quickly lost interest. I even held my breath, fearing that my bubbles might give me away. This was futile, since the shark had already sensed us from far away, beyond our field of vision.

You cannot outswim a shark that is hellbent on consuming you. I wasn't entirely sure what we could do in the event the shark made a move on us. As I examined the puny three-inch knife on my calf, and Jason's blade, which looked more like a machete than a knife, I realized I was clearly outgunned. As the shark approached, I could see its large, blue-rimmed eyes moving in their sockets, studying us. Its enormous pectoral fins swayed in the current. Even the small pelvic fins near the posterior of the shark were the size of large dinner plates. The crescent-shaped caudal fin of the beast stood four or five feet tall.

Its rows of gills were fully open, giving me a ringside seat to gaze into its massive maw. Bloody hell, it was so silent. We watched with great interest as it turned and made a few passes before swimming onward. Eventually, it appeared to lose interest and ascended to the surface. The throbbing in my neck began to ease. Jeff looked up at us, his grin evident from his wrinkled cheeks behind his regulator, followed by two thumbs up. Janet was busy taking shots with her camera rig. I slowed my breathing and followed the creature with my eyes until it left my sight. My hands were still trembling, but I was ecstatic.

I had dreams of coming face to face with this predator in the open, a once in a lifetime encounter. Preferably, from behind bars made of reinforced steel. Thankfully, it had been uninterested in us and probably saw us as nothing more than a curiosity. Now that we'd experienced the high point of our dive, it could only be downhill from here. I was perfectly fine with that. No need to tempt fate again.

After our extraordinary experience with the great white, Jeff signaled us to follow him toward the reef's edge. The group was a little slow to react. I had the feeling that some of the guest divers wanted to stay put until our most recent visitor had definitively left the area. Jeff pointed to our pressure gauges and his watch. Eventually, come hell or high water, we would need to ascend. I took a deep breath and moved out from the safety of my foxhole.

Schools of jacks and snapper paraded in front of us. The schools would split up and pass by on either side and then rapidly change direction, which was quite disorienting. The terrain on our left was changing, and soon we found ourselves inside an underwater citadel. The lava tube appeared out from an escarpment below a ridgeline, revealing an enclosed room of sorts. The vaulted room we found ourselves in was probably thirty feet tall. It was not a closed compartment as there were large vertically slanted openings on both sides of the chamber, acting like light guides into its inner sanctum. During pre-dive planning, Jeff had marked this site on the whiteboard as *The Cathedral*. Along the ceiling, endemic fish swam in and out of cracks. Beams of light from the surface penetrated the room, giving it an almost religious aura. I looked out of one opening, hoping for one last glimpse of our large barrel-chested visitor. At this point we had been down for almost thirty minutes. Jeff made his way about the group to check their tank pressures.

Satisfied, Jeff exited through one of the openings in the lava tube. We carefully exited the chamber to avoid striking the coral and tunicates that lined the openings of the tube. I could feel tidal forces pushing out through what appeared like a naturally formed venturi nozzle. Nature was spitting us out from the church.

Out in the open water, we ascended slowly toward the harbor. I poked about the nearby coral structures, looking for interesting macro life. Several soldierfish darted along the sand. I ventured a little way from the group to examine a large coral overhang. I was probably no more than twenty-five, thirty feet from the others.

The sound of Marco's scooter passed overhead, but I did not look up. I had an odd feeling at that moment, though I wasn't sure why. I scanned the area around me but saw nothing. Beneath me, nestled in some rocks and coral, a fairly large moray was studying my movements. Its skin was mottled brown, and rows of sharp teeth decorated its lower and upper jaw. I swam over and watched it open and close its mouth as it sucked water through its gills. Morays are interesting in that they have two sets of jaws and two sets of teeth, one for capturing prey and the other for eating. This configuration reminded me of a well-known cinematic horror figure from my youth, the Xenomorph from *Alien*. I reckoned the eel was five or six feet long.

The sound of Jeff banging his rod again filled the water. I looked up and behind me but saw nothing, so I figured he'd found something interesting for Janet to capture on her camera. I swam around to the left of the moray and studied its movements. It eyed me with suspicion, but I kept my distance to avoid stressing it. After a few seconds of floating still, it came further out of its burrow and approached me. I held onto some dead coral to steady myself against the current.

I heard Jeff banging on his tank again, but this time it sounded louder and more urgent. I was about to turn toward the noise when I noticed the moray sink rapidly back into its burrow. The sudden motion—which I could hear as well as see—confused me.

Suddenly, the world around me moved rapidly in one direction. Something struck me with enormous force from behind. All the air was expelled from my lungs. I tried to breathe but couldn't. My mask slid down toward my mouth from the force of the water passing by. The collision thrust my regulator from my mouth, leaving it to dangle behind me in the current. I felt terrible pressure around my waist, as if a vise had closed on them, and despite not having my goggles on, I saw the surrounding water turn an ominous green. There was a terrible grating sound, as if my dive tank were rubbing against stone. I couldn't get my hands up to adjust my mask and the pain of the salt in my eyes prevented me from seeing anything. I saw the sea bottom rapidly moving below me, and I thought for a second that maybe Marco had collided with me. But I was still moving, and my vision was rapidly fading. *This can't be right.*

I found I could rotate my head a little to the right, but the scene presented made me even more confused. A large, unfocused black orb filled my field of vision. At this point I no longer felt pressure, or pretty much anything else. With my eyes barely open, I pondered the meaning of the large orb, trying to make sense of it. It was then that I realized it was not an orb but an enormous eye, whose pupil was studying me.

What remained of my consciousness made a connection that filled me with absolute horror as the world around me dissolved.

Crossing the Abyss

The seafloor in front of me appeared tranquil. It took me a few seconds to realize I was still underwater. I was pretty sure something hit me. My mind was still reeling from the force of the collision. Was it possible Marco barreled into me, maybe by accident? Perhaps he was distracted and didn't realize I was directly ahead of him. However it had happened, he had some serious explaining to do. Aside from some unusual grogginess I felt fine. There was some pressure about my waist, but it wavered, and I wondered if it was just residual pain from the collision. Another memory entered my mind, that of a moray backing into its hole in the coral. Its expression, if it was at all possible to read, had been one of alarm, so far as I could tell. Yet another recollection that made little sense.

A small, dual-shaded wrasse was hovering by my left eye. It approached and retreated repeatedly, as if unsure what to do. I watched it twitch its tail as it moved. *Quite the neurotic little fish*, I thought. A short distance away, a small group of Bumphead parrotfish were hiding under some coral. Beyond, an eagle ray flexed its wings and then drifted back into the blue. Schools of fish meandered into the scene.

The last thing I recalled was the dive guide hammering his tank with a metal rod and then me getting rammed from behind. A very vague memory of a large black eye suggested a more sinister situation, but that couldn't be, since I was still here. Besides, the shark had lost interest in us. My surroundings were still familiar, though I must have moved a bit, since none of the coral outcroppings I had been looking at earlier were nearby. As best as I could recall, we were outside the harbor, making our way up to the surface.

But where was everyone?

It took a few seconds for me to realize that I was completely alone. There was no cacophony of bubbles from multiple divers exhaling air from their tanks. It was far too silent for my liking.

I was operating under the assumption that the dive guide had been trying to get my attention. I probably should have listened. *Stupid me.* Caught up as usual with whatever critter had my attention. What do they always say to you before you enter water? *Never turn your back to the ocean.* I was going to kill Marco. The man had ruined my holiday. Cecilia was going to eat me alive when she heard about this. That was it for my diving. I'd be spending the rest of the trip by the kiddy pool.

I was startled to realize that I was lying sideways on a sandy surface some forty-fifty feet underwater, near to where we had been diving. The lava tubes from our earlier exploration were barely visible at the edge of my field of view. The water was shallow enough to see the surface and visibility was still quite good, which was weird since I recalled my mask sliding off my face. In my subconscious state, I must have put everything back in place and used my supply air to clear my mask. Some small baitfish lingered in front of me and a moray, a different one, eyed me suspiciously.

I felt groggy but well enough to look around. My vision was all over the place. It was hard to focus, as if I'd lost coordination between my left and right eye. But that did not explain why some parts of my vision were crystal clear. Maybe I'd never lost my mask, perhaps it just partly flooded, and my recollection was all wrong. Like a bad dream, nothing made sense.

I was pinned on both sides by rough, solid structures, most probably lava or coral. I could sense my hands and arms but could not see them. The same went for my legs. I rolled back and forth a little to free myself from whatever was holding me. I tried lifting myself, but my arms were too weak. My head was pounding, probably from overexertion and lack of oxygen. *I can't imagine I have much air left. I'd better get up and make my way back to the boat.* Without knowing how much time I had been at depth, it would be risky to attempt a direct ascent. *At least I wasn't too deep.*

I kicked a few times with my legs and that seemed to push me forward a bit, but I was still stuck. My dive computer was nowhere to be seen. Normally the thick rubber tubes would dangle over my right shoulder, held in place with Velcro. I tried craning my neck, but in my current position it was too difficult to move my head.

I could make out a dark form approaching from the depths. My mind was playing tricks on me. Whatever it was, it kept its distance and remained just outside my field of vision. But I could sense that something was there, like a tingle, but it was hard to explain. I watched silently. After a while a small, white-tipped reef shark appeared. *Probably a six-footer,* I thought. Why was he waiting so far out of my range? Not that I was happy about it at all. It gave me motivation, however, to work harder in extricating myself.

I kicked furiously. My flopping around was certainly not helping. Sand was whirled up around me, reducing visibility. The small reef shark moved slowly but hesitatingly in my direction. Every time I made a little progress it would recede and move further away, which was good, but again made no sense. *Twitchy fellow.* Then it would turn and approach me from a different angle. I was concerned that eventually it would approach me from behind. A couple more thrusts with my legs and arms and I should be free. The reef shark was probably thirty feet away when I finally came loose from the rocks that pinned me. Suddenly, the shark turned and quickly vanished. What had happened? I followed it briefly, but it went deep and I decided I should get back to the boat.

My swimming was awkward; I kept side-slipping the whole way, as if my weights were all on one side, and I was sinking all the time. It was such an effort to ascend. With a diver's buoyancy compensator or BCD, the tendency was always to drift upwards as one ascended because of added buoyancy caused by the expansion of the vest. It felt as though all the weights from one side of the vest had fallen out, creating an imbalance. Now every time I stopped kicking, I drifted slowly downwards, which was odd. Maybe my vest was empty of air, or worse yet, damaged from the collision. I still could not turn my head. Perhaps in the collision my neck had got locked due to an as-yet unknown injury. All I knew was I had to get to the surface and get medical attention immediately.

My air supply must be near its end. *Better find that boat.* I peered from side-to-side, as much as I could, and made my way slowly to the surface. Ascend too quickly and I would get the bends, and that would mean a quick trip to the nearest decompression tank, which was probably on Oahu. *Another disaster awaits.*

I figured that due to my downtime and last depth reading I needed to decompress for at least fifteen minutes at twenty-five feet, and five or ten minutes at fifteen feet. That should do it. Add in a proper scolding of the dive guide. Definitely a one-star performance. Tipping was out of the question. He should have worked harder to assist me. I mean, bloody hell, that idiot had probably rammed me with the scooter. No one had come to check on me afterward. *What a bunch of assholes.* It was probably scary as all hell to witness; I guessed I could give them that. But Jeff should have looked for me after the collision. Maybe the great white had come back, and they'd all panicked. *Fuck.* It was a long swim back to Maui. Ten miles of open water and current to boot. Might as well swim to shore and wait for another boat.

After swimming for a bit and nearing the surface, I noticed a boat in the distance. I was probably still a hundred feet out from shore, but there was no mistaking the rows of tanks and black-suited figures. At this point my nitrogen levels should have dropped, so rising to the surface should not be a concern. I could see the divers exiting the water. Something was weird, though. They were rushing to get out of the water. This was really infuriating. My experience with divers who are finishing a dive is that they exit the water lazily. There's no sense of urgency. They chat endlessly on the surface, bobbing like corks, waiting for their comrades to remove their gear and make their way up the ladders.

I swam toward the boat with all my strength. I could hear the diesel motors starting. *Oh no you don't. You don't get to leave me here to rot, you fucking bastards. I'll complain to the tourist board, the Maritime Board, the Maui best business practices bureau. You'll suffer a lingering and protracted sexual illness with postulating anal warts, you ingrates! And months in court for abandoning your client.* Cowards, all of them.

And then they were gone. *What the hell?* It was as if they were in a rush to get out of here. *What did I do to piss them off?* At least the shore was nearby. I could swim in and hang out until another dive boat arrived. I had never felt this much disappointment in people. Not in all the years working in tech had I ever gotten summarily dumped by a mob.

I looked around, scanning the shoreline for other boats. There *had* to be other boats. This was a popular place. In the distance to the south, I saw another boat, and people on it. Swimming toward it, leisurely this time, I was feeling better and felt my energy was returning. I was so looking forward to getting back to Cecilia and the girls. I couldn't wait to get this gear off me. I was feeling really heavy, almost bloated.

I was about a hundred yards out from the boat when I saw people clambering up out of the water. Some swimmers headed directly for the shallows; the ones closest to the boat climbed quickly up the stern ladder. Had they seen something I couldn't? Another shark, perhaps? I looked around under the surface, but the coast was clear. The water was so clear around here. I didn't know what was causing such a stir. After witnessing that massive great white earlier, I felt I could handle anything.

Carefully, I swam toward the boat. Several people were looking in my direction—pointing, even. Maybe it was behind me. That's all I needed, another surprise from behind. I turned and checked my six. Nothing. What on earth was freaking these people out? I noticed the boat was one of those nice new catamarans. The hull had a glass section that was partly below the waterline, and it was highly reflective. Someone had paid a pretty price for that boat. I planned on getting a lift, no matter what.

As I approached the boat, I noticed something odd. The reflections were really off, or my mind was playing tricks on me. Where I expected to see the reflection of my tanks, I saw a blurred vertical structure. I could sort of see something moving in the reflection, but it made little sense.

The people on the boat were now making lots of noise and they were looking directly at me. *Really, what's so funny?* I swam back to the ladder at the rear of the boat and tried to grab it, but my arms couldn't reach for it. I made several attempts, water splashing all around me. The people just stared at me, literally dumbfounded by my spastic exertions. Nobody extended a hand or thought to assist me.

I pulled back a little and swam back to the front of the boat. Facing the reflective surface once again, my jaw dropped a thousand feet. I saw part of a large conical object that appeared mostly submerged, and what looked like a large vertical fin tall enough to reach the gunwales. Was there a shark directly behind me? A chill passed along my spine. *This is it, the end. There's nothing you can do. It's the shark you don't see that gets you.* And here I was with a boatload of witnesses who hadn't even bothered to tell me I was being stalked.

I expected the attack to come shortly. I closed my eyes. *Goodbye Cecilia, Sarah, and Amelia. Goodbye Ben.* I could feel the space between my heartbeats.

Nothing happened.

I looked up again and saw the same reflection. I turned slowly to meet the apex predator that was about to eat me for lunch.

As I turned, I nearly jumped from fright. I could see a tail, but not the body that was attached to it. So there *was* something behind me. Paralyzed with fear, I refused to turn all the way around and confront it. I looked up at the reflection again, hoping to make some sense of what was going on. I started sinking again.

From my understanding of shark behavior, it wasn't possible for a great white to remain motionless in the water. Not for long, anyway. Coast a little, maybe even pause for a moment, but the animal needed to move. How was it possible for the shark to sit squarely behind me without sinking or drifting into me? I wanted to yell for help, for anyone to lift me out of the water. There was no sound other than the splashing from my repeated efforts to climb the boat. But the boat passengers and crew just stared at me.

Suddenly, they started to yelp and shout excitedly, but it was hard to understand what was being said. Sounds from above water were odd. I could hear people talking, but it all sounded muffled, as if my auditory range was reduced. Maybe my ears were full of water. I expected my hearing to be a little clearer upon raising my head out of the water, but the continued muffled quality of sound confused me.

You need to calm yourself, I told myself. *Get a grip.*

I turned once more and tried to see the tail. It was still there, as if the shark was directly behind me. The cognitive disconnect was reaching epic proportions at this point. *Will somebody explain to me what the fuck is happening!*

I turned my gaze up to the crew and passengers gawking at me. A young deckhand came down to the railing near me and poked me with a long pole. This was getting infuriating. I heard some shouting from the boat's captain. This, I understood.

"Jake, we need to get the other passengers onboard!" he yelled.

The young deckhand looked back at him and replied, "How? As long as the shark is here, we can't risk getting the dinghy in the water. He could puncture it."

The captain was losing patience. "Well then, chase it away, scare it!"

The young man again poked me with the long wooden pole.

What shark are they talking about? Isn't it just me here, or am I missing something?

I drifted in front of the glass nose of the boat again and studied my reflection. There was indeed a large, partially submerged conical object in the water and a large fin protruding vertically. I also noticed that as I rolled, so did the fin, and that got me worried. I rolled and pitched myself in the water. The reflection in the glass did the same.

Suddenly, the door to the bridge opened, and the captain emerged with what looked like a sidearm. He was running down the steps toward me. Something inside of me put two and two together and my sense of self-preservation subconsciously commanded me to dive. As I submerged under the boat, I saw bullet tracings pass through the water within a few feet of me. There was no other large shark in the vicinity. The captain was deliberately shooting at me.

I let myself drift to the shallow sea bottom beneath the dive boat while I tried to piece together what had happened to me. A few more bullets passed by, their watery traces dissolving until there was nothing but a tumbling projectile. One bullet came within a few feet of my head, but by the time it neared me it had lost most of its momentum. I watched it tumble harmlessly into the coral.

Above me, I could see the dinghy cruising to the beach to pick up the stranded guests. As I rested on the sea bottom, I began considering the idea that perhaps the shark had attacked me and that I'd subsequently been consumed. The collision in my memory was indeed violent, but it was also unexpectedly brief. I didn't believe I'd suffered terribly. It was actually hard to recall the pain. But how, then, was I in control of the shark? Was this reincarnation? I thought about Hawaiian culture and the power of their legends, their connection to the animal kingdom. In Hawaiian mythology, sharks spawned humans, and priests changed the ghosts of the dead into sharks. Every family had a guardian, so-called Aumakua, which was usually a shark. Their role, as I understood it, was to protect the family from harm. Incredible what information you could glean from airline magazines these days.

But I wasn't Hawaiian, and I was pretty certain that I had zero Polynesian DNA. I had a hard time accepting that this had happened to me, but what were the alternatives? I couldn't find a way to rationalize what had happened. However, I could not deny the reality. I had to accept that I was still *here*, and conscious inside this apex predator. This was not a dream. Explanations would hopefully come later.

If indeed I commanded this beast, what of my corporeal remains? The thought that I was slowly digesting my own body while occupying an apex predator was depressing, to an extreme degree. I felt a headache coming on again, most likely due to having lain idle. Sweeping, or rather kicking, my tail a few times raised me from the sea bottom. The headache dissipated. It became apparent that I needed to keep moving. One thing was becoming abundantly clear: now that I had accepted, or at least partially acknowledged, my change of *state*, the next step was figuring out how to *survive*. Sharks are the product of millions of years of evolution. They possessed perfect adaptations for hunting, but unfortunately, I did not. And then there was the question of the original owner of this body. What happened to its consciousness? I'd never thought of sharks as being conscious or sentient like dolphins, but large great whites had been observed to be inquisitive. During the act of it killing me, had I killed it?

The sound of the diesel engines attracted my attention. Looking toward the surface, I saw the boat sail away from the coastline. Once away from the coast, the engines throttled up, and the boat was gone. I was alone.

It was then that the full weight of my ordeal weighed in on me. After all the excitement and subsequent horror, I'd totally forgotten my family. Their faces flooded my mind. The authorities would inform Cecilia of my passing, my death. This would send my family into a spiral. Cecilia would be left to raise our girls alone. I was pretty certain of that. They, along with my colleagues at the firm, depended on me. I had life insurance, but I wondered if the insurance broker would balk at the payout due to me taking part in risky activities. I knew this would be the last thing Cecilia would be concerned about. The pain of intense loss was building inside of me. What of my future? Would I ever see my wife and children again? I was overwhelmed with grief.

As I swam through the shallow bay, I caught sight of something familiar on the bottom. Swimming closer, I noticed the yellow outline of one of my diving fins sticking out of the sand. I thought I was going to be sick. It must have fallen off in the attack. For a moment I was too scared to look closer and perhaps find the remnants of my foot still in it. Thankfully, the fin was empty. For some odd reason, that brought my level of concern down a notch.

I followed the coastline for a while. Lanai is a small island, so it would not take me long to complete a circuit. However, this was not my plan. I needed to cross the ten-mile gulf between Lanai and Maui. The waters surrounding this archipelago are extremely deep. The thought of crossing that narrow strait and sinking to the bottom scared the hell out of me. I still had much to learn about my new body, and I would have to master buoyancy and attitude control quickly. My knowledge of fluid dynamics and propulsion was helpful, but still inadequate for the challenges that lay ahead.

Race to Maui

I figured that, after the chaos of the morning, the dive boat I'd arrived in had a one-hour lead on me, but the dive guide would probably contact the authorities first by radio, and then the emergency services would arrive and spend the next few days scouring the area for human remains. As far as I knew, there wouldn't be any; other than the fin I'd found, there wasn't much to come after. The public inquest would be short. Yet another clueless human sapiens who had succumbed to a fatal shark attack, in this instance having been completely consumed. I'd always wondered about the cases where the remains were never recovered. I mean, who were we kidding? When they don't find the remains, you have officially become part of the food chain. Really an awful thought, coming out as fish waste at some point.

As awful as my own situation was, my greatest concern was the news of my death reaching Cecilia and the girls. The authorities would attempt to contact my family, but there was no way to prepare them for this. Because of that, I felt absolutely wretched that my family would soon face this coming nightmare. But none of that would have transpired yet. The girls would probably have hit the pool or beach by now. In their minds, it was just another day on the beach and Dad would be back in the afternoon. *God, this is going to be awful. I can already see it now.*

I picked up the pace, keeping myself just beneath the surface. My swimming style was in need of improvement. I kept drifting over to my "port" or left side and having to correct. My buoyancy control was all over the place; somehow, I was expecting my nonexistent vest to correct my position in the water. Pausing briefly in my strokes, I sensed my body descending. If I ever made it out to deep water, this was something I needed to get under control.

One of my favorite pastimes was swimming with a monofin. Years ago, these fins had been all the rage, and had even spawned new events in competitive swimming. For me, they were also a lot of fun to dive with, and very effective, far more so than traditional fins. I could cross the breadth of a fifty-meter pool in seconds. With a monofin your legs moved in unison, much like a dolphin tail. The fin itself can be quite large and usually very stiff. The locomotion resulted from up and down motion.

A shark sweeps its tail from left to right, which I was learning was quite different. Since I didn't have my sea legs yet, I would have to concentrate on my application of force. I still had phantom sensations of my legs, which was very odd.

One thing I had noticed with fish—and cetaceans and pinnipeds, for that matter—is that they don't use a lot of motion to achieve forward locomotion. No big sweeps of the tail or empennage. It was quite subtle. This was going to take some practice. If I moved my legs with what in my mind was side-to-side motion, I found myself propelled forward. Another problem was that I lacked the necessary flexibility to achieve optimal locomotion because I was used to having legs with few joints, resulting in a limited range of motion and fixed points of flexion. The human body derives most of its motion through bending of the legs for forward locomotion. A shark's skeleton is mostly cartilage, and because of this it is extremely flexible. I was convinced that my locomotion would improve with continued practice.

From Lanai's east coast, it was a ten-mile trek over open water to the west coast of Maui. I recalled the map Jeff showed us of the dive site. On this same map was a depth chart of the waters around Maui, Molokai, and Lanai. In general, the underwater topography surrounding the Hawaiian Islands is characterized by steep slopes that quickly plunge into deep waters. If my memory served me right, on that map there was a spit of raised terrain connecting Lanai with Maui. Apparently, the sea bottom connecting the two islands was surprisingly shallow, which ought to help orient me as I made the crossing. It didn't get any deeper than fifty feet, which again would make navigation easier and less frightening.

With newfound resolve, I pushed off into the depths toward Maui. After several minutes of consistent swimming, I ascended to the surface to judge my progress. Lanai was already in the distance and Maui was just ahead. I descended again and followed the sea bottom, looking left and right to ensure that I did not veer into the depths. It was frightening to be so alone out here. Sometimes a school of jacks or tuna would pass in the distance. A lone manta gently soared below me. A pod of dolphins was swimming parallel near the surface. The local sea life was acutely aware of my passage. It was not like the fish scampered to safety at my approach, but deliberately gave me space. Visibility was clear, and the surface conditions were pretty smooth. The sea bottom was visible in all directions.

Now and then I'd peek above the surface to get my bearings. The coast was coming up quickly.

I hadn't realized I could move so fast. In my mind, my legs were moving up and down, but something was converting these signals to left and right tail movements. Was it possible that the sensations I was feeling were related to the phantom movements of my appendages? My arms were now pectoral fins, which explained why I could not see them. I could control them, and they affected my orientation in the water, but I lost the fine dexterity I associated with individual finger movement. Now, it felt like I was wearing mittens all the time.

Like miniature airfoils, these appendages gave me a lot of attitude control. My challenge was to coordinate these frontal control surfaces with my tail, which was essentially two-thirds of my body length. When my tail flexed during a stroke, my nose exhibited an excessive yaw, making my field of view shift dramatically in the horizontal direction. I found this somewhat disconcerting. Relaxing my stroke and making smaller sweeps eradicated some of this yaw, but what really helped was lowering both of my pectoral fins so that they were nearly vertical. Suddenly, I was moving in a straight line. It was not possible to maintain this for extended periods, since I needed my pectoral fins to steer. Easy to forget that a shark does not have a rudder. I still didn't know how to use my pelvic fins, which were small and located two-thirds of the way down my body, and which should eventually provide more nuanced control of my empennage.

Occasionally my body would rotate onto its side and drift due to one fin being incorrectly oriented. More than once I ended up sliding into or skimming the sandy bottom. It was not possible to manipulate these fins as if they were paddles, but only as control surfaces allowing me to change the angle of attack, or to raise or lower them for directional control. Slowly and with persistence, I tried different approaches, with the goal of controlling my locomotion and direction. My dorsal fin was also quite flexible and controllable, giving me added control over roll stabilization. Managing my motion became challenging as my mind was overloaded with inputs from this new body.

I reflected on the submersible drone my company was developing. I was essentially inhabiting a biological extension of that device. This living entity came with a new suite of sensors and a flexible but strong hull that I would have to adapt to, and master.

My vision was very acute. I estimated I could see somewhere between fifty to one hundred yards in front of me, depending on the local visibility. But the field of view of my vision was something to adjust to. I had a blind spot both in front and behind me. My snout was part of the problem, and… well, everything behind me. Subconsciously, I was focusing on my frontal field since as humans this is what humans are used to. The bizarre thing was that I could rotate my eyes all the way back into their sockets. It is common knowledge that great white sharks roll their eyes back into their sockets when they attack prey, to protect them. Unlike other sharks, the great white evolved without eyelids.

The other thing, though, was the extended field of view of my vision. It kind of reminded me of fisheye lenses, only this time I had two of them. Looking to the side was really weird, in that both eyes now worked independently. Except for looking forward, where I had stereoscopic vision, looking to the side and behind was done one eyeball at a time. The shark had undoubtedly evolved to view the world this way; I had not.

There was another thing. As I looked out from the eyes of the beast, I realized I was also looking through the same eyes that had hunted me down. What had made the shark decide I was the ideal prey? Was it opportunism? Was I preoccupied with the moray and thus not keeping an eye out for threats? What form of intelligence was there at work? I tried imagining the experience of it bearing down on poor hapless me. It gave me cold comfort that I had no recollection of the actual bite.

My snout was reacting to all sorts of signals in the water. It was as if I was tasting water through pores in my nose. My initial reaction was one of befuddlement. There was a tingling response as well, probably due to other receptors picking up electric currents in the water. My poor human brain had no idea what to make of all the inputs. Some of the tastes were distinct and recognizable, like fish oil and boat fuel. Others were completely foreign to me. There was also a subtle but distinct taste of iron in the water, indicating the presence of blood. Perhaps something else was feeding nearby.

I also had strange sensations along my back, nerve impulses that acted up when there was motion in the water. Depending on the strength of the signal, I could sense movements from nearby fish and even sounds from the surface. Shadows in the distance played with my perceptions. Sometimes I found myself swimming deeper than I liked, so I thrust upwards toward shallower water. It was obvious I hadn't mastered my propulsion, or my direction, for that matter. Like a drunk swimmer I was fighting my new state, and I was not attuned to my new body. I could literally hear the water rushing by my snout. My memory of breathing, the urge to inhale and exhale, was still there. But I didn't experience the painful struggle for air as when one dives deeply without diving gear. The characteristic response from CO_2 buildup was absent. The only telltale sign was when I stopped moving, which usually resulted in a splitting headache. My gills fluttered as seawater passed through them at high speed. My mouth was a whole new concept for me. I needed to keep it open if I was to allow water over the gills. All those years of family and friends telling me to close my mouth when it wasn't doing anything useful was not very helpful.

The deeper implications of what I had become had not really sunk in yet—pardon the pun. I was wondering how I would survive. I mean, sharks had millions of years of evolution to help them get through the day. What did I have that could be of any use? How would I hunt? What would I eat? Nothing on the shark's menu was particularly appetizing, except maybe raw tuna. I was a big sushi fan, so that might help. Cecilia could make amazing inside-out rolls. She would prepare tempura shrimp and roll them with scallions, avocado, and daikon. Then she'd wrap the roll with thin slices of raw tuna and slobber chili mayo over it.

Just thinking of it made me hungry. There were no such luxuries down here. *It's going to be meat, bone, and brains in three bites.* I was becoming furious with myself. Had I just listened to my wife, I would have been enjoying a croissant and a latte by the pool this morning, in my own body. I had gone from being an insignificant human to a fairly large apex predator. An apex predator undergoing a midlife crisis and with an insecurity complex to boot. There was something oddly surreal about the thought of slowly digesting oneself. Gives fresh meaning to the phrase *You are what you eat.*

I was perhaps three or four hundred yards off the coast when I stopped to look around. I could see beachgoers milling about on some beach. They reminded me of a seal colony. Was that me thinking, or a version of me as a shark? Large sharks have relatively small brains, so how was it that my consciousness could fit in that space? Would my mental health suffer as a result of my transformation?

A few paddle boarders floated past, not more than fifty feet from me, oblivious to a large fin and a fat fish in their immediate vicinity. I watched them, waiting for someone to shout "Shark" or go fully ballistic with panic. No such luck. This crowd was pretty chill.

Sinking beneath the waves, I made my way up the Kaanapali coast. The hotel was probably a mile north of me, and there were lots of familiar landmarks, so navigating was not all that difficult. The Black Rock promontory in front of the Sheraton stands out, and there are usually catamarans beached on the sand in front of it. A little farther up and you get to the Westin, a mix of hotel and short-term apartments. Cecilia and I had played this really pathetic game during our early years:

Let's pretend we have lots of money and design our dream vacation. We'd fantasize about staying a few weeks at the Ritz-Carlton or maybe the Fairmont, having waiters and staff at our beck and call. Eating Sunday brunch at the Grand Wailea, gorging on an endless supply of pastries and fresh tropical fruit. As the years went by, the dream shifted to buying property, a house by the sea. The thought of just getting on a plane at a moment's notice, for a weekend jaunt, without having to make reservations. We dreamed of that kind of freedom. Instead, we had maxed-out credit cards and a mortgage that ate into our savings. I'd freely admit that we were unrealistic, but the dream kept us going. Right now, those dreams seemed silly and pointless.

Those nights studying hotels had paid off. Soon I approached the beach in front of our hotel. It looked so small and insignificant now, except for a woman and her two small children lying on a small blanket in the middle of it. It was pretty obvious it was Cecilia lying on the blanket, totally oblivious that her world was about to be shattered. She was reading a book, probably the one she'd picked up at the airport on the way over. Amelia and Sarah were hard at work building a sandcastle at the water's edge. Sarah was putting wet sand into a bucket while Amelia was carving rivers in the sand.

The utter helplessness of it all was devastating. I so badly wanted to exit the water and embrace Cecilia and my girls and apologize for all my foolishness and tell them everything would be fine.

But there was no solution to this mess. It was agonizing to watch them. I couldn't even kill myself. I mean really, how? Stab myself with coral? Perhaps I could find a large cruise ship and swim through the massive propellers. That would be quick and final. *I need to get a grip on myself. What's done is done. I'm not helping them or myself by giving up.*

Another paddle boarder coasted not more than twenty feet

from me. Really? Was I that invisible, or were these people absolute morons? I established some distance between myself and the moron.

I was oddly relieved that Cecilia didn't know yet. She was blissfully unaware that her partner in life had left his human form and had now become Mr. Teeth. I rolled to my side to prevent my fin from breaking the surface of the water. I could feel my tail dragging along the sandy bottom. This meant that only one of my eyes could view the beach. It would have to do. I swam back and forth slowly to keep myself oxygenated.

Cecilia looked up from her book, and I swear she was looking directly in my direction. It was probably my fantasy, but it was comforting all the same. I wondered if she was daydreaming about me, probably thinking I would be back soon from a day of diving.

I hovered right underneath the surface with one eye just above the waterline, watching. Cecilia looked at her watch, probably wondering why I was late. Looking around, I could see that the sun was beginning its downward trend. My dive took place in the early morning, so how was it conceivable that it was afternoon already? There had been an unexplained passage of time. *Did it take time for the shark to absorb me?*

Cecilia got up and walked up to the water's edge. From her pacing in the sand, I could see she was getting impatient and worried. She was probably watching the dive boats returning from the day's excursions. It was doubtful she knew the name of the boat I'd been on. She probably figured I was on one of them. I could hear the propellers of the boats as they passed behind me. Cecilia's gaze followed each boat as it returned to the harbor to the south.

I spent the next hour watching her, suspended by her presence, but most of all frightened by the inevitability of what was to come. More than anything, I wanted this nightmare to end. I wanted to wake up from this twisted dream that defied any rational explanation. I was a casual observer of my own demise, unable to bring comfort to those that meant everything to me.

I thought back to the moment when I had awoken. It had felt as though I was awakening from anesthesia after a surgical procedure. It was so calm. But what happened in the interim? I recalled being struck from behind, but not much else. It had happened so fast that I questioned whether I had dreamt up the memories of it. The rushing of water over my eyes as my face mask and regulator tore away. I wondered about the other divers. Had they witnessed the entire event? If I had seen one of them attacked and consumed, the trauma would have been palpable, and unrelenting. An act so horrible and visceral as to defy description. But I guessed it was no different from watching an antelope getting ambushed by a lion in the Serengeti, or a snake swallowing a frog. I had simply not been high enough in the food chain.

I raised my head and eyeball ever so slightly over the waterline to view my family again. Cecilia was looking at her phone. I could see her typing in a number and trying to call someone, most likely the dive company. It didn't appear that anyone answered her call. She put the phone back in her pocket and began pacing the beach. The girls looked up momentarily at their mother, clearly wondering why she appeared concerned. I felt a pain developing in my gut.

Out in the parking lot behind the beach, I saw several police vehicles arrive. They did not have their lights on. Three officers, two women and a man, exited the vehicles and walked toward the hotel entrance. Cecilia remained oblivious to all this as she firmly focused her gaze on the ocean. After several minutes passed by, the officers returned to the parking lot and walked toward the beach, along with one of the hotel personnel from the lobby, a young woman who had assisted us with our check-in. Discreetly, she pointed out Cecilia and the girls to one of the female officers. The same officer walked slowly forward and came up to Cecilia from behind and called out to her. The officer's voice clearly startled Cecilia. Even from my viewpoint I could see anxiety etch itself across her features, her shoulders tensed, drawing inward as if seeking protection, while her eyes squeezed shut, bracing for the worst.

The officer rested her hands on Cecilia's shoulders, and focused directly on her, speaking slowly. After the officer had finished talking, Cecilia crumpled to the ground. She was crying. Sarah ran to her mother's side. Amelia looked shell-shocked, still sitting in the sand, watching the event unfold in front of her. The officer leaned down and hugged Cecilia and then helped her to her feet. The other female officer walked over to Amelia and asked for her hand. I watched as they all walk back to the officer's vehicles and be driven away.

Struck by what happened before me, I felt a primal urge to rend the earth asunder, to obliterate everything in my path and unleash chaos upon the cosmos. When rage proved futile, I resorted to desperation. I found myself beseeching the gods to reverse time and undo the events of the day. When met with silence, I unleashed a torrent of curses at them, railing against their indifference in the face of such profound tragedy. My wife did not deserve to suffer like this.

Slipping back into the depths, I mulled over my options. Without the means to communicate, I had no possibility of conveying my situation to anyone, let alone my family. For the time being, I lingered in the area and hoped for some sign, despite the evidence to the contrary, that there was some kind of path forward for me. One thing that life had taught me was not to make major decisions when in an emotionally charged state. Easier said than done. Now I needed to figure out what to do. It was absolutely critical that I focus on something in the interim, as events played out. I needed to get my buoyancy and locomotion in order, so I deliberately distracted myself with this task while my subconscious worked on a solution to my personal problems. For a short while, fear left the room.

As I moved a little offshore, I sensed motion in the water. Sharks possess sensors all along their body length that can detect vibration. They also have an extraordinary sense of smell. I regularly felt a tingling sensation along my snout and back, but without the experience and knowledge to interpret them, that was all they were. It felt like someone was applying delicate pressure along a line on my back, on either side of my dorsal fin. I could apply some determinism to get at least a basic understanding of their function. There were several boats in the vicinity, and some people riding around on jet skis. I approached these crafts carefully and used the opportunity to register the cyclic response of mechanical systems. Then, with some practice, I could move on to more organic sources of stimuli. Splashing in the water was easy to distinguish from other activities. Passing by a beach, it surprised me how far I could go offshore and still hear people splashing around. I was astounded how easily I could sense people.

Maui is home to a large population of tiger sharks. Many return to the island to pup in the fall, but from news clippings I knew there were a few permanent residents. The tigers kept their distance on my approach, which reduced my angst level. A few of them were collared, with sensors mounted onto their dorsal fins. I attempted to approach one of them out of curiosity, or stupidity, to see what kind of reception I would get. Sure enough, the tiger withdrew upon catching a glimpse of me.

Size meant everything down here. That was comforting to know. Given the few documented attacks every year, I saw a potential form of employment for myself, as a protector. That might upset the ecological balance around Maui, although it was not unusual for animals to move into a new territory and affect the local balance.

Darkness came quickly and, with it, so did my fears of predators and other strange creatures that only emerged at night. With the vanquishing of daylight, I was left to navigate in the darkness using my other senses. Senses that I had yet to master. I had no way of orientating myself using the vibrations I felt in the water. As for smell, I had no clue how to use it.

Years ago, I had done night dives, but they were always close to shore, using a bright strobe to get around. It was the closest I had ever got to feeling like an astronaut, floating in space. Back then I had found it a blissful and peaceful experience. Now I was effectively blind and just scared.

This would be my first night alone in the ocean. Out of fear that I would be hunted, I stayed close to the coastline. This was, of course, completely irrational. I was an apex predator now; there was nothing to fear. Taking stock of my current situation, I came to the conclusion that of all the white sharks that lived in the oceans I was the first pussy great white.

My vision eventually adjusted to the darkness, though the world appeared now more like a contrast image of lights and darks. Colors had vanished. Even in daylight, my color acuity had diminished, although it was possible for the brain to be trained to adjust the color response. I wasn't entirely sure if I was observing actual color, or if my brain was filling in color from memory. On the whole, the colors underwater appeared more subdued and less saturated. Seawater absorbs a lot of light which ruins whatever color response the eye has, anyway, but when I looked above the surface, I perceived a difference. It appeared as though someone had placed a polarization filter over my eyes.

I was also dealing with a lot of field distortion in my vision that was making me uncomfortable. The effect was dizzying, to say the least. Distortion was most dramatic at the edges of my field of view. Moving my eyeball compounded the effect. It didn't help to have that massive snout in front of me. With time, my mind should be able to correct for this. There was also the problem of controlling each eye independently. For this reason, I was only looking in the forward direction.

I poked around in the darkness, swinging my head around whenever the senses in my snout picked up something. As I coasted along the sandy bottom, I saw silhouettes of different animals exiting from their burrows. Spiny lobsters with their antennas extended were the first to come out. A squadron of mantas appeared at the edge of my vision, executing somersaults in a plankton cloud. Below me, a large moray eel exited its hiding place in the coral and chased an octopus, leaping from one coral colony to another until it grabbed hold of its prey. The two animals twisted and struggled beneath a coral overhang. To their misfortune, a group of small reef sharks arrived and took them both in a feeding frenzy that reduced both animals to a cloud, with guts spread everywhere as the sharks worked to remove any evidence of either animal. *That was brutal and efficient.* As I circled above them, I caught the sharks watching me. If I descended, the sharks would retreat into the darkness. After the limited experience I'd gained today with tiger and reef sharks, I decided I should be safe for the time being.

Mental fatigue was setting in from the day's events. It had been a long day. A horrible day. I was getting drowsy thinking about it. I had been cruising over a featureless sandy bottom for some time. Then, without warning, I fell asleep.

When I woke, I found myself surrounded by the blue ocean. The sun was shining through the surface, its rays refracting through a multitude of microscopic organisms and particles. It appeared quite serene—until I looked below me. There was no terrain, only blackness, and it produced in me an upwelling of panic. I rushed to the surface and looked around. The islands were gone. *Fuck!* I bobbed like a cork on the surface as wave after wave crashed into me. The waves were considerably higher in the open sea, making it difficult to make out objects in the distance. Following the swells, I made out the lonely peak of an island in the distance. It was the only sign of land on the horizon.

Apparently, while I slept the shark continued swimming and functioning like a normal shark, which raised two questions in my mind. One, where was the shark while I was awake? My understanding was that I had full control of this body while I was conscious. Was it possible we coexisted without knowledge or awareness of each other? I couldn't sense another presence. It was completely quiet, except for the usual noise in my head. Perhaps it was for the best. I mean, how would we coexist? It defied logic that we could communicate. A sentient human and an instinct-driven predator—I think not. And two, did this mean it would hunt while I was asleep at the wheel, as it were? This latter possibility, if proven true, might actually save my ass.

The white shark has no qualms about going deep. Having dived countless times off vertical reef walls with no bottom in sight, the deep blue void had never bothered me. Back then, I'd welcomed the experience. Now I was terrified of sinking into the abyss. Peering down into the depths gave me shivers. This was a really bad time to develop thalassophobia. Perhaps I was ignoring signs of something else that could have been at the heart of my response: trauma. I was wondering if I had blocked out certain parts of the attack, to protect my tender soul. Eventually, I would have to address it.

After getting my bearings, I descended to about twenty feet and plotted a straight course towards the islands. Given that this archipelago is isolated from any land in all directions for several thousand miles, it was reasonable to assume that I was swimming back to Hawaii. It took me several hours to get back, despite all my huffing and puffing. I was relieved to pass the outer reefs, at which point large schools of trevally appeared. Suddenly, I could see the sea bottom again. I'd read somewhere that sharks travel about fifty miles each day, on average. A half day would logically result in half that distance, which is what I'd experienced this morning. This was yet another thing I needed to address. On the one hand, I needed to feed, and on the other I needed to have a certain level of authority over my movements, both when awake and asleep. I needed to convey my wishes to the absentee captain of this vessel.

For several days I wondered if Cecilia and the girls had left Maui. It was pointless for them to stay, knowing that I had perished. Still, I couldn't let go, and felt compelled to return to the same beach. The beach where officers had confronted my wife with the bad news. As before, I would raise one eye above the waterline to peer at the families that populated the small beach. All I saw was happiness: adults embracing their small children, older children playing in the shallows, and a few adults standing on paddleboards. I saw smoke rising from grills, and young couples drinking on beach chairs. I came back the next day, and then the next. Hoping beyond hope I would catch a last glimpse of Cecilia and our kids.

Three days after my transformation, I returned in the late afternoon. Most of the families had gone back to their respective hotels, but a few folks stayed on the beach, enjoying the night air. I was about to descend into the depths when suddenly I spotted the silhouette of someone familiar walking toward the beach from our hotel. Even in this light I had no difficulty identifying my wife. I saw her sit down in the sand by the water's edge. Trying to avoid making any commotion on the surface, I slowly swam closer to her. Incredibly, I managed to come within fifty feet of her. The depth of the water was simply too shallow for me to come any closer. Getting beached was not an option.

The sun was setting quickly, but my eyes had no difficulty making out Cecilia's face. She was hunched over in the sand, her eyes downcast, her lips curved in resignation. *Where are the girls?* I thought. Maybe she needed time to herself, to be alone to grieve. Was Cecilia receiving any help or support from anyone? *Someone from my company should help her.* After an hour, she rose from the sand and made her way back to the hotel.

For several nights, Cecilia came to the same spot on the beach. Sometimes she walked the length of the beach, her head hanging low, her mind elsewhere. I would follow her movements in the darkness. One night, to my surprise, she gave out a primordial scream toward the ocean. It was like nothing I had ever heard before. It was raw anger, directed toward an unfair universe. A tiny voice whose shards penetrated the cosmos. I'm sure the god Neptune heard that. Shaken by my wife's suffering and rattled with guilt, I slipped back into the darkness of the sea, hoping for a better day that probably would never come.

And then, one day, she was gone.

Island Time

Three weeks had passed since I'd last seen Cecilia on the beach. Once again, I became consumed by thoughts of self-annihilation, to escape from the painful reality of my situation. I could imagine no path that would lead to a possible reunion. I was finding it exceedingly difficult to accept my new life. Cargo ships in the distance offered an easy, calculated remedy to my demise. But they rarely came close to shore, and I was too scared to swim beyond the deep falloffs surrounding the island. Even the owner of this vessel I occupied was sticking to the island periphery. Somehow, it had got the message. I was no longer concerned about the prospect of ending up in the distant ocean without a clue where I was.

I was probably on my third circuit of the island. With each circumnavigation, the shallow seas around Maui grew more familiar and less intimidating. The vast emptiness and mystery of the sea further out pushed back any immediate urge to escape. The trauma of my circumstances still made it difficult for me to enjoy the underwater scenery and the life below the waves, the very thing I had loved since my youth. It made no difference that I was a large predator on the outside; it was still me inside and I felt vulnerable.

I still hadn't figured out what happened when I slept. I would wake and it would take time for me to adjust to the surroundings and remind myself what had happened. Most marine animals do not sleep, at least not in the same sense as humans do. Whether fish or mammal, in the depths it paid to have one eye open. It was the norm for most cetaceans to shut down one half of their brain, and then switch from one half to the other.

While I relied on my alter ego to feed, I was still experiencing hunger during my waking hours. The level varied, depending on the success of my owner the night before. There were plenty of tarpon and tuna in the local waters. I even spotted a monk seal once, which would have relieved my needs for several days, but there were too few of them and, well, Sarah and Amelia wouldn't have approved. Dolphinfish, or mahi-mahi, were also plentiful, as were wahoo. Both fishes made hunting challenging for me, being small and agile, but I developed a trick, or rather a cheat, to catch them. Private fishing charters went out daily from the local harbors to lay lures and patiently wait for the fish to bite. The lures were often hundreds of yards behind the boat, and any fish that bit were then ripe for the taking. I recalled videos of fishermen losing their catch to bull sharks in the Caribbean. It certainly made things easier for me. To avoid getting caught on the hooks myself, I would bite the fish behind the head and take everything behind it. Occasionally, I surfaced to watch customers pull a fish head from the water with expressions of chagrin on their faces. It provided me with some small measure of amusement.

With each passing day, I grew more familiar with the body I had inherited. Swimming was becoming almost effortless, and my sense of direction was improving.

Occasionally, I would pass a familiar spot, a place I had dived or snorkeled at some point earlier in my life. I recognized the entry to Honolua Bay in the distance. It was impossible to miss the cliff walls flanking the bay, and the catamarans parked in the middle of it. Imprinted as it was on my recent memory, the bay brought me great sorrow. It had only been a short while ago that my wife and daughters had explored the reefs of this lovely place. Barry, the barracuda was probably still swimming within that enormous school of scad.

I surveyed the outer reefs of the bay, reluctant to enter the shallows for several reasons, the least being frightening the visitors. Swimming just beneath the surface, I imagined my girls kicking their small fins next to their mother. With heavy memories, I exited the bay, not giving it another look. I couldn't imagine ever going back there.

Continuing down the coast toward Lahaina, I came across what was left of the Mala Pier. A cyclone had destroyed the pier over thirty years ago, leaving the seafloor littered with large concrete blocks toppled over each other. It was close to the shore and quite shallow. The familiarity of the location was comforting. A wooden pier on the beach was all that remained of the structure above water. Divers would enter the water from shore and swim out to the awaiting undersea garden. The large, monolithic blocks made for fun passageways. After spending a quarter of a century submerged, coral had completely encrusted the concrete blocks of the pier. During the day large sea turtles parked themselves on some flats, keeping a vigilant eye toward the open sea.

I swam the full length of the submerged pier. On my first visit to Maui, many years ago, I'd dived in this very spot with a private guide. With just the two of us in the water, it was relatively easy to approach the reef sharks lying beneath the concrete overhangs.

As I approached, three large green sea turtles stood guard on a large concrete plateau a few feet below the surface, keeping a watchful eye on approaching predators. The closest turtle raised its head to look in my direction, evidently alarmed at my presence. A sea turtle to the left of this fellow launched himself into a narrow crack in the concrete. I turned away and moved parallel with the sunken jetty, giving the local denizens a wide berth. It all appeared small and very shallow compared to what I remembered. The swim-throughs beneath the concrete slabs were far too small for me to pass comfortably. The place no longer held the charm I once thought it had. The underwater scenery further out to sea was much more interesting and varied.

After a few passes, I turned out to sea and headed south toward Kihei and Wailea. I kept a little distance from the coast, as it was quite shallow. The sandy bottom extended some distance from the breakers. There wasn't much to see other than the occasional clusters of hard coral. The rapid growth of hotels in the seventies and eighties had impacted much of the local underwater terrain along the western shores of Maui. Inshore reefs had suffered terribly from sediment deposits caused by water runoff from construction and landfill activity. Since then, there has been a slow but continued recovery, but the constant exposure to boating traffic and tourism has not helped. I saw evidence of human passage all along my path, the occasional hotel slipper, food wrappers, plastic water bottles, and other items. There was plenty of it all around. As I moved further offshore, there was less of it.

Occasionally, I sensed a vibration along my snout, or along my back, a prickly feeling, and I would turn instinctively in the direction of its source. It was quite a tool for registering life around me. I was getting better at understanding how to use it. With motorboats I would hear or sense very distinct mechanical patterns, cyclic in nature, the intensity of which varied with distance. With sailboats, it was an irregular sloshing sound caused by the passing of water over a hull, albeit much quieter than powered boats. Dolphins had characteristic sounds as well, aside from their social communication. I could sense their presence by their activity: the clicks of their echolocation or persistent jumping from the sea surface as they passed nearby.

From what I could tell, visibility was nearly a hundred feet. I sensed a weaker vibration in the water, but one that was familiar to me. It was rhythmic, but not mechanically consistent like a motor. I looked around but saw nothing. The signal grew ever so slightly. I ascended above the rock shelf on my left and, in the distance, spotted a lone swimmer. I approached carefully from behind, keeping just out of sight to avoid alarming the individual. From the body profile and long ponytail, I surmised that it was a young woman in a wetsuit. Her freestyle strokes were both smooth and strong. Her legs barely created a ripple behind her, which was probably why the signal had been weak. Despite her obvious vulnerability, I admired her confident stroke. She was perhaps a hundred yards from shore. It was quite possible she was training for a long-distance swimming event, several of which were held every year in the Hawaiian Islands.

I stayed deep and followed along like a member of her private security detail. It was comforting to be near another human. As she swam above me, I studied the ocean floor below. Ancient lava tubes and stratified coral terraces passed beneath me. Even after an hour of swimming, the woman was still pushing a solid pace.

Out of nowhere, I experienced that odd tingle again. I didn't recognize the pattern, and it was even weaker than the swimmer's. I swam a loop and scoured the sea bottom for the source. Was it a monk seal or turtle? It was difficult to tell. Each fish or animal had its own characteristic signature, and I was still learning. The signal was definitely coming from behind me, so I turned and awaited the interloper. I was definitely sensing something moving in my direction, but the sea remained elusive. What was it?

I turned back to attend to the swimmer. That was when I noticed the torpedo-like shape of a large tiger shark slowly ascending from the seafloor and trailing in the swimmer's wake. I recognized the characteristic dark stripes on its body as well as its size, which was between twelve and thirteen feet. From the claspers positioned at the rear of the shark, I could determine that it was a male. It was quite a chubby specimen. There was still a good hundred feet between it and the swimmer, but the shark could close in on her in no time if it wanted to.

I sped up along the sea bottom as fast as I could, so that I could put myself between the swimmer and the shark. The shark elicited a little fear in me as I did not sense any significant level of threat from it, and I had no intention of letting it attack the unsuspecting swimmer.

Unfortunately, the tiger shark had no interest in playing nice. With a few, rapid flicks of its caudal fin, it revealed its intentions and closed in on the swimmer. With less than twenty feet between them, I swam up from below the tiger shark and rammed it from the side, effectively blocking it, but not without breaking the ocean surface and creating quite a commotion. The young woman stopped and turned in the water to be confronted by not one but two large sharks fighting it out. *This is not good.* I could hear her gasping and screaming underwater, but I was too busy dissuading the large fellow from making a meal of her. I snapped repeatedly at the tiger, carving large marks on its tough hide. Unlike the tiger sharks I'd passed while circling the island, this fellow was not going down without a fight. The tiger shark twisted its head and bit back, repeatedly lunging toward me, clearly irritated at my intrusion. Its jaws extended from its skull every time it lunged, then slammed shut with an audible crunch near my head. Thankfully, it had missed me. Annoyed at its persistence, I pushed my snout deep into its gills with all my strength, driving the animal over the near-shore reefs and into the shallows, inverting it. I heard its jaws snapping wildly. My goal was to distract the shark enough that it would relinquish its intent to feed and move out into deeper waters.

Now the shark lay in the shallows, gyrating its tail in spasms in an attempt to return to deeper water. I wasn't sure how I could help it get back out. It wasn't like I had hands to grab onto something. It necessitated a few tries, but the shark eventually extricated itself from its trap in the shallows and jettisoned itself into the depths, clearly done with fighting.

I watched the shark as it vanished into the depths. Convinced that the danger had passed, I turned back to the woman who had, by this time, reached the safety of the beach. The woman was clutching her chest. Her mouth was wide open, and she was breathing heavily. There was no mistaking the shocked expression on her face. I backed off from the shallows and continued to watch her, concerned. The poor woman sat down on a partially submerged rock and gazed out at the sea. She was looking at my dorsal fin which was clearly protruding above the waterline. I couldn't imagine how she must have felt. This experience would probably put her off swimming solo for a while. I descended beneath the waves and continued my journey down the coast. For the first time since that day, I felt something positive. I was feeling satisfied. *Mark vs Shark, 1–0.*

Later in the afternoon, I arrived at Wailea. The surfers were out in droves, but most were lazily drifting on their boards when I arrived. There was a lull in the surf. I passed beneath the outer lineup and watched as their boards rose and fell with each passing wave. The sound of chatter from the surface filled the silence in the depths. I swam further offshore so that I could view the above-water scenery without causing alarm. The Grand Wailea Resort stood prominently behind the beach, the vast complex appearing like a gigantic spider, with the large central structure dominating the scene. Uniformly spaced palm trees swayed in the light breeze between the beach and the resort. Bright green grass interspersed with flower beds laced the grounds behind the beach. Cecilia and I stayed here once. We were both very fond of the resort's Sunday brunches, filling ourselves to the brim until we could no longer move, like lions on the savannah after a hunt. Back in those days we would park ourselves on the beach on inexpensive towels and snore through the afternoon. I experienced waves of nostalgia as I thought about the good times we'd had. Nostalgia followed by guilt.

The beach was full of guests today, enjoying the sun. Families frolicked in the shallows while servers milled about and took orders. How I missed just relaxing with the family. A lone surfer passed by within twenty feet of me, which startled me, but the guy was completely oblivious to my presence. My dorsal fin was partly out of the water, and he was riding the world's smallest wave. *Bloody amateur*, I thought. Long, wet blond locks and not a care in the world. A similarly clad but brunette version slid up beside him, ending in a fist bump. It appeared that I had inadvertently drifted closer to the beach. That was my signal to move out. The prankster in me was tempted to give these guys a scare, but that would likely result in panic amongst the beachgoers and ruin some swimwear. I resigned myself to the depths and made my way further south to Makena Beach.

Having had lots of time to think, a plan was forming in my head, and with it a decision. Rather than giving up or accepting my lot in life, I decided that my best option was to make the journey to the West Coast from Hawaii. At this point, what I wanted more than anything else was to be home, or as close as I could get. Watching Cecilia on those few nights on the beach had confirmed that to me. But I knew deep down it would not be easy. I would need to cross an expanse of open water spanning thousands of miles, and that was only if I didn't deviate from the path at any point. The average depth of the ocean along this path is fourteen thousand feet. The thought of making that crossing made my stomach sink.

To prepare, it would be necessary for me to familiarize myself with this body as much as possible. Practice using my senses in a variety of scenarios. Apply risk analysis from my engineering training. It would be necessary for me to build up my confidence swimming in deep water and work on honing my skills as an ocean predator. Training would include multiple circuits of Maui and the neighboring islands.

I would have to learn to feed, to navigate, and to fend for myself out in the deep blue. I had little to fear from predators around the islands, but I wasn't sure this logic would hold any weight out in the heart of the Pacific. Killer whales, or orcas, were fond of great white livers. I'd need to keep an eye out for them and other large predators. One thing was certain: very little is known about the deep ocean. Over eighty percent of the ocean has never been mapped or explored by humans.

Despite the richness of sea life around the islands, I was still having challenges feeding. I was simply not adept enough to capture prey and relied on this vessel's owner to compensate while I slept. To prepare for the long journey, I would need to stock up on reserves. The seas are not exactly bountiful in the open space between coastlines.

As for navigation, I had the benefit of swimming east toward a very long coastline. As long as I could keep myself eastbound, I should strike the American or Canadian coast at some point. As I saw it, I had several options to keep me moving in the right direction. First and foremost, there was the sun. As long as there was fair weather, I should be able to note the sun's position and align myself. At one point I even considered using my dorsal fin as a sundial, using the extended rotation of my eyeballs to observe my fin's shadow along my back. The problem was, once my eyeball was far back, I couldn't keep it from rolling all the way into my head. On the few occasions I could get a glimpse rearward, it was clear that my vision did not extend to the area near my dorsal fin.

Ships regularly traverse the Pacific on established routes. Though large and heavy when ladened with cargo, they still move faster than most sea life, pushing between fifteen and twenty knots, but I should be able to follow them for reasonable distances and then wait for the next boat to follow. There are five or six main trade routes connecting Hawaii with the mainland. The thing is, the destinations can vary between Vancouver BC and Los Angeles. To be honest, I would be happy just to make contact anywhere along the West Coast. Having grown up and spent a lot of time on the West Coast, I was familiar enough with the coastline to navigate my way to San Francisco Bay.

Nighttime voyaging brought other challenges. My dead reckoning skills were rusty as hell. Not since my days sailing with my dad had I done any navigation by stars or landmarks. And there was another thing: I would need to accommodate my sidekick's habit of roaming off the chosen path. Ideally, if I could cover fifty miles a day, the trip would take between fifty and a hundred days. This, of course, was if nothing went wrong. Worst case? Maybe a year or more. I was counting on somewhere in between those extremes.

I still had to address the elephant in the room: How on earth was I going to communicate once the opportunity came? I thought deeply about different modes of communication. Without the means to use verbal language, I would be restricted to simpler, more binary forms of communication. I couldn't generate sounds like a whale. My Morse was rudimentary, but effective. But without proper limbs, my body could not construct messages or manipulate objects. There was no practical way to create messages in the sea that would be visible from above.

I would have to figure out some kind of physical

mechanism for communication, and then I would have to attract the attention of curious individuals willing to engage with me. The only parts of my body over which I had precise control were my eyes and my jaws. I could control my eyes independently, rolling them back into the socket, but the process was slow. Writing out a sentence was going to take some effort. Still, it was better than nothing. If that didn't work, there was the possibility of extending and manipulating my jaws rapidly. Trying to decipher a message coming from the jaws of a large shark would require a recipient with a serious set of cojónes.

It was also very clear to me that this was going to be painfully slow. How would I get anyone to sit still enough in my presence to actually recognize my actions as communication? How would I communicate with a diver who panicked in my presence? A diver in a cage was a distinct possibility. For this to succeed, I would have to travel further south. Best bet would be Mexico, off the Baja coast, or even better, the island Guadalupe.

Departure

I'd probably circumnavigated Maui six or seven times before summoning enough courage to depart the islands and make my way to the West Coast. Lately, my sense of time has become more of a gut sensation. I figured it had taken me two days to complete one circuit of the island. Six passages of the island periphery would cover two weeks, give or take a day.

With each circuit, I'd made several attempts to feed. The situation had reached a stage where I could no longer afford to be selective. I loved tuna meat, but the fish were just too fast for me to capture. I needed to work on my predation techniques, using nature as my guide. Relying on fishing charters only worked near the islands. Feeding out in the Pacific would be a whole different matter. I also held preconceived notions about feeding, like avoiding small whales or their offspring. From a practical perspective, consuming a juvenile whale would take me a long way. I might not need to feed at all during the crossing. I mulled the possibility but heard my older daughter's voice in my conscience, telling me to leave the large cetaceans alone. Dolphins were also a possibility… but then it was Amelia's voice scolding me. *Shit, I better eat a lot of fish.*

I used the beach near our accommodation in Kaanapali as a point of reference. There was no rational reason to show up at that beach after each passage of the island. It had simply become a longing. I desperately held on to the memory of Cecilia sitting alone on the beach at night. I took a last, long look at the beach. Since Kaanapali was on the west side of the island, I needed to head north and then east toward Hana. From there it would be a forty-five-degree northeastern swim to the Californian coast. On paper it sounded relatively uncomplicated. I could follow ships along the shipping lanes heading east, as long as my own vessel's owner followed through as well. My fear, other than navigating a deep and menacing ocean and possibly ending on the bottom, was losing direction and wandering aimlessly without ever again seeing land. It was weird that the islands were a source of comfort for me, despite my circumstances. Staying, however, was not an option. The trip was not without risk and my mind was only beginning to fathom the multitude of outcomes. *Fuck it.*

The immediate terrain around Maui is pretty shallow for a few miles and then it drops precipitously to insane depths. I remember looking at marine depth charts of the islands, and the drop-off a few miles off the coast of Maui was staggering. About ten miles offshore as one heads northeast, Hana Ridge appears like a submerged cliff and leads into the Hawaiian trough. An abyssal plain if there ever was one. Here, the ocean drops from two thousand feet to eighteen thousand feet in short order. If it was possible, I could try using the Molokai fracture zone to navigate my way east. The vertical rifts in the zone make a beeline to Baja, Mexico, but would require staying at a depth of over twelve thousand feet for extended periods. I didn't think my nerves could handle all that darkness, not to mention the limited oxygen and the intense cold at those depths. The typical temperature profile of the thermocline starts at a balmy fifty-five degrees at six hundred feet and drops to thirty-nine degrees at three thousand feet. Below that the water temperature stays just above freezing. Swimming shallow sounded like a plan. *Now where did I put my GPS?*

The Hawaiian Islands are volcanoes at various stages of development. I recalled years ago driving up Haleakalā, the big volcano on Maui, and listening to a volcanologist explain that the islands were slowly crumbling and that in a few million years they would erode down to sea level. He also mentioned that the weight of the volcanoes was sinking the seafloor at a rate of one inch per year. I guessed if you owned property here there was no reason to worry, just yet.

As I made my way to Hana, I occasionally stopped to marvel at the coastline. This part of Maui had a more dramatic coastline than the low-lying terrain of the western coast. I could see the headlights of cars making their way slowly to Hana, a slow drive with endless turns and a waterfall every few hundred yards. Cecilia and I had made the complete trip around the island before we had kids.

Though it was further south along the eastern coast of Maui, some of my fondest memories with Cecilia were of during our time wandering through the bamboo forest along the Pipiwai trail. Fifteen years ago, it was rare to meet people there in the early morning. I don't think I have ever been so enchanted with a woman as while walking through that endless forest of bamboo. Cecilia would spontaneously run between the weaving stalks, appearing and disappearing, teasing me to follow. Sweating from exertion, I chased her toward the Waimoku waterfall at the end of the trail. When I arrived at the end of the path, all I found was a small pile of clothes dumped onto a wooden platform. In front of me appeared an emerald pool, fed from copious amounts of water provided by the waterfall. Sheets of water cascaded from above, obscuring everything. Great mists of vapor rose from the rocks behind the pool. The water level was high from recent rainfall, so the pool was deeper than usual. Somewhere in there, she was waiting for me. I felt like I was being lured to my doom, with a smile on my face.

How I longed to be with her now. Just thinking about it reinforced my desire to get home, whatever the costs.

As I approached the eastern side of the island, I recognized the lighthouse at Hana. It was more of a beacon than a lighthouse. The shores on the east side of Maui are black from the solidified lava and very rocky, and the seas are turbulent. Inhospitable is the word I would use. Once I reached the most northeasterly point of Maui's coastline, I paused. I took one last, sad look at the island that had been my home the past few weeks.

For a while I floated on the surface, letting the waves and current carry me further eastward. I looked up at the cloudless sky and gazed at the stars. Digging deep into my memories, I tried to access whatever knowledge I had of star constellations and celestial navigation. The data was coming up a little short. Polaris, the North Star, was clearly recognizable in the night sky. Lying toward the north near the horizon from my position, it should provide a steady reference. It took a while before I could recall the star Betelgeuse within Orion's constellation, and the track it takes over the Pacific, rising at dusk in the east and passing directly overhead as it makes its way west. Ancient mariners used this celestial body and others to navigate the oceans. Combined with the sun's daily movements, I had some basic tools of navigation.

I summoned the little courage that I had and peered toward the eastern horizon. Looking eastward, I noticed a lighted beacon. These were ocean buoys used for sea level measurement and wave activity. I came across a few buoys separated every few miles. It felt comforting to have these lights pave my way toward an uncertain future. When the last of the lights passed me by, I took a final look at the night sky and descended.

The familiar underwater terrain around Maui was now replaced by a foreboding darkness. I avoided looking down. I kept myself near enough to the surface that I could see the waves from below. Angst built up in me again. A part of me desperately wanted to return to the comparative security of the islands. Overcoming my fears, I moved steadfastly forward, focusing on getting closer to the mainland. *Only a few months*, I told myself. It was all that really mattered to me at this point: to get as close to home as possible. I still had a lot of distance to cover. Any number of things could happen. I hadn't slept in days and mental exhaustion was setting in.

Then, almost as if on schedule, I fell asleep.

When I awoke again, I was unaware of my depth or whereabouts. I could see light coming from the surface and made the decision to ascend and look around. A rather futile exercise, I might add, since there was nothing to see other than sky and waves. There was no turning back, since the islands had long retreated from the horizons. The ocean waves gently raised and lowered my hulk as I looked around. My orientation had suffered, and it was hard to make out what time of day it was. If it was morning, was I looking east, or was it the afternoon sun? It was very confusing. I would need to wait a few minutes and see if the sun was rising or setting.

Gazing at the horizon, I saw a large cargo ship approaching. I figured I had a 50–50 chance it was heading east. From its name and flag, I gathered the ship was of Danish origin, and was heavily laden. It was probably sailing from the ports of Shanghai. Hundreds of containers stacked up high, heading to the west coast. I hung out by its port side and followed alongside it for several days. A small school of fish hung out by its stern. Sure enough, the sun set behind me.

Because of their speeds, following transport ships for extended periods is impossible for a shark. There is too much energy expenditure involved. Underwater, the ships are very loud. While swimming in its slipstream saved me some effort, the noise level often became intolerable. Despite this, I tried cruising close to the ship, but at ten knots it was moving too fast for me, and I could sense both hunger and fatigue building up, so I backed off and slowed my pace. This helped reduce the hunger issue and I could think more clearly. But pretty soon I would need to find food. In general, large sharks can eat a single large meal—a big fat seal or other large mammal—and go for weeks without feeding. Out here, most of the prey lacked the necessary fat to sustain me for weeks on end. The open sea was surprisingly devoid of life. For days I saw absolutely nothing. The ship was now far ahead and beyond my vision. However, I could still see the smoke rising from its stacks.

Remarkably, the owner of this vessel had also failed in finding food. I was delirious from hunger. If I let myself sleep, then there was a possibility the shark would feed on its own. The thought of waking up in the deep was the only thing holding me back, but I had little choice in the matter. I, or rather we, needed to feed, so I relaxed and let go.

When I woke the following day, I was disappointed to find myself still insanely hungry. This was not good. After swimming near the surface for several hours I came across a small pod of humpback whales, comprising several adults and a calf. The calf looked mighty interesting as a potential source of food, but there was no getting past the presence of the adults, which were conversing. They were many times my size and probably well aware of my presence.

Sensibility and common sense went out the window. Deep down, I really didn't want to upset a whale's day, but I was starving. Humans do surprisingly dumb stuff when famished. Your blood sugar drops, you lose patience, you yell at everyone, and you can't concentrate. Where is that energy bar when you need it? It wasn't my finest hour. I snuck up from behind, between the two adults and tried to nip the calf in the tail and slowly drag it backwards. On my first attempt, I unfortunately barreled into the side of one adult. Not good. I got a strong swish of its tail, and the message was clear. Great whites roll their eyes back into the socket when biting prey, as a reflexive act. This made coordination between a starving brain and my jaws problematic.

I was still behind the calf when I sensed a large presence behind me. Another large adult whale was creeping in from behind and below me. I could sense its bulk as it pushed forward beneath me. At first, I was concerned about this, but not enough to put aside my hunger, so I persisted in my half-assed attempt to nab the calf. I could hear the whales conversing amongst themselves, though it was a pity I couldn't understand them. It might have prepared me for what was about to transpire.

The adult below me began to rise and lift me toward the surface. Soon I found myself beached on the whale's back like a bloated slug, unable to move. This was not good. I was literally asphyxiating. My vision was blurring, and I could sense an oncoming headache of epic proportions. There was no escaping the ridiculousness of my situation. Thankfully whales don't like to sit forever on the surface, and the whale that had lifted me up eventually descended again beneath the waves. I rolled off into the water. After getting my bearings, I moved off and started looking for easier game. Lesson learned: don't mess with whales.

I had a bit of luck later in the day when I came across a school of yellowfin tuna. I had the advantage of coming in from behind, so they never saw me coming. Tunas are fast, but they are not exactly clever. I charged in and grabbed the closest fish. The remaining tuna caught on to my presence and scampered, making any possibility of an encore performance impossible. The tuna I nabbed was a good size one, maybe three or four hundred pounds. It should keep me going for a while. I could feel the fish writhe in my jaws. Blood from the fish's wounds trailed into my gullet and through my gills. That I could taste the meat in my mouth revealed to me the existence of a tongue, but unlike my own I could not move it. The senses in my mouth and nose went absolutely wild from the taste of blood. It was almost a kind of euphoria, a rush, and it felt wonderful. Though probably not for the tuna.

I was getting a sense of how powerful my jaws were. Once I nabbed the tuna, it was easy to consume the fish in three or four bites, shredding muscle and sinew between my teeth. The taste was actually familiar, like eating raw fish, but with more blood. It was funny to think that as a human several ounces of tuna would satisfy me, but here I was pounding down hundreds of pounds of meat as if it was nothing. There was hardly a struggle. Anatomically, the body of a tuna is mostly muscle with minimal fat content, so I would need to hunt again in a few days.

Oddly, it seemed I had inherited something from the shark. I didn't notice it at first, but upon replaying the scene in my mind, I recalled my eyes had indeed rolled back when I lunged for the tuna. So there was a little crosstalk between the two of us. Would there be any others? Time would tell.

For a short while, my famishment subsided. This was very satisfying. I realized if I was to survive, I would need to get more efficient at hunting. Or just let my owner take over.

Days turned into weeks as I progressed across the Pacific. As the sun arced overhead, I got a sense that I was still moving in the right direction. If I kept going at this pace and direction, it would only be a matter of time before I saw land. I used every trick I could muster to keep myself engaged mentally. I would think back to my childhood, to my parents and my life growing up. Every argument at the dinner table became a cherished moment. Shouting matches between my brothers and my father were replayed in my mind ad nauseam, to my giddy amusement. But many unresolved moments from childhood crept up between the fond episodes of family life. My mother and father had had many difficulties in their marriage, most of it because of my father's stubborn nature. My father was a sweet man, but very much a product of his generation. There was not the slightest doubt in my mind that he loved my mother, but it was also clear to me he was a serial misogynist. My older brother inherited some of this, but being the middle child gave me some perspective. Whatever misogynism remained in me was wiped clean when I married Cecilia.

I thought long and hard about my father's death. Though he'd never been a big smoker aside from the occasional cigar, my father liked to drink. As a sober person, he rarely revealed his feelings, but if he drank a libation or two his emotional meter rose a notch. Funny how alcohol brings out the best and worst in people. He never drank to drunkenness—rather, he simply became too tired and would fall asleep. Thankfully, my father had the sense to call my mother to come and pick him up when he had a little too much. A few drinks elevated him, and he became a much more empathetic and affectionate person.

Despite his faults, I had many fond memories of my father. His love of music and his trove of albums in the basement were what stood out most. My father collected music from different genres, but his love of jazz was clear from the size of the collection. On weekends, he would engage in some carpentry project in the garage, and Miles Davis would be belting it out on his cheap cassette player. On his deathbed I played Miles to ease his suffering. Though disease wasted away his body, his forefinger tapped jubilantly on his chest to the beat of "Bitches Brew." In my head I played "Bags' Groove" and "On the Corner" on repeat as I made my way east. I had found at least one way to maintain my sanity.

My memories were intact as far as I could see, which was

an encouraging sign. Despite my transformation I was still the same old Mark, just bigger and meaner on the outside. I could traverse the length of my life in my memories without effort. Sometimes I tried concentrating in an attempt to connect with the beast whose body I now inhabited. Even in my dreams, all I found were my own thoughts, my own weird distortions of reality. No visions of battles with other sharks or other creatures of the sea. Could the creature observe me while it waited for me to sleep? Was it witness to my thoughts and memories, however alien they would appear to such an animal? Did it understand or even register its current predicament? My rational side accepted the simple version of the story: that the shark was unaware of its surroundings while I was awake and simply resumed being a shark when I slept. We coexisted, unaware of each other.

Lapse

I was in the midst of another quiet day in the ocean when the barnacle-covered bottom of a fishing trawler passed above me. Extraordinary, I thought, that with so much ocean around me, this boat had to pass right over me. The monotonous rumble of its engines broke the silence as it trudged along. I could feel the cyclic beat of the pistons passing through my body. Perhaps I wasn't being too attentive, as there was no mistaking its characteristic sound from beneath the waves. Sound travels farther in water than in air, so I had no excuse for not picking it up earlier. It was becoming a habit of mine to approach and follow seagoing vessels; perhaps it had become a subconscious tendency. Being close to ships meant being close to people.

I had seen similar boats miles out from the coastlines of Hawaiian Islands, but never this far out in the open sea. Trawlers have a respectable range and are often out at sea for extended periods. One summer in my twenties, I decided to work on a trawler out of Seward, Alaska. It was the hardest job I ever had. The boat was called *Leaving it to Cod*, so on that alone I was probably asking for trouble. On paper I was both a deckhand and freezer loader, but my duties didn't end there. Even after returning from the sea, we were required to spend several hours unloading, cleaning, and preparing for the next day's haul. Ten- or twelve-hour shifts on a rocking vessel made for an unforgettable summer. I alternately froze and sweated in my bibs. Despite this, I respected the crews I worked with above all. I couldn't imagine a more dangerous and exhausting enterprise. It took weeks to get the smell out of my skin.

The sea was quite rough today, more so than usual. I estimated I was cruising along at one hundred feet, though depth was often difficult to gauge in these conditions. The water was more turbid today than usual. Light is completely absorbed at five hundred feet, but this again depends on the clarity of the water. Sometimes I would find myself in absolute clear water, with visibility extending several hundred feet. Then it would change and drop to where I couldn't see more than forty or fifty feet. In those conditions, I could genuinely observe the plankton passing by my eyes.

It had been a month since I'd left the islands, but I had no means of judging the distance traveled. The days slipped into one another. I thought about Ben and the company we'd started five years ago. Prior to our departure, Ben and I had finished the second major funding and put together a revised business plan, to counter the comments and concerns of our first investors. We presented it to the board, who then bombarded us with questions regarding our financials and any contingency plans should we arrive at our dry well date without any new funding in place. We debated bridge loans and potential staff reductions. These meetings pained Ben, but they were necessary evils if we were to survive for the long game. I took the punches for him. Like much of the varied sea life I had encountered, the investors we met were, for the most part, hardened individuals, responsible for allocating tens of millions in investment funds with nary a blink. Reckoning would come later.

While I was recalling a spreadsheet in my mind, I noticed the edges of a vast net being pulled alongside me. The warp wires were slowly being winched toward the vessel up ahead. The otter boards were only fifty feet ahead of me and were clearly ascending. I looked around quickly and was shocked to see that the opening of the net had reached up to me, together with a lot of unlucky fish. Looking behind me, it was clear that the back of the net was still far behind my position. There was a large, dark section visible in the middle of the net, which I guessed to be a mass of catch.

I powered forward to reach the front ring of the net. Small red floats lined the warp wires all the way to the surface. How I'd missed the cables of the ship in the first place was beyond me. This was deeply unsettling. Even though the trawler appeared to move slowly on the surface, the edge of the net was not getting any closer. If I didn't slip out of the front opening of the net I would become bycatch, which could mean any number of things. The rule is that great whites and other large sharks are normally tossed overboard, but who knows what really happens out in the open sea. Finning was still occurring in some quarters. Large fish or dolphins, when caught, tend to get tangled in the netting, which leaves their fate up to the empathy of the fishing crew.

All I understood was that I had to stay ahead of the lines and bail out. The net was being pulled forward and upward. Powering forward with all the effort I could muster, I got within twenty feet of the buoy lines of the net. The otter boards were directly in front of me, swaying in the current. If I could maintain my current pace, I ought to be able to slip between the cables and out of the net altogether.

Just then, a few large tunas barreled into me from behind, striking me on both my left and right flanks. They were going all out in full-blown panic, in a last-bid attempt to escape the ensnaring net. Two tunas rammed the otter board and flailed in panic, in the process falling back in the current and striking me in the snout. In the tumult that ensued, we all fell deeper into the net. Instinctively, they were attempting to outrun the net, as I was. They were certainly better equipped, from a speed perspective, but in the spirit of natural selection and with poor cognitive skills, they had messed up, taking me with them.

The net was rapidly closing as it was being winched up. The narrowing of the net meant that we were getting slowly packed in, making movement nearly impossible. I tried biting into the net, hoping to tear it, but to no avail. There was simply not time enough for me to punch a hole big enough for me to get through. To journey all this way and then end up getting slaughtered and packed in ice was a dismal prospect. As far as I could see, my options were seriously limited. I could feel the squirming of hundreds of fish behind me.

Being at the head of the mass of fish entitled me to a front-row view of my future tormentors. From below the surface, I could see the gunwales of the trawler, the winch pulling the net, and the fishermen waiting eagerly for their catch. As the winch raised me above the waterline, I heard screams from multiple people. One of the men nearest me had his hands on his head and his mouth wide open in a sign of shock and disbelief. I was hanging in midair, suspended in the net. The winch strained under the load of my weight, with sounds of groaning and creaking coming from the boom. Although the guide wires supporting the booms were not intended for this kind of load, they still managed to hold for now.

Several men ran to the winch controls and stopped the hauling of the net. The captain stepped out from the bridge and took a long, hard look at me. He removed his cap and scratched his head. The boat heaved from the load in the nets. I could feel myself swaying. The water had drained from my gills, making me dizzy and lightheaded. I'd heard of stories of beached sharks surviving for hours before returning to the ocean when the tide returned. This meant I had some time. My attention turned to the fisherman closest to me, who examined me at close quarters. He touched my snout, squeezing the tip. I tried to react, but without a voice or other means to communicate, there was little I could do. I snapped my jaws at him a few times to let him know I was not happy. He stepped back and turned to the captain.

"What do we do, Cap?" he hollered over the din of the engines.

The captain cocked his head sideways. He replied sarcastically, "We don't have space for him in the freezer. Great whites are not on the menu yet."

That was reassuring. The captain yelled at some deckhands and commanded them to release me over the side, but it was apparent that the young men had no interest in carrying out his order. They just stood and stared at me, bewildered and frightened by the large creature in front of them, and then back at him. I remembered from my fishing days the horror stories of large sharks being brought up and then biting anything or anyone in reach when they were released from the netting.

"For fuck's sake, lads, pull it over the side and cut open the net. I still want to save the rest of the catch. So no fucking it up," the captain shouted.

Still no action. An older, grizzled fellow wearing a bright orange bib and massive green wellies came up from below and shoved the young deckhands aside. He walked right up to my left eye and peered deeply into it. I stared right back. I don't think I have ever stood this close to a fisherman. While he fretted, I studied his sun-worn face. My lightheadedness reduced my overall stress level a little, but my fate was not yet determined, so I tried to concentrate. Not that I could do much. I tried rolling my eyes to get his attention, but this just confused him.

"This one is very much alive," he yelled to the captain. *You are very much observant, numb nuts,* I thought. He stepped back and walked about the net. He pulled at it, trying to move its contents—that would be me—towards the edge railing. He tried heaving the net around to get better traction. Leaning forward from a position of leverage, the man pressed with all his strength. The boom creaked loudly from my weight. He gasped and cursed under his breath, and at one point he let out a roar from his exertions. Despite his best efforts, I was just too big for him.

Unsuccessful at hauling me over the side only made him angrier, and he yelled at the younger fellows to assist him. I surmised there was not much harmony in this team, at least where sharks were concerned. Clearly reluctant, the younger lads each grabbed a part of the netting and pulled. The deckhand nearest my head was the most uneasy and jumped back when I moved my jaw. After a time, the crew managed, with a lot of shoving and cursing, to get me hanging over the starboard railing. The boat heeled under my weight, but at this point I didn't care if it capsized.

The captain screamed for the remaining deckhands to move to the opposite side of the boat to act as counterweights. *Really*, I thought, *eight men against one large shark. Someone needs a physics lesson.* The same grizzled fellow from before came up to my head with a long spear. I gazed apprehensively at the length of the blade and watched it pass within inches of my left eye. The blade edge turned away to cut at the netting, but the metal backside scraped against my skin, causing quite a bit of discomfort as it sliced both my skin and the netting. Another fisherman showed up with a spear and assisted. Now I hurt in two places. Every time the boat heeled, the blade edges would dig deeper into my skin, adding to my already extreme physical discomfort.

After cutting through several feet of netting I began to slip through the hole they were enlarging. Then the unthinkable happened. Since I was quite heavy up front, and they were cutting right beneath my head, as soon as the last thread of the netting beneath my head broke, I fell back into the sea. But not all of me. My head was dragging in the surf and colliding with the hull of the boat, while the rest of me—my so-called empennage—hung still in the netting. The boat heeled hard starboard from my weight. This was a serious pickle to be in. At least I had some water running over my gills, but the violently churning water about by head made it impossible for me to see. I shook myself as hard as I could to break free, but I was still stuck. Looking upwards, or rather backwards, I saw a brave deckhand crawl up the netting that was holding my tail. While gripping the supporting boom above him with one hand and thrusting the spear with his other hand, he attempted to cut more of the netting to set me free. Eventually the last strands of netting holding my tail were cut, and I fell back into the sea in a plume of bubbles created by my splash.

The boat quickly righted itself. I heard the engines throttle up and the propellers reengage. The boat and the remaining net that was still submerged passed by me unimpeded. With large, pained eyes, the tuna inside the net looked at me in astonishment. Were they actually thinking?

I was relieved, but I was also furious at myself. This should never have happened. I had been complacent. If I was to survive out here in the open ocean, I would need to focus on what was going on around me. It was incumbent on me to investigate any noise or change in the environment. With the senses I was given, I would hear and feel things long before I could see them. Most of my days were going to be monotonous, so noticing the occasional change in routine should be well within my capabilities. *There endeth the lesson.* The first of many.

A week later, I came across another fishing trawler, but this ship did not place a massive net in the sea. Keeping a safe distance and following from behind, I recognized several large pelagic fish being pulled along in the water. Upon closer inspection I saw that this was a longline fishing boat. Judging by the size of the vessel, I estimated that the main line dragged behind this boat probably extended for miles. Every hundred feet, a shorter branch line or gangion extended from it. These lesser lines connected to baited hooks and, more often than not, something had already taken the bite. Not everything that had been hooked was aquatic. A poor albatross had drowned while trying to pull the bait off a hook, only to find itself ensnared. Though lifeless, it drifted pass me with its wings outstretched as if in flight.

This longline ship did present a unique opportunity for me. It was sailing relatively slowly and there was fish catch as far as the eye could see. I was captivated by all the tuna I saw, but I was looking for something bigger. A large ten-foot blue marlin caught my eye, as it would make for a spectacular meal. Careful to avoid getting hooked myself, I bit behind the head. As I ate through its carcass, the tail section fell away and began to sink. The marlin was quite large and beefy, and consuming it all ended up being quite a challenge. In the end, I got lazy and simply returned to the longline ship for more game. *Now if I could get these guys to sail all the way to the West Coast...*

Cruise

Ideally, crossing the Pacific between Maui and the West Coast would take me between forty-five to fifty days, give or take. If I could manage an average of fifty miles each day, and maintain my direction, then I should see land in two months' time. This optimism would only hold if I didn't waiver from the course. Truth is, I was course correcting the whole time, which meant that my true course was probably more zigzag in nature. It didn't help that this vessel's captain had a tendency to wander from the chosen path.

With this in mind, I believed the trip would probably require double the estimated time or more. One bad course correction and it was possible I could lose weeks or months—but it didn't matter to me. I was only interested in the endgame, though, ironically, I did not know how it was going to play out.

Most of my journey, I imagined, would be uneventful and pretty monotonous. Ninety-nine percent boredom punctuated by one percent absolute terror. This guesswork was, of course, updated from time to time by equal parts optimism and frustration. The open ocean was often quite empty, literally devoid of life, except for microscopic organisms. Currents and changing visibility conditions, both above and below water, could play havoc with my sense of direction. Occasionally, I found myself unintentionally heading north. It wasn't like I could call up the GPS in my palm and get an immediate status on traffic and roadwork. I recalled a discussion among marine biologists that sharks had an innate sense of direction, possibly derived from the earth's magnetic fields, or perhaps smell. It didn't seem to matter which way I pointed or sniffed; my ability to derive quantitative information from my senses had not evolved to the level of usefulness.

Periodically, I would ascend to the surface to see the stars at night. It was an easy matter to find the Big Dipper or Taurus and keep their positions locked, as long as the night sky remained clear. Polaris would remain a fixed reminder of the north. I had become accustomed to Betelgeuse's passage in the night sky above me. Dead reckoning, when all else fails, is not to be undervalued. Knowing my average speed and distance covered, I could estimate my position. I was not terribly concerned with accuracy. Weather could throw a wrench in my plans. A few cloudy days or a dense fog could set me in the wrong direction. I had been pretty fortunate so far. All I needed to do was make landfall eastward. If I was too far north or south, it would make no difference to me.

As a shark, there are some advantages. For one, my night vision was pretty exceptional. It took a little adjustment to get everything sharp above the surface, but there was no doubting how much I could see with these new eyes of mine. There were no city lights to blot out the night sky, just millions of stars to delight in. The Milky Way was truly magnificent out here, a mottled dark and light band arching across the night sky that reminded me of my insignificance. Somewhere in its middle, a gigantic black hole ruled my local universe. With its characteristic and dominating shape in the night sky, the Milky Way was added to my navigation toolset.

My wide-field vision allowed me to see the entire night sky without panning my head. I had no difficulty stitching images from both eyes into one large contiguous image in my mind and filtering out the subtle black region separating them. I could stay on the surface like this for hours, but a sense of urgency reminded me to move on.

Whales and large sharks are known to raise their heads above the surface in an activity called spyhopping. They are simply looking around, checking out the life above the waves. Is it curiosity that drives them, or something else? Do they raise their heads above the waves at night to see the stars? I wondered if these specks of light had some meaning to both the sentient and the instinct-driven animal. Could they discern patterns in the night sky and use them for navigation?

Hunting in the vast sea had its challenges. Stealth was pretty much impossible. It came down to speed and agility, both of which were difficult when you were my size. Prey could sense me long before I had visual contact. There were no games of cat and mouse in the open, unless the odd ship showed up. Large tankers and bulk carriers were particularly useful. I found hiding between the screws and the large tiller gave me some advantage against certain types of prey. However, I tried to jump a mako once, and what a fool's game that was. I could literally see the cheeky grin on the bastard as he left me in the dust. Sunfish, on the other hand, were far too easy prey, and I felt guilty feeding on them.

In my solitude, I found myself having conversations with Cecilia. She would sit next to me on some beach or on the sofa back home. It took me some time to block out the anguished expression on her face, which was clearly induced by my guilt. Sometimes conversations came from our past, when we first met, or during our early years as a married couple. Cecilia had been entirely supportive of my ambitions, even when it cost her. She could also be tough on me on occasion, pulling me down when I became too self-absorbed or overbearing. Cecilia could also be moody, and downright menacing when there were dark clouds in her mind. Lately, her discontent at the progress of my company and its constant intrusion into our lives has been taking its toll. And now this. I honestly couldn't imagine what she was going through.

"Don't let them walk all over you," she would say, gently preparing me for the onslaught to come. Be it a crucial meeting with an investor or a board gathering, she would get up early and help me prepare in the mornings. Later the same day, we would meet for coffee at our favorite cafe and review my experiences. Despite the secrecy and discretion sometimes required in my job, I told her everything. I wanted her to know what I was up against. In my experience, too many relationships soured from the lack of disclosure between partners. I needed a sounding board to bounce off, someone to share my fears and concerns. Sometimes our conversations in my mind drifted off topic. We could be discussing something as mundane as a car repair bill, or damage to the house caused by a recent storm. In other conversations, our girls interrupted us. Sarah would barge in on our private discussion and complain about her boredom. I would walk through the house looking for things for her to do. I missed my decrepit old house.

While I was thinking about Cecilia, I picked up a strange scent in the water. It was particularly pungent, reminding me of old fish in the garbage, or fish offal tossed by deckhands off the stern of fishing trawlers. The sea was empty of mechanical sounds, so that was not a possibility. Under normal circumstances, I would have found it repulsive. Now, it piqued my curiosity; against my better judgment, I followed the scent. Whatever it was, it was directly ahead and, fortunately for me, in an easterly direction.

The silliness of following a stink trail from a boat to be guided home was not lost on me. Navigation by smell. The olfactory sense of a shark is legendary, and I was privy to its marvelous effectiveness. Whatever it was, it was getting closer. I rose to the surface and peeked around to catch a glimpse of the source. In all directions I saw nothing but waves and clouds. The scent was quite specific and increased in intensity as I continued further along.

Earlier, the scent had had a rotting, offal character to it. Now the scent struck me as oily, as if I was swimming through an ooze of fish entrails. Normally by this point I would be gagging from the stench, but apparently, I was fine with it. There was no directionality to the smell any longer; it was intense everywhere. The water had also lost some of its clarity. Up close, I could see tiny, white filaments passing before my eyes. The surrounding water was saturated with the same substance, giving it a milky consistency. It resembled shredded tissue. Whatever was in the water had once been part of something bigger.

It was then that I saw the chalky outline of a semi-submerged blue whale. The massive carcass was severely bloated and bobbed just below the surface. I swam around it to get a better look. Its enormous mouth was open, and I marveled at the size of the tongue and the layer upon layer of bristles in its baleen. A large tiger shark was feeding near the tail, pulling chunks of blubber off in a frenzied fashion. Smaller sharks cowered in the distance and fed only when their larger cousins gave them berth. Animals approached from far and wide and made off with the spoils.

I counted five or six species of shark in the immediate area. A blue shark darted in and grabbed what it could, avoiding eye contact with the other sharks. They all made space when I arrived, though I wasn't quite ready to indulge in the buffet. I circled the whale several times, observing nature recoup its losses.

The abdominal area of the whale was no longer dark, with most of its outer skin bitten off or ravaged by scavengers. I noted the large, scalloped bite marks made by large sharks, revealing a milky white layer of blubber. The whale was so large that despite all the feeding going on, none of the feeders had penetrated to its vital organs. Eventually, the gas in the whale would release and the carcass would sink. In the meantime, it would serve as a mid-ocean buffet for all. I could hear Cecilia's voice in the background, urging me on: "Are you going to let it go to waste? What are you waiting for?" as if this was equivalent to eating the four-day-old chicken leftovers in the fridge. I didn't have a clue how long this putrefying carcass had been floating around, but given the limited availability of food, I would have to consider stocking up. The whale blubber would stem my hunger for a few weeks at least.

I moved in for a closer look. The cloudy, lifeless eyes of the whale stared into the depths. This expired cetacean had probably been quite old when it died, judging from its size and girth. I also guessed it had been floating for a while before any other life-form had come across it. When whales die, they sink. It's only through the putrefaction process and the subsequent generation of gas that they come up to the surface again.

I followed the grooves on its skin, looking for an area that was untouched and therefore the least unappetizing. Opening my jaws, I grabbed hold of meat just below the right pectoral fin. I had never bitten into something so large, so it didn't occur to me that my jaws would get stuck. The outer hide of the whale was actually quite tough. I could sense the pulling and tugging of other sharks as they bit again and again into the carcass. Using my limited knowledge gained from the internet, I attempted to cut through the meat by shaking my head in a lateral motion. I made a bit of progress, but I was still stuck.

Looking to my left, I watched with disdain as another large white shark charged the whale and clamped its jaws deep into the tissue. With intense vigor, it shook its head from side-to-side, tearing off large, scalloped shaped chunks of blubber. It repeated this act several times before retiring to the depths.

Here goes, I thought. Using all my strength, I shook my entire body. Eventually, I succeeded in disengaging myself from the whale, removing a small piece of whale skin and the underlying blubber. I swallowed the meat as quickly as I could. To ease my ingestion, I took smaller bites from the whale. I was at the very least comforted by the fact that my competition would not judge me for my pathetic eating style.

Once I reached the blubber, it became much easier to eat. I tore chunk after chunk from the whale, gorging on the meat and fat, filling up for the long voyage home. As for the taste, the seawater was so rancid around the whale that it made little difference. The taste reminded me of venison. For an hour I ate, eventually making a sizable hole in the beast. I could feel my belly fill and spread. Simultaneously satisfied and disgusted, I parted ways with the blue whale and continued on my journey. I now had one less thing to worry about. I resumed my imaginary conversation with Cecilia. She was baking something delicious, and the entire house was filled with the smells of cinnamon and cloves. The girls were sitting with anticipation in the kitchen.

Neptune Speaks

Now that I was all fueled up, I needed to tend to my mental health. It was very lonely out here in the blue. To maintain my sanity, I would need some form of daily routine, some mental exercises to keep the gray cells in line. The goal was to keep Cecilia and the girls fresh in my mind, and to not wonder about the potential horrors that lurked in the deeps below me.

To start, I'd pretend to go through the rhythms of a normal working day. My day would begin with me waking up and peeking in on the girls to see if they had awakened. Then it was a trip to the kitchen to start the coffee machine. Cecilia would still be sleeping; her gentle but loud snoring audible from any room in the house. I'd muse over the contents of the refrigerator and dwell on my personal needs: yogurt and cereal or toast and eggs. Leftover waffles? The coffee machine would let out its characteristic *ding*, marking the official start to my day. I would usually receive an early message from Ned the IT guy that our internet was on the fritz again, or that overnight backup had failed, or some other thing. Janet, my head of marketing, would remind me to call Charles, our principal investor. Ben would call and state emphatically that he was ready to torch the office.

I would be on a telephone call when the girls would scramble down the stairs, followed by the slow steady steps of my wife. The kitchen would hum with frenetic activity, from packing lunches to partial consumption of the morning meal, and once the girls were on their way to school, the dust would settle, and I would be alone with Cecilia. We'd drink our coffees in silence and gaze at each other lovingly from across the table. This would go on for at least five minutes before we would each take a deep breath and let reality barge into our private space again.

I would replay these scenes daily to enforce some attachment to my old reality. I was deeply concerned about forgetting details of my life, that I would eventually become defined only by what I was now, after all my memories had faded.

Replaying these memories also had a downside. They were always the same, or at least that's what I thought. Much like an overplayed cassette, the recording would lose its original character. Holes would develop in the timeline and sometimes events would go out of sequence. I could correct some of these omissions, but it took a concerted effort to reconstruct them as faithfully as possible. I was convinced that my wife looked different from how I currently remember her, which concerned me.

And then it was back to wagging my tail back and forth and scanning my surroundings for any evidence of life. For weeks, the ocean refused to reveal anything. Then, as if out of nowhere, I suddenly found myself in an immense swarm of small pencil squid. The school was enormous, in the thousands, but the mollusks were far too small for me to catch and consume. Between ten and sixteen inches in length, the tiny squid moved rapidly using their biological thrusters, or siphon. Combined with their ability to change color and self-illuminate, they were putting on quite a show for me. The swarm would generate a cascade of color that brightened and darkened, depending on their level of excitation. The light pulsating synchronously between the animals was disorienting as they swept around me. I wondered if I was going to be privy to a rare event. Would they spawn?

It was rather frustrating, since I actually liked eating squid, and here they were for the taking. I imagined them deep fried or grilled in garlic and served with chili mayonnaise. It appeared that the squid were perfectly aware of my shortcomings, as they displayed little fear in my presence. I was enveloped in a cloud of these small creatures, but they left ample space about my body, and moved rhythmically in unison whenever I changed position.

The surrounding water churned with life, the squid darting haphazardly as males hunted females. The water about me soon became turbid with eggs and squid semen. For several hours I engaged in a game of swimming in and out of the cloud of squid. I would circle outside this massive bait ball and then charge it with my mouth gaping open, in a fruitless attempt to scoop up one of my favorite delicacies. I imagine a marine biologist observing my actions would find it all too absurd to present it to any colleague and would just as soon be rid of the data. And then, just like that, they were gone. The sea was empty, and the water became clear again.

As a result of my fooling around, I had become disoriented. I did not know where I was or which way I was going. What a fool I'd been to let my guard down and allow myself to be carried away by whimsy! I rose slowly to the surface and scanned the horizon. Thankfully, I could see a ship in the distance, moving away from the setting sun. I recalibrated and resumed my course. Aside from the low-frequency ambient noise generated by the ship, the ocean was quiet. Or so I believed.

I heard an unusual rumbling, very faint at first and rather random, I thought. It was definitely not mechanical in nature. I slowed my speed and listened carefully. The pitch would rise and fall somewhat and then stop for a short period. Following a few minutes of near silence (the sea never really became completely silent), the noise resumed and then deepened in tone. I pitched my nose downward and descended until I could barely see the surface and leveled off.

The sun was setting, and darkness was encroaching rapidly in the depths. The sound grew again; this time it was clearer, and the water resonated with the changing tones. The frequency pitched up a little, but for all intents and purposes appeared random in structure. Sometimes it seemed like metal grating on metal, or like distant muffled explosions. The sound pitch and intensity varied considerably. It was definitely not whale song, and not organic in origin, from the sound of it. Could it be possible that I was listening to the tectonic plates groan under their strain? Was I listening to the Earth breathe? I had once read about a sound picked up by a passive sonar array in the Pacific that was nicknamed "Julia", most likely caused by an iceberg that ran aground off Antarctica, which lasted over two minutes. The intensity of that event was so great it could be heard worldwide.

I could not locate the source since it sounded like it came from all directions, but logically it was coming from the deep. For several days the sound persisted, keeping me enthralled, and then it eventually faded. Maybe Neptune was speaking to me, unaware that a member of the homo sapiens club was directing one of his apex predators across the Pacific. I could not imagine his horror if he knew. The oceans were a respite from humanity.

For a week I heard nothing unusual. I had almost given up when I heard the most unusual sound of all. First there was a low-key rumble, followed by a period of relative silence. This pattern repeated itself for several days. The sounds were in the low-register range of my hearing but increased slowly in pitch and tone. I was moving closer to its source. In the beginning the sound had little character, but as I approached its source, it became more interesting and varied. It was as if I was listening to a baritone singing voice, modulated with background ocean noise. I was awestruck at the possibility that I could hear this out in the deep emptiness of the ocean. Maybe it was not as empty as I'd thought. This idea left me in a quandary. As scared as I was of venturing into the depths, my curiosity would not let me be.

The idea of descending was still a frightening prospect. How would I navigate? How would I know which way was up or down, in complete darkness? Oxygen content drops with water depth, so at some point I could literally asphyxiate. However, great whites are known to descend to four thousand feet, so in theory I should be okay. I reasoned I could experiment with a few shallow dives and build up my confidence. During the nights my eyes adjusted quickly to darkness, so I wasn't completely blind. Sharks have a marvelous reflective layer in their eyes that concentrates light in low conditions.

Baby steps, I reminded myself.

Briefly, I closed my eyes and relaxed while summoning my inner courage. Then I tilted my body ever so slightly downwards. Spreading my pectoral fins wide, I managed to dampen my rate of descent. I watched the darkness rise about me. I felt like I was falling in a glass elevator into a deep, dark chasm, with no end in sight. The light above waned to a small patch of dark blue. At that point, I stopped descending and waited for my eyes to adjust. I recalled having to wait for my eyes to adjust whenever I went out of the house. It usually took several minutes to fully adjust. My new shark eyes adjusted much faster to the darkness.

I swam for a while at a constant depth, adjusting to the new environment. From my knowledge of gases in water I knew that gas saturation decreases by ten percent for every three feet in depth because of hydrostatic pressure. Just thinking of the weight of all that water above gave me pause. At around three thousand feet there is a region known as the oxygen minimum layer. I was beginning to feel a growing headache, the likely result of a steady decline in oxygen at my current depth. I knew that if I persisted in my descent, the oxygen levels would rise, at least for a while before dropping again.

Satisfied with my progress and confident I could find my way up again, I decided to continue diving for another thirty or forty seconds. Again, total darkness enveloped me, as did the cold. My eyes were adjusting to the extreme low light conditions. When all the light vanished, all that was visible was a contrast image. Occasionally, there appeared blips of light from small, bioluminescent lifeforms that were endemic at these depths. These allowed me to observe particulates passing by my eyes, conveying to my severely stressed brain that I was still descending, with gravity providing a major assist. Fatigue was setting in due to the cold and low oxygen. It would take some exertion on my part to return to the shallows.

The low-pitched rumble came again, but much louder now and more distinct. Oddly, it was reassuring to hear it. This was the deepest I had ever been, and the sound gave me something to think about other than the water pressure, the cold, and the darkness.

I leveled off, orienting myself by watching the direction of particulates near my eyes. This was sometimes deceiving since currents can displace water both vertically and horizontally. Years ago, while diving in Indonesia, I experienced a downward current behind an ocean pinnacle. It caught me off guard and sent me and a few of my fellow divers to the sandy sea bottom, which was thankfully not far below us. From start to finish we dropped fifty feet, a small distance by ocean standards, but it scared the hell out of us. We had no control over our descent, and had it been a deep section of ocean, even a few hundred feet could have been fatal.

In my current situation this was not so much of a dilemma, but leaving my fate to the currents was problematic in many respects. I lost all sense of direction, and I did not know how deep I was. The particulates near my eyes were more or less horizontal, which was encouraging, but occasionally I could feel a current pulling me downwards. A sudden upwelling of unusually warm and turbulent water lifted me. This continued for several hundred feet, and then I was released from its warm grip, to be surrounded by familiar cold water again. It dawned on me that I might have passed over an erupting seamount, deep below me. The cackle of exploding rock was definitely audible. Looking down, I thought I could see the faint glow of molten rock being spewed from the peak of an underwater volcano. At these depths, thermal vents provided an environment conducive to certain types of marine life. I considered descending further to explore, but an inner voice told me to move on.

This was my first foray into the depths. My runaway imagination had got the better of me. Comforted by a plausible explanation, I slowly ascended toward the surface. My fears were receding, and I was growing accustomed to my new skin. The ocean was perhaps not the fearful environment I had conjured in my imagination.

The Bull

When I read Herman Melville's *Moby Dick* as a boy, the immensity of the large white sperm whale and the diminutive, almost meaningless size of the whaling crews traumatized me. They were powerless against not just the whale's ferocity but also the unrelenting sea that cast them about in their fragile hunting boats. And yet the whalers could inflict great pain on the whale with their harpoons, which returned again and again to smash the boats and the ship that had sent them.

I had been cruising along the surface when I observed a large male sperm whale rise from the depths, cruising ever so slowly toward the surface. It moved its broad tail in slow, confident undulations, unhurried after its long journey from the deep. Rows of teeth glistened in the morning light, the jawline pocked with wounds from battles with countless adversaries. I wondered if the sea contained leviathans beyond what deep-sea voyagers had revealed. Legends and myths spoke volumes about monsters, but were they simply constructions of man's fertile imagination?

The bull exuded immense confidence. The massive whale was out here alone, appearing unfettered by its solitary existence and the sea's mysteries. Did it meet other whales during its long journeys?

As is the case for most large mammals, male bulls must often leave the flock to wander the seas alone to avoid confrontations. This was the first time I had felt truly overwhelmed by something so much larger than myself. I did not experience fear, but kinship and respect. Its skin was a midnight black, with deep scars spanning the entirety of its body. Countless acorn barnacles clustered in dense groups that riddled its body. The humpback whales I had met earlier had not elicited fear from me in the same way as this whale, even when they tossed me above the surf like a sardine, to convince me that consuming their calf was not in my best interest. This fellow, however, was fearsome in appearance, and I had no desire to provoke it or enter its safe space. I kept my distance but followed him out of curiosity.

The water was alive with clicks and snapping sounds. Occasionally a trumpet-like squawk came from deep inside the bull. At such a close distance, these sounds were very intense, and made the water vibrate.

I marveled at the size of his head. Most sperm whales that I had seen in photographs and nature programs had rather diminutive heads, lacking the squarish prominence of this bull, which made it appear more like a submarine than a marine mammal.

While maintaining my distance, I moved carefully alongside it so that I could study it. It rotated its massive hulk ever so slightly to get a good look at me. I tried winking, to communicate with it. He was probably wondering what an odd shark I was, making googly eyes at him. I rolled a few times to get his attention. He was completely unfazed at my exploits and let out a deep bellow in response, making vibrations pass through me. I guessed it was his way of saying that I did not impress him. The bull rose to the surface to breathe, the long body arcing and the spray from the blowhole falling on either side. It did this several times, probably preparing for its next dive.

The bull took one last breath and then descended. It slowly

adjusted its attitude until it was nearly vertical. With a few thrusts of its tail, the bull began descending at great speed. I attempted to follow but could not keep up. My fascination was getting the better of me. This was better than any nature program or dive I could ever imagine. I had a ringside seat to watch one of nature's great actors. Soon the bull was out of my sight, but I could still feel the energy of its wake rising from below.

Moving in its slipstream, I hoped to make use of the column of falling water to keep up with him. The thing is a full-grown sperm whale is many times more massive than I am. The vortex wake generated by the sweeping of its enormous tail sent me spinning and tumbling. The analogy of a small Cessna flying behind a Boeing 747 was an adequate comparison. I had no choice but to fall back. The large eddies eventually subsided to a manageable level.

The world around me was rapidly becoming dark. However, even at these depths small bubbles rose and gave me solace that I would eventually find my way to the surface. This was not my first time experiencing the deep, and I would not give up. The thought of witnessing a deep battle in the sea consumed me. My imagination was running at full steam. I could no longer see the bull, but I could hear him. Even though he was far below, his clicks were loud and clear. Using the strength of the vibrations, I figured I could estimate his distance. Steadily, the sound diminished until it was barely audible, and then it was gone. For a while all I heard was the ocean, and I longed to hear his clicks again. I had grown accustomed to the whale, and it comforted me, reminding me I wasn't completely alone. I persisted in following him in the darkness, hoping that a sound would eventually penetrate the lightless world I found myself in. Looking upwards, I saw only blackness. Now and then, small bubbles rose around me, reminding me which way was up.

I hadn't realized how much colder it had gotten, but it was clearly chilly down here. I didn't believe I had ever descended this far. Great whites have higher core temperatures than smaller sharks, and my body was spending more energy to keep its core warm. The low oxygen in the water was also affecting me. I was becoming more and more sluggish. This was certainly risky on my part. I made the decision that I was deep enough and that I'd better ascend if I wanted to keep my wits and survive. I waited for some bubbles to give me some sense of direction. It didn't take long. A series rose in a line rose in front of me, and I followed them toward the surface.

Then I heard the clicks again, faintly at first, then growing steadily stronger. Then there was another sound, a high-pitched, horrifying screech. I looked below me but saw nothing. I continued upward until I could see shades of blue appearing, light penetrating the ocean depths from the world above. The whale made a bellow in response to the screeching, which was now increasing in strength. I looked down again and could barely make out the form of the bull as it ascended. It was moving fast, its tail oscillating at a high rate. What was it fleeing from?

Then the screech came again, this time louder and shriller. The bull was still some distance below me when from the depths below it a pair of enormous tentacles reached out and grabbed the tail of the bull. Whatever it was, it was very large, and the bull was running from it. The bull shook its tail violently, trying to release itself from the grips of those tentacles. I stopped moving and gazed in shock at the scene below me. The bull clicked and bellowed more often now, apparently in the throes of a struggle for its survival. It filled me with a sense of dread and great empathy for this creature. What could I do? I was insignificant to both the bull and whatever was pulling on it. A sense of overwhelming futility filled me, yet my inner voice was screaming at me to ascend. I looked up at the light blue above me and moved upwards. This lasted for about two seconds, and then I rotated my insignificant hulk towards the battle being engaged below me.

I really don't know what came over me. Maybe I pitied the bull too much. Though I was still lacking in a strategy, a plan formed in my head, which at first appeared deranged and probably suicidal. There weren't many options at this stage. I descended quickly, racing directly toward the bull. As I passed by the writhing body of the sperm whale, I glimpsed an enormous squid just below it. The creature was absolutely massive. Its body glowed in the darkness. Chromatophores along its body sent waves of color across its entire length. The center body or mantle was the size of a large greyhound bus, and the two feeding tentacles were very long and thick, like the trunks of an old oak tree, dwarfing the remaining eight arms. These long tentacles were holding the whale in a death grip, clearly intending to drown the bull.

I thought that if I could pass directly under the whale and nip at those tentacles, they might release the whale. I just needed to make sure that I didn't find myself near the many suckers that populated each arm. Up close, I could see serrated teeth on the rim of the suckers. I had to make sure it never got a grip on me. Because of its constant struggling, the whale was making a little headway to the surface. I swam straight for the tentacle attached to the whale's belly. I bit deeply into the arm and removed a sizable chunk of its flesh. The surrounding water vibrated from the squid's screeching. It reminded me of someone running their fingernails over a blackboard. It was awful to listen to.

As far as I understood, squids don't vocalize. Could it be this variant of a giant squid could do so, and perhaps even hear? There was little time to evaluate the monstrosity before me. I took another bite and gnawed at the tentacle until it released the whale. The bull shook its tail violently and pushed upwards. The wake generated from its powerful tail was impressive, loosening the remaining tentacle and forcing the injured squid to retreat. At that moment I got a good look at the squid, its massive bulging eyes staring at me in rage or resentment. One problem with swimming as a shark is that you cannot back away from something. You can only swim forward, or sideways. In front of me was a large beak and several extended tentacles. I decided, out of blind faith, to swim directly at the creature, figuring its eyesight was better suited to distance than up close.

Despite the creature's size and apparent strength, the tentacles could not move quickly because of water resistance. I swam directly at the huge eyes and, as I passed over them, I exposed my teeth and made mashing sounds with my jaws. I imagined that up close, my jaws and serrated teeth would make an impression, and they did. Each time a tentacle approached me, I rushed the squid's eyes with jaws agape. Circling repeatedly, I made several thrusts toward its eyes. Each time, the squid quickly retreated. Soon after, it began to descend, and I circled it a few times to let it know I was watching it. Accepting its defeat as final, the creature retreated to the depths.

The bull surfaced and lay motionless. I rose alongside it and gazed at it. Deep scars ran down the length of its bulk. I could see deep red striations where the wounds penetrated the thick outer skin layer. Blood trickled into the seawater. Circular wounds from the powerful suckers were on full display. I wondered what it was thinking—what was this creature that had come to its aid that normally would opportunistically feed on the carcasses of dead or injured whales? We stayed like this for a while; me swimming alongside him as he rested.

Today was the first time since my departure from the islands that I was in the company of an ocean creature that I could relate to. A kinship was perhaps forming between two unlikely beings. From my perspective, this whale had seen a lot of life. Every scar, every barnacle told a story, like rings on a tree. It was sentient. I could feel it observing me, studying me. I was hoping we could achieve more, but any kind of relationship requires communication, and here I was still at a disadvantage. From time to time the whale made sounds, but to whom and for what purpose was still a mystery to me. Was it watching me react to his communications? I did not have the means to comprehend or communicate back to it. Or did I? I tried mashing my jaws underwater to generate sounds, to form a reply. It was the only part of my body that could create sounds.

I even tried Morse, knowing full well it was useless. This must have looked odd to such a creature. After a few attempts of mashing and gesticulating, I did get a response. Clicks and pops sounded in the water, bouncing off my body. The communication continued back and forth, neither of us understanding the other. Nevertheless, I enjoyed the companionship. To be honest, I had more difficulty explaining to a French waiter that my coffee was too cold. At least this fellow kept his tone polite.

I wondered if Cecilia would have believed me if I could tell her of my adventures today. She certainly would have called me out. *Bullshit, Mark*, she'd say with a smile. I missed her laugh, and her hearty giggling when I spouted nonsense to amuse her. My heart was aching just thinking about her. From time to time, I played back those few precious days back at the hotel. I even looked back fondly on our fights.

Did my daughters still think of me? How does a child handle grief? How were my daughters processing the death of their father and the intense grief of their mother? I couldn't imagine the hell I was putting them through. Here I was, cruising next to this whale, coping in this vessel as best as possible. And they were picking up the pieces of their life.

I hadn't thought about it, but there must have been a funeral held in my honor, a memorial. With nothing to bury, what do you do? Put keepsakes and photographs in a small box and bury it? I once heard of a cenotaph, a gravestone for those lost at sea. Was I lost at sea? *Not yet,* I told myself, and added sarcastically, *but I might be if I don't keep an eye on my navigation.*

Ben was on my mind, too. I hadn't thought about my colleagues for some time. How had the company reacted to my death? Years ago, a colleague of ours was killed in a car accident. Everyone, from the leadership down to the office assistants, was stunned by his death. He was well liked. Nothing in life prepares you for death of a colleague or friend, and each time it happens it hits you just as hard. In a business, there is a protocol of sorts. The atmosphere is somber, and a week goes by during which people talk quietly in corners or keep to themselves. Some attend the funeral. And then it's as if the person never worked there. Someone else takes over the desk. Conversations about the person become muted and everyone moves on. I wonder if this had transpired in my case. Had they forgotten me already? It was the ultimate reminder that a company is not family. It is an enterprise with but one purpose.

The bull and I remained side by side for several days, and I played wingman on several of his hunts. Occasionally, he let me take a bite here and there of his kills. Thankfully, the other squid we found were much smaller and consequently easier prey. The bull and I were such unlikely bedfellows, but I was enjoying myself. A new phase in my life had started. On the fifth day we parted ways, as he started turning south and I needed to make my way east. I hoped we would meet again someday. He let out a long, soothing bellow, and then he was gone. He haunted my dreams for some time after that.

Seamount

It had been several weeks since the bull and I had parted ways. I was moving east toward the North American coast at a steady clip. With each passing day I checked my orientation during the day and again by night. Having both the sun and stars to navigate gave me some redundancy, some confidence that I would eventually strike the West Coast. Every evening, I sought out two stars: Betelgeuse in Orion's belt, and Sirius. Polaris, the bright North Star, would be on my left, clearly marking north. As I swam eastward, at sunset Betelgeuse would show up on the horizon toward the east and would traverse the night sky above me until morning came. These landmarks in the sky gave me hope. During the day it was not essential for me to surface often and reorient. Nighttime was a different matter. If a ship sailed by, heading east, I simply followed for as long as I could. When I felt confident, I would drop below the surface and swim deep.

Even from a distance and in near darkness, the outline of the submerged ship was clearly recognizable. The light from the setting sun topside no longer reached the depths, but there was still some light in the shallows. Darkness expanded below me. There is no mistaking anything man-made. I believed I could see the ship before I saw the seamount that held it, almost weightless in the deep blue. The bow of the great ship rose above the pinnacle like a spear, pointing toward the surface. Its hull was laced with barnacles and coral. All manners of life swam freely through the many openings that lined its fractured hull. In the vast expanse of the Pacific Ocean, the occasional seamount rises like a rare oasis, its highest point still many fathoms below the surface. Born of primordial volcanic activity, this seamount might have breached the surface at one time. Over time, erosion and ocean floor movement will bring any island back beneath the waves.

The summit of this seamount was quite close to the surface, perhaps fifty or sixty feet from it, which explained the surplus of life in these waters. In contrast to the vast emptiness of the open sea, life can be prolific at a seamount. Bluefin trevally, bonitos, and yellow snapper moved in unison in vast shoals through the deep-water grotto behind the ship, their scales shimmering in the faint light from above. Within the schools, larger predatory barracuda and tuna swam unhindered. A few pelagic whitetip sharks patrolled the shallows above the schools. A squadron of eagle rays made large sweeping circuits between jutting spires of undersea rocks.

There were fields of colorful coral nested throughout the open regions of the seamount where sunlight could reach. Scores of soft corals of every color swayed in the ocean currents. Large gorgonian fans reached out into the passing current, their tentacles catching all manner of small organisms. The place was alive and pristine. Except for the ship, this seamount had probably remained undiscovered and untouched by man.

The ship's hull was broken into several pieces, the largest being the bow and bridge. Shattered and unrecognizable, the stern was nothing more than large, twisted chunks of metal strewn about the seafloor. Severely corroded from years of submersion, the great armor plating was a shadow of its former self. Layers upon layers of organisms were slowly consuming the iron-rich shell of the massive ship. Large sections of the hull bore the telltale signs of a bygone battle. Beneath the blast holes and large openings were piles of debris, mostly fragments of corroded metal. Several turrets lay inverted and sunken into the surrounding terrain, their encrusted cannons pointing uselessly into the abyss.

Upon closer inspection, it appeared to be a battleship from the Second World War, perhaps a destroyer or a cruiser, though my knowledge of military ships was limited. The condition of the ship made it impossible to determine if it was Japanese or American. Most shipwrecks from the war were much farther west, so it was odd seeing it here. I figured there would be some evidence of its identity near the bow or stern. I reached the bow first and then made my way toward the bridge, slowly navigating between cables and other structures. The heavy lids of the forward hatch were buckled. Two large windlasses near the bow were still holding the ship's anchors. To get to the bridge involved a two-hundred-foot swim over the forward decking and two large turrets. The center structure, or conning tower, was more or less intact, rising considerably above the wreck. A collapsed radar dome stood sentry on the top. Behind it were the tilted remains of the funnel.

The large windows of the wheelhouse were no longer present, but the openings were too small for me to slip through. I reminded myself to be cautious. I could not afford to get stuck or severely injured mucking about in the remains of an old ship.

From my vantage point I could survey the cockpit and its contents safely. I was half expecting to see the remains of crewmembers and perhaps some clothing but was relieved to see only small debris. The ship's wheel was clearly visible behind the officer's station, the brass bell next to it shimmering in the near darkness. A lone boot lay on the floor in the middle of the cockpit, its owner long gone.

Having fulfilled my curiosity at the bridge, I moved toward the lower decks. Several machine gun stations populated the lower part of the tower. Below the main deck, a massive gaping hole presented itself, the likely result of a torpedo or some other form of detonation. Great shards of corroded metal hung from the upper edges of the hole like knives. I felt uneasy about entering. Would I be able to turn my bulk if no passage was possible through to the other side? Curiosity was getting the better of me, and after the long periods of solitude on my journey, this ocean pinnacle presented something meaningful. A sense of purpose suddenly overwhelmed me: to seek out the origin of the ship, to chronicle my passing that one day I could convey to a future audience, whoever they may be.

Cautiously, I looked about the interior, searching for evidence of light indicating a passage. After surveying the interior for several minutes, and confident that I could double back if I got trapped, I entered. As I passed slowly through the opening, I tilted myself sideways to avoid catching the metal shards with my dorsal fin. In front of me and below, the deck walls had breached and blown back, revealing several bulkheads and twisted piping. On my left there appeared to be an entrance to a compartment. Looking up, I saw faint rays of light penetrating through a long, jagged crack in the deck. I wasn't sure whether the damage had resulted from the initial detonation or the rapid sinking of the vessel.

As I cruised my way amidships, I saw another opening below me that was large enough to accommodate me. I let gravity do its work and performed a smooth glide toward the opening. Initially, I thought I was clear, but I felt the sharp scrap of metal on my skin and abruptly stopped. It wasn't particularly painful, but I needed to be careful. Glancing to my left, I noticed a passageway towards what appeared to be the engine room. The engine room on a warship is two-thirds the way down the hull, so it was well away from the obliterated stern. I jimmied my tail a little to push myself, applying small kicks until, eventually, I could turn. Normally the corridors of ships are very narrow, but the walls here buckled outward, probably a result of the impact of the collision when the ship struck the seamount. This gave me ample space to maneuver, so I carefully propelled my girth along the passageway until I reached the engine room. I paused momentarily, trying not to whip up the silt on the floor, entombing myself. The limited light that penetrated from above was enough for me to see.

The large engines of the vessel appeared intact and retained much of their detail, despite the overgrowth of organic material. From my position I could see the twin drive shafts exiting toward the rear of the chamber. Many of the dials on the engines were frozen in their final settings. Some of the brass dials had kept their luster after decades submerged. It was possible the engines had still been running as the ship sank. I caught sight of a large engine dial to my right, and I noticed that the needle was firmly set at full speed. It was quite possible this ship had been trying to outrun something. Unless some record of this vessel existed, the mystery of its fate would remain sealed.

I swam slowly over to the first engine, studying the large transmission box that was just behind it. I missed having my hands to touch and manipulate objects. My dorsal fin rubbed along the ceiling and occasionally bumped against a crossbeam. Despite the close quarters, the engine room was quite large. I stayed near the ceiling to avoid kicking up the thick layer of silt all over the floor.

I noticed some motion in the corner of my eye. I had to look twice to convince myself that I had indeed seen a long tail slither beneath a large pump. Slowly, with a few kicks, I floated over and rested myself on top of the transmission box, where a gentle current let me stay immobile for a short while. As I looked beneath me, I observed a long white tail that snaked about the machinery. Its width grew steadily along its length, and behind the machinery I could see that it had become quite thick. I shifted my weight around to find myself literally face to face with a massive moray eel. Shocked by the size of the animal and unable to retreat, I stopped moving and stared at it. I wasn't entirely sure it was a moray, but it certainly looked like one. In all my years diving I had never encountered such a large specimen. At its thickest, the body was probably close to a few feet in diameter. Other than its size, it looked like a conventional spotted moray. Conger eels are known to grow to six or seven feet in length. This animal was more than twice that.

It gazed at me as if startled. The mouth of the beast opened, revealing a healthy set of teeth. Now I was the one startled. Just two large fish inside a wreck, with little room to wiggle. I could see from the creature's reaction that it was not sure what to make of our situation.

Morays can appear sinister, with their snakelike motion and the sucking of water through their gills. As an experienced diver I knew moray eels to be very timid, and they only attack if provoked, except for the ones I'd heard about on Clipperton Island. Those morays are outright aggressive and come on land to hunt crabs.

In my current predicament, I had one minor problem. For me to get out of the engine room I would have to swim above the creature and circle back, which meant it would have to duck to let me pass, and I wasn't particularly happy about that. Nor was I certain the animal would oblige me and let me pass overhead. I needed to move soon; I could feel myself slowly fading. I thrust forward with my tail, feeling parts of me bang into objects. Thankfully, the eel sank below me, but in the process of slithering along the floor it kicked up a lot of silt. With one rapid stroke, the eel vacated the engine room, turning it into a cloud chamber.

The visibility in the engine room went from clear to nothing in just a few seconds. Eddies of silt filled the room, refracting what little light there was in all directions, making navigation downright impossible. My one chance was following the visible parts of the animal and hoping for an opening I could slip through. The room was much darker now. I could see a thick cloud of silt particles near my eye. The motion of millions of small particles was almost mesmerizing. *This is not good.*

Proceeding cautiously, I slowly made my way down a passageway. I could hardly make out the outline of the corridor in the cloud of particles. My snout bumped repeatedly against machinery and every imaginable object. The walls seemed to converge upon me, though it was probably my mind playing tricks on me. The white tail was still within my vision, barely. I gave it my all and pushed my body into full gear. I could hear metal falling and crashing behind me, propagating through the ship's hull. There was no stopping now. I barreled forward until I saw what looked like an opening through the silt cloud on my right. It was not large by any means, and I was worried my empennage would get snagged and bring the entire ship down around me. I made a sharp turn, pushing through the dangling metal shards, rotating my form as best I could to exit.

I was most of the way out of the ship when I felt a tug from my tail, and my motion stopped abruptly. Being a shark gives some advantages. Despite my great size, I could flex my forward half enough to see the predicament I was in. From my perspective, several bulkheads had collapsed during my hasty evacuation and a large, corroded beam had fallen on my tail and was lodged between two armor plates. Thankfully, the full weight of the beams was not on my tail. There was pressure, but it was tolerable.

I swung my body from side-to-side to loosen it but made very little progress. I tried not to panic as I swiveled the forward half of my body into the current to get oxygen. Again, I turned toward the beam and tried pushing it with my nose, but I could not reach it. I had reached the full extent of my flexure, and no matter how much effort I endured there was no pushing the beam. The surrounding wall, however, was weakening due to my efforts, and if I persisted it, too, would collapse. Sure enough, the metal plating holding back the beam buckled and then broke into large fragments and the beam slid outward, freeing my bruised tail.

This had been very reckless of me. All that effort to cross the Pacific and to come home would have been wasted had I been unable to free myself. It could have ended badly for me. The world still didn't know I existed. Cecilia didn't know. *I need to be more careful.*

Still, I enjoyed the mystery the ship offered. An unknown vessel hidden from the world. I wondered what kind of battle had ensued on the surface. Was it an aircraft or submarine that had dealt the final blow? Did the ship sink quickly? Were there survivors? Without identification, there was no way to be certain. I observed the ship from a safe distance. Voluminous clouds formed in the sublevels where the bulkheads had collapsed, resulting in the further collapse of the rear section of the ship. The maritime heritage societies would send their finest after me. I had to admit it was a handsome ship, though I still wondered how it had got here, so far east of the islands.

I approached the dismantled stern, passing over a large, dark rock formation and making a mental note to use it as a fix point. Out here, the water was brilliantly clear. Passing over the last vestiges of what must have been the very tail of the vessel, I found no demarcation nor any reference to a country. It was likely that the paint had dissolved long ago. My best guess was that it was a large destroyer, and that it could have been American, British, or Japanese.

Turning again toward the side of the ship, I made for the

large rock formation to orient myself but couldn't find it. Confused and concerned for my mental welfare, I looked about agitatedly. Frustrated, I turned my eyes from the ship, and then caught sight of something very peculiar. As if enjoying a ringside seat, a large—and I mean a *very* large— goliath grouper was observing me with small, confused eyes. It was lumbering and slow, with large, pursed lips that opened and closed repeatedly.

The largest grouper I had ever seen in my early dives was probably around five or six feet long. I'd heard of titan or goliath groupers reaching over six feet, but this fellow was well over twelve feet in length. The girth of the beast was enormous, and I paled by comparison. Had I been a diver, he would have had me for starters. The maw of its lower jaw spread as wide as a tractor tire. It was, however, very timid in its behavior and not in the least threatening. I would say that it probably feared me more than I feared it, but then it didn't know that a serial entrepreneur with severely limited hunting skills inhabited this white shark. Had my alter ego been present I'd be quite full now and not in need of any sustenance for the rest of the month. *Your lucky day, big fella*. We faced each other for a few minutes, sizing each other up. Obviously, I had encroached on its territory, and it was waiting for me to leave. Its small, beady eyes watched me intently. Its jaws opened and closed as if mouthing or trying to communicate, but I believe it was simply adjusting the flow of water over its gills. The movement of its lips, though, gave me an idea. Slowly, I shifted to my left and gave the creature a wide berth. This had been quite an eventful day. I stuck around to explore and see what other fantastic beasts awaited me.

The terrain on the other side of the ship had a very different topology. The slope of rock and sand fell precipitously, with the opposite side of the seamount revealing a terraced appearance. Large clusters of cabbage coral populated both the plateau of the seamount and the terraces, intermingled with large and small sponges. Tiny angelfish darted in and out of the shadows. It was difficult for me to get close, but I tried anyway, occasionally bumping into coral and cursing myself each time. It is considered poor buoyancy to collide unintentionally with coral, which is quite fragile. I kept my distance and only moved closer when I felt I had achieved the required degree of control. Even after several months, I was still learning to control this massive fish I inhabited.

Eventually the terraces stopped, and a wall descended below me into the abyss. I swam beneath the edge of the last terrace and observed the nooks and crannies of the wall, looking for small critters. Magnificent fan coral, probably gorgonian, swayed in the current below me. As a diver I had always enjoyed diving on reefs and searching for rare fish, nudibranch, or crustacean. I missed having a camera to record everything I was experiencing. If I could just get some intrepid researcher to mount a critter-cam on me... think of all the discoveries that could be made!

It was incredible how the ship had got lodged here. A few more feet over the edge and it would have slithered down the sharp embankment into the abyss below. A seamount is an extraordinary place, mainly because of its isolation and its ability to attract life, no matter how far it is from the mainland. However, not all seamounts are welcoming to life. Some are just too deep, like the ones that encircle the Hawaiian archipelago. Having traveled in isolation for so many months, I decided I would stay for a while and regain my strength. I must admit my soul had suffered from the angst of passing through vast distances with nothing below me but darkness and mystery. The ocean is a frightful place and having spent some time here has not made it less so.

Pillars

It's hard to hum to music when you no longer have vocal cords. There was simply no way to generate sound with this body, other than mashing my jaws. I had even attempted varying the opening of my jaws or adjusting my speed to increase the inflow of water, with the poorly thought idea that I could somehow generate a resonating pitch. The gills flutter as water flows between them, but they are otherwise silent. Water is not like air. It's not compressible. It can transmit sound over long distances but creating that vibrato that was so easy as a human was impossible for me now.

Ironically, the ocean is full of sounds, though most of it is indecipherable and occupies the lower registers. The sound band is not always so featureless, however. On my journey I listened to sounds from humpback whales, the cacophony of large schools of fish moving in unison, the rupture of magma, mechanical noises from ships, and the sea floor that occasionally sends its eerie greetings up to the surface. In my dreams I was regularly reminded of sounds I experienced as a human, like that of wind, passing automobiles, and the voices of people. I consciously looked for reminders of my old world, but in the deep ocean there were few, except for the occasional passing ship. Sadly, sometimes it was just trash. It was extraordinary how soda cans and plastic bottles ended up out here in the middle of nowhere.

I once found a large empty plastic bottle, one of those large five-gallon types used for office water coolers, floating on the surface. I played with it as if it was a soccer ball, pushing it along with my snout, pretending to play against imaginary opponents, striking against a nonexistent goal. Occasionally I head-butted it and sent it flying, pretending I was Pele or Ronaldo. Then I tried punting the bottle by sinking deep and coming up at full force, to see how far I could jettison it. This kept me occupied for hours. Eventually the bottle sank due to my rough playing.

Then one day I came across a container floating listlessly. It was orange and had the name of its owner inscribed on it. This container was probably one of many that fell overboard each year from the cargo ships that plied these seas. The container was slightly submerged at one end, but the opposite end was lifted above the water and had one door open. *That is so odd*, I thought. I swam closer to the opening. Lifting my head out of the water as far as I could, I looked inside the long container. Rows of large wooden crates lined one side of its interior. I could almost read the shipping labels closest to me. *What a strange sensation to read text again.* From what I could read on the manifest, this container had originated from Japan and had been en route to Los Angeles when it was lost. From the type of packaging, I assumed these were parts for automobiles, or maybe something industrial. Hopefully the shipper had insurance.

Something metallic was reflecting light near the rear of the container. Looking inside, I caught a glimpse of something that made me stare in amazement. A spanking new Harley Davidsen motorcycle stood on its parking legs, covered in plastic. I was willing to guess that it was a Harley Cruiser, maybe even a Softail. *What a beauty.* And it was out here in the middle of the ocean. *Holy shit.* It was still dry. No evidence of corrosion. It couldn't have been out here very long. The salt in the air would have eventually claimed it. Ever since I was a kid, I'd dreamt of owning a Harley. I just could never afford one. What an incredible reminder of home and humanity. And it was here for the taking. Now if I could just place a tracker on this container. And get my legs back.

What the hell am I thinking? Who am I kidding? I was getting used to my new existence, and then to be painfully reminded of my past made me depressed again. The combination of childhood dreams and my recent trauma and the loss of my family was weighing on me again. It was to be expected, I supposed.

My best estimate was that I was now probably halfway through my journey, if I didn't mess up. These feelings were going to rise up again and again as I made progress. I shook the depression off and focused on moving east. I left the container where it was, hoping one day it would make its way across the Pacific to its rightful owner.

As often as I could, I played music in my mind. When it all got too much, I would just close my eyes and think of songs from different periods of my life. It is often noted that listening to a particular song can evoke a long-lost memory. Figuring that nothing lay before me, I cruised onwards with my eyes closed, listening to an imaginary concert in my mind.

When I eventually did open my eyes, I was presented with a vision that confused me at first. I shook my head to assure myself that I was awake and not dreaming. The water was thick with plankton, and it didn't help that the surface lighting from above was fading. It appeared as though I was approaching some great acropolis. Let me correct that: a *floating* acropolis. It was as if someone had placed the Parthenon underwater, and then removed its base and roof. All that remained were the vertical columns, which were quite large, perhaps ten to fifteen feet in diameter and over fifty feet in length. I counted over twenty columns. They were quite dark and were situated relatively close to each other, with nearly uniform spacing between them.

The columns hovered motionless some thirty feet below the surface. I swam arcs around the pillars to get a better look. I must admit, this was very mysterious. Had I discovered something that no man had seen before, or was there more to this than what met the eyes? What were they? One thing was for certain: I was captivated by it, and it was a welcome respite from the quiet and routine of most of my days. There was nothing menacing or remotely threatening about the columns. I spent around a half hour swimming around the structures, studying them, making mental notes. Out of curiosity, I approached one column and observed it up close. It was then that I realized that the columns were not completely still, but slowly rising and descending. Had I not come so close, I would not have noticed it at all.

I descended slowly along one column to hover near the bottom end. The surface was riddled with barnacles and vertical striations. I noticed a small protuberance near the bottom and closed in on it. While I was observing it up close, the protuberance opened up to reveal an eye. It blinked at me a few times. Startled, I rolled away to let the creature reveal itself. There came a sequence of familiar clicks followed by a loud bellow, a sound I had heard before. I now realized I had come upon a pod of sperm whales sleeping vertically, evidently waking one of them in the process. It reminded me of a congregation of blade fish, which also orient themselves vertically. These were just a lot larger. The sperm whale that I had unceremoniously awakened righted itself and pushed itself toward me. I had little choice other than to give it berth. More members of the pod began to move and reorient themselves in the water. I gathered that this group was not particularly happy with my intrusion. They had been having a blissfully peaceful evening until I showed up.

The ocean filled with the sounds of their clicking. I had read once that sperm whales were the loudest animals on earth —so loud that listening to them up close could be fatal. I needed to create space between myself and the flock. I observed as the whales moved on. Eventually their clicks grew faint, and I was alone again.

I was deeply appreciative of the adventures I had accumulated in the past few months. My mind had conjured up a variety of terrors prior to setting off from Maui, only to be surprised again and again. And yet here I was, still standing, sort of. I cannot deny the occasional shitstorm that happened: I couldn't forget the big squid from a month back. But on the whole, things had been okay. I was almost looking forward to the next experience. All I wanted right now was to get to the West Coast as quickly as possible. Hopefully there would be no more leviathans along the way. Weather conditions, for most of my journey, were good and had mostly kept me on the path. I knew this could change as I neared the coast, where fog and currents would play havoc with my senses.

Hull

I often wondered about my paradoxical relationship with the shark whose body I inhabited and controlled during the day, and sometimes at night. No other voice or thought entered my mind. I searched constantly for some sign that I was not alone in this magnificent beast. When I woke, I found myself still oriented east, or nearly east, which gave me confidence that some sort of control was in place. Was it my subconscious that was directing commands to this instinctual beast? Or did it understand me and my needs in a way that were beyond my means to understand? Was it learning from me? Was it observing me and adapting to me? There was just no way to know for certain. At any rate, my anxiety levels had dropped considerably from a month ago.

I was beginning to dream again in my sleep. And in those dreams, I often dreamt of Cecilia. Tonight, I saw Cecilia lying next to me, asleep. I could smell her perfume and her hair. The scent of lavender was everywhere. The room we were in was unfamiliar, and dimly lit. I couldn't move my arms or touch her, but I could feel her next to me. The warmth of her body radiated against mine. Why could I not move? I wanted to talk to her and reassure her that I was okay.

This dream persisted for weeks. My vision was always fixed in one direction, as if I were looking through the lens of an immovable camera.

***

I felt an excruciating pain in my ears. The pain spread through my head and down to my chest. It took a moment for me to comprehend that the source of the pain was some terrible sound in the water. Eventually the pain eased and almost vanished, but then it came again. This time, the intensity was so severe I was forced to close my eyes. It sounded like the world's largest tuning fork placed right up against my ears. The ringing was absolutely deafening. I shook my head in pain. For weeks, the sea had been resoundingly quiet. Now the sea came alive again, painfully so. I swam a large circuit to identify the direction of the source. The sound came again, and this time massive vibrations coursed around me and through me. Localizing a powerful sound underwater was still nearly impossible for me.

For a while after the last blast, there was another period of relative silence. Then it came again, but from a different direction, and less intense. I looked above, below, every which way I could, and still there was no sign of the source. A slender blue shark in the distance was writhing from the sonic onslaught. I thought of the sounds I had occasionally heard from the deep during my crossing, but this was very different.

Then a new, unfamiliar sound came to my ears. It was more of a cyclical, mechanical sound, not at all unpleasant, but definitely not natural.

I looked below and almost jumped out of my skin. No more than fifty yards below me, the massive, bulbous head of a large submarine loomed into view. As more of it emerged from the gloom, I wondered how big this thing was. It was like watching one of those science-fiction movies where a vessel of endless proportions passes overhead. Once the entire vessel was in view, I estimated it was well over a hundred and fifty yards long, and the width of its thickest section, near the conning tower, was over twenty yards. The bloody thing was huge. From the shape and girth of the hull, I gathered it was a Russian sub. American submarines are typically longer and more slender in design, with the conning tower placed farther forward on the hull. I couldn't say which class it was—the Cyrillic writing along the hull encrypted its specific identity— but I gathered it was a relatively new submarine, gauging by its lack of scrapes and dents.

The submarine lumbered along below me, moving slightly quicker than my relaxed pace. I watched with interest as this long, man-made vessel slowly passed by. It filled me with elation to be close to humans again, even if I could not see them. Beneath that thick iron hull, men went about with their duties. I was curious. It had been some time since I had seen a human being, let alone be close to anything man-made, so I felt some kinship to whatever this was. I swam up just behind the conning tower, sitting in its wake. This made it easier to follow along. As I lay there, I wondered what was going on inside the hull. I wondered about the contents of the conversations between crewmembers. Did they talk about their families, or did they play games like chess or backgammon? At this depth, there could be no communication with the outside world. They were just as isolated from the world as I was. I could just sit here quietly for a while, hiding behind the tower, using the sub's slipstream to save energy, for as long as they continued toward the American coast.

As a boy I read with interest about the life of submariners. They were a special lot, though these days life aboard a modern submarine is much more comfortable than the vessels from history. Modern submarine interiors are so enormous you can run laps around the missile compartments. Just below and behind me I recognized the long section and the circular outlines of doors marking locations of missile silos. The nuclear reactor driving this machine of war was just behind them, and two sets of props at the tail pushed the dreadnought along. I could hear the steady drone as it propelled itself through the seawater.

As I settled into this new rhythm, I heard other sounds underneath the drone, the sounds of metal on metal, perhaps the closing of a hatch. I lowered myself slowly to a position just behind the base of the conning tower until I landed on the metal surface. Interestingly, I no longer needed to exert any strokes to maintain my position; the stream of water passed the tower on either side of me, nipping at the tips of my pectoral fins. I was pleased to hear chatter below, transmitting through the hull. It sounded clear, though it was completely unintelligible to me, as I didn't speak the language.

Yet it was fascinating to eavesdrop on another culture deep beneath the sea. I imagined I was positioned just above the control room, with officers barking orders and sailors running around executing them, like in some old war movie. Truth be told, it all sounded very relaxed. They were, like me, in the zone, away from the world and its problems. Occasionally, roars of laughter passed through the hull. For the moment, this took the edge off my current predicament. Deep down, I longed for human contact.

Here I was, lounging on the back of a sub like some deep-sea hitchhiker, eavesdropping on conversations within a foreign power's weapon of war. It seemed weird that I hadn't immediately considered that not so insignificant detail in this most unusual of circumstances. But that was what this was: a weapon capable of cataclysmic devastation on a scale I could barely imagine. The entire premise behind submarine warfare is its inherent sneakiness, the ability to strike offshore and disappear, leaving a wasteland in its wake. Much like the ambush tactics of a great white shark, though that seemed far too inadequate a comparison. There wasn't much I could do about the sub. I was far too small to affect any change in this vessel's course or to antagonize the crew within. Nibbling on the hull was out of the question. Besides being ineffectual, I would lose too many teeth in the process. The owner of my own *vessel* would not be happy.

After an hour of coasting along, a thought occurred to me. I slowly backed off my position and floated down the length of the submarine until I neared the propellers. A pair of large fins, mounted onto the hull just ahead of the large props on either side of the hull, stretched some distance out like small wings. The outer edge of these fins was thicker than the center part, and jutting out of the rear of this bulge was a cable that stretched some fifty, sixty yards behind the sub. At the end of the cable was a slender torpedo-shaped object, with what looked like sensors mounted alongside it. I was confident these were hydrophones, tasked with listening to anything within a specific audible range. The acoustic signature of a ship, or a whale, is unique. I wondered if they could hear me swimming alongside.

Without the slipstream of the conning tower to protect me, I found myself in the turbulent wake generated by the sub's twin props. Near the propellers the buffeting was quite substantial. I was able to observe cavitation bubbles forming at the blade tips. Increasing my distance from them lessened the intensity and allowed by to approach the sonar array.

The urge to gnaw through the cable connecting the probe to the submarine was growing within me. What a story to tell, to whoever I could tell it to, one day. I slowly approached the towed object. The cable was thick, but it was not completely solid. I could peer through the structure of the cable and see bundles of smaller cables, and connectors and sensors, covered in a mesh-like sheath. I prodded the cable with my snout to test its resistance. It was quite stiff. This was probably because of the intense drag of the probe and speed of the sub. The senses in my snout detected electricity passing through the bundles. Getting electrocuted was not high on my bucket list.

The cylindrical object being towed was about the same length as me, as far as I could judge, though not as plump in the midsection. Sonar arrays have but one purpose, to passively listen to noises in the sea. Increasing the intensity of my strokes, I reached the midpoint in the cable, and in one motion I rolled over into the cable and clenched my jaws down onto it. Electricity surged through my mouth. I was beginning to regret my decision.

My presence in the submarine's slipstream was acting as a disturbance, causing the probe to oscillate behind me. Soon, both the sonar probe and I were swinging uncontrollably behind the vessel. At the least, I was inducing some serious drag. Somebody on board must be picking up on the situation back here.

The intensity of the electrical surges soon overwhelmed the sensor organs on my snout, but I was not letting go. I shook my head vigorously to cut through as much of the sheath and cable as I could. Looking forward while still biting the cable, I could see the props of the submarine spinning faster. Undoubtedly, my efforts were being registered and someone on board was not happy. There was no way for me to discern how much damage I was inflicting, but I figured I would hang on as long as possible and induce as much damage as I could. A few teeth flew past my eyes. They would grow back. The electricity I sensed surging through the cables was strong but not debilitating. However, my ability to smell anything or detect vibrations was compromised, and there was some numbness in my snout. I could still control my jaws.

The probe shifted violently, pushing me sideways. I could see the rudder up ahead swiveling, fishtailing the whole assembly to sling me off the cable. The hydraulics pushing the large control surfaces were clearly audible, like large rusty doors on massive iron hinges. The sub's captain was probably very concerned by now. I could imagine that the previously relaxed mood onboard was probably now replaced by urgency and panic. Without the array, the sub would probably have to return to port for repairs. An expensive and embarrassing plight for a ship's captain of a brand-new ship.

It was at that moment I heard a snap, and the frayed end of a cable appeared before me. Now that the cable was partly cut, the probe began to swing back and forth in the current, generating increased drag. The sonar array remained connected to the sub, but it probably lacked power. A few more teeth floated past me.

Unable to sling the saboteur off, the sub ascended. Air bubbles blew from openings beneath the sub's hull, signifying the purging of the ballast tanks of water. The cloud of bubbles was slung rearward from the ship's motion, reducing my visibility and plunging me into a carbonated bath. The ocean surface approached rapidly. I imagined the captain must be very irritated by now. The cable, or what was left of it, was being spun up to save the probe. I worked harder and, thanks to the submarine's reduced speed, I could put the leftover cable deeper into my mouth. The cable was being spun up into an opening in the rightmost fin, and me along with it.

Abruptly, the propellers stopped spinning. The submarine surfaced and drifted without power. Waves crashed over the hull from a stormy sea. The swells were perhaps twelve to fifteen feet in height. Despite its mass and colossal size, the submarine rolled in the large swells. At my depth, I could feel the waves above me, pounding the vessel. The array lay just below the surface, with me ripping apart the rest of the cable holding it together. I pulled away from the cable as it was drawn into the hull.

A crew member emerged from a rear hatch, which landed with a thud as it struck the hull. More than once, the intense waves striking the vessel nearly knocked him down. I kept myself below the surface, just out of sight. Doubtless this fellow was probably forced to inspect the probe by his commanding officer. I watched intently as he stumbled and struggled to gain a better perspective of the cable. Fear was written all over his face. He was in uniform and wearing a life vest wrapped loosely around his waist. His cap blew off in the wind. I swam back to the remains of the damaged cable extending from the submarine and inspected my work. The damage was quite extensive. In fact, the sonar array could not be fully retracted because of the frayed sheath. It just hung there lopsidedly some thirty feet behind the props, adding resistance to the boat. Satisfied with my work, I swam back to see what the poor sailor was up to.

Unable to hold on to anything on the sub's exterior as it rolled, the lone crew member lost his footing and slipped, sliding along the smooth, curved surface of the sub and headlong into the water. That must have hurt. I stuck my head above the surface and watched the scene play out. Though the hatch was still open, no other crew member came up through the hatch to assist the beleaguered sailor. The head of another sailor did eventually pop up, but still no one came to the aid of the fallen sailor. Some of the seawater pelting the submarine made its way to the hatch and poured in. Over the howl of the wind and wave action, I could hear someone barking orders. The crew would need to think fast if they had any chance of saving their comrade.

I swam over to the stricken crew member in the water, who was now being buffeted mercilessly against the hull of the submarine. He would not last long in these waters. He had been smart enough to wear a vest, but this would not save him. Without cold water gear, he wouldn't survive long in these waters.

In his panic, he did not see me. I could see he was struggling to breathe. Blood ran down his cheeks from the battering. I was feeling a little guilty for putting him in this predicament. There he was, facing his mortality, and unknowingly in view of the apex predator that had set the events in motion. He was just a lowly sailor, forced to exit the ship at the captain's behest.

In an act of extraordinary self-sacrifice, he pushed himself away from the hull into the open water, relinquishing any hope that the other crew members could save him. I watched him pass over me, drifting helplessly in the surf.

Several other crew members did eventually emerge, tied to each other with rope to form a lifeline. Like a drunk conga line, the crew held on desperately to the hull, swaying back and forth as the ship leaned. The sailor at the end of the line made it to the waterline, but they were too late. The lone crew member was drifting further and further away from the vessel.

Okay, enough, I told myself. I carefully swam up to the sailor from behind and slowly nudged him toward the vessel. Surprising how small and fragile human beings are. I had grown accustomed to the toughness and resilience of this new body, even if I didn't completely own it. At first, he didn't quite know what was going on. Then he turned his head. He closed his eyes in terror. The surprise and shock on the man's face after getting a first view of his savior was palpable. He probably thought this was the end for him, after an already terrible day. He was muttering to himself, perhaps praying, or saying goodbyes to his loved ones. Tears ran down his face. I could relate to his hopelessness and despair.

I nudged him gently from the side, though my snout had the tendency of pushing him under. Eventually, I got him close enough so that he could swim to the sub on his own. The crew member closest to him stood in shock as I floated just beneath the surface. The crew member beside him spontaneously vomited. I rolled back my eyes a few times, as if winking, but nobody noticed.

The crew stood staring at me in disbelief. They were

definitely going to remember this day for the rest of their lives. Only the man closest to the sailor had the wherewithal to act and respond. I moved away and watched from a distance as the seaman was pulled from the ocean and embraced by his comrades. A few sailors stood frozen on the rolling deck, unable to tear their gaze away from me. Then a barking officer ordered them below. Once they had closed the hatch, the propellers started up again, and the submarine sank beneath the waves. I watched as the massive boat made a wide turn and headed west again, the broken probe dangling uselessly in its wake. Eventually, the cyclical sound of the props vanished in the background noise of the sea, and I was once again alone.

It was an odd feeling, having been so close to people, and yet my actions, through some odd sense of duty, had brought that moment to an abrupt close. I felt some guilt at having put that poor sailor's life in jeopardy. Next time I would just keep my distance and observe. I could have just exploited the transit assist and saved some energy. Politics have no place in the deep ocean.

I would have loved to hear the official report from the ship's captain when they returned to port. If I ever communicated with the outside world again, I would inquire about weird encounters with Russian subs. My feeling was that they would probably bury the story because no one would believe it, despite there being witnesses. They would blame it on the vodka. There were countless tales and myths associated with the sea. This would be one of many. I floated on the surface for a while, bobbing like a cork, replaying the day's events. The sun was preparing to set and, taking this as my cue, I turned east and resumed my journey.

As I kicked off, I thought about all the songs from my youth that had something to do with the sea. "Yellow Submarine" by the Beatles popped up first, for obvious reasons. This was followed in quick succession by the Beatles

"Octopus's Garden" and Led Zeppelin's "The Ocean." I couldn't leave out the Beach Boys' "Surfin' USA" or even Irving Berlin's "How Deep is the Ocean." Growing up, my dad had vinyl LPs packed away in boxes. I couldn't recall how many boxes there were, but there were many, and each album was filed and sorted alphabetically. The vinyl records were adorned with plastic sleeves, reflecting the consummate audiophile he was. Depending on his mood, Dad would meticulously search each box for a certain song or songwriter and tell me and my siblings a story about how he discovered them. He would then lift a record, blow any residual dust off it, place it carefully onto the turntable, and play a number. The pop and crackle of the needle was as buried in my subconscious as were the songs that were played on that turntable. I played back the tunes in my head.

Espresso, Anyone?

My best estimate was that I had progressed beyond the midpoint between Hawaii and the West Coast. Over the past few weeks, the ocean had remained tranquil, refusing to startle or test me, which I appreciated. *Thanks, Neptune.* After weeks of relentless solitude with nary a lifeform since my run-in with the bull and the sub, restlessness was building in me. The water had such clarity that occasionally it gave the sensation of floating in air. I understood that this was an illusion, but it needed some effort on my part to acknowledge. Sometimes I would break the surface and look above to remind myself of how the real world, my old world, appeared. Apart from the clouds, sun, and the occasional bird, there was little to jog my memory of my past life. Unsatisfied, I would sink beneath the waves again and continue my quest to the West Coast, counting down the days to the best of my ability.

Apart from the ocean crossing, a multitude of other challenges presented themselves, some of which seemed insurmountable. I was experimenting with different approaches to potential communication. I couldn't speak, nor did I have the use of opposable thumbs, and I could neither draw nor write. Scraping messages onto boat hulls using my teeth did occur to me once (I did think to try, but I was miles from Hawaii when the idea came to me). Tapping onto a boat or structure using Morse seemed like a good idea, but people might get too rattled by the appearance of the sender. Then there was the minor detail of finding a person who could recognize Morse code. My little Sarah knew Morse, but that was only because we had made it into a game and, well, because I was a nerd. Less than one percent of the population knows Morse, and today it is very much the province of ham radio operators. Seamen are expected to acquire some knowledge of it as part of their training, but most would have probably forgotten it since everyone communicates using satellites these days.

I spent much of the morning pontificating about Morse and other things communication related. I also started to feel hungry. In the distance I saw a small, perhaps insignificant dark spot just below the surface. As I neared it, I could perceive it was moving, at a much slower pace than myself. It crossed my mind that it might be a sea turtle. As I approached, I recognized the slowly undulating flippers of a large green turtle. It seemed not to have sensed my presence yet. The sea turtle appeared to be relatively young, maybe twenty or thirty years old, and its carapace lacked the mottled pattern of older turtles.

The motions of the turtle made it appear unhurried and unstressed, and I felt a little guilty being so close to it, knowing full well sea turtles were Sarah's favorite creatures. I watched it for a while, but the damn thing was so slow I lost patience. I swam up alongside it and studied it up close. The turtle looked over at me and continued on swimming, albeit at a slightly raised tempo. Vacillating between hunger and guilt, I made the decision to swim onward and leave the poor thing to the elements.

Due to my ever-increasing hunger, I started dreaming about food. Human food, that is. For months now I had subsisted on a pure seafood diet. Catching tuna was both challenging and rewarding, as were mahi-mahi and other large game fish. Sunfish were easy pickings, as were rays and other slow-moving denizens of the sea. Unfortunately, there were no fishing boats to be seen. *Where is a longline boat when you need one?*

Images of steak started popping up in my mind, as well as pasta and chicken dishes. I recalled standing behind Cecilia while she cooked pasta Alfredo, saltimbocca, crab cakes, or the many other dishes into which she put her heart into. And I didn't stop at the entrees. How about fresh homemade tiramisu or chocolate mousse or crème brûlée? As a sea creature, it wasn't possible for me to salivate, but the mind has its way of torturing its owner with thoughts of tasty cuisine. And now that would never be possible again. Even if given the opportunity, would my taste buds even recognize these foods? It would have to be a sizable portion to even fill my mouth, but would my buds react to the hints of coffee and cinnamon and cocoa? Oh God, now I was thinking of chicken tikka masala and onion bhajis. Would this torture ever end?

I was in the middle of thinking about cream puffs and Sacher torte when the silhouette of a great white rose from behind me. It was a large male shark, with two claspers dangling beneath it. Amelia called them double penises, which is essentially what they are. I examined its exterior, noting the bite scars from battles with other sharks. The scars ran the length of its body. The beast simply reeked of testosterone. I recalled our neighbor's dog, Geralt, that would mate with anything on two or more legs if given the chance. The neighbor refused to castrate the poor fellow, so we all suffered. I hoped great whites were not the same, unable to contain outbursts of testosterone-driven libido and rage.

Further afield, I saw the outline of yet another shark, rising from the depths. I monitored both creatures, not knowing precisely what was going on, but on the safe side I made the decision to swim away from these brutes. My nerves were on edge, so I picked up speed. Executing a roll gave me the opportunity to get an overview of my surroundings and, sure enough, the waters were slowly becoming populated with white sharks, large and small. A few pelagic whitetips entered the fray as well, but quickly scampered off when a large female great white arched her back. It appeared as though they were all moving in the same direction. There were more sharks just below me, emerging out of the ether.

As my courage increased, I decided to examine my fellow citizens of the deep up close. *Why am I suddenly surrounded by large sharks? And why now, in this place, of all places?* I swam slowly up to a large female and inspected her markings. She did not appear threatened by my presence, nor did she show malice in any way. We swam parallel to one another for a while. To aid with identification, I gave some of the sharks names, reflecting some aspect of their appearance. I called the large female Molly. Her caudal fin had a sizable piece of flesh missing and one of her pectoral fins displayed painful-looking scars. The trailing edge of her dorsal fin had injuries from multiple bites. Her gills flexed as she swam, and her maw was open, revealing an unbroken line of serrated teeth.

I had a sense that Molly had lived life on her own terms, and that she had survived for a long time. I sensed her studying me in return, but she did not sway from her course. I slowed my speed to observe her tail markings. Her bulbous white belly contrasted with her slim empennage. There were large scrapes, made by teeth, I imagined. Some had the distinct patterns of the teeth of male sharks. Not all the scars on her body were semi-circular in form. Some markings were long and stretched several meters along the length of her body. I was looking at my future, I supposed, fending off other sharks during territorial disputes, or simply being in the wrong place at the wrong time. So far, I managed to avoid close encounters with these behemoths, for which I was grateful.

It was impressive to be in the company of such mighty predators and to be accepted by them. But it didn't last long. While enjoying a serene moment, I was rammed from one side by a smaller shark that bit my right pectoral fin and twisted as it tried to align its body toward mine. Like a small, overexcited dog, it wiggled its body uncontrollably. Without thinking I turned, pulling my fin from his mouth and bit into it. I could feel the smaller shark squirming in my mouth. Having made my point, I released my bite and watched the shark swim rapidly away from me, with deep gouges in its gill area, clearly revealing where I had bitten him. The bite I had administered was quite deep, and flakes of flesh hung loosely around the wounded area. I gave the young shark a second look and realized it was a juvenile male. Was the shark confused? The shark fell from view, but I was not taking any chances.

Later, another pair of sharks came up from behind, slowly but steadily. *Opportunistic bastards*, I thought. It seemed they were clueless to my gender and, like my neighbor's dog, were taking out their libido on anything that moved. To deny them, I turned to confront them and swam directly toward the larger of the two. The large male veered off below me while the smaller shark, lacking in moral compass and good judgment, attempted to latch on only to find a pair of larger jaws clamping down on its dorsal fin. Its body writhed violently in panic. I relinquished my hold and witnessed the poor soul swim away in defeat to tend to its wounds. *Hey, I'm getting good at this.* I swam a large arc between several other males to remind them of the consequences should they try again.

It took me a moment to deduce my location. Apparently, I must have entered the region of the Pacific known as the White Shark Cafe. There was no other explanation for the multitude of sharks I had encountered. It would be essential for me to be vigilant until I was far enough away from this crowd of libido-stricken males.

Observing the other sharks coupling made me realize the intensity and brutality of the process. There existed no gentle term for it; in the wild kingdom, it was rape. A large male had an even larger female locked in its grasp. Seeing the two bodies coupled and twisting and sinking into the depths made for an unappetizing show. In these deep waters, concealment was impossible, so I made haste to exit the area. After a few hours, the number of males in sight decreased to a point where I could relax. *Onward*, I thought.

I had just dropped my guard when I was broadsided by a large male hellbent on latching onto me. His teeth penetrated deeply into my right pectoral fin. Pain spread along my right flank. Rotating my body, I attempted to disengage him, but he held on. I snapped at him repeatedly, but I could not reach his snout, since he was some distance behind me. I could feel him struggling, trying desperately to mate. He was quite large, probably as large as I was, and he wasn't taking no for an answer. My mind ran through different scenarios, but the only way I was going to get him off was to shake him off. I twisted my body away from him to the maximum extent possible. He countered by flexing his powerful tail to push himself against me. I shook as hard as I could. My pectoral fin was in pain, like a thousand sharp pricks. The more I struggled, the more painful the experience became. I found that if I rotated and snapped at him simultaneously, his grip would slip just a little. He would struggle to regain his grip, but then I would lurch again and again, until he eventually let go.

He made another attempt to grab my heavily lacerated fin, but I was waiting for him. I bit down on his gills as hard as I could. This time, I was taking a pound of flesh. I was using my limited knowledge of predatory behavior and applying it to the max. Biting down on the attacking shark's gills forced it to disengage. I shook my head in a lateral motion and let my teeth do the work. As my jaws closed, the shark pulled away. I stared in horror at the gaping wound I had made on the male shark. The entire gill area along one side of the shark was gone—or rather, I was consuming it. The male shark struggled to swim and was rapidly losing blood. With limited ability to exchange oxygen from water, it was drowning, fast. I watched as its limp body sank into the depths. It was sad to see, but I felt no remorse. I was angry, and I had been assaulted.

The harsh reality of the submerged world I was living in was that there was no distinction between good or evil. Morals had no meaning here. I existed as an outsider in this world, even though I appeared as one of these creatures. They were merely performing a mating ritual that had been regularly occurring here for millions of years.

After all that had transpired, I decided to ascend. Upon breaking the surface, I looked at the setting sun behind me and, in my mind, sighed deeply. My pectoral fin was still sore, though I was certain it would heal. Gazing at the sun gave me some sense of familiarity and calm. The orange light bathed the slowly rising waves, dulling the memory of the violence. I had never experienced that kind of assault during my time as a human being. Perhaps I should consider myself fortunate. However, the experience had shaken me. I still tasted blood in my mouth. I had also, in literal terms, become a cannibal. To survive out here, I would need to compartmentalize some of my human beliefs. It was eat or be eaten. Fucking was out of the question.

Landfall

After heading east for six or seven months, it only remained a matter of time before I saw the first hint of land. It startled me when the coast suddenly appeared one morning. No island, no atoll, just one long endless coastline extending north and south. I assumed it was the North American coast, since realistically it was the only coastline that was reachable within the time that had passed. There was literally nothing between here and the Hawaiian Islands. I was certainly relieved to see it, and I even felt pride in accomplishing my goal, but I had no clue where I was along that long coastline. Was I looking at Mexico or Canada? Oregon or southern California? I genuinely hoped it was not Alaska.

The water temperature had dropped precipitously from a week ago, which indicated I had left the warmer Japanese current. I was guessing it was May or June, so the water should have kept some of the heat. As I got closer to the coast, the water temperature rose a little. There was another hint that I was approaching land: underwater visibility. The water was murkier and greener close to the coast than out in the deep Pacific.

Having lived along the West Coast most of my life, I was familiar with many of the coastal landmarks. I would need these to get my bearings. I pushed on until I was within viewing distance of the nearest beach. As I approached the shallows, I immediately recognized the mist-shrouded forests and rugged rocky outcroppings of the Pacific Northwest. This meant I was far north of my destination.

After heading south for nearly a day, I recognized a jutting spire of rock that reignited memories of my teen years. When I was growing up in Eugene, Oregon, my family often took trips to the coast during the summer months. Among our favorite destinations, Cannon Beach stood out. Smack dab in the middle of it was Haystack Rock. No other sea stack along the west coast came close to it in size and presence, so it was hard-wired in my brain. I had my landmark. The high tide allowed me the luxury of getting up close and visiting the ocean-facing face of the stack. It remains just as impressive now as it was in my childhood.

This marked the beginning of the next chapter of my journey. I had successfully navigated from the Hawaiian Islands to the American coast. It amazed me that I had survived the passage. The next phase would take me south along the western coast, all the way to San Francisco. In a car, this would take me eleven or twelve hours from my present location. Swimming fifty miles a day, it would take me a good two weeks. I had better get cracking. The water was extremely cold, and my hunger was intensifying. There were plenty of seals around, so my host would have ample opportunity to feed, so I wouldn't starve. I was still at a loss regarding what I would do when I finally arrived at the Bay. But I had two weeks to figure it out. The shallow waters near the coast were both inviting and comforting. I no longer worried about demons, either real or imagined.

It took me a full week to arrive at Crescent City, which lay midway on my journey. Along the way, I recognized another landmark from my memories: Castle Rock. Thick layers of guano covered the massive rock, and there were seals everywhere. Elephant seals, California seals, and even harbor seals sunned themselves here. It was probably best to hang here for the night and let my partner get some nourishment. I had no interest in taking down a seal for food myself. Tuna or a mahi-mahi I could handle, but I drew the line with mammals. I didn't want to be there when it happened, and I didn't want to wake up with one in my jaws, like the tarpon I'd experienced a little while back. This was all irrational, of course, but I had an easier time accepting fish as my food source.

As I swam around this rock, I came across a dense kelp forest. Long vines with intermittently placed pneumatocyst that acted as floats rose from the ocean floor, ending with a mat of fronds at the surface. I entered the underwater forest carefully, gliding between the stalks as they swayed with the current. Beneath me, a pair of yellow tangs and rockfish darted between the stems. The seafloor teemed with black, spiny sea urchins. A California sea lion stuck its head out from behind a large frond, eyeing me suspiciously. The poor animal darted from stalk to stalk, expecting me to give chase. At one point I found the seal following closely behind me.

The scene below me was quite pretty, with sunlight cutting through the grove of kelp and casting its rays over the shallow floor. In the past, while diving through a kelp forest, I used to think that I would be safe from large predators like sharks, yet, despite my size, it was fairly easy for me to navigate through this forest. *So I assumed wrong.* To pass the time until sunset, I poked around the forest, watching life here up close, without the limitations of an air bottle. I'd learned to dive around kelp forests, having gotten my certification in Monterey. Contrary to what many think, there is a lot of life in cold water, especially in the shallows. I preferred the warm waters of Indonesia, but that was because I hated cold water suits, finding them claustrophobic. Had I been smart, I would have invested in a drysuit, which would have made my diving a lot more pleasant in cold conditions. As a large shark with internal heating, the cold did not bother me too much, though it was chilly. If I remained as a shark for the rest of my life, I would certainly return to this place and explore some more.

Light started to fade as sunset drew near. Time to sleep.

I woke with a jolt. As the sun rose over the horizon, I found myself near a cluster of rocks, on the surface. I didn't recognize the location. Had I headed north again? *Fuck!* The taste of iron lingered in my mouth, as if I had unintentionally bitten my lip. Seagulls and cormorants dove into the water all around me, resembling a scene from the old Hitchcock movie, *The Birds. Chaos* would be the word that best described it. Several birds displayed outright aggression, with one even landing on my snout. The rocks were overrun with seals in a state of panic. The sounds of their barking filled the air. Some hid in the shallows or in sheltered tidepools due to the lack of space. The roughness of the early morning sea did not help their efforts. Large waves buffeted the poor seals mercilessly as they clambered high up on the rocks. As if it were a sea of undulating blubber, the seals slid from one side of rocks to the other as they pushed and shoved each other.

Shit, I woke up too early. There, directly before me, lay the partially consumed body of a sizable elephant seal. Lifeless and gray, it bobbed with the incoming tide. Blood spread from it, making the water cloudy. Evidently, I'd taken part in a feast. Observing it underwater, I saw that a large part of its torso was absent, and there were remnants of entrails hanging below it. The head remained above the water; its lifeless eyes fixed on the heavens. My host must have been feeding for some time. From the looks of it, it had fed well. Despite the carnage, this was good, as I would probably not need to feed for a while.

I put some distance between me and the carcass to reduce my guilt and resumed my southward passage. Both Sarah and Amelia were extremely fond of seals, so I wasn't earning any brownie points. As I recalled, they had between them a dozen seal cuddle toys, most of them acquired during visits to local aquariums. Thinking about my girls reinvigorated my motivation.

It would be another week before I reached another favorite landmark of mine, Point Reyes. Shaped like a horse's head, the cape of Point Reyes jutted out some distance from the mainland. With miles of undisturbed beaches and more seal colonies, this would be an ideal pit stop before I attempted to enter the Bay. Like Cannon Beach, I had a soft spot for Point Reyes. Memories of oyster farming and camping on the many bluffs toward the south of the cape seeped into my consciousness. I recalled one winter—February, I believe— when the temperature rose over seventy-five degrees and large female gray whales and their young clung close to the beach shallows for safety. During my teenage years, my family relocated to Santa Rosa, marking the beginning of a sequence of moves throughout California. I spent a significant portion of my youth in northern California, starting with high school in Vallejo, and eventually settling in Berkeley for college.

I surveyed the landscape around Drake's Bay. On the left side stood the high rocks and majestic bluffs of Chimney Rock, culminating in the dramatic yet no longer operational lighthouse. To the right, Limantour Beach extended endlessly into the haze. Here, I surfed with my college buddies for weeks on end during the summer months. The clear conditions today provided me with splendid views.

Cecilia and the girls were not far away. As I approached the beach, I saw people milling about. These beaches never got crowded, so people were spread quite thinly. Some were out walking, while others hid themselves in the high grass a little away from the sand to avoid the winds. A group of young men played touch football near the water's edge. All of this filled me with feelings of nostalgia and joy, joy, knowing that I would be soon home.

It took a half day of swimming to reach the mouth of the Bay. The orange trusses of the Golden Gate Bridge soared above me. Cars and trucks passed noisily above. In the distance, a kitesurfer was navigating his way around the harsh surf at breakneck speed. What an amazing experience to be back home and surrounded by humanity. After months of isolation in the Pacific, it was a welcome respite.

Directly in front of me and inside the Bay, the lonely outpost that had once been Alcatraz prison stood guard. To my left, the Marin headlands with its extinct bunkers faced the Pacific. I let the ingoing tide push me in and watched the scenery unfold with interest. Our house was in East Bay, a few blocks from a beach.

A tingle on my back grew quickly, and I turned to face a cargo ship, a very large one, passing a short distance from me. Rows of cargo pallets stacked up high lined the ship from bow to stern, so many that the ship's bridge was barely visible. I thought of the container I'd found, and the Harley Davidsen within it. The ship was probably on its way to Oakland and was slowing after entering the Bay. I figured I could tag along, since I was going that way. The water in the Bay was quite murky, which made navigation problematic. I was a little biased against poor visibility. While sharks evolved over millions of years to handle these environments, I had not. I opted for the old-fashioned approach and kept my eyes above water, though I knew it might bring me unwelcome attention.

I followed the ship beneath the Bay Bridge, then turned north toward Alameda Beach, which would bring me within a block of our old house. Cecilia enjoyed walking along the beach on calm evenings. With luck, I should be able to see her on one of her walks. Then again, what good would it do, besides giving me a moment of joy? What would Cecilia think of having a white shark stalking her, the very same shark that killed her husband? The shark her deceased husband now controlled. This was insane. I really needed to get my act together. My emotions were getting the better of me, and I decided for the interim to let them ride through me while I settled into my new surroundings.

I recognized the beach near our home instantly. Standing on the beach gave an unhindered view of San Francisco. Though it was more a sliver of sand, when living in a large city, you take what you can get. Families and couples populated the small beach. It still felt good to be home, or at least near it. West Alameda is a small island connected to Oakland, or Alameda County. A narrow tidal channel separates it from Oakland proper. I debated circumnavigating the island to kill the time. It was possible that Cecilia was still at work. I wasn't sure if it was the weekend or a weekday.

Searching my memories, I recalled a small bank on the adjacent side of the island that had an outdoor digital screen in the parking lot, right next to the water's edge. Large yachts often berthed along the boardwalk. I would wait for darkness and then proceed around the island to see if I could garner any information from the sign, though I wasn't sure whether it would be possible to read it from the waterline.

I loitered near the beach for several hours, even passing a few unsuspecting kayakers, but there were no signs of my beloved. Eventually, the beach emptied. Frustrated, I followed the contour of the island. I was a little concerned that my host would wander back out to the Pacific, so I made a plan to swim to the southernmost part of the bay and overnight in the salt ponds. With only one narrow entrance, it might act as a barrier and prevent my partner from fleeing the scene, resulting in me having to work my way back the next day. The other possibility was to venture out to the Farallon Islands and wait there until my partner got fed.

As I entered the tidal canal, I immediately recognized the construction company on the opposite bank. Five bridges connected West Alameda to the mainland. The first was the bridge at High Street, a bridge I normally took to get to the highway on my way to work. The railroad and car bridge at Fruitvale Avenue was next. Directly after this bridge, several shops and banks lined the canal, giving me an unobstructed view of local life. I could see people walking through the parking lot. There was a large electronic billboard outside, but it was too far away for me to read. A long pier that ran parallel with the bank had a few boats moored to it. The space between the bank and the pier was probably around thirty feet, so I swam into the narrow channel and lifted my head out of the water to get a better view. The water was deep enough for me to navigate, and now I could read the billboard. In the lower right corner, the outside temperature was displayed, a balmy seventy degrees Fahrenheit. The date was displayed on the opposite side of the sign. Could read the word *May*, but I couldn't make out the day or year. All the same, it made absolute sense that I had journeyed eight months since the event.

While watching the sign, I heard the voices of people walking on the pier above me. Looking up, I noticed there was a small gap in the floorboards, giving me a brief opportunity to observe anyone passing by. I heard the voices of a man and a woman approaching. The couple passed over the gap and continued onwards, but then I heard the man stop. He walked back to the gap in the floorboards and looked down, apparently curious about something in the water. It was quite dark, so I held my position. My snout was above the surface but the rest of me was below. In the darkness, it would be difficult for the man to understand what he was looking at.

He called out to the woman, "Hey Trish, see what I'm seeing?"

The woman walked over to the gap and squinted. "No, no idea. What is it?"

"I don't know. Shall I go down and have a look?"

"Oh, come on, Joe, it's late as it is. C'mon," she replied hastily.

It was evident to me that what he saw bothered him. Good thing it wasn't daylight. *He would probably have shit himself.* To avoid creating even more problems for myself, I dipped my snout underwater and attempted to pass through the trusses of the pier. Of course, I ended up barreling into some of them and shaking the entire structure. It took a bit of work to extricate myself, breaking parts of the submerged wooden structure. I surfaced a short distance away and looked back at the couple. I could see the man jumping on the pier and yelling.

"It was a fucking shark! I told you there was something!" he yelled.

"Shut up, Joe. Let's go home", the woman replied, clearly irritated.

Curious about the commotion the man was making, people began approaching the pier. *Time to leave*, I told myself. Submerged, I made my way around the island and pressed on toward the South Bay. My plan was to swim to the Dumbarton Bridge and *lock* myself in the southernmost "pond" until morning. The visibility in the South Bay was quite poor, so I swam near the surface. The water was also shallow, save for a narrow, dredged channel that continued all the way to the southernmost point of the bay. Within this channel, the water depth varied between twenty-five and forty feet. Outside the channel, the depth fell to two or three feet at most, far too shallow for a big fellow like me. Once I'd passed the bridge, the water depth persisted for about a mile before beginning to shallow. An old defunct rail bridge acted as a natural barrier. I figured my host and sidekick had no interest in beaching itself, so I should be fine. Night had fallen, and I was tired. Enough excitement for one day.

When I woke in the early morning, I was gazing directly at Pier 37, smack dab in Fisherman's Wharf. A large group of seals were congregating on rafts, barking at me, obviously upset at my presence. Who could blame them? It seemed the cheeky bastard had figured out my plan and escaped from the South Bay but became sufficiently enamored by the local wildlife to stick around. For this, I was grateful. I felt the beast's hunger, but it was not so bad that it couldn't wait a few days. In a day or two I could swim out to the Farallon Islands and let it feed in peace.

I turned away from the noisy pier and followed the city coastline. It was morning, and I didn't expect to see anyone familiar on the beach at this hour. To kill time, I poked around the harbor. While coasting along the surface, I paraded my dorsal fin with pride. Even while I was up close to the city's jetties, not a single person noticed me. People were so caught up in their phones and other electronic devices that they rarely looked up to see what was going on in the water. By early afternoon I was growing tired of cruising the internal waterways and headed east to Alameda.

In the late afternoon, I placed myself near the beach off our street and waited with trepidation. Families came and went, but mine didn't show up. The water near the beach was quite shallow, so I had to stay at least a few hundred yards offshore to avoid beaching. I surveyed the sandy beach from one end to the other, looking for any sign of Cecilia or the girls. As I did so, I noticed a hand waving in my direction. The hand belonged to an older gentleman sitting on a lawn chair on the beach, wearing a beret and smiling in my direction. Of all the people on the beach, he was the only one who had noticed me. He had identified the large fish in the water, fin and all. I raised my dorsal fin and swayed it back and forth to acknowledge him. In response, he smiled and waved his hands high in the air. Nobody gave him the time of day or responded to his gesticulations. Children went about their games, and parents talked amongst themselves. The natural world was apparently unimportant and uninteresting. In their minds, great whites did not swim in the Bay. *But they do.*

After a few hours of waiting, I became frustrated and disheartened by my situation. What did I expect to achieve? Even if Cecilia or the girls came to the beach, there was nothing I could do. But it would have been nice to see them, even from afar. To see them living and healthy would have made my day.

I spent the rest of the afternoon feeling sorry for myself. This was getting ridiculous. It was getting clearer to me that if I was to connect with my old world, if I had any chance at all, my best bet would be to reach out to ocean scientists. Those with the skills to see beyond my predicament and help me cross the communication gulf. To get to them, I needed to travel further south to Mexico.

The Boat Incident

On my way out of the Bay, I came across a modest-sized sailboat moving along at a brisk pace. It was tacking southwards near Tiburon, so I followed it out of curiosity and because I figured I could do with some distraction. At one point the boat slowed, probably preparing to ease into one of Sausalito's marinas. The boat was still a good half-mile offshore. I could see the Golden Gate close by, its towers peeking through the fog above the hills of Marin. By mid-afternoon, most of the fog had burned off, revealing a bright blue sky.

Boat traffic in the Bay was intense. Ferry boats filed back and forth between the city and Angel Island, Alcatraz, and South Vallejo. Sunset tour boats had already started their early evening runs, their guests lined up at the bow. Mono-hull and multi-hull racing boats moved in pairs across long stretches of open water. A few, brave kitesurfers battled the waves and currents beneath the bridge, occasionally lifting themselves aloft and gliding above the surface when the wind afforded it.

I caught up to the boat I was stalking and watched with interest as its occupants moved about the deck. As I came closer, I saw it was manned by an elderly couple. The husband was wearing an old sailor's cap and sat behind the wheel, holding it with one hand, a wine glass in the other. It was a pretty boat, probably a forty-footer and relatively new, with a fiberglass hull and a mahogany trim. Most of the hardware looked unused, and the mainsail had a lovely tri-colored pattern stitched into it. As a boy, I loved sailing with my dad. It was the only activity we had ever really enjoyed doing together, aside from listening to his many records. We had a short twenty-five-footer that my dad had refinished with the help of one of his pals. It had an open cabin and limited facilities but was a joy to sail. It also had one of those adjustable keels that you could raise or lower, a rare sight these days. As I grew older, my interests moved elsewhere, but I never lost the love of sailing.

I watched the older couple from a distance. The wife was going on about something, speaking into the wind. Not sure if the husband could hear her. He nodded a few times in response, but my guess was he couldn't hear a word she said. He just smiled. They looked happy. Maybe they had been happily married for decades, had grandchildren, and were enjoying their sunset years together.

The husband slackened the mainsail, and the boat coasted to a stop. The man walked up to one of the winches along the port side and pulled on the rope. From his repeated tugging, I surmised the winch had jammed. I swam in closer for a better look. He alternately raised and lowered his eyebrows, bobbing his head side-to-side, giving the impression of some competence, but this being a new boat, I was willing to bet he was stuck. The jib sheet had only partially slackened, and his attempts at freeing up the winch by pulling on the line were not succeeding. I couldn't see what he was doing from where I was, but I assumed he had fouled the lines by being inattentive. His wife sat down in the cockpit, apparently uninterested in his exploits, and gazed longingly at the San Francisco skyline. She was pouring wine into glasses. Finally, she grew impatient, stood up and walked over to her husband, watching with concern as he pulled and pulled on the line to free it from the fouled winch. It didn't take long for the prankster in me to come up with a devious plan. Their grandchildren would certainly retell this story of Grandma and Grandpa and the white shark. A twisted take on Jonah and the whale.

I sank beneath the waves and descended some distance, keeping an eye on the boat above me. A hundred feet or so was enough, I figured. I pivoted upwards, making a beeline for the surface of the water beside the boat. I moved slowly at first, then picked up speed and thrust forward with all my might. When I was just beneath the surface, I gave two or three really powerful strokes with my tail. Suddenly I was airborne. Oh, this was incredible. This actually worked.

After watching countless videos of white sharks breaching, the raw power they had for this kind of display never ceased to amaze me. I should have tried this earlier. The view was decent. I must have gotten pretty far from the surface, since it took some time before I fell back into the sea. I landed with a large splash and came up to the surface to see if the couple was gawking at my display. To my surprise, they hadn't even noticed. They were still fussing with some rope near the main winch, utterly oblivious to my performance.

Disappointed, I decided to give it another try. This time, my plan was to rise closer to the boat and try to get the occupants wet from the spray. I descended again and swam deeper to build up more speed. As I ascended, I increased my stroke rate and adjusted my course. As before, I pushed with all my might just below the surface. In slow motion it would have looked comical, this magnificent large shark aiming for the stars, soaring from the surface of the water, jaws agape—and then the shocked look of the couple as they watched this multi-ton fish fly above them, right into their mainsail. The look on their faces *would* have been priceless... but they weren't looking. They were so preoccupied with the winch that they hadn't even noticed the massive shadow I cast onto them.

For a moment I was hanging in mid-air, my body pressing against the mainsail. It didn't stop there. I had too much lateral momentum, capsizing the boat and catapulting the occupants into the water along with me, wine glasses and all.

Upon reentering the water, I looked upwards to find the couple struggling at the surface. The boat lay on its side but did not sink. Several wine glasses passed me on the way to the bay bottom, along with a rather salty bottle of wine. I watched sadly as the mucky water of the Bay quickly diluted its contents.

The wife managed to grab a lanyard floating in the water, which stopped her from drifting too far from the boat. She pulled herself back to the boat and crawled up onto the semi-submerged cabin. The husband was not so lucky. He had nothing to grab onto and floated away from the boat. Fortunately, he was wearing a vest that kept him afloat. It was obvious from their angry reactions that they were shocked to find themselves immersed, but they still had no clue that it was due to my actions. There was no alarm in their response, other than that the wife was very irritated at her husband. She was literally cursing him out. Colorful vocabulary, I might add. That he was drifting slowly away didn't seem to concern her.

I had made a mess of things. This was rapidly turning into a shitshow. Looking above the surface, I noticed that many onlookers from the marina were watching with interest. From this distance I don't believe they could see what had caused the capsizing, only that the boat had flipped. A harbor patrol boat was making its way out to them, which meant I needed to make myself scarce. Embarrassed at my shenanigans, I promised myself never to try something that dangerous so close to people. I could have crushed them. A waste of a good Chardonnay, too.

Flight

I had this recurring dream, where I would wake up in a dimly lit room. The contents of my dream were blurry, and I could not change my point of view. A small amount of light penetrated the curtains covering a nearby window, but I could not recognize anything in the room. My vision improved a little, but it was still difficult to focus on anything, either in the foreground or background. Peripheral vision was nonexistent.

There was a dark object to the right of my meager field of vision, such as it was. It was also very quiet. I sensed that I was breathing, though it was not something that I could actively control. The dark object in the foreground slowly coalesced into the shape of my wife's head. She was asleep, lying next to me. Her face was mere inches from mine. I tried speaking, moving, anything to get her attention, but it was all fruitless. All I could do was watch her. Then like a mirage, the room and Cecilia vanished. *Waking really sucks sometimes.*

The surface ripples were just visible from my current depth. Wave height was probably between five and ten feet, but from my perspective they could have been only millimeters. For weeks the ocean revealed nothing to me. Sometimes a large pod of dolphins would pass overhead, their noisy chatter audible for several minutes prior to their approach and then after their passage. I would watch them enviously from below as they played and communicated with one another. Individual after individual would leap from the crest of building waves and then plunge into the sea, leaving behind a stream of swirling bubbles. Sometimes the din of their physical exploits drowned out all other sounds. After their passage, the ocean was again silent, and I would feel terribly lonely.

I had just completed a loop, something I did from time to time to avoid any surprises, when in the corner of my eye I noticed a group of aquatic mammals in the distance, frolicking just below the surface. I couldn't make out whether they were dolphins or whales and thought little of it until I noticed a lone figure that had separated from the group and was coming at quite a clip toward me. I watched with curiosity, thinking dolphins normally don't hunt great whites or even approach the larger apex predator for mere curiosity's sake.

A few strokes of my tail and I began swimming away to keep some distance between myself and the approaching animal. It was then that I heard chatter, similar to that of a dolphin pod, but sufficiently different—deeper and a little slower—to raise concern. Occasionally, I could hear a light whistle and a pop, but most of the sounds were clicks, which suggested echolocation. I wondered if the clicks I heard were intended for me. The ocean was empty except for myself and the pod of mammals approaching me. I still had difficulty determining which cetacean was gunning for me, and it certainly made no sign of breaking off its pursuit. Some of the other individuals were quickening their pace in my direction. The clicks were getting louder.

I decided not to stick around, and moved as quickly as possible to deeper waters, tipping downwards and kicking with all my strength toward the abyss below me. The clicks were not fading. If I had to guess, I was most probably being hunted by a pod of killer whales. Panic welled up within me. The pod had identified me from a distance as potential prey, and probably considered I was an easy target out in the open. If memory served me correctly, orcas are relentless pack hunters, capable of taking down prey much larger than themselves. These mammals were already much bigger than me. Orcas can dive deep and are skilled hunters, which nullified any advantage I might have. I would need to apply some unique skills to avoid being decoupled from my liver.

The clicks had not abated, and I could sense that my pursuers were closing in on me. I observed the sea bottom rapidly approaching. These waters were not deep, a thousand feet maybe, which was problematic. Unfortunately for me, the sea bottom was also quite flat and featureless, an endless field of organic material and mud. I looked frantically in every direction for anything that could give me protection from these marauders.

The clicks suddenly ceased, and for a moment I wondered if they had broken off their chase. Orcas are clever animals, and I was not about to drop my guard. I was about to see if my years of watching nature programs were going to pay off.

Suddenly, a trench opened up below me, expanding in width, the bottom dropping several hundred feet. I took refuge between the narrow walls and made for the bottom that was beyond my field of vision. There were no overhangs or ledges nearby for me to hide under, so I continued my descent, searching for a place to hide. It was quite dark, but I could see evidence of life along the walls of the trench. Deep-sea corals grew in large swaths along the rough surface. Small anglerfish, startled by my presence, moved aside. Sadly, there was little time for me to inspect the life-forms here. The characteristic clicking was still not audible, but I was still worried that they were stalking me, observing me from a distance, waiting for me to make a mistake.

The visibility here was good. I flexed my starboard pectoral fin a little so that my body rolled clockwise. I figured I could still move forward and have some sense of what was going on above me. I could see some faint light above me, but the center of my vision was quite dark, as if a large oval object was persistently blocking my view. The darkness followed me, slowly, stealthily, patiently. Whatever it was, it kept its distance.

I held this position for a while as I moved forward, transfixed by the dark outline. The object did not appear to descend toward me, but because of the faint light it was impossible to determine just how close it was. The only sound was the low-level rushing of seawater.

Ahead of me, the channel narrowed, but the downward slope of the trench continued. A bridge-like structure, festooned with deep-water life, presented an opportunity to hide. I slowed my speed by deliberately rubbing against the trench wall. This had the added effect of creating a swirling storm of particles in my wake. The walls continued to narrow to a point where I had to squeeze in sideways. I bumped my head into the wall just beneath the bridge and eventually came to a stop inside a chamber of sorts. In colliding with the rock wall, my body tumbled over itself. I found myself inside a small compartment below the rocky structure, the only opening a narrow slit through which I had somehow blindly slipped in during the commotion. My head was facing outward through the narrow opening and my tail was above me, bent due to the tight space.

Suddenly the water thrummed with an intense clicking noise, echoing off the rock walls from every direction. The vibrations were so powerful that the water vibrated, as if trembling in response. Through the narrow opening, dark forms shifted and weaved—a ballet of massive shapes in the murky depths. The cetaceans circled, their movements hesitant and searching, their confusion casting an aura of palpable frustration into the surrounding water.

There was a steady but low current of water entering the chamber, which kept my gills busy. I kept as still as possible, hoping the pod would quickly lose interest. The orcas only made things worse by swimming through the mass of particles, and occasionally butting their heads into the walls of the narrow channel, creating even more particles. The floating silt reduced the visibility to zero.

It was an unusual situation, in more than one sense. I needed to move to extract oxygen from the seawater, and the orcas needed to ascend to the surface to replenish their own. After several minutes, I felt the first effects of oxygen deprivation. They had not quit just yet, but the obvious agitation in their movements was revealing. *They must be running low*, I thought. A large adult took a stab at the narrow channel where I lay patiently. It came down to within ten feet of my snout. This male orca was much larger than me, and its enormous head dwarfed mine. The beast exuded unbridled ferocity. Despite the darkness I could see its head sticking out below the dust cloud, and I realized that it could see me clearly, but there was no way for it to approach, as my gaping jaws were clearly in the way and the opening in the rock was far too narrow for the large beast to penetrate. It attempted to bite at the surrounding rock, to enlarge the opening. Small rocks tumbled into the depths as it rubbed its white teeth against the wall. I thought I heard it groan in frustration. It even attempted to butt the edge of the opening in the futile hope that the rock would break apart.

Eventually, it seemed as though the beast had grown weary of the chase, knowing full well it could never get to me. Both of us were deep underwater, and I firmly believed it needed to rise to the surface soon. The large orca used its buoyancy to rise from the trench bottom and evaluate the situation before retreating into the dense particle cloud above. It was evident to me that this was an intelligent animal, much like the sperm whale I had met earlier in my travels. Those large, black eyes studied me intently. Likewise, I was probably unlike any shark it had met before. *How irritating to meet a clever shark!* It was not cleverness that had saved me, but blind luck.

The clicking was still audible, but it was fading. I figured I could wait another few minutes before extricating myself from my cell. The cloud of particles dissipated, and I watched as the magnificent animal rose to its companions. The water was alive with clicks and pops as the orcas communicated amongst themselves, probably discussing whether I was worth the effort. I could only guess.

My thoughts were getting cloudy, like the surrounding water, but I could still focus when needed. As soon as I felt it was safe, I kicked my tail a few times and pushed myself out of the opening and toward the depths again. I continued to look upwards until I was satisfied that it was safe to ascend again. Once my excitement had died down, I realized how sore and drained I felt.

As I ascended, I saw the pod of orcas regroup in the distance, near the surface. I swam away from them with all the energy that remained in me. The unrelenting emptiness of the ocean was now very welcome. *No more surprises from now on,* I demanded of fate and destiny. *Good luck with that.* Weeks had gone by without incident, and suddenly, in the space of a few minutes, absolute terror had replaced the draining solitude. *This is how you die,* I told myself. I would need to be more vigilant and, most of all, careful when approaching, or when approached by other species. In most situations, my apex status would keep me safe. But the sea is a cruel mistress. She likes surprises, and she awaits the right moment to strike, at the height of complacency. *Here endeth the lesson, once again.*

Upon reaching the surface, I realized that I no longer knew where I was. It was dark, and the coastline was nowhere to be seen. I told myself not to panic. *Just relax and wait until sunrise, then I'll get my bearings again.* I parked myself on the surface and watched the evening sky. Sometime later, I slumbered off.

When I awoke the following day and came to the surface, I was surrounded by an impenetrable fog. I simply had no way to judge direction. Should I just stay put until the fog burned off, or take a chance? I heard a ship's foghorn bellow in the mist. It sounded far away, but I would not take any chances. My most recent dive hadn't been horribly deep, so perhaps I could use the topography of the sea bottom to navigate. In the old days, a weighted line was dropped over the side of the vessel to determine the depth of the water. Instead of using a line, I could count at regular intervals in my head as I descended. Moving in one direction across the surface I would make multiple dives and determine if the waters were getting shallower, an indicator that a coast was nearby.

After descending leisurely for what seemed like ten minutes, I reached the bottom. During my descent I counted slowly. From my rough calculations, I estimated the depth at roughly a half mile. I was not too far from the coast, but if I chose the wrong direction, I could make things worse for myself. Then I thought about the prevailing trade winds along the West Coast, which were usually from the west. As a large shark, it was difficult to ascertain where the wind was coming from. I hated plastic pollution, having seen plenty of it on my crossing, but a small section of plastic film was moving consistently along the water surface. I followed it. After following it for nearly an hour I made another descent to the bottom. This took roughly five minutes, so the water was getting shallower. I kept my orientation constant and continued in the same direction. When I surfaced again after another hour, the sound of the waves crashing on a beach greeted me.

It was at that moment that I realized that a large group of tarpons were trailing in my wake. I did not know how long they had been following me, but it was quite the entourage. It was still foggy, so I didn't want to shift position and lose my orientation again. I followed the sound of the surf until I could see the breakers. The fog was also beginning to lift. Relieved at my progress, I made a sharp turn and faced my followers. There must have been thirty fish in the school. It was beyond me why they had followed me. Perhaps to pick up scraps from a kill. As I faced them, the individuals scattered now that I was onto them. And then they were gone.

Following the coastline for about a mile, I got the sense I was being shadowed again. Turning around, I saw a young male sea lion swimming in my wake. Upon noticing me, he darted over to my blind spot, just out of my line of sight. This game went on for several minutes. There was nothing threatening about this sea lion; perhaps it was simple curiosity that made him follow me, or maybe it knew from experience that great whites are ambush hunters, and it was better to watch from behind than be in front. The seal watched me constantly, rolling and darting as it did so. It provided me with a small measure of entertainment to watch this oversized puppy. Eventually, the sea lion lost interest in me and not seeing me as a threat, it moved on.

Contact

I would have to say that it felt like a year. Maybe a bit more, who knows. Some of my memories of Cecilia and the girls seemed a bit faded, blurred after playing the same record in my head over and over. I fought hard to recollect those precious moments, unconsciously filtering out the difficulties we had endured. As for estimating the passage of time, my crude mental calculations were gross approximations at best. Getting the date off the billboard did wonders for resetting my inner clock which was so mangled. I did my best to count the days and weeks after that.

Three weeks had passed since I left the Monterey peninsula. Thereafter, a cursory pass of the Channel Islands, depriving it of a seal. This was followed by the island of Catalina, which was lovely, after which I was helped on by heaps of smooth water and sunshine.

A week later, the rugged coastline of Guadalupe Island stared me in the face. Situated nearly eighty miles offshore from Baja, Mexico, the high rocky cliffs of this volcanic island are hard to miss. It is well-known that several times a year, many great whites congregate here. I had run into a few of these characters during my crossing. I recognized one of the large males that had attacked me, a heavily scarred individual with his half-bitten dorsal. The wounds I'd inflicted with my bite had healed, but the scars were pretty obvious. My handiwork. I figured he was older than me, from the heavily mottled pattern beneath his chin. A large rusty hook dangled from his mouth. *That can't be too pleasant.* The large female I had named Molly showed up later in the afternoon, swinging her large, bulbous belly. Wow, she was big. She left soon after. Most of the time I saw juveniles, young great whites chasing smaller fish and staying in the periphery when the big guys showed up. Here, the pecking order was firmly in place.

Later in the afternoon, I discovered two ships moored close to the island. One was clearly a scientific vessel from its designation, while the other appeared to be a liveaboard dive boat. The two vessels were practically adjacent to each other. As always, I was curious and slowly approached, but kept some distance, unsure if it was a shark cage operator or just illegal fisherman operating where they shouldn't. As I got closer, I noticed that the research vessel was owned and managed by the San Diego-based Scripps Institute of Oceanography and was named the *R/V Relentless*. I had read about this boat before. A general-purpose research vessel, the ship often sailed between the California coast and Hawaiian Islands, conducting a variety of deep-water research.

The institute had been on my list of potential customers. Funny, considering that now I might be a source of interest for these people. This was my first encounter with a research ship of any kind. I would have to be patient and not get too discouraged if things didn't go my way. *Baby steps,* I reminded myself.

As I approached, I saw that there were two cages lowered into the water, one from each boat. Both cages were roughly thirty feet underwater. The divers within them were wearing scuba gear, and streams of bubbles from their regulators rose upwards. *Oh, how wonderful to see people up close again,* I thought. And yet at the same time it was so strange to see them, as if they were the uninvited visitors to my realm.

Who am I kidding? I swam in slow circles around each cage. In one cage, three male divers were holding what appeared to be video camera gear. One man was hanging outside the cage, holding onto the trusses of the cage, tempting fate. As luck would have it, the other sharks were not interested. At the urging of his mates, he returned to the safety of the cage.

The other cage contained a lone diver. I swam up for a better look. When I was within a few feet of the cage, I noticed the diver was a young woman. She was standing just behind the bars, watching me studiously as I made several cursory passes, exhibiting no fear. Her long, brown hair billowed slowly in the current.

The woman placed her arms on the cross trusses and smiled at me. At least, I supposed it was a smile. The regulator made expressions difficult to read. However, her eyes were wide open, and I could see creases in her cheeks.

I had long imagined what it would be like to have my first moment of contact. Now that it had arrived, I wasn't sure where to begin. I thought about executing some maneuvers to pique the curiosity of the divers. My thinking was if I could get them to realize that I was different, by simulating human-like behavior, I might get their attention. Cetaceans, like orcas and dolphins, are known for their extensive playfulness. Sharks are not. Ultimately, the crew of the research boat were of more value to me, so I decided to use the recreational divers as targets of some controlled pranks, though I wasn't sure how this was going to play out.

I swam back to the cage containing the three men and lowered myself until I was just below the cage. I edged closer to the center of the cage and slowly raised my dorsal fin between the bars of the cage floor, forcing the men to separate. The men were clearly getting rattled by my tactics. One of them tried stomping on my fin, to little effect. I repeated this a few times until the men were scampering for the side walls of the cage.

The spacing between the bars was, for the most part, too narrow for a burly chap like myself, but in the midsection there was a gap of sixteen, maybe twenty inches between the bars, to accommodate camera gear. Carefully, I pressed my snout between the bars of this wide section and tried with all my might to expand the space. The flexure was minimal, but the wide-eyed looks of the gentlemen inside was priceless.

Then I swam back to the other cage to see if I got a reaction. I swam between the cages several times, repeating my efforts to entertain the sole occupant of the research cage. I could see she was laughing from the cacophony of bubbles coming out of her regulator.

The prankster in me was determined to take this to the next level. Feeling some mild intestinal pressure, I slid up closely to the men's cage again and expelled the contents of my bowels. Throughout the course of my travels, my experience of purging waste had always been: *it's behind me, don't look, and don't care.* I had never bothered to see what kind of shitstorm I could create. The clear water about the first cage became slowly enveloped in a dense, yellow cloud. Soon large schools of fish congregated around the cage, feeding on my exhaust with great abandon. Particulates of waste were everywhere. *Oh dear, I might have overdone it.*

I watched with intense pleasure as the divers inside the cage struggled hopelessly to escape the oncoming cloud of shark poo. Soon the cloud erased the cage from view in a large yellowish-orange ball. I saw arms and legs flailing at the edge of the cloud. Looking back at the other cage, I saw the young woman rolling backwards in her cage, profuse amounts of bubbles emanating from her regulator. This was seriously funny. *Don't lose track of why you're here*, I reminded myself.

Having satisfied my prankster urges I swam back to the woman's cage. I glided forward ever so slowly so that my snout passed a few inches within the cage bars. Carefully, she stuck out her hand and touched the tip of my snout. To sense a human hand touching me was exhilarating. Watching those tiny fingers gently probe my enormous snout got me excited. It had been a long time since I had felt the touch of another human being.

Hovering is challenging for a shark as big as myself. To make it work, I would let myself sink backward and then thrust a little with my tail so that water still passed through my gills, but I could hold my position for a short while. The problem with this approach was that I would eventually tip over and would have to swim to correct my pose. I had the same challenge swimming around the tight passages in coral reefs. It took some doing to get it right, and many times I had to give up. I was just too damn big.

I wondered if the woman could sense that I was cognitive. I mean, one minute I'd been terrorizing a group of divers in one cage, and the next minute I was flirting with another. That couldn't be normal shark behavior, but what did I know. I couldn't be sure that I was the only example of a possessed shark out here in the blue. My behavior could be mistaken for genuine curiosity, which is sometimes exhibited by large great whites. I needed to convince this young lady that I was more than an inquisitive shark.

While hovering in front of the young woman, I began tapping my snout slowly on one of the horizontal cross bars of the cage. I had played with the idea of repeatedly sending signals with either my snout or my teeth banging on metal. Since I could not try this in the open ocean, I had to improvise. It was challenging carrying out any kind of repetitive task underwater. I had no leverage. So, I repeated myself several times until I found a way forward.

Most young people today have limited to no knowledge of Morse code, but I figured some researchers on board would have come out of the naval academy or even a sailing course, where knowledge of Morse was still a requirement. I took a chance. My Morse was surprisingly still good, so I introduced myself by tapping on the bars, albeit sluggishly and with some error, *My nme is Mrk.*

At first, the woman didn't respond as I had hoped, and she looked confused. She scratched her head and just stood there.

I repeated the same message three times, carefully separating the long and short taps. The tapping from my snout was quite low and soft. I tried again by tapping with my upper jaw against the bars, so that my teeth struck the metal. The next attempt was perfect. Suddenly, the woman thrust herself back to the middle of the cage and pressed her hands against her goggles, shaking her head in disbelief. She looked over at the beleaguered men in the other cage, then back at me, strangely. This was what I had expected, but would she respond?

She gestured to me to repeat my action, aiming to verify what she just observed. I repeated the message several times, pausing between attempts to ensure it didn't appear accidental.

I saw her reach down and grab an underwater pad and pencil from the pocket of her BCD. She wrote something and showed it to me. The letters were small but there was no mistaking it: *My name is Lucy.*

My shock was profound. It took me several seconds to absorb what was happening. This was my first contact with another human being in over a year.

Lucy then scribbled, *How is this possible?*

I tapped out, *you r nt going to beleve ths.*

She was still shaking her head, bewildered. *Please don't give up on me,* I thought desperately to myself. Floating uncomfortably close to the cage, I attempted to tap again on the bars when suddenly she lifted her hands to make the familiar OK sign and pointed toward the surface. I pulled away and nodded my head in acknowledgement.

At that moment I wanted to hug that young woman. I swam large circles around both cages for a while before coming back to Lucy. Was I up to the challenge of communicating in Morse? This was going to take some doing. It's one thing to construct a few simple sentences, a full-on conversation was something else. I came up to her cage again and tapped carefully, *Please kep an opn mnd*. She nodded.

It was a struggle to tap out Morse on the cage bars. Sometimes the sentences came out all wrong. It had been a while since I communicated in Morse, the last time being with Sarah in the technical museum, just before we left for the islands. When tapping on the bars, there was nothing for me to hold on to, not that I had hands for gripping, and I couldn't remain still for extended periods. It was an exercise in frustration. But I could see Lucy watching me and thinking, and that encouraged me. There was hope.

The men in the other cage were still recovering from the poop onslaught and started waving at Lucy. She communicated to them in diver sign language. They responded with that typical dismissive gesture: a nonchalant shrug that seemed to say, *what are you even saying*? I was counting on Lucy's intuition to move things forward, but I knew it wouldn't be easy for her. She had a lot of people to convince.

She started writing again on her pad and placed it up against the bars for me to read. I could only imagine what the fools in the other cage were thinking. She had written, *We have a platform onboard. Will you come up?* I did my best up and down motion, hoping she understood me. Lucy pulled on a cable to inform the crew to raise the cage.

From the surface I watched as the crew maneuvered a large platform into the water. I had seen these platforms on nature programs, allowing sharks to be tagged and released, usually by coaxing the shark with a big chunk of tuna at the end of a rope or by heaving it in by boat. As expected, one deckhand launched a tuna head at me, and it splashed a mere five feet in front of my snout. I ignored it. The deckhand placed his hands on his hips and raised his eyebrows in surprise.

The platform was lowered by a crane until the wooden decking was five feet underwater. Carefully, I swam forward. To the surprise and to the shock of her colleagues, Lucy jumped directly in front of me, placing her hand on my snout. She signaled for the team to raise the platform. They raised it until I was halfway out of the water. The brightness of the sunlight reflecting off the metal surfaces temporarily blinded me. It took me several minutes to adjust to the visual onslaught. Lucy sat down next to me and caressed the skin near my eyes. She started talking to me. Her accent had a southern California vibe to it. Hearing it for the first time in a year was soothing.

"Mark, we are going to find a way to communicate with you," she whispered to me. "We have a lot of minds to convince today."

As I glanced at her, the furrow between her brows deepened, and her lips pressed into a thin line, betraying a mounting concern in her eyes. It was clear to me that she was watching the crew, trying to gauge their reactions.

A young fellow jumped down to the platform and brought over several high-pressure hoses. He and another fellow opened my jaws as far as they could, which was difficult to do above water, and pushed in the pipes. Oxygenated water streamed through my gills. So far so good.

This was not my first time dealing with gravity—I recalled my unplanned ride on a whale's back. Sitting fixed on the platform was very limiting, and to a degree uncomfortable. The only part of my body I could move fully were my eyes. The pipes pumping water and the weight of my head heavily constrained the movement of my jaws. My fins were effectively useless. *Like a beached whale.*

I attempted to communicate with my eyes using Morse, rolling them back quickly and slowly, but it proved to be very difficult and imprecise. Lucy could see I was struggling.

"Let's keep this as simple as possible, Mark," she whispered, "I'm going to ask you a series of questions. Just roll your eyes once to agree, okay?"

I acknowledged by rolling my eyes.

Lucy raised her voice to get everyone's attention. "Hi everyone, can I have your attention please."

Everyone on deck stopped what they were doing and watched her intently.

"I'm about to do something that is going to ask a lot of all of you" she said. "I know some of you are going to think I'm off my rocker, but please give me your time for the next few minutes. They say life is stranger than fiction. It's going to get really strange in a moment, so please bear with me."

Most of the crew nodded back, but a few had contorted expressions on their faces, squinting their eyes and turning away from the speaker as if offended. *Pockets of resistance*, I thought. There was also plenty of mumbling and murmuring between some of the crew.

"I don't know how to put this any more succinctly than this: it is quite possible we have a sentient shark here," Lucy explained earnestly.

I heard a few gasps in the audience. Some laughed at her statement. I mean, the idea of a sentient shark does sound ridiculous. It was critical to me that Lucy persevered, regardless of the fallout. Lucy had her work cut out with this bunch. I looked around at the crew, watching their facial expressions change from moment to moment.

"Look, this is really important to me. Think of it as a Turing test. Can I please have your attention for five minutes?"

Briefly, everyone was quiet.

A tall, tanned young man stepped forward and asked,

"Does it have a name?"

"Yes, its name is Mark," she answered. Some of the crew laughed out loud, saying repeatedly, "Mark the shark". *Jeez.*

"You're fucking kidding me, right?" the young man retorted, cocking his head at an angle as if annoyed. Lucy just nodded, which seemed to irritate him even more.

"Josh, can you just give me five minutes? Please. That's all I ask," Lucy implored.

This was getting unbearable. If the crew did not give her this opportunity, then all was lost.

Josh paced back and forth for a short while, then walked up to Lucy. "Okay, let's see where this goes. You have a considerable number of individuals to convince here, me included. You have five minutes, Lucy."

"Thanks," she replied. She faced the crew again. "I'm going to ask a series of yes and no questions. Mark will answer by rolling his eyes. Everybody got that?" she said loudly.

She shifted her gaze towards me and asked, "Is your name Mark?"

I acknowledged with an eye roll. She asked again, and I responded in the same manner.

"Are you, or were you once human?"

I rolled back my eyes.

Someone yelled, "Bullshit!"

Voices of surprise mingled with hints of doubt rippled through the audience.

"Has it been a long time?"

Too long… but yes. Eye roll.

"Are you pulling my leg?" met with no response.

"Are you of sound mind?"

Really? Rolled back eyes twice.

"How many years?"

I rolled my eyes once to signify a year.

"One year?" she asked. I responded again with an eye roll.

"Are you, or were you a man?"

Eye roll.

"That's interesting, because you are inhabiting a female shark."

Really? I thought.

She continued, "Did you know?"

No response.

"Well, how could you know?" she said.

I thought about that. Apparently, I had been cruising the seas in the body of a large female great white shark. My host had been revealed. *So I'm part of a sisterhood.* It would explain a few things, like the aggressive behavior of other male sharks. In my defense, I was too caught trying to fend off the attacks to think about it. Not that it bothered me all that much knowing my host was a female. Still, it was odd to have it confirmed after so much time had passed. I thought back to the day of the attack, when the shark had appeared to us. At the time, I was so impressed by the beast that I never considered the creature's sex.

How would Cecilia take to this? *Honey, I have been inside another female for the better part of a year.* As funny and odd as it sounded, it was the least of my problems. First, she would have to contend with me being alive, and then the fact that I was inside this massive fish.

Lucy stepped away from the platform to discuss with her colleagues. The building tension was palpable in their raised voices. It seemed to be Lucy against the skeptics, although Josh appeared to be relenting, evident from his more relaxed posture. While Lucy's determination may have swayed a few, the majority remained steadfastly opposed. Concern gnawed at me as I feared the outcome of this discussion.

Lucy, Josh, and a few of the crew separated from the rest and stood in a circle, my guess was that they were batting ideas back and forth. The tension was really getting to me. I was just lying here, feeling useless. After about ten minutes, Lucy and Josh stepped down to the platform. She spoke to me while pointing at her colleague.

"Mark, this is Josh. He is our resident engineer. We have an idea that we would like to try. But it will take us the evening and probably most of the night to put together a prototype. Could you come back tomorrow so we can try it?"

Absolutely, I thought. I rolled my eyes three times in succession. A sense of relief washed over me. The past hour had seemed an eternity. The crew supporting Lucy gave thumbs-up gestures.

They lowered the platform and set me free. For the next couple of hours, I loitered up and down the coast. I was so excited about what tomorrow would bring. I was grateful this young woman had taken a chance with me. I imagined what this might have done to her career and reputation, if the others had not given her their backing. I recalled stories of engineers claiming a particular AI system had become sentient, only to be rolled by their peers.

I began reviewing my knowledge of Morse. *Keep it simple*, I reminded myself. I considered shortcuts and simplifications so that I didn't waste energy conveying irrelevant information.

That I had inhabited a large female white shark all this time didn't really faze me. I knew who I was, and more importantly, *what* I was. The large males that accosted me did so out of instinct. Yes, I had felt threatened when they attacked, but for the wrong reasons, apparently. If the bastards had impregnated me, I would have been absolutely livid.

Along the coast I saw other great whites. Most passed without showing the least iota of interest. I came across a large gray whale and her calf floating in the shallows. It was most prudent to give them a wide berth. I recalled vividly what had happened the last time I came between a large whale and its offspring. Visibility was quite good this close to shore, but the depths were calling me, and it was getting late. Today had ended up being a great day, but who knew what tomorrow would bring. With that thought, I fell into a slumber and let my host take over.

When I woke, I rose to the surface to figure out where my owner had wandered off to. Thankfully, the coast of Guadalupe was not too far away. Now I just had to figure out whether to swim north or south of the island. I recalled the topography of the coastline from the day before and made an educated guess. I recalled groups of cliffs, rather tall ones that lined the background. To the south, the coastline looked less dramatic, so I ventured north. Sure enough, the black hull of the *R/V Relentless* came into view near one of the bays. I powered forward and stayed on the surface, giving the team ample time to see me and prepare the platform.

As I approached, the ship's crew was lifting the platform from the ship into the water. On cue, I swam toward it, and again ignored the block of tuna tartare that was hurled at me. I guessed it was a litmus test, but there were easier ways to identify individuals. Weird, though, that I had very little recollection of the shark I had seen at Lanai, which would have been helpful in knowing how I appeared. *I'll ask for a self-portrait.*

Lucy and Josh popped down to the platform as it was being lifted. Josh was carrying an object that comprised two moving plates, separated by an accordion-like structure. It looked like one of those old cameras with a bellows structure separating the front part from the film plate. Several wires came out of one plate, and a cable ran from the device to a laptop. It looked like something cooked up at a science fair.

"Good morning, Mark," Lucy said to me. "I hope you are well. We've been busy all night turning the lab upside down. If we appear dopey, it's just because we are tired. We sincerely hope this works."

I rolled my eyes in acknowledgment.

She continued, "Josh is going to place this contraption between your jaws. We designed it to withstand a bite force of five hundred pounds per square inch, which is nothing for you, but it's the best we could do on short notice. We repurposed a lab jack for this. It's important that you do not press too hard when you bite down. You might break it."

Josh leaned forward with the device. Other crew members assisted with the cables. I slowly spread my jaws apart and let him place the device near where the two halves joined, closest to him. Another crew member placed high-pressure hoses along the other side of my mouth. Lucy stepped forward and assisted Josh in aligning the apparatus in my mouth. I could feel their fingers prodding inside my mouth. After several minutes, the two of them stood up and gave thumbs-up signs. Most people would shriek in fear at being this close to a large great white, but not these guys. I was very proud of them.

Josh said, "Mark, could you please open and close your mouth slowly."

As I did so, I could feel the device expand and contract. They placed a large flatscreen display in front of me for all to see. Josh placed a tripod to one side of the display and fitted a camera. Another camera was placed closer to my head, near my eyes. The flatscreen displayed the live feed from both cameras in two small windows on the right side of the screen.

There I was, in all my glory. I dwarfed everyone on the platform. Despite my imposing size, a profound sense of humility washed over me, humbling me in the face of it all. It was astounding to realize that not only did I inhabit this colossal creature, but I had also managed to endure a whole year navigating the ocean within it. In the feed from the closeup camera I could see striations, scratches, and wounds all across my right side. The height of my dorsal fin was astonishing, and there were many notches along the trailing edge. Like a fingerprint these are unique for each shark.

Then reality came back with a vengeance, along with the terrifying sense of being locked in with no way to escape my prison. I experienced no pain or discomfort, other than feeling like a beached slug on the platform.

A narrow but wide window at the top of the display showed a running time history of my jaw motion. As I opened and closed my mouth, the signal would rise and fall like a sinusoidal wave.

Lucy leaned down to me and said, "As you can see, the signal represents the motion of your jaws. Josh is going to tune the width of those signals so that we can translate them to long and short pulses. In the window below, the software will attempt to decipher the incoming signal. We obviously didn't have time to build a full AI stack for this, if you understand what I mean."

I replied with an eye roll.

They also placed a poster near my right eye featuring Morse conversions, just in case I forgot. They had thought of everything.

"Are you ready?" Lucy asked.

Oh yeah, I thought.

"Let's try a few short simple phrases first."

I considered what to say. Perhaps it was most advisable to take it slowly. Short, succinct sentences.

My name is Mark Forster. A year ago, while diving off the island of Lanai, a great white shark attacked me. The same shark you see before you.

It took a while to get the words out, but the system was working. All eyes were on the screen. A few of the crew were scanning their phones, presumably looking for news articles. Their expressions spoke volumes—eyes widening in disbelief, brows knitting together in surprise—as the information sank in.

The next thing I remember is that I woke up on the seafloor as this shark. I guess I died. That is the only explanation I have.

Little by little, the system translated my jaw movements. Occasionally there were spelling mistakes or a missed word, but the crew got the gist of it. Josh examined the apparatus to see how it was holding out against my thrashing. He would also correct the phrases as they came on screen. Identifying pauses between the words was still an issue, but easy to fix on the display. As I looked around, I could see more and more of the crew listening in. I observed a remarkable transformation in their expressions. Initially marked by disbelief, their faces gradually softened, replaced by expressions of wonder and admiration.

"We're good, Mark." Josh reassured me. The impact of my story registered unmistakably on his face. It was evident from his expression that the magnitude of what I had conveyed was sinking in, leaving a weighty impression on him.

The process of communicating was sluggish, but with practice it should go faster.

Lucy asked, "You said a shark attacked you off Lanai, correct?"

I replied yes. Her expression was a bit odd, so I prodded her: *What do you know?*

She replied, "Not much. It was a year ago. It was all over the news, and then it faded, like everything else."

That was the issue I had with shark attacks. Of all the trauma, pain, and suffering one could read about in the press, why do shark attacks get so much coverage? Three to five fatalities a year and the media go absolutely bonkers for several weeks after each incident.

Before we discussed anything further, there was one thing I desperately needed to express.

Can someone, any of you, contact my family and let them know I am okay, I implored.

It became obvious that I had not thought this through. How on earth would this happen? How would they explain it? Would Cecilia even listen to them?

Sorry, I don't know how else to ask. You are the first people I have spoken to in a year.

For a moment I forgot I had the device in my mouth, and I let my upper jaw descend too quickly. I could both feel and hear the metal buckle between my jaws. The screen suddenly filled with noise.

Josh leapt up to retrieve the device from my mouth and raised it up. The modified lab jack was nothing more than scrap metal now, crushed beyond recognition on the platform floor, with twisted pieces of metal scattered around. The bellows structure between the plates of steel was shredded, and several cables were cut. Seeing the mangled unit brought back memories of the sonar array I'd damaged on the Russian sub.

"It's alright, Mark," Josh said reassuringly. "I didn't think we would get this far. I'll build a better one next time."

Lucy sat down in front of me and gazed into space. She turned to me and said, "Mark, I need to ask a favor of you. I need to discuss this with my boss, Dr. Holloway, from the institute. It's not going to be easy. But we are all witnesses to something truly extraordinary here, and we want to help. There isn't a person here who doesn't feel touched by your situation. Here's the big 'but': we need to convince the grown-ups back home, because we desperately need their help. On another note, we will sail to Maui in two months' time, arriving in mid-July. That will give you six months. Can you meet us out there?"

What the fuck? Having covered half the width of the Pacific, now I had to head back? With the device broken, I had no way to express my irritation over this. Could we not find some place closer? It had taken me nearly a year to get here, so close to home. The thought of having to retrace my steps back to the origin of all my transition and all my problems was terribly upsetting.

Lucy just smiled at me, which made it all much worse. She simply had no clue what she was asking of me.

I attempted a few eye rolls to show my indignation. She just smiled in response. *Oh fuck.*

"We also need to build a better unit and more software, and I don't know where to go from here with all this. Time will tell." She looked at me with concern. "I'll see what we can do about your family. I can't promise anything right now. I worry about inviting more trauma."

She was right about that. As much as I knew Cecilia, I could not imagine her response to all of this. Lucy scratched my nose to get my attention, almost as if I was a puppy. "Can we place a tracker on you so that we can follow your movements?"

I confirmed by rolling my eyes.

That stung a bit, I thought as two members of the crew punched a small hole in my dorsal fin and attached the transponder. I guessed this was how it felt to get your ears pierced. Now I had something else in common with my wife and daughters.

"The satellite tracking tag that we attached has enough juice to last ten years. Though we expect it to fall off much sooner," Lucy informed me. "It will capture your location, and record depth, and water temperature. Every time you surface it will upload to the satellite."

They lowered the platform and released me. As I swam away, I brooded a bit. I should have been relieved and happy that I had finally got in touch with people again. But I couldn't help but feel a little disappointed. Expectations would need to be managed. *Baby steps,* I reminded myself. The crew of this boat were mostly young, but this experience would have affected old salts as well. I had six months to make it to the islands, which was plenty, as long as I did not veer off course too much.

And then it dawned on me. The Hawaiian Islands are mere specks in the vastness of the Pacific Ocean. There is nothing close to these islands for over two thousand miles in all directions. Despite my recent challenges, finding a coastline that runs for thousands of miles north and south was infinitely easier in all respects. I could have done it blind, almost. *Holy shit, I really need to think about this.* With no way to communicate with Lucy or her colleagues, I would need to figure out a way myself.

I thought long and hard. Locating the Hawaiian Islands in the middle of the Pacific was a terrifying gamble. If I missed the islands, which was likely, I could end up far west of my desired location and miss my rendezvous with the *Relentless* altogether. Somehow, I needed to come up with a solution to reduce my risk.

The ancient Polynesians knew a thing or two about navigating the Pacific. Islands act as blockers and reflectors of currents. The north equatorial current strikes the islands head on and splits into the North Hawaiian Ridge current and a continuation of the equatorial current. If I followed the equatorial current without slipping into the countercurrent, this should bring me within a few hundred miles of the islands. I would need to apply dead reckoning and evaluate my drift as I progressed across the Pacific. Clouds have a way of forming over high islands because of the thermal gradients between land and water. These cloud formations ought to be visible from far away. Since none of these approaches were guaranteed to work, I would also need to sweep a large area of the central Pacific. My one fear was having to iterate and backtrack based on intuition. I could end up lost out there.

There was one other consideration: great whites regularly visit the cafe, a region smack dab between Hawaii and Baja. A select few also undertake the journey to Hawaii from this hot spot in the Pacific. If I was fortunate to find great whites traveling further west, I could tag along. This might reduce the reach of the sweep. From my previous experience, I would need to be vigilant passing through the cafe again, but once I was clear of it, it would be a beeline west to the islands. *I hope.*

Good Golly

It took a good month to get to the cafe, heading west. I followed a few unsuspecting great whites that I spotted along the way, one of whom I named Curly since he had an unusual mane of green algae growing on his head, right above his eyes. He was a large male with a broken jaw that looked positively painful. I gather he was the bully in the schoolyard who had got his comeuppance. There are always bigger, meaner fish out there. Nevertheless, I pitied him, and followed him for several weeks. As I approached the cafe, I put my senses on full alert and moved out to the periphery. I knew full well that the waters here were deep and great whites are the masters of the ambush, even if an ambush only meant getting shagged.

Despite the risky nature of the area I was approaching, deep down I was relieved I had gotten here without too much difficulty. This was the halfway point. Was I feeling more confident in my navigation capabilities? A little, perhaps, but I also accepted the notion that I needed help, and that help came from watching, following and sometimes collaborating with my brethren. Deviate a fraction of a degree north or south from the path and this expedition would all be for nought. Not even the night sky could help me. I needed to feel the water.

One morning I witnessed Molly defending herself from the amorous charms of a would-be suitor. She was double the size of her amour. The male shark accosted her repeatedly. For a while she tolerated him, occasionally giving him side glances to dissuade him, but from his aggressiveness it was inevitable he would try to copulate. From my perspective, he was way out of his league.

There was something stately about her countenance. Judging by the size of her ever-growing belly, I wondered if she was pregnant. She had certainly gotten bigger from a few months back. *It can't all be food*, I thought. Molly probably made this journey every year, persevering through the gauntlet of guileless males. It was riveting to watch. This young male was certainly persistent. From time to time, he would grab one of Molly's pectoral fins and attempt to latch on, only to be dispatched with great haste. Then, as if a light switch had been flicked, the young male lost interest and disappeared into the depths.

A gut feeling told me to keep following Molly, in the hope she would continue westward. Several sharks were turning north or south, which usually meant they were heading back to the mainland. Molly kept plodding westwards. For a few days I followed near her flank as she held course, and then one day, for whatever reason, she decided to descend. I had followed whales and other cetaceans into the deep before, but this was an unfamiliar experience for me.

No one really knows what white sharks do or what they hunt in these waters. I figured I was about to find out. Unlike the cetaceans, Molly was moving at a relatively easy pace as she dived. Her large tail undulated in large sweeps. I followed close behind, and before long, we were in complete darkness, but I could still sense her movement directly ahead of me. Like a stalker, I followed her. Every few hours she would ascend to three or four hundred feet, as if getting her bearings, and then descend again into the darkness. Why she did this was an absolute mystery to me.

This process repeated for several days. With each descent

the water temperature dropped dramatically relative to the surface, robbing me of vital energy. I was wondering about all this energy expenditure when she suddenly began diving at high speed. Keeping up as best I could, I picked up signals in my snout, coming from further ahead. The surrounding water was coming to life. And so was Molly. The once stately and relaxed queen of the sea was now maneuvering—aggressively, I might add. She would inexplicably dart after shadows. Something moving in absolute darkness doesn't necessarily qualify as a shadow, but that was how it appeared to me. Occasionally I saw flashes of light, most of it short-lived. It was a lot of work keeping up with her.

Sea creatures of all sizes exert forces in the water when pursued, the strength of which is roughly proportional to their displacement or size. When a seal or fish dodges a pursuer, the sharp turns they make send very characteristic wakes in all directions. I can best describe them as a series of pulses or waves. The intensity of forces I was sensing along my lateral line was quite varied, making me think that I was surrounded by creatures both smaller and larger than myself. Being in near darkness did not help to reduce my angst.

Inexplicably, Molly came to a stop and just drifted ahead of me. There was no swift movement in the water, just shallow undulations revealing to me that she was eating. Giving her space, I swam a large arc, stopping a short distance away, facing her. Somehow, I could just make out her silhouette in the darkness, and then I realized why. The lifeless remains of a large Humboldt squid lay in front of her, glowing eerily in the darkness. Molly quickly consumed the squid in several bites. For a moment her mouth had a frightening glow, teeth glowing in a pitch-black sea.

I followed Molly back up to the shallows and lay in her wake. The setting sun in front of us reassured me we were on a westward track, but to where exactly? I wondered how she maintained her course, if she maintained one at all. Thinking back to that large topographical map of the Pacific in the museum, I recalled the seamounts, the volcanic spires that rose from the sea bottom. The abyssal plain was littered with them, stretching from Baja, Mexico to the Hawaiian Islands and beyond. Could Molly sense them? Did she have a map of each pinnacle laid out in her mind, like breadcrumbs, giving her guidance?

Fatigue was setting in with a vengeance, and I had to make a decision. I'd forced myself to stay awake for several weeks now, holding desperately onto consciousness. Occasionally, I nodded off due to sleep deprivation, but woke quickly, startled, to resume control. Falling asleep now for even a few hours could potentially throw a wrench into my plans. I just needed to get close to the islands. Molly was taking her sweet time, but she had the means and sense of direction that I did not. Again, I was assuming that Molly was indeed heading to the islands. This was a big if. What would I do if I surfaced way west of my destination? *Keep it together, brother.*

Seeing Molly devour a squid made me think of my own hunger. On my left, I saw a school of yellowfin tuna. Sneaking up on them was not without risk, but I saw little choice. I extended the distance between myself and Molly. Visibility was good, so she was still in view even when I was more than a hundred feet from her. Descending slowly at first, I tried to make my way under the school. The spontaneously conceived plan had me boxing them in, pushing them towards Molly. Once the school got wind of Molly on their right flank, they altered their course and scattered. I rose to meet them. One unlucky fish darted directly into my maw. That worked out nicely. Momentarily spared of hunger I pressed on and caught up with my guide. Now only if I could find a good sized mola.

Leviathan

Molly had been calling the shots for what seemed like weeks, but she had been keeping a reasonably shallow depth for most of it, for which I was thankful. Weeks of darkness with only my senses and Molly guiding me were beginning to grate on my nerves, so running at a depth where some sunlight filtered through was uplifting for my soul. Having Molly as a constant companion, even if we never shared a word, reduced my anxiety.

It came as a surprise when one day Molly began to charge toward the depths again. This time it seemed we were going much deeper than before. Without time to react, I followed blindly behind her, trying to keep up as best as possible. I never would have expected such a large and majestic shark to be in such a rush, which made the whole situation so odd. Was she reacting to something? Darkness surrounded us rapidly, but her speed did not abate. *What is going on?* I thought, concerned. I could see her flanks working intensely as we descended further into the depths. My guess was Molly was familiar with the region of the ocean and wasn't going to explain to me, the novice, the goings on of the deep. Not that she could. The drop in oxygen and temperature had the effect of making me sluggish and slow.

Molly made several turns in our descent, following a map in her mind only she could understand. *She knows something's up*. It was then that I registered the first of several faint stirrings in the depths. The low frequency vibrations had little strength at first but grew steadily. My experience up to now has been that vibrations come and go; they never continue to grow unabated. The vibrations then stabilized in intensity. I had the impression that we were being pursued by something very large.

Molly picked up her pace again, her tail making rapid sweeps. The tingling in my back was rising again, only this time it was continuous. Molly made another sharp turn and then plummeted headlong into deep sea mud, which had seemingly come out of nowhere, then came to a full halt. I followed suit, coming to rest a short distance from her. We must have struck a deep-sea pinnacle, one of many that lined the path before us. My right pectoral fin was buried deep in the soft sea bottom and my mouth was filled with organic material. I was about to shake it all out when I noticed that Molly was not making any attempt to move. She was, in fact, completely still. *Why?*

The tingling along my back sharpened to stabbing levels. Lying still, I tried looking around in the pitch blackness. Some bioluminescent fish passed between Molly and me. In the faint light generated by the creatures I caught Molly scanning the water above us. Something was coming. I also noticed that both Molly and I were lying in a shallow channel carved into the seamount. The surrounding water began to move, slowly at first, as if we were at the edge of an approaching storm. I still did not know what it was we were about to experience, but Molly's absolute stillness was troubling, to say the least. The current had increased to the level where it simply lifted off any loose debris into the maelstrom above us. I looked in all directions, wondering what was creating the massive movement of water this far down.

More bioluminescent creatures passed us. In the dimness I

could see Molly pushing her snout deep into the mud. The current had grown so powerful that I was beginning to slide. I doubled down and pressed my snout deeper into the sea bottom. Even with the bioluminescent animals dimly lighting the immediate area, the visibility in the water above us had dropped to near zero. All I could see was a thick soup of mud and particulates sweeping above me. Now and then, faint shadows of creatures passed by at high speed, those less fortunate caught in the storm. Some were very large. Water still moved through my gills, but the lack of oxygen at this depth still made me uncomfortable. A bad headache was coming on. I rolled back my eyes to protect them.

Frightening as it all was, I was no longer concerned about getting pulled into the storm. I figured all storms have a beginning, a peak, and an end. Molly was waiting out a deep-sea storm, something I never knew existed. Her experience and her knowledge had probably taught her long ago what was coming and how to survive it. I pitied the creatures who were caught up in the onslaught of water and suddenly displaced, or worse, drowned. It was tough enough for large creatures like us to maintain our position in the mud.

Most surface storms last a day or two and eventually subside. Without the rising and setting of the sun I had no way to gauge time down here. My best guess was that a week passed, and the massive underwater current was showing no sign of abating. Lifting off the bottom now would throw me off completely, without a hope of ever finding the islands again. Patiently I waited, headache and all. I hoped Molly was equally patient. On top of it all, I was fighting exhaustion and sleep deprivation. I tried nodding off briefly to take the top off the fatigue, but I feared falling asleep and getting sucked into the storm above me. Or worse, waking up my partner, who might have other plans.

By the third week, the current dropped a tad. A few days

later, it dropped to a manageable level, but the visibility was still nil. Not that it mattered at this depth, but the occasional organism passing would have provided enough light to view the surroundings. The water around was finally quiet. I listened intently for life or activity. I then felt a sensation of water being slowly swept aside, like a mild current caused by the swish of a large tail. This was my cue to lift from the bottom and follow Molly to the surface. The sweeps of her tail were more relaxed now, and from her body's orientation I noticed that she was pining for the surface, just as I was. Three weeks of oxygen deprivation was enough. Ascending, my spirit lifted as the first rays of sunlight reached my eyes.

Full Circle

Despite some navigational challenges and the underwater storm, the trip back to Maui was, thankfully, uneventful. Passage through the cafe was quick and, with few run-ins besides the occasional cargo vessel and a few rumblings from the deep, the trip was smooth. At one point I heard a pod of orcas, but they left me alone. Molly had done a splendid job of bringing me to the islands, even though the entire passage had probably just been part of her annual transit across the Pacific. I felt very fortunate to have her as my guide. Funny thing, though, I don't believe she ever acknowledged my presence at any time during our passage.

Exhaustion barely describes how I felt now. Sleep was high on my schedule, but it would have to wait. Deep down, my greatest fear was still that Cecilia would not be there. Would they have even tried to reach out to her? Would Cecilia entertain the notion of me being alive? I could imagine her slamming the door in Lucy's face in a fit of rage, or even sending the police after her and having her charged with harassment. Lucy had enough challenges with her own crew. From any perspective, the situation was fucked.

I shook away these negative thoughts and dreamt of little Amelia, who was probably not so small anymore, and probably stubborn, like her mother. Sarah was probably entering her teenage years, if not fully immersed in them. I often wondered how Cecilia had coped with bringing up the girls alone. Would she ever forgive me?

The coast north of Hana was the first sign of landfall, emerging from the mist from recent rainfall. Molly was no longer around, having left me to my own devices. Once she had approached the islands she had wandered off, uninterested in these isolated isles. Just as well, I supposed, now that I was back in familiar territory. If I ever had to make a crossing like this again, I would search her out.

The sun did not greet me on my arrival. I followed the northern coast for a day until I rounded the point. Lucy and I had agreed to meet a few miles offshore to keep inquisitive eyes at bay.

By late afternoon, the sea had calmed and most of the tourist boats had returned to port. A lone ship lay before me. Even from a few miles away, I was pretty certain that it was the *R/V Relentless*. The boat had idled and drifted with the current. I could hear its engines shutting down. Back in Mexico, Lucy had fitted me with a tracker so she could keep up with my progress across the Pacific. I wondered if they had any concern I could find my way back. Approaching the boat, I could see her leaning on the rear railing, smiling. She had certainly spotted me. I swam up slowly and rolled my body in the water to show my pleasure. They lowered the platform to just a few feet so I could ease myself in. I was getting good at this sort of thing.

Josh and another fellow hopped down onto the platform and placed a hose into my mouth. Lucy came down into the water and patted me on my back, or at least that's what it felt like. Shark skin is not sensitive to human touch. You'd have to hit me really hard or drive a boat over me to get me feeling serious pain. Or bite me on my pectoral fin. *Fuck, that hurts.*

The platform lifted a little, giving me a little possibility of movement, but, as before, I was essentially stuck like a slug.

Lucy was holding some kind of device, which she brought up close to my left eye. I recognized it as a new iteration of the original communicator Lucy's team had developed after our first meeting. The device appeared considerably more robust than the original, with thick metal parts and a hinge that looked like it could take a beating. The upper and lower surfaces were lined with layers of thick, hard rubber to keep the device from slipping out, and probably cushion it against a crunch if I closed my jaws a little too quickly.

"It's an improvement over the device we cobbled together on our first meeting," Lucy said with a smile. "Josh put a lot of work into designing a more rugged system. The software got a serious upgrade as well. We also made three of them as backup, just in case."

What a clever group of kids, I thought.

Lucy placed the device gingerly at the corner of my mouth, near where the upper and lower jaws met. I could taste the rubber block designed to protect the device from my teeth. Lucy waved her hands slowly up and down as a signal for me to move my jaws. Carefully, I pressed a few times to get a sense of how it worked. Josh placed a laptop and a large flatscreen display on a small table in front of us so I could read what I was sending.

Lucy made some minor adjustments and reached into my mouth to test the fit of the device. I watched her closely and made certain my jaws didn't clamp onto anything human. Up close, her prominent cheekbones, high forehead, and brown complexion made me think she must have some Hawaiian blood in her.

She turned her head toward me and said, "There are some days when I truly envy you. To travel anywhere and see ocean life up close on a daily level. A true explorer of the unknown."

I wanted to remind her of the perils of the oceans, but that would have to wait for another day.

I miss being able to walk on my two feet. I miss the feelings of touch To hug my children and embrace my wife. I envy you.

Josh watched the screen patiently as I relayed my thoughts via their device. He looked at me sympathetically.

"I still have to pinch myself that we're doing this," he said while shaking his head.

While Josh and Lucy adjusted my communication device, I noticed an older, bespectacled gentleman move down the transom. He had quite a mop of gray hair that followed the direction of the wind, like a windsock. He was wearing a rather worn wetsuit, the colors of which were heavily faded, and the edges tattered through many years of use. It made me think of my old dive suit, which I wore for years but never properly washed. I could almost imagine the smell of aged neoprene. The man appeared lithe, though he was probably in his early sixties. Tucked into his arm he carried a yellow notepad fixed onto a clipboard. With his right hand, he presented a small memory stick and inserted it into Lucy's laptop. He tapped the keyboard to bring up an image on the screen. A crewmember brought a plastic chair for him to sit on.

He then redirected his attention towards me. "Hi, Mark. My name is Dr. Peter Holloway. I run the research station on Maui and am visiting professor of marine biology at the Scripps Institute in San Diego. I am very excited to meet you and talk with you in person."

I sized him up. It was hard to tell if he was someone I could work with. I imagined that at the outset even Lucy had had a hard time accepting the grim reality that a supposedly dead man was still alive and cruising the oceans inside a large fish. But she had managed it. Patiently, I heard him out.

"I must confess that when I learned about your existence, I had doubts about every aspect of this claim. But Lucy made some very convincing arguments, as did the rest of the team. The video recording of your first meeting was... how should I put it? Astonishing. As human beings, we can be stubbornly inflexible when introduced to something novel, especially something that defies immediate explanation. We often lock ourselves into our own fixed version of reality. There is no recorded event in history in which any sentient individual's consciousness had been observed transferring to another creature. And yet here you are."

When he finished, I thought about what I would say next. I bit down carefully on the device, making sure I didn't overstress it.

Nice to meet you, Peter, or should I call you Dr. Holloway? The software Josh had put together auto corrected my input, which was a wonderful addition. Sometimes the text was just too garbled, and I would need to repeat my inputs.

The doctor smiled as he looked at the screen. I wondered if he had emotionally prepared himself for my response. It's not every day you have a conversation with a fish.

"That will not be necessary, Mark. Peter will do. We are very informal here. Morse is bad enough and spelling out titles every time is unnecessary," he replied, looking at me directly, the afternoon sun glancing off his glasses. His relaxed posture and calm demeanor gave me the impression of someone willing to navigate through the complexities of a challenging scenario.

"Mark, I would like to ask you some questions, if you don't mind. I'd like to establish the framework for our conversation, for the sake of science. The purpose of this is to set the stage for our conversation, ensuring that the process and the evidence cannot be questioned, no matter how outlandish the claims. This is for my benefit as well as yours. It is very possible the information we gather today will never be disclosed to the public. To safeguard everyone's reputation."

I acknowledged, *Please do. The isolation has weighed heavily on me. I am just so happy to speak to people again. Has anyone reached out to my family, my wife?*

Peter looked sympathetically at me. "Before I can give you an answer, I need to ask you some questions. Can you please bear with me? First, indulge me by recounting your experiences, so we can all grasp what actually happened to you on that day nearly eighteen months ago. There are so many questions that need answering."

Have you read the transcripts from my conversations with Lucy? Those should give insight.

Peter replied, "Yes, I have read the transcripts. I have also viewed the videos taken by the team. But I need more information. First, how well do you recall the day of the accident, the attack?"

I reflected for a minute and recounted the events as clearly as I could.

I remember diving around the lava tubes of Lanai, the Cathedral site specifically. I remember the shark arriving and then passing over us. It was so exhilarating. So unexpected. We were all hiding in the rocks, but it knew we were there. Then it left. We assumed it lost interest, so we continued diving.

I watched the text being written letter by letter on the display in front of us. I figured this was going to take some time. Josh had certainly improved on the device. There was a trick to Morse that I had been working on during my passage over. With some words the Morse structure plays out like a song with a characteristic beat. I would play that rhythm over and over in my head. Translating that beat to jaw motion was pretty straightforward. Keeping sentences short was key to conversing in Morse.

The blasting of water through my gullet was not exactly comfortable, but I intended to hold out as long as I could.

Peter made some notes and then asked, "What do you remember of the attack itself?"

Not much, I replied. *I recall the impact, my mask and*

regulator falling out of my mouth. Seawater in my eyes. The intense pressure. It all happened so fast, but I recall glimpsing the shark briefly, its eye, up close and realizing that was it for me. I remember the seafloor passing below me and then it all went black.

Peter leaned back in the chair. "What happened after that?"

When I came to, I was lying on the sandy bottom, in a shallow area. I remember being stuck between coral and unable to move. Disoriented. I could no longer control my limbs. And my vision was suddenly clear. The seawater no longer stung. Colors and textures were off. I could hear things far away. It took some time to realize I had changed. I saw a dive boat nearby. When the divers saw me they jumped out of the water. The boat had a glass bottom. I saw my reflection, and I didn't believe it at first, but there was no way I could deny it.

Peter interjected, "What were you feeling upon this realization?"

I was terrified and thinking about how it would affect my family. The reality of having to fend for myself to survive had not dawned on me. That came later.

Painful memories of that time started flooding back. I recalled my confusion and despair. Denial had not been an option.

"So once you knew, really knew what had happened to you, how did you cope?"

I was more concerned with my family and their well-being. I made my way back to Maui, hoping to see them before the authorities did.

Peter looked up from the display. "But how could you see them?"

I was desperate. I made it to the beach, and I saw them for a short while. They were sitting on the beach. They looked so peaceful. I was in the shallows, watching them. It took an hour for the authorities to show up.

"And nobody saw you? Nobody raised the alarm?"

You'd be surprised how inattentive people are when they go in the water.

The yellow pages of Peter's pad fluttered in the wind. He reviewed his notes and looked up at me. "I know this is all painful to relive. But it is important that we document the details. Is there anything else you can remember?"

When my family had left the island, I had to figure out how to survive on my own. I did not have the skill set to survive in the ocean. But I was not completely alone.

Peter asked, "Not alone? How do you mean?"

I am not alone in this body. I am sharing it with its owner. When I am awake, I completely control my movements. But when I sleep the shark takes over, doing what sharks do. It was a lifesaver. While I slept the shark hunted and fed. When I woke the sense of hunger was gone.

I knew this question would come. Peter smiled, "Did you ever try to hunt yourself?"

I knew you would ask. LOL. I am terrible at hunting. Pathetic. I do not have a million years of instinct to draw upon. Once I woke with a large tarpon in my mouth. That was quite a shock.

"Did you eat it, then?"

You enjoy torturing me, don't you, Peter?

"I'm asking, did you exploit the situation and consume your kill?"

Obviously. I hunted tuna and other sea life, and some mola. I did hunt, but I wasn't good at it.

I figured there was no reason to talk about the half-eaten elephant seal. That still gave me the chills to think about.

Peter laughed. He seemed to think it was all good fun. He then became serious again. "Have you ever thought about what had happened to you, your corporeal form?"

That seemed an odd question.

It consumed me. Fish food, I replied. I was a little unnerved by this line of questioning.

Peter stared directly at me. "What makes you think that? Based on what evidence?" he asked pointedly.

Obviously, I had been consumed from head to toe. There was nothing left, no remains. How else could I be here, inside this immense fish? What about the fin on the sea bottom?

"Are you sure?" Peter repeated.

I thought back to the moment I woke and approached the dive boat. I struggled with my memories.

He pressed, "How much time passed between the attack and when you woke?"

I don't know. I thought I saw my dive boat leave, in a hurry.

Peter looked down at his notes. "On October 3ʳᵈ you took part in a dive trip organized by Maui Reef Tours. It was the morning of the 3ʳᵈ when the attack occurred, around 10 AM as marked by the local authorities and the operator of the dive boat. Your wife, Cecilia, was first notified in the afternoon, around four o'clock."

I was stunned. So, the dive boats in the area were afternoon boats. What happened in the hours between?

I'm confused. You're saying several hours passed. Perhaps I was unconscious.

Peter adjusted his glasses and leaned toward my left eye. "Mark, have you wondered why you are here?".

I pondered this for a while. None of it made any sense. I'd considered everything, from the Hawaiian legend of reincarnation to a crazy notion of mind transfer. It was all speculative.

Lucy came down to the deck and sat down with her back against the platform wall. She stared at Peter. I saw her jaws tighten and her nostrils flare, as if troubled by something.

Peter, I do not understand how this happened to me, or why. Lost doesn't begin to describe how I am feeling. But I know who I was then and what I am now.

The professor adopted a different line of questioning.

"Mark, how much of your childhood do you recall? Your parents, for example."

I thought about my dad, his music collection, all our arguments while I was a teenager. And my mom, the quintessential homemaker, making life bearable for my siblings and myself. We moved around a lot, from house to house from Oregon to California.

"Tell me about your parents, Mark," Peter pressed again.

Martin and Catherine Forster. Both deceased. My dad died of liver cancer when I was in my early twenties. He was a salesman. My mom died of ovarian cancer during my late forties.

"Any siblings?"

Three. Two brothers and a sister. I am closest to my older brother, Matt. There's a seven-year gap between me and my younger brother and sister.

Peter made some notes. "Do you remember the names of your younger siblings?"

David and Lacy, why?

"I need to confirm all the information about your personal background. It is simply an acknowledgment that I am speaking with Mark Forster, who was born in 1965 to Martin and Catherine Forster. Confirmation of indisputable facts will ensure the trust that is needed to establish that the events described did, in fact, occur."

So you accept the possibility that sentient sharks exist?

"Nope, not at all. They don't, at least not yet." He smiled, "Mercifully."

He continued, "You see, in science if you have confirmation of something with a single data point, no one will accept it as absolute truth."

He was right, of course. Working as an engineer alongside scientists for decades had taught me to repeat measurements, to convince the more conservative members within the scientific community. There would need to be more instances of creatures like me, or of sentient examples of other lifeforms that exhibited human traits as I did. Backed up by a ton of irrefutable data. We regard cetaceans as sentient, equals to us in the oceans. A single sentient shark might turn heads, but it would be marked as an outlier.

From Lucy's fidgeting I sensed she was getting impatient with Peter.

"Pete, you need to tell him. This has gone long enough."

Tell me what? I asked.

Peter sat up in his chair and looked at me briefly.

"Mark, you asked me earlier if we contacted your family. We did, in a sense."

Explain?

Peter's brows furrowed. "Mark, after all that we talked about today, the astonishing reality of what has happened, there is something I need to tell you which most probably will upset you further. There's no getting around it, so here goes. Mark Forster did not die on October third."

It took me a second to absorb what he said. A panic attack welled up from within me as the shock of those words rippled through my being, tearing at every vestige of confidence I had. It was so frustrating that I couldn't scream. I was suddenly undone, as if the ground had opened beneath me and pulled me under. My heart was pounding from within this cavernous body. It took me a few minutes to collect myself. Peter sat patiently waiting for my response.

Please explain.

Peter pulled out a picture from beneath his pad and placed it close to my eye. It showed a man lying on a hospital bed, his chest and head heavily bandaged, and a gastric tube placed up one nostril. Intravenous catheters were fitted to both arms. Electronic scopes were visible in the background.

Despite the bandages, I could clearly recognize the man in the image. It was me. I looked gaunt, my mouth hanging open to one side.

I was alive. The image proved it. But how could this be possible?

Peter lifted a document from beneath the picture and began reading the contents. "On the third of October, Mark Forster was attacked by a large great white, and was in the process of being consumed when a fellow diver on an electric underwater scooter collided intentionally with the shark. I'm reading the official report here."

Please continue, I replied.

"The collision and the subsequent ignition of the scooter's lithium-ion power source evidently led to the shark releasing its victim. Several divers, including the scooter driver and the dive guide, quickly brought the victim up to the surface and subsequently arranged transit to the nearest port, where emergency services transported the victim to the nearest hospital."

My mind was reeling from the implications. I had been physically alive the whole time. It was both confusing and weirdly satisfying to hear.

How can I be in two places? Am I a fucking copy? I asked desperately. I watched as the letters slowly filled the screen. I was getting impatient with the speed of communication.

"My firm belief is that no, you aren't a copy. But that is all it is—my belief. It's the only thing that makes sense to me."

Could you please explain in more detail? The world as I perceived it, was not making sense anymore, and I was desperate for answers.

Peter put his hand on my snout. "Mark Forster has been in a coma since the day of the attack. Your body lies at UCSF hospital in San Francisco under the care of their staff. Your body is there, but *you* are here."

I fully believed in my death and reincarnation, or whatever one could call it. A deep fog of confusion had settled in my mind. I didn't know what to believe.

Peter continued, "You sustained serious injuries during the attack. The medical report describes your injuries in some detail: crushed ribs and vertebrae, internal bleeding, blunt force trauma, and an artery in your arm was partially severed. You would have died had it not been for the other divers in your group. The dive team were exemplary in getting you to the surface, stemming the bleeding, and resuscitating you, which ultimately saved your life. Not an easy thing to do under those circumstances."

I thought about the other divers in the group. I had never thought of them as exemplary. Maybe I was being a bit too harsh—I mean, Janet was cool. Marco had infuriated me with his noisy scooter, and yet of all people, he was the one who had saved my life. I should be more grateful.

On to more pressing matters. I needed answers.

I am remote controlling an apex predator thousands of miles away? From a hospital bed?

"That's one possibility. I spoke with a close friend of mine, a physicist. Your situation absolutely fascinated him. In broad strokes, his line of reasoning was this: The collision of the scooter and the subsequent electrical discharge initiated a so-called quantum tunneling effect—entanglement, if you will—between your brain and the shark's. He drew a diagram showing how it might work, though he lost me after five minutes. But imagine a strand that represents your consciousness, stretched so that it binds your mind and the subconscious part of the shark's brain, which is most of it. How you are able to project your awareness and control the shark is a mystery. Somehow entanglement has made this possible. Mind you, this is all conjecture at this moment. Like I said, we have just one data point."

Just when I thought things couldn't get any weirder, I said. *So I am having a discussion with you from my bedside.*

"I cannot imagine your frustration, Mark. This is the reason we couldn't contact your family. Not yet. We can't even tell our fellow scientists. It's simply not ready for prime time. There is much work to do."

I paused, playing back the concept of quantum tunneling and its implications in my mind. It had been a while since I had looked at my college physics textbook. I thought of Cecilia and the girls. Suddenly it seemed that there was a possibility, albeit a remote one of coming back. I would do anything to make it happen. I recalled reading an article about how some neuroscientists were changing their views on how the brain, or more specifically consciousness, worked. For many years the prevailing theory was based on a classical approach. Now scientists were beginning to mull over the role of quantum entanglement in even some of the basic functions of the brain. I believed my current situation supported that notion.

Peter, did you ask your physicist friend if the connection could it be severed, or disconnected? I asked.

"He wasn't optimistic. His take on it was that the science behind entanglement is purely theoretical at this point. We should tread carefully. Whatever connection there is, it's beyond our ability to just... *snip*, and hope it all goes back to normal. Even if we considered euthanizing the shark, the outcome is far from certain."

I needed clarity, and I was getting information through a firehose. It was not possible to compartmentalize the different parts of my transition.

Lucy was more relaxed after the great reveal. It must have weighed on her heavily that I didn't know the full extent of my situation. I'd made history, yet we couldn't tell another living soul. Reigning in my overdeveloped imagination, I took stock of my reality. I was surrounded by a sympathetic group of people. They had my best intentions at heart.

What do we do now? I asked.

"We continue this study and keep quiet, for now. I will eventually reach out to Cecilia. But Mark, this will take time. I ask you to prepare yourself, because the eventual outcome may fall short of your expectations." He seemed to be choosing his words carefully.

Understood. I am exhausted from my journey, and I need time to process this, I replied, feeling overwhelmed by the contents of our conversation. Resting was high on my agenda.

I need to get back into the water.

"Sure. Can we meet again tomorrow?"

I'll make every attempt to come by in the morning, but a lot depends on the owner of this body. She sometimes likes to wander off, I answered.

"You call the shark your owner?" he asked, with a smirk on his face.

I got used to feeling like a secondary person in this relationship, I replied. *I control the shark only when awake.*

Peter signaled to the crew to prepare the lowering of the platform. Josh carefully removed the communicator device from my mouth and inspected it.

"Not bad for a prototype," he said with a smile.

As I reentered the water and shoved myself off the platform, I couldn't help but think about the endgame. There were so many unknowns in the equation, and roughly half of them were beyond my control—or anyone's, for that matter. Would, or could, Cecilia even accept my current existence. To her I was just an unfortunate man confined to a bed, the victim of a tragedy. It would send shockwaves through my family and my colleagues if they knew the truth. *Baby steps.*

I dipped my nose and descended, deliberately cruising away from the ship and the islands.

When I woke early the next day—at least, I hoped it was the

next day—I found myself just north of Kauai. There was no mistaking the high island and the town of Princeville before me. I was perhaps a mile offshore. This meant I would have quite a swim if I was to meet up with the boat. It was quite possible I'd slept for several days due to exhaustion. Kauai is over a hundred and fifty miles northwest of Maui.

I was no longer famished, which was a good sign. I wondered what had been on the menu. Well, maybe I don't. When I got my bearings, I deduced I was on the north side of the island, and that Oahu would be my first waypoint toward the southeast. There was no way I would get to the *R/V Relentless* today. I would need to pull an all-nighter.

By the next morning, I'd managed to reach the Kalohi Channel between Molokai and Lanai. The last time I was here I'd avoided Lanai, for obvious reasons. Now I didn't care. The northwestern coastline of Maui was within view. Would the boat still be here after so many days? Would its crew wait? As I headed toward the island, I noticed that the surf was getting noticeably rougher, with increased swells. Clouds were gathering over the islands and beyond them. I scanned the nearby coast for the ship but could not see it. Discouraged but not beaten, I swam in for a closer look. After swimming a few miles down the coast, I recognized the *Relentless* hiding in one of the many coves along the coast. It was funny that I kept forgetting that I had a tracker on me. If it still functioned, then it was likely the crew had been tracking me the whole time. I saw Lucy and Josh come out on deck, waving at me. They did not lower the platform as I approached, but instead signaled for me to come closer. With my head out of the water, I attempted to listen to Lucy while she yelled over the howl of the wind.

"There is a severe cyclone warning in effect around Hawaii! Category five! It will be here tonight! We need to return to the harbor ASAP. Let's meet again in three days!" she hollered.

I rolled my eyes back twice to confirm the message.

I guessed I should move offshore. Cyclones are a nasty business. A category five storm means sustained winds of over one hundred and thirty knots. That kind of storm would tear up the landscape and wreak havoc in the surrounding seas. I was concerned for the crew's safety and contemplated following them until they were back in Maalaea Harbor. But the *Relentless* was a tough boat, and I was sure they had weathered rough seas in other parts of the world. It was a one-hour sail to the harbor, so they should be good. Judging by the cloud formations, I determined that the cyclone was coming in from the southeast. With this information, it would be prudent to hang out on the leeward side of the island, and then go deep.

Storm

The sky had grown darker and more menacing over the past few hours. Even below the surface, the onset of darkness seemed a tad early. I poked my head above the surface and surveyed the horizon. Wave activity was definitely increasing with whitecaps as far as the eye could see. In the distance, lightning arced across the sky, portending the chaos to come. Thick, dark, billowy clouds rolled across my field of view. Beneath the darkest clouds, I could see bands of rain obscuring anything behind them. Fair weather had characterized most of my days, with occasional strong winds and waves.

It had never occurred to me that some of the wildest storms on the planet occurred out at sea. For me, this was actually exciting. It would be my first foray into an ocean storm. Seafarers typically avoid even the mildest sign of inclement weather, for good reason. Against all common sense, I wanted a front-row seat to the approaching theatrics. What did I have to fear? I was in my element. I recalled watching videos of large cargo ships getting tossed around by the monstrous waves. The white crests of the waves near me were already gaining in strength. An hour later, the waves were already over twenty feet in height.

To make good headway, I swam parallel to the waves, even swimming up the side of one enormous wave to get a view of what was coming. The scene in the distance was beyond description. Some waves were over fifty feet tall from crest to trough, or perhaps more. These massive waves were colliding, creating great spouts of water. I would get seriously tossed around in that surf. Did I consider retiring to the depths? Not a chance.

After a serious toss from the top of one massive wave, I looked up toward the surface and saw bright flashes of light. Within the flashes, I saw arcs of lightning streaking across the dark sky. It was getting really furious.

It was then that an idea spawned in my brain. I thought of the lithium batteries and the collision with the scooter that had set in motion my connection to this beast. What if I could expose myself to a large surge in electricity brought upon by lightning strikes? The bolts that rained about me were far more powerful than any that a scooter could provide. *Too much of a good thing might not be a good thing.* As a human, it was highly unlikely that I would survive a direct strike by lightning. However, the shark I inhabited was a significantly larger and tougher organism. There was a lot at stake here and my impatience was getting in the way properly thinking things through. I desperately wanted to return to my old life, to Cecilia and the girls, and nature was providing a potentially risky solution to it all. *Here goes everything.*

The sound of multiple lightning strikes crackled through the air above me. Bobbing like a fat cork, I stuck my head out of the water again and watched the light show from my perceived position of safety. The waves lifted me all the way up, and sometimes I would roll over a crest. The flashes of lightning saturated my vision, creating blotches similar to when a photographer doesn't warn you about a flash. I sank below the waves to recover, waiting for my vision to clear.

I swam up to the surface, only to be met by a sight that took my breath away. An enormous wave was heading in my direction. A wall of water over a hundred feet high had somehow formed in the melee and was barreling forward with a massive crest forming at the top. *A rogue wave!* The crest extended as far as the eye could see. I was tempted to sink and let it pass, but in my excitement, I swam toward it. I wanted to ride up that vertical wall more than anything. With that wave I could reach a height that would expose me to more lightning. Despite the electrical activity around me, it was nearly impossible to get close to a strike. I was simply not fast enough to get close to one.

With the wave still building, I figured I could move parallel across it, just beneath the surface, and slowly gain altitude while traversing the front face of the wave. There continued to be a lot of lightning activity in my area, and one bolt landed near me. The bolt penetrated the water surface and spread out in a myriad of tendrils until it dissipated. The resulting undersea flash illuminated the billions of plankton and other microscopic organisms around me. It was getting quite surreal. And beautiful. I had to get higher up.

As I moved parallel to the frontal field of the wave, I heard the crashing of water behind me. Looking back, I could see the crest of the wave violently collapsing. I was riding the wave partially submerged, and perilously close to an ocean break. I heard the thunderous sound of water crashing. Lightning danced all around me, crackling as it propagated in multiple streams in the air above me. The sky was as violent as the sea that suspended me. This did not feel like Earth anymore. It was rapidly becoming a truly inhospitable and downright frightening place. Even so, I still felt indestructible in my large form. I climbed further and further up the face of the wave.

At this point, I could see above most of the nearby waves— not that it mattered, since the heavy rains diminished visibility. I needed to keep ahead of the crest, though at some point I would need to sink and pull away if I did not want to be *drilled*. I noticed that there wasn't much in the way of fish life in these tumultuous conditions. In fact, I could see nothing. Perhaps sea life thought better than to challenge the forces of nature. Only I was insane enough to test the waters. The pounding of water behind me was getting louder. I pushed onward. Again, the night sky was lit up by an extensive network of lightning strikes.

Suddenly, several powerful bolts struck the surrounding water in multiple arcs. The air sizzled with electrical activity, and rings of bright light spread in all directions, bathing me in its intensity. My body began to spasm uncontrollably, starting with my tail and then followed by my pectoral fins. There was no pain. I wondered if it was a super bolt, which could be hundreds or sometimes thousands of times more powerful than any lightning found on land.

Suddenly, another massive bolt of lightning struck the water near my snout, sending a massive surge through me, disabling me. I could no longer swim or move or feel anything. Again, there was no pain, and I was still conscious. *What's happening? This is not what I expected.* Rolling with the wave, I saw that the wave crest had finally caught up to me, but I could do nothing as my body was plunged into a maelstrom. I was powerless. There was another bright flash and then the world went dark.

Reset

I heard sounds, faint at first of people walking in and out of a room. As I woke up the sounds became louder, clearer. There was some clanging of metal objects, and a periodic beeping sound in the background. There was a drip-drip sound, like raindrops on a hard surface. Echoes of voices in hallways, indistinct at first and then clearer and louder as they entered a room—my room, I believed—wherever it was. The familiar sound of the ocean was no longer present. My mind was spinning, my senses unable to assimilate to this new normal. Then it occurred to me: *I'm back! I actually made it back.* I was no longer surrounded by an endless sea, and I was no longer alone.

The smells of alcohol and medicines reminded me of hospitals. I wanted to get up, but drowsiness and fatigue overwhelmed me. For a short while, I listened with my eyes closed, trying to make sense of my condition, until fatigue took over again and I fell asleep. *No, no...*

I awoke again, in the same room as far as I could tell, relieved that I was still *here*. I heard shuffling noises, like tennis shoes on a smooth floor, followed by more voices. I recognized them as both male and female, though I couldn't make sense of what was being said. It was really hard to follow anything. Light filtered through my eyelids, but it was too bright for me to open them. I tried moving my head to the side, but it was difficult.

A reassuring voice near my ear said, "Mark, can you hear me?" I did not recognize the voice.

I tried to move my lips to speak. They felt stiff and parched. A latex-covered finger gently probed my chapped lips. Someone was pouring a sweet lemony liquid into my mouth, drop by drop. I slid my tongue forward to taste it. The sugar went straight to my bloodstream, bringing with it small doses of energy. My lungs filled with air, and the smell of medicine again filled my nostrils. *This is a hospital.*

I was overjoyed with the fact that I was back in my own body, even though I now knew I never left it in the first place. Before I met Peter, I was moving muscles and teeth thousands of miles away, fully convinced that I had met the hereafter, or some version of it. But instead, my mind had stretched some distance around the earth, in a mind meld with one of the ocean's great predators. And despite everything I experienced, I was never in any true danger. Though I would have to contend with the fact that on several occasions I did put Marci's life *in* peril. I wondered what became of the shark after the lightning strike.

My body felt sore, with a dull pain emanating from my shoulder and downward to my pelvis. Carefully, I opened my left eye and almost immediately closed it again due to the brightness. In that brief instant I had seen a room with bright yellow walls and the piercing blue of the daylight sky through one large window. My eyelids had become crusted over with layers of hardened mucus. Barely opening my eyes so that only a sliver of light passed through, I saw dark, unfocused blobs moving about me.

Another voice spoke to me, and at the same time a hand touched my forearm. "Mark, can you feel my touch? Please twitch your nose or press your index finger into my hand if you can."

More voices were entering the room. I twitched my nose.

"He's conscious. I have a response. Call the doctor. And his wife, please."

Another voice responded, "She's down the hall. I'll get her."

Yes, please call her. It took a few seconds to recall Cecilia's name. Even the memory of her was blurry. Slowly, an image of her face formed in my thoughts. I was ecstatic at the thought of seeing her again. I remembered seeing her on the morning I'd left for the dive. She was sleeping peacefully.

Several hands gently lifted and rotated me. The hospital staff was washing me. Warm sponges passed over my back. A nurse was examining my shoulder and then my back. Her fingers gently probed between my shoulder blades. Getting touched by humans again was so delightful.

A male voice in the washing party said, "The scars have healed nicely. Inflammation is down." I did not know what he was talking about.

Another voice, this time a female, confirmed his observation. This was all very confusing.

The owner of the deeper male voice touched my shoulder, speaking as he examined me, "Mark, if you can hear us, try nodding your head or moving a finger."

I did my very best to nod, though it wasn't much. It was, however, enough to elicit joyful responses from the nurses: "Wonderful to have you back!" Another roared, "Yeah!"

In all the din, one voice was clearly recognizable. It had been more than a year since I heard it. Someone took my hand. This time, both my eyes opened. In the intense brightness, my eyes focused on the face of my wife, who was in tears. Her face was inches from mine. She looked a little different from the image in my memory, her dark brown hair shorter than I remember, and there were strands of gray hair mixed in. She also looked tired. Dark circles shadowed beneath her eyes, etched with weariness that weighed heavy on her features. Cecilia reached over and put her hand on my face. Her lips trembled, and she appeared so overwhelmed with emotion that she was unable to say anything.

Wiping away tears, she managed to get a few words out. "How are you feeling?" she asked, her voice breaking from emotion.

It was so comforting to hear her voice. I tried raising my hands to embrace her, then grimaced in pain. Something was wrong with me.

"I feel like a truck drove over me. Breathing is hard," I said, wincing.

The sense of overpowering fatigue was frustrating. The urge to close my eyes and drift off was ever-present. *Hang on, don't slip.*

Cecilia and I stared at each other for a while. I managed a weak smile. Then it started coming back to me, a flood of memories. The storm, then blacking out. After that, nothing. I couldn't believe I was still alive. How was this possible? *Never mind—be happy, dude. You should be thrilled.*

I looked at Cecilia and muttered to the best of my ability, "Hi honey."

In response, she squeezed my hand so much it hurt, and I flinched. She realized what she was doing and released her grip. "God, I'm so sorry. I can't help myself".

Several doctors entered the room and came over to my bed, standing in a circle over me like village elders. One of them was tall, with thinning gray hair. The room became quiet.

"Hello. Good to have you back with us. Can you tell me your full name and birth date?" he asked me. At the same time, he squeezed my hands, which hurt a little.

I replied weakly, "Mark Forster, born December 7th 1965."

He smiled and put his hands on my forehead and studied my eyes with his ophthalmoscope. He then listened to my heart. When he was done, he brought over a chair and sat down next to me.

"Mark, do you have any recollection of being brought here, of being treated by the individuals in this room?" he asked.

I considered this but could not place a single memory relating to my convalescence. I thought about the dreams I had while making my way across the Pacific. Dreams of Cecilia and the girls. Looking around, I vaguely recognized the room. Was it possible that I had been waking up in the hospital for brief moments? Other than occasional visions of this room, I could not recollect anything else related to my rescue and recovery. I replied, "No."

"Mark, this might come as a surprise to you, but you have been in a coma for a little over eighteen months," he said in a monotone delivery. "You have been slowly waking over the past two weeks."

My jaw dropped. *So it took two weeks to return after the lightning strike?* It only took me several hours to wake up in the shark after the attack. The added complication of being in a coma and weakened physical state probably played a role. It dawned on me that I had a more pressing problem to deal with.

Nobody in the room would believe where I had been all this time. Eighteen months of cruising the depths of the Pacific would not go over well with this audience, least of all my wife. I could imagine the outcome of explaining my adventures in great detail to the hospital shrink—the resultant diagnosis would see me put me in straps. To everybody here, I had been an inert vegetable. *I need to bide my time and focus on recovery.*

"You had an accident," the doctor said. "Your injuries were quite severe. Before we go into details, do you know why you are here? Do you remember anything from before you lost consciousness?"

I thought about my meeting with Dr. Holloway. Given all

that had happened, I needed to tread carefully. No one here was witness to my communication with the *M/V Relentless*. No one knew of my unique connection with a shark located thousands of miles away. Peter had made it clear that I had been in a coma, so for all intended purposes, I needed to keep that part hidden, for now. I would need to play along. This included lying to my wife, which seemed deceitful, but I had no choice.

"Something struck me from behind. Then I felt something or someone dragging me in the water for some time, and then it all went black. You said eighteen months?"

The doctor nodded. "My name is Dr. Healey. I was one of your attending surgeons at UCSF when they flew you in from Hawaii. Do you recall any part of that journey?"

"None," I answered truthfully. At the time I was somewhere else.

"I'm not sure if you recall the specifics, but the short answer is a large shark attacked you while diving off Lanai. A fellow diver drove his scooter into the shark, which ended with the shark releasing you. However, your wounds were very severe, with considerable blood loss and massive tissue damage. You were also at depth and suffering from pulmonary edema. In short, you were drowning. Your fellow divers brought you up to the surface and contacted the authorities. The local hospital on Maui patched you up as best they could and, when you stabilized, they flew you here. Those surgeons worked through the better part of the first night and used many liters of blood. During your transfer, I spoke with the attending surgeon on Maui. He was not optimistic about your chances for survival. In those scenarios, it's nice to be wrong."

"The feeling's mutual, Doc," I said with a smile. *God, this is awful. I really did not want to take part in this charade.*

"Normally, when a patient has critical injuries, as in your case, we will put them in an induced coma. This was unnecessary in your case. You did that all by yourself. We changed your dressings, stimulated your muscles, fed you, changed you. The team you see here has been with you the entire time. There are cases where patients have been in a coma for years and then suddenly wake. But there is usually a cost."

I surveyed the team—lots of smiles. I guessed I'd made their day.

I said, "You said there is a cost…"

"Lying inert is never good for the body. Just lying in one position on the sofa for several hours for a few days is simply not healthy. Imagine doing that for more than a year. You will need a lot of training and therapy. I need you to understand that there are no promises of a full recovery. But you were in good physical shape to begin with, and this will undoubtedly help. Let's take it one day at a time. We have a team here that will assist you."

The doctor continued describing the physical regimen I would need to maintain if I was to have any chance of full mobility. Recovery was going to be tough. It was tiring just to lift my arm. How on earth I was going to get out of bed and walk was a whole other matter.

I still can't believe I'm here. Cecilia looked on from the bedside, smiling and wiping her nose. I wanted to talk to her in private, but that would have to wait.

It was marvelous to have people around me again. To converse in full sentences without the need of a lab jack in my mouth. Watching the people in the room reminded me of what I had lost. For eighteen months I had been completely alone in my thoughts. Would I be the same person again? Would I be able to socialize as before? It was weird to speak again, to use my mouth to enunciate words. The voice came out naturally, as if I'd never left. I was breathing again, or at least I could control it. *I was always breathing, you idiot.* Still, it felt weird not to have seawater pass through my gills.

The doctor directed his attention to the nurse on the other side of my bed. "Let's remove the nasogastric tube and start feeding him liquids. After a week, we can begin on solids." The nurse acknowledged this and took hold of the part of the tube that stuck out of my left nostril.

"Mark, this will be a little uncomfortable," the nurse informed me. "I'm going to pull the nasogastric tube from your nose. It's been there for a while, so it's probably lost some of the lubricant."

Slowly, she started pulling on the tube. I could feel it running all the way down my esophagus. *Oh God, it hurts. It feels like someone is trying to pull my stomach up from the inside.* And it seemed endless. *How long is this thing?* The back of my throat was sore from rubbing against the tube.

The nurse patted me on the shoulder and said, "That was the worst of it."

I was relieved until I looked down at the edge of the bed and noticed a catheter leading to a bag filled with yellow liquid. One more tube to remove. The nurse asked if I wanted some privacy. *Of course.*

Once I was free of tubes, the doctor continued making a list of tasks for his team to start. All I could think of was food and talking to Cecilia. God, I was hungry. I looked at my arms, which were thin and emaciated. There was not an ounce of fat on me. Or muscle, for that matter. Looking beneath the sheets, I saw a pair of toothpick legs. My toenails seriously needed clipping. The third leg and his two buddies were too sad to look at. Looking down at my side, I noticed lots of scars, inch-long puncture wounds from the shark's bite. I wasn't sure I was ready for the grand reveal. *One day at a time.* I still had both arms and both legs. I flexed my toes and fingers, counting them in succession. So far, so good.

"The shark struck you from behind," the doctor explained. "The tank gave some limited protection from the bite, and your wetsuit held you together until the local surgeons could work on you. But it was that diver with the scooter who saved your life. Had he not charged the shark and struck it with as much force as he could muster, we would not be having this conversation."

During my time in the ocean, I hadn't really given much thought to Marco. We'd never chatted on the boat. Underwater, I'd found him and his scooter to be a nuisance. Once Peter had explained to me what Marco had done, I experienced pangs of regret. I would certainly reach out and thank him, one day.

What else did I remember from that day? Memories were beginning to come back, but it was all garbled. It was hard to distinguish actual memories from dreams, and some of the stuff was pretty messed up. Fatigue was setting in again, and for a moment the room became silent. Voices receded into the background, and the light in the room faded.

I woke up again a few hours later. But just before that I was dreaming, or thought I was. It was so bizarre. I was deep underwater again, poking around some reef like I did back on Maui. Was I still connected to the shark, or were these just memories? It was, however, incredibly peaceful. Oddly, I almost didn't want to wake up.

I heard some noise, then a large male nurse entered the room with some pouches of IV solution. "You awake?" he asked.

I opened my eyes and nodded. "Yeah. How long was I out?"

He replaced the nearly empty IV pouch with a new one. "About six or seven hours. You went right out like a lightbulb. It's pretty normal to have a few spells before you are fully back."

This encouraged me. It was dark outside, and the room was

only lit by the monitoring equipment. The sunlight I experienced before was overpowering. Multiple sensors on my chest lead to a monitor above me, tracing the performance of my heart.

"I was afraid of falling back into that darkness," I said.

"I get it. Take it one day at a time." He took my hand. "We're all rooting for you."

"What's your name?" I asked.

"John Bradley, but you can just call me Pops," he replied, smiling.

"I'm almost afraid to ask… where did that name come from?"

"It was my nickname from my time in the corps. Long story."

"How many tours?"

"Three, then I became a medic. I got tired of shooting at people."

I nodded in understanding.

"How about yourself? What do you do?" I sensed he was testing me, testing my memory. I thought for a minute, then Ben, Jenny, and the rest of the gang filtered into my thoughts.

"I was running a startup. A buddy of mine I knew from college, Ben, helped me put together this company, and we had just got funding when I went on vacation with the family… and then this. Jeez, I actually do not even know if the company is still running. I was the boss. Ben and I worked on the company for five years. It was our fifth startup together."

John looked at me sympathetically. "Maybe ask your wife tomorrow to look into it. Maybe she knows something."

"Speaking of my dearly beloved, where is she?" I asked.

"Everyone went home soon after you fell asleep," he answered.

I lay there quietly, watching John go about his work. He then came over with a tray containing soup and other liquids.

"So this is how it starts," I joked.

"Not exactly Cordon bleu, but it's a start," he grinned. "By the way, while you were out your peristalsis more or less stopped, so don't be surprised if you receive a surprise package," he said, smiling.

"Thanks for the heads up," I said with a grin.

The soup was pretty tasteless. Water and salt. *Everything a growing boy needs.* I was so looking forward to solid food. The juice was at least passable, even if it came out of a plastic package. When I finished, John took the tray away.

"While I'm here, would you like to try standing up and see if you can get up on your own?" he asked.

Sitting up was the first challenge. My stomach muscles were so weak, I could barely lift myself. I grabbed the gurney's sidebars for stability. My arms shook from the strain. Gently, I moved my legs, one at a time, off the gurney so that my feet touched the cold floor. Despite me leaning against the gurney, my legs were shaking. John helped me adjust my position.

"Jesus, I am so skinny," I remarked on viewing my legs again. A mirror across the room revealed the true nature of the trauma I endured. I let the gown drop away and looked at myself in amazement. Along my back I saw the deep marks where the jaws of the shark had locked onto me. A circular pattern along both sides of my back stretched all the way down to my buttocks. Had it not been for my aluminum tank and Marco's extraordinary bravery, the bite would have meant my most certain demise. Besides the teeth marks and other scars, there were bed sores and blisters.

"The first few weeks are going to be the hardest. But I got your back, you got me?"

I took a few deep breaths and let myself slide off the bed. John caught me and held me, as if I were a sick child who could barely stand. He was holding me up with one arm, as that was pretty much all it took to hold me. On the day of the attack, I had been one hundred and ninety pounds. I was probably half that now.

"Are you okay?" John asked gently.

"This is both horrifying and fascinating at the same time," I remarked. It was fascinating from a morbid perspective, like watching one of those black and white war videos about concentration camps. Victims emaciated and hollowed out. Bone and skin.

We ambled slowly toward the bathroom. Balancing myself was nearly impossible. Nearly two years of immobility had made me like this. John held onto me the entire way. It was extraordinary to think that just a short while ago I had commandeered a massive ocean predator and crossed a major ocean on my own power. I felt invincible. *Who is this scrawny dude?*

I now had a more pressing issue.

"We have one of those wheelchairs with a built-in toilet, would you prefer that?" John asked.

I glared at him. I was going to walk across the room to the toilet, no matter what. After what seemed an eternity of walking, sliding, and slipping, with a massive man to hold me up, I made it to the throne and sat down. I collected my dignity and took my first voluntary piss in eighteen months.

I am now humbled.

The next morning, after another exciting breakfast of tasteless liquids and juice, several physical therapists entered my room. The sun was shining outside and, thankfully, my eyes had grown accustomed to the light. Anne, the morning nurse, helped me sit up and brush my teeth. She also gave me a soak, which eased my bed sores. A young female therapist came through the door and introduced herself.

"Hi Mark, my name is Colleen, and I will be your PT coordinator for the duration of your DOC recovery. How are you feeling today?"

She couldn't have been more than thirty years old, but what she lacked in age and probably experience, she more than made up for in spunk.

She introduced her colleagues, "This is George. He specializes in mobility. And this is Nicholas, our spine and balance expert." I shook hands with each of them. From where I was standing, they had their work cut out for them.

"What is DOC?" I asked out of curiosity.

"Disorders of consciousness," she replied pertly.

Really? I thought. I had to remind myself constantly to play along. *No one here is going to listen to a story of shark possession.*

Colleen continued, "As soon as you are ready we will start basic motion and strength therapies. We need to get you up and about. At first, you'll feel weak and shaky in your movements. That will dissipate in time."

I was just hoping my trip to the loo was going to get easier. *Baby steps.*

"How is your tactile sense?" she asked.

"Okay, I guess. I can sense my fingertips and my toes," I replied. "But my back feels funny, as if waves of electrical sensations were moving up and down."

"Probably nerves that were severed when you were attacked," she explained nonchalantly, as if a small dog had bitten me. "Nerves can repopulate an area, and the ability to feel in the region will resume, but it takes time."

"You realize a massive shark bit me? The bite extends the length of my torso," I replied, annoyed.

"I do. Do you mind if we look at your back for a moment?" she asked politely.

I tried raising the gown over my head, but it proved too difficult. Nicholas reached forward to assist and helped remove it.

At that moment, Cecilia walked in with both of my girls. I was both surprised and delighted to see them. They had both grown up during my absence. Sarah had grown at least five inches and Amelia looked more like her mother in every way. The three of them stood at the foot of the bed, clearly stunned at seeing me in the flesh. Nicholas deftly pulled down my gown again to hide the scars. The man deserved a medal.

It thrilled me to see my family, despite the shocked expressions on my daughter's faces. The girls must have known of my injuries. It's just something else to see it up close. Amelia started to get all teary. I called them over and got massive hugs from all of them. The fact we had spectators meant nothing.

Colleen tapped me on my shoulder and said that she and the others would return in an hour. I nodded in agreement. All I wanted was to see my family and hear my girls speak. To divert their attention from my current condition, I said, "So great to see you all again. What's going on in your lives? Tell me everything."

Sarah and Amelia looked at each other and then back at Cecilia, whose head was dipped in mock shame.

Cecilia said, "When I got the message that you were waking, I also got a phone call from the principal's office telling me that Sarah had a run-in with a boy in her class."

Sarah has always had a knack for timing, I thought. I couldn't help but grin.

I was curious. "What for? Was it that bad?"

Sarah's head lowered.

Cecilia said, "Sarah got into a fight with a boy in her homeroom. And she ended up planting the poor boy in the infirmary. I was on the phone with the principal when the call came in from the hospital."

Amelia added to the mix, "Sarah also has a boyfriend."

From her brooding expression, Sarah was clearly feeling

antagonized by both her mother and her sister. "This isn't fair. You know Gavin is a bully and an idiot. He had it coming."

Cecilia reminded her that actions have consequences.

"Sarah, we already talked about this, you are grounded". She said to her eldest daughter, who responded with foot stomping and a growl. Someone was clearly unhappy. No phone for a week, which meant no contact with whatever his name was.

I tried to spin the situation a little. "Sarah, you can use the week to help me catch up on stuff, right? I would love to spend some time with my oldest girl." This brought a little smile, and a shrugged shoulder.

Cecilia turned to the girls. "Now that we've cleared the air, can you girls go downstairs and get me a coffee and something for yourselves so I can speak with your dad alone, okay? Thanks." She gave them her credit card and off they went.

Cecilia hopped onto the bed and lay next to me.

"How are you doing, my dear?" I asked, somewhat embarrassed at my state. Cecilia pushed my unwashed bangs from my eyes. It was then I realized that my hair was shoulder length. *Not since high school*, I thought, and grinned.

"Sometimes I am so tired raising those two," she replied, "but they saved my sanity. We all missed you so much. I'm really looking forward to you coming home. I still can't believe this is happening."

"Me too," I replied. "I'm so sorry for the way things ended up."

She ran her hands through my hair. "You smell funny, dear," she said cheekily.

"It's my new aftershave: old piss and antiseptic. But I can't smell anything," I replied with a snarky laugh.

My response made her giggle. She took a deep sniff and said, "Oh God, you need to be fumigated." She squeezed her nose shut. Despite my pungent aroma, though, she continued to lay close to me.

"You've been in the news since you woke," Cecilia informed me.

"What are they saying?" I asked.

"Miracle man wakes up, and some other nonsense. You know the tabloids."

"I wouldn't say a miracle, but certainly lucky," I said.

"How are you feeling today?" she asked.

"Still very weak. I can barely sit up, and standing requires someone to hold me up. It's really depressing."

Suddenly, I missed the ability to power myself beneath the waves. The feeling of near invincibility. Returning to my old reality was a shock to the system. But I was still relieved I'd come back. I missed Cecilia and the girls terribly during my time away. Still, adjustment was going to be rough.

"You are recovering, dear," she said reassuringly.

"I'm getting better at staying awake, but I fear falling asleep, falling back…" I said, almost without thinking.

"Why?" Cecilia asked.

"It's just too weird, and I'm afraid you would not understand. That *any* of you would understand," I emphasized.

"What, like out-of-body, flying-over-the-bed kind of stuff?" she asked wryly.

"See, I knew you wouldn't understand," I responded sourly. I knew it was too early, but I couldn't resist testing the waters a little. *Definitely too early.*

"Try not to get all hung up over those sorts of thoughts. There are a lot of people who want to see you and will probably show up in the next few days. Friends, colleagues and more family. Do you think you can handle it?"

Cecilia reminded me that as a survivor, I had a responsibility to the people who were affected by my situation.

"Sure, in a few days when I get more of my strength back. Let them come and visit. I have PT most days and I'll probably be tired in the evenings, but I can handle a few visitors."

Cecilia gazed at me sympathetically, "I'll help manage things at my end."

A week later I started getting regular visits from family and friends and the occasional colleague. Cecilia made certain that only a few could visit at a time and spaced out their visits. The limitations annoyed some of them. The press tried to get close to me a few times, sometimes even sneaking into the building in hospital garb, just to get a passing look or a photo op. Cecilia and the staff were pretty good at sniffing them out and having them escorted off the premises. Some of the altercations provided much amusement. As for the other patients and the staff, everyone gave me privacy and respect.

Ben showed up one afternoon, smiling at the sight of me. He was wearing a bright red flannel shirt and blue jeans, which gave him a Paul Bunyanesque aura. I was both happy and a little frightened to see him. His hair had thinned, and streaks of gray had woven their way through his dark locks. He appeared gaunt, but that could have been my memory playing tricks. As I recalled, he was always a bit wiry. My partner of many years looked relaxed, evidenced by the cheeky grin on his face and his saunter into my room, no doubt inspired by my recent recovery. Looking at him got me thinking about the state of the company.

"Nice to see you, Ben—have a seat," I commanded. He promptly pulled up a chair and studied me from head to toe. I was lying on the bed wearing a bathrobe and socks, trying to hide the skinny guy.

"I can't believe it's really you," he exclaimed. "How are you, buddy?"

"I'm better. It gets better with each passing day. Can't

believe I've been sleeping it off for eighteen months," I said sarcastically. "I'm almost too afraid to ask…"

"The company's fine, Mark," he said, anticipating my question. "It was quite a shock to all of us. We thought we lost you," he said sorrowfully.

"I'm so sorry," I said.

"You have no reason to be sorry. Take that up with fate, the creator, or whatever was responsible. But since you woke, the company unanimously agreed never to allow you to go on holiday again. And diving is out of the question," he added with a mock tone of authority. We both laughed.

"Guess I deserved that," I said. "I mean, I took almost two years off, right?"

"Yep, there you are. We're going to dock that off your pay," Ben said in his usual cheeky manner. Laughing was beginning to hurt. "We actually had a good year, financially. Kyle was all smiles at the all-hands last week."

"That's good to hear, and thanks for looking after Cecilia and the girls, Ben. I mean it," I said with as much sincerity as I could muster. It meant a lot to me that friends and family had looked after my girls while I was in limbo, cruising the Pacific. *It really sucks I can't talk about it.*

"Don't mention it. Many people chipped in to help," Ben reminded me. "We kept your salary going. I mean, you were still alive, so we had to pay you. You weren't helping much, but you were there in spirit. Not that it was any different when you were there," he said jokingly.

"So you're saying the staff was more effective in my absence?"

"Oh, definitely. It was actually measurable. Remote work really suits you." Ben was really having fun at my expense, and I was thoroughly enjoying it, but without knowing it he hit the nail with his last comment.

"You know, Max came in a couple of times to see you," Ben

continued. "I never thought of him as empathetic—always distant, that guy—but I could see it affected him, watching you in that state. The dude really felt something. He even talked to you."

I was touched by the observation. *So Max has a heart after all.* Max had been with the company since we founded it, and in all those years I'd never saw a rise in emotion from the man. He wasn't much of a talker.

"So how goes it with PT?" Ben asked seriously.

"Hard, but fruitful. I have a feeling I'll be doing this for a while."

"What about going home?"

"Maybe in a few weeks. It all depends on my recovery."

Ben brought me up to speed on the company and the changes that had occurred during my absence. As expected, a few key employees left the company shortly after my accident.

"Some of the staff were personally affected by your situation and lost faith in the company. It was probably too much for some of them to bear," Ben explained. "But the rest of us hoped for the best and when you stabilized, we thought you were on your way back. But fuck, dude, you really took your sweet time."

"Sorry."

"So, any thoughts about when we can expect you back?" Ben asked.

"I don't know," I replied. "I was an absent father and husband when I worked, and I was truly absent when I nearly died."

"What are you thinking?"

"I was thinking of selling some of my stake in the company and taking a year off. Spend some much-needed time with the family. Recalibrate."

Ben looked up at the ceiling and sighed, which to me meant that he was not altogether happy with my response. He then turned his gaze back to me and shook his head.

"I see. I get it."

"Look, Ben, it doesn't mean forever. I just need time with Cecilia and the girls."

"Understood. Can we do our chats again?" Ben asked. "I could use a friend."

"Sure. Always. By the way, I haven't been completely honest with everyone. Not even Cecilia knows. I can't say anything specific at the moment, but there is more to this story of mine."

Ben looked at me curiously. "That sounds ominous," he said.

"If I say anything now, the docs will put me in the nuthouse," I explained with trepidation.

Ben's eyebrows rose.

Another two weeks passed, and I was getting impatient and testy about going home. The doctors repeated the same tests every few days and informed me I was improving. Things had escalated to the point where Cecilia and Ben were bringing in food from outside or sneaking me out to the cafe across the street from time to time. I no longer waited for John to show up with the requisite wheelchair. I often stole one from the hallway and made my way over to the training facility. It was becoming routine for John to find me there, stretching or bench-pressing weights. Today, he had a smile on his face, so something was up. Our banter had changed somewhat from the first weeks.

"Good morning, Mark. Glad to see you are up early," he said. "A minor change to the program today."

"Really? Enlighten me," I said curiously.

"You've done an awesome job getting your weight up and building up muscle mass, but your legs, dude... I mean, look at them," he chafed me. I gazed at my legs, eyeing them wistfully and then lifting the left leg up with my arm and squeezing the flesh. They were still quite thin.

"I guess you might have a point. What do you recommend?" I asked.

"Your PT coordinator recommended we work on those toothpicks for a while. How is your walking?"

I stood up and balanced myself against the nearest wall. Then I put my hand down and walked until I reached the weight equipment along the far wall. I turned around and walked back, albeit with a little unsteadiness. It was getting better, but it was clear my upper body was getting the most workout. I looked like a competitive kayak rower. Muscular torso, but spindly legs. I could see from John's expression I had my work cut out for me.

We worked on my toothpicks for a good hour, balancing strength exercises and stretching. Then we were on the bicycles for another thirty minutes. My face became flushed from the exercise. Seeing that I was spent, John passed a water bottle to me and invited me to the cafeteria.

"The cafe is just across the street—we could sneak over," I said.

"Your friends and family can do that with you, but I can't. Against the Rules." he answered emphatically.

"So you knew?" I asked.

"Everyone knows. It's common knowledge," he said, smiling.

"And no one says anything?"

"Nah, we all kind of feel sorry for you," he said with a grin.

"Stop feeling sorry for me. I don't want your pity," I implored.

The cafeteria was full of people when we arrived. The queue extended out to the hallway. In the past, I had never been into crowds of people. I couldn't stand the noise and the hustle and bustle of crowded urban environments. Now, watching all these people mill about a hospital cafeteria brought pleasure and delight. *I could sit here all day and watch.*

"Hospital busier today?" I asked.

"It's not exactly Grand Central," John responded laconically.

After getting our coffee we found a table near the entrance and parked ourselves. The coffee was certainly better at the cafe across the street, but I decided against arguing. Cecilia and I could sneak over later. For now, I enjoyed just sitting there and observing people. Across the room was a family of four. The husband had his head between his knees and the wife gazed into space, her eyes downcast. Two children sat quietly at their feet. Next to them, a young mother cradled an infant in her arms, an oxygen tube attached to the baby's nose. A young man—her husband, perhaps—sat across from her, chatting. They were both smiling, so I surmised their situation as being less bleak than the other family's. So odd to see such diametric opposites sitting within an arm's length of each other.

"You shouldn't spy on people," John said, interrupting my new favorite pastime.

"I don't mean to eavesdrop, but I just love watching people. Cut me some slack. I've been in a coma for a while, right?"

"Right," he said with a smirk.

It was then that I noticed a familiar middle-aged man and a young woman sitting at a table a short distance from us. The fellow was wearing faded jeans and had long, gray hair tied in a ponytail. He had these big-rimmed glasses from the seventies. I wondered if they were back in fashion. The woman sitting across from him was of Polynesian descent and probably less than half his age. It took me a moment to realize that it was Dr. Holloway and Lucy.

I turned to John. "Do you mind if I go over to the pair sitting there by the table? They look familiar. Be back in a sec," I said innocently, knowing full well the absurdity of what was about to happen.

I rolled my chair slowly over to the couple, trying my best to pretend that I was greeting old friends. There was no mistaking Peter's long gray mane and metal-rimmed glasses. He looked like a throwback to the seventies in unwashed jeans and an aloha shirt. I couldn't help smiling as I approached them. Lucy turned her head and raised her one eyebrow in surprise.

"Dr. Holloway, I presume? Lucy?" I asked.

Peter responded with a question. "Mark? Is that really you?"

"In the flesh, or rather, as a homo sapiens," I answered.

We all discreetly looked around to make sure no one could overhear our conversation. John was still sitting at our table, drinking his coffee and looking at his phone.

"I'm still in shock," Lucy said. "When Peter told me that you had come out of your coma and you were recovering, I couldn't believe it."

"How long has it been since we met off Maui?" I asked, to get a sense of the true time that passed.

"I would say five or six weeks ago," Peter replied.

"The doctors explained to me I was slowly waking over a two-week period, so it sounds reasonable," I said. "I still can't get over the fact that I'm back. It defies explanation. But look at me—I'm happy, but I'm also a mess."

"I'm astonished we are speaking, Mark. All things considered, you look well," Peter said in a low voice, "But remember, we need to be careful in public."

I nodded in understanding.

"So, what did happen to you out there? Perhaps you could enlighten us," Peter asked with a smile disguising his inquisitiveness.

"Do you recall the storm, or rather the typhoon?" I asked.

"How could we forget?" Lucy said. "We had quite a ride

back to the harbor."

"There was a lot of lightning and thunder that day. I came to thinking about Marco and his damned scooter and the electrical explosion that created this connection in the first place. So, I looked for lightning. Apparently, I had success," I said with a smirk.

"Mark, you do realize that lightning is several orders of magnitude more powerful than any power supply found in a scooter, right?" Peter reminded me.

"I admit there was some risk involved. But this shark was a far larger and stronger animal than I am."

"You could have died along with the shark you inhabited. That was reckless," Peter said quietly, knowing full well if anyone overheard our conversation, they would think we were off the range.

"Aside from recovery, I feel fine. The storm presented an opportunity which, as you may well understand, I longed for. I was desperate. Speaking of which, are you still able to track the shark's whereabouts?"

"We can. It apparently survived the event, like you," Peter said.

I felt strangely relieved.

"We named her Marci, in honor of you," Lucy said proudly.

"Really? She has a name now?" Would Marci approve of her new name? *I'm so sorry they named you Marci.*

"How is your recovery progressing?" Peter asked.

"Better today than yesterday. You should have seen me on my first day. Skin and bone. Lots of discomfort."

I described my experience to them in detail. Then I asked, "So where is Marci headed?"

"She's moving southwest. We'll know more in a few days," Lucy said.

"I'd like to address the proverbial elephant in the room,"

Peter said to both of us. This part of the conversation was inevitable.

I said, "My feeling, after speaking with the doctors, my wife, and colleagues, is that nobody here is prepared for this. For the moment, people are just overwhelmed by my survival and recovery."

Peter looked thoughtfully at me. "Anything we can do to help?"

I looked back at John, who was now watching us. "I'll reach out to you when I've recovered and put some space between myself and this hospital," I said.

Peter pulled a card from his pocket and discreetly passed it to me. With that, the two of them stood up, and we parted ways.

I took a brief nap in the afternoon. When I woke, I found I was not alone in the room. Sitting across from me was a middle-aged woman who looked vaguely familiar. She had short hair, streaks of white mixed in with the gray. She was petite, and her feet floated above the floor. *I know this woman,* I thought. She was staring at me and, after a moment, smiled faintly.

"Do I know you?" I asked.

"We met, once. Maybe you might remember me," she said.

I cocked my head and tried very hard to remember where I had met her before. It took a couple of moments and then I realized. "Janet?"

She nodded. "I'm so pleased you remember me." Her smile grew.

She was sitting with a bag on her lap. On top of the bag was an iPad.

"You were there with me," I said.

She nodded. "How are you?"

"I've seen better days, but I am OK now. Recovery has been rough. Looking forward to going home and being with the family."

"I can believe that," she said.

"Is it okay that I'm here?" she asked softly.

"I'm actually thrilled you're here. Finally, someone from that day to speak with. Is it alright with you to discuss it?" Despite the severity of the incident, I felt fine talking about it, and I wanted to know more.

"It's still a struggle for me to open up about it. But sitting here with you makes it okay for me. That you are alive helps," she said.

"I understand. Look, I have a lot of holes in my memory of the actual attack. It's all very hazy. It would help me greatly in coming to terms with what happened to me," I said. I thought carefully about all I could remember from that day. "I remember diving around Lanai. The lava tubes, Marco's annoying scooter, and the shark."

Janet shuddered from the mention of the last word.

"I'd like to know more about the event from someone who was there. Do you think you could help me?" I asked patiently.

"What would you like to know?"

"I guess what I'm trying to ask is, what happened after we saw the shark the first time?"

Janet took a deep breath then closed her eyes briefly. "Here goes…"

She turned toward me. "We had just seen the shark. I think we were all in awe of the experience, on top of being frightened out of our wits. But then it swam off. The assumption was it had lost interest."

She paused, gripping her bag firmly. "Jeffrey proceeded up to the Cathedral, where we stayed for a short while, and then we returned to the boat. Most of us had spread out a little by then. We were at a low depth, maybe forty feet. I was exploring an ancient lava vent. You were about fifty feet from me when I heard Jeffrey's furious banging on his tank. When I turned in his direction, I felt an enormous pressure of water hit me flat in the face. It was then that I saw it. The shark passed within five feet of me, moving fast. It completely ignored me. My mind didn't even have time to process what was happening. I saw you looking away at something in the coral. And then you turned."

Janet's eyes were welling up with tears. There was some Kleenex by the bed, so I offered her the box. My body was knotting up as I listened to her account. Having someone describe the moment of my death almost two years after the fact was surreal. The fact I didn't die only compounded the confusion. It was like an out-of-body experience.

"The official report stated that a scooter, Marco's scooter, rammed the shark. Is that right?" I asked.

"This is the part that's hardest for me to talk about. I went to therapy for six months to find peace with it. I still haven't entered the water since that dive. Before that, I had dived for thirty years, and had seen hundreds of sharks. But after that, I was done."

She took a deep breath. "When the shark took you, there was a loud sound. We all heard it. It was probably the sound of your tank under the force of the collision. It was awful, the force of it. I recall feeling a pit in my stomach, thinking you were done for. And then, out of nowhere, Marco rammed his scooter into the shark and there was this bright flash." Janet paused again to regain her composure.

I sat and digested the story. I had a weird disconnect with it all.

"Janet, you said you saw a flash?" I asked, somewhat confused.

"It was most extraordinary. After that flash, both you and the shark sank to the seafloor. The shark had gone completely limb, and you fell out of its jaws. We picked you up and brought you to the surface as quickly as we could. Jeffrey did

CPR on you and cleared your airway. The rest of the team helped stem the bleeding. That suit of yours held you together."

While I had clear memories of my time after I woke up inside the shark, there was a period between the attack and that point that had eluded me. The information Janet was providing lifted a veil from that period and provided a clue to what set everything in motion after the attack. I wished I could explain to her the extraordinary adventure I experienced as a result of them saving my life. *Maybe one day, Janet.*

The story was so engrossing that I almost forgot it was about me, but then I was jolted back to the living. Janet sat quietly for a few minutes, her hands still rubbing the handles of her bag. I pointed at the iPad. "Was there something you wanted to show me?"

She looked down. "I have images from that dive. I wasn't sure if you were interested in seeing them. But you were my spotter."

Actually, I was very interested.

"Janet, would you like some water or coffee, tea?" I asked.

"Water would be lovely."

I took a clean glass from the nearby table and poured some lukewarm water into it. I got up from the bed and sat in the chair next to hers. Janet unlocked the iPad and selected a folder marked with the date of the event. Rows of thumbnails populated the small screen. She clicked on the first image to enlarge it. It was a picture of us preparing for the dive. Our kit was everywhere. Marco was there with his scooter.

"You took a picture while we were suiting up?" I asked.

"Yes. I always test my gear before entering the water. You were all such excellent subjects," she said with a smile.

We went through picture after picture. Since I had been her spotter, I was occasionally in the images. There were images of all the critters we'd encountered: some ghost shrimp, a couple of nudibranchs, a lone frogfish. Viewing these images filled me with joy, reminding me why I loved diving in the first place. As we worked our way through the pictures, I noticed a thumbnail image that filled me with dread.

I clicked it. Then I sat silently, not really knowing what to do with the emotions I felt. Janet had taken the image of the shark from where we had seen it the first time, just as I recalled it. Marci floating above us in the current. I realized how lucky I had been to survive But it wasn't aggressive towards us at all, at least not then. It was checking us out.

I had a hard time reconciling Marci with the same shark that had attacked me. I simply do not remember much from the incident. In the time I spent with her I had grown fond of my host. Within her I saw some wonders of the world, and some of its mysteries. In that period, the horror of the original attack had diminished, but looking at these photos now was bringing the trauma back. I took a deep breath.

I scrolled down the list to the last row, my curiosity piqued. Janet put her hand on the screen.

"Are you completely sure you want to see this?" she asked. "I didn't intend to take the last image. It was a reflex."

I gently moved her hand aside and enlarged the last image.

The image appeared to be at an angle, as if the camera was rotated. On the right side was a large, blurry object. Whatever it was, it was moving fast. I assumed that was the shark. In the distance I could barely make out a diver who was facing away, preoccupied with something.

"That's me, isn't it?" I asked. She nodded.

The image was taken mere seconds before my fate was sealed. I sat quietly and absorbed the immensity of the event. It was going to take some time to process. The authorities hadn't gone into the same level of detail in their reports. I guess nobody had furnished the information.

"What of the others, Janet? Where are they now?" I asked.

"I don't really know. We saw each other last at the public inquiry." She paused, then continued, "I saw Jeffrey briefly after the event. He closed his dive shop after that. Sold his boat. Pretty broken up about the whole affair."

"What of Marco?" I asked.

"No idea. He didn't come to the inquiry. Nobody knew where he was. He just disappeared."

I took a deep breath. "Thank you so much, Janet. I really appreciate you coming to see me. This has meant a lot to me."

With that, she stood up and then turned to me. "Mark, take care of yourself. I'm glad you're okay."

She gave me a big hug, then packed her device into her bag and left. I wondered if I would ever see her again. It filled me with sadness that she had given up her passion because of the event that connected us. I played back the last image in my mind. I guess it was good I hadn't seen it coming.

The Visitor

After three months of physical therapy, I was given the green light to go home. Cecilia and the girls packed my things while John brought over the wheelchair. Standing for brief intervals was possible, but then my legs would start trembling, requiring me to sit and rest. I made it a goal to walk at least one tour of the hospital grounds each day, without stopping to sit. Despite my progress and weight gain, I was still a long way from my former self. My clothes hung loosely from my shoulders, and I had to use the tightest setting in my belt to keep my pants from falling down. My socks rolled limply around my ankles. Looking in mirrors did very little for my self-esteem, so I avoided them.

For weeks, I'd consumed food at every opportunity, from foul-tasting protein drinks to piles of mediocre hospital roast beef. My weight had measurably increased. I was so looking forward to going home and getting some decent food. On top of eating more, my energy level and general outlook had improved, and I could stay awake for hours before fatigue set in.

Cecilia caught me looking at myself in the mirror one day, and said, "In a few months we'll have you back to normal, dear."

I loved her optimism; it was a massive confidence booster. I still found it hard to accept that this room had been my home for nearly two years, although I was only awake in it for three months. Looking around, I realized I had grown attached to it. It felt familiar and safe. Those pastel green colors worked wonders on my soul. Thoughts of going out the door made me uneasy. I knew they would eventually pass.

Sarah came over with my bag. "Are you ready?" she asked.

"Yeah, I'm so looking forward to coming home," I replied. "Do you have any plans tonight?"

"Not really. I cleared my calendar," she said proudly.

I gaped at her. "You have a calendar now?"

Sarah looked at me quizzically. "Duh, yeah."

John rolled the wheelchair in front of me, smiling. "Ready, champ?"

"Do I really need to sit in that thing?" I asked.

"It's a long walk to the parking garage."

Reluctantly, I planted myself into the chair and let the gang transport me to the car. I was pretty shocked to see our old red Volvo still making the rounds. I felt kinship with it.

John helped me sit in the front seat. I confidently snapped the seat belt in place myself and looked up at him.

"Thanks for everything, John. I mean it," I said.

"Don't mention it, Cap. I'll see you on Monday at PT. Have a great weekend with the fam," he said kindly, patting me on the shoulder.

The girls jumped into the car and buckled in. Cecilia started the engine and soon we were on our way home. I gazed out the window as we passed familiar landmarks. It all looked familiar and yet oddly alien at the same time. Driving over several large potholes on the highway cured me of any doubt that this was real.

The house looked exactly as I remembered it. Maybe a little more battered, with a few more cedar shingles missing. Below the fascia, the shingles were nearly black from sun exposure.

I recognized Cecilia's handiwork in the front yard.

Climbing roses of every color adorned the trellises along the front wall. Roses were her favorites, along with Camelia plants. Interspersed between the roses she had planted lavender bushes.

"I'm behind in the yard work, given all the stuff that's been going on," Cecilia said as we entered the driveway.

"Still looks great. I like what you did with those tree stumps over there..." I said, pointing at the far corner of the yard.

She frowned at me. "No jokes about my gardening. You can make fun of everything else, but not my pride and joy." She grinned.

All jokes aside, it was great to be home. Our home was small, more of a rambler. Cozy and compact. Not exactly representative of a typical company CEO. I was going to ask Cecilia about our finances but decided to wait. There was plenty of time for me to go through them in the coming days.

"We're ordering in tonight. Pizza okay with you?" Cecilia asked.

"Wow, I've been away for how long and I don't even get a home-cooked meal?" I teased her.

Cecilia threw an icy stare at me.

"Honey, I'm just messing with you, and you said I could make fun of other stuff," I reminded her. She was not pleased.

As we approached the front door, I heard a bark. I looked at Cecilia.

"We have a guard dog now," she said seriously.

As we stood by the opened front door, an excited small black lab ran out and circled us several times before letting us into the house. Someone was thrilled by our presence. But who was this little fella?

"Mark, say hello to Jordan," Cecilia said.

"Hello Jordan," I said to the excited puppy, scratching its head. "So how old are you? And are you house- trained?" I asked.

"Eight months, and yes, almost. He occasionally pees on the carpet. He's getting better," Sarah replied. She and Amelia took the puppy and ran into the backyard with it, no longer interested in their once long-absent father. *That was quick.*

Inside, the house looked unchanged, though the rooms seemed smaller, like when one revisits a childhood home, and memory and experience collide. The sofa was showing some sign of wear, and the dining table needed some sanding and refinishing. At the very least, I would not be bored, as there would be plenty of jobs to do around the house. Cecilia ordered food over the phone and then sat at the kitchen table. I sat next to her, smiling like a giddy teenager.

"What? What are you all worked up about?" she asked.

"I'm just happy to be home with all of you. That's all."

"Hmmm… I recognize that twinkle in your eye," she replied with a smile, which slowly vanished. "Look, Mark, we're all relieved to have you home. But it's also weird to have you here. I mean, you've been absent for so long, I can scarcely believe that you're sitting next to me. I have to pinch myself," she said, looking at me as if I were a ghost.

"Is it hard to have me back?" I asked, a little discouraged.

"In a way, yes. But I'm so happy, too. It's just that my head needs time to get around all of this. For so long, we were expecting the worst. The girls need to adjust to having their father around. They've grown up a bit in your absence. It's not like we can pick up where we left off."

I sat quietly, absorbing her words.

"I can't imagine what it must have been like for you, for the girls," I said. "Eighteen months is a long time. I can completely sympathize if you felt lonely and needed, well, someone."

The words appeared to strike a nerve, judging by Cecilia's hurt expression.

She took a deep breath. "We managed. Ben was very

helpful through it all. I can understand why the two of you are such good friends. But to be honest, we were never given any indication from the doctors that you would one day wake up."

We both sat quietly for several minutes. Cecilia's words resonated with me, and it made me depressed to think about my physical condition. I got up and walked toward the back door and leaned against the door frame. As I stood there, Cecilia's arms wrapped around my waist, and she rested her head on my shoulder.

"Give it time, Mark. We have all the time in the world. The most important thing is that you're home. Nothing else matters."

I looked at her. "I can't stand looking at myself. I don't think I've ever felt this kind of self-loathing before in my life. My body's so scarred. And to top it off, I have a ton of guilt."

Cecilia hugged me tightly. She whispered into my ear, "I'm here. We're *all* here. We love you the same. I'm just so glad to have you home again."

We stood there for several minutes, watching the kids run around the backyard chasing Jordan. We went back into the house and sat down in the living room. I looked around, still in disbelief that I had been absent for so long. I breathed deeply, taking in the smell of our old house. I had missed it. Part of me just wanted to forget everything from my time in the ocean, to go back to my old self.

Deep down, I knew this would be impossible. That experience was as hard-wired in me as my previous life. Reconciling both was going to be hard. One day, I would need to explain to Cecilia what had happened.

Cecilia pulled out a phone from a drawer. "Oh, Mark, here's your old phone. I charged it up. It's pretty full, and there's a ton of spam. I tried my best to clean it up, but it keeps filling up." She handed it to me before heading to the kitchen.

I stared at my phone in disbelief. There were literally

thousands of unopened messages and emails, many from people I'd never met. Occasionally, a familiar name popped up. In the process of deleting large groups of spam messages I almost deleted a message from Ben. I did a cursory pass of my message queue and copied the important mail items to a private folder.

"Wow, this is definitely going to take a while to go through," I remarked as I sorted line after line of text messages and emails. Cecilia stood by the door to the kitchen.

"You don't have to do it now, dear. It might be easier to do it on the laptop," Cecilia said.

"Maybe I should just get a new number and email," I said, frustrated. This was just too much.

"Since you woke, the tide of messages has been endless. There are so many people that want to meet you and talk to you."

The situation was spiraling out of control. I put the phone face down onto the coffee table and closed my eyes, absorbing the sounds from the backyard and Cecilia doing housework. One thing was clear: I had a lot of adjusting to do. Looking out the window, I could see curious neighbors talking to each other on the sidewalks, gawking at our house. How had Cecilia dealt with this after the incident? It would never be the same to talk to neighbors again. *Maybe we should move.* I heard Cecilia walk up from behind.

"A year ago, there were news trucks lining the street in front of our house for weeks. It nearly drove me over the edge. I wanted to chase them off with your chainsaw. This, I can handle," Cecilia said, resting her head on my shoulder.

Just who is this woman I'm married to?

The next day I got up early and took a walk around the backyard. The family was still asleep. I walked around the flower beds Cecilia had been working on. She had pruned the rose bushes and removed the old bark from previous years. New growths of lavender were sprouting here and there between the rose bushes. I opened up one of the lounge chairs on the patio and laid down on it. The sun's rays pierced the branches of the large oak tree in our backyard and bathed my face in warmth.

The neighborhood was quiet, except for the birds and the occasional dog barking. I closed my eyes and breathed in the morning air. It was delightful. *Good to be back.*

I had no idea how long I napped before the sound of coffee beans being ground punctured the peace and quiet. Soon the aroma of fresh coffee drifted out into the yard. Cecilia came out with two large mugs, which I held while she moved a small garden table and another chair into place.

"Good morning. How did you sleep?" she asked as she adjusted her chair. She was wearing my old robe, which was a little too large for her. It was touching to see her wear it.

"Nice to be back in my old bed, sleeping next to you," I answered with a smile. *I've dreamt of this moment for so long.*

Cecilia gazed over her garden. She was looking less tired and weary today. The deep creases along her brow were less apparent.

"It's so odd that the girls have just accepted that their father is back," she said.

"I noticed that too yesterday. An hour with me and then off with the dog," I replied with a hint of melancholy. "Two years. Is it okay if I ask how you managed it?" I said carefully.

I saw lines of worry develop on her forehead. Briefly she gazed at her hands, then looked up at me.

"I'm not sure I'm ready to talk about it. I still feel the pain of those early days," she explained. "I don't blame you, at least not anymore. We were just extremely unfortunate."

I thought about the moment on the beach when the officers arrived. Cecilia's reaction to my attack at the time was seared into my memory.

"I remember how we fought the day before the attack," I said. "The restaurant, and those idiots at the beach."

"You remember that?" She chuckled, followed by a sigh. "It fills me with so much sadness every time I think about that time. So much was lost. You know, I went down to that beach every night for a whole week while we waited for the doctors to stabilize you."

I was about to reply *I know* but caught myself.

"I'm so sorry for all of this, Cecilia, for the pain I caused," I said, holding her hand.

"I was angry with you, and the world, for a long time. Eventually, I became exhausted by it all. I had the girls to think about. I learned to move on. Sitting with you now brings some of that pain back."

I hadn't counted on the difficulties of separation. Occasionally, I caught myself wanting to say something absurd like *I missed you while I was gone,* or *I dreamt of you and the girls constantly*. It was both hard and irritating having to censor my thoughts to avoid uttering an inconvenient truth. We had lived separate lives for two years. I was like an astronaut returning from a multi-year voyage. Sailors and submariners on deployments were regularly away from their spouses for six months or longer. I would have to treat this the same way. The only issue I had was introducing my wife to the idea that I had actually been away on my own adventure. At the moment, I was without a clue about how to approach this.

There were stilted pauses in our conversation. It was obvious that we both felt awkward, and that we were being polite to one another, trying to figure out how we functioned together. We also had unresolved problems to deal with. I loved my wife, but how do you talk to someone you haven't seen in two years?

I was resolute in wanting to explain my time away, but I

restrained myself to avoid antagonizing my wife. She had suffered enough.

"Do you recall a few weeks ago when I told you that something happened to me while I was in a coma?" I asked, watching her carefully.

"Yes, I do. Though I wasn't sure you were being serious."

I tried not to look disappointed at her response.

"There were moments when I thought I was there with you in the hospital room, like someone locked in, unable to speak or move," I explained.

"Really?" she asked, suddenly curious.

"I could smell you, your perfume. But I couldn't hear anything. My eyes remained fixed in one position, barely open. It was so weird."

"How often did this happen?" Cecilia asked.

"Probably a few times," I replied.

"Strange that the doctors didn't pick up on it," Cecilia said.

Talking about these visions was at least a start to the larger, more demanding conversation we'd need to have later.

"There are other things too, Cecilia," I said.

"Like?"

"Watching you and the girls wasn't the only experience I had," I added.

"Are you sure you weren't dreaming? Have you thought about talking to someone? Maybe your trauma is somehow connected to these dreams."

Cecilia was a little too tied up with the concept of *dreams*. People usually associate dreams with fantasies, constructions of the mind. What I'd experienced was not a construction of the mind at all, that much I was sure of. I needed to think how I would go about describing what happened.

I realized how ridiculous it would all sound. Without proof, without witnesses, it would be a hard slog. Even with my wife.

However, I did manage to convince a boatload of people that I was a human inside a shark. Why should this be any different?

Like an old married couple, we sat there in silence for what felt like an hour. Jordan popped his little head out of the back door and then walked out into the yard, taking a piss on Cecilia's roses.

"Thanks, Jordan," Cecilia called out sarcastically.

Despite my personal frustrations, the pup's actions elicited a hearty chuckle from me.

"It's nice to just sit here quietly with you, before the world wakes up," I said.

Cecelia smiled and took a sip of her coffee. In response to a ringing sound from the kitchen, she leapt up from the chair and walked into the house. I could hear her humming as she went about pulling something out of the oven.

A familiar, sleepy young lady stood in the doorway. Amelia was in her pajamas, yawning. She walked out on the patio in her bare feet and laid down on her mother's chair.

Cecilia came out carrying a small basket covered with a cheesecloth. Something smelled divine.

"How are you this fine morning?" I asked Amelia.

"Something smells good. Did Mom bake something?" Amelia asked, monitoring the basket.

Cecilia shoved Amelia to one side of the lounge chair while protecting the contents of the basket as Amelia attempted to pull the cheesecloth off. "Hey, hands to yourself, Amelia!" Cecilia chastised her.

It was absolutely wonderful watching them. It was extraordinary how much Amelia had grown. She was a clone of her mother. Her once round face had become oval, her features more pronounced. She was already wearing braces, on the cusp of being a teenager.

In the afternoon, we took a stroll down the block to the beach. Cecilia did a quick scan of the street and saw that it was empty. I wore a hoodie and took on a pair of sunglasses.

"Incognito? Really. The streets are empty, Mark," Cecilia teased.

"I'm just not ready to talk to people."

When we got to the beach, Jordan immediately stuck his nose into the sand and his paws dug deep as he attempted to retrieve some phantom object. The two girls followed the puppy down the beach as it jumped from hole to hole.

I recognized an elderly gentleman sitting on a tattered fold-out beach chair, his chin resting on his cane. He was the only person to notice me in the water all those months ago, when I had come here in an unsuccessful try to see my family. He never took his gaze from the water.

Cecilia was looking at the city skyline as we walked past him.

"There's a big one out there!" he blurted out.

I turned to face him.

"A big what?" I asked in surprise.

"It's George—he caught a big one, and it got away," the man replied, "I'm keeping an eye out for him."

"You mean a fish?" I asked.

"I would have to ask George. But one day he just appeared and waved to me, with his big fin, like a whale."

I was wondering if this fellow was playing with a full deck. *So he remembers me.* I assumed he was in his mid-eighties, and he was alone. He was wearing a green beret that had seen better days.

Cecilia and I continued walking along the beach.

"He moved here about a year ago," Cecilia informed me. "I think his son is taking care of him. They live down the street. The son usually comes down in the afternoon and helps him home. We see him often. He's always looking out at the water. The girls are a little frightened of him."

"He seems harmless, if a little off the range," I said.

* * *

A few days later, after I had come back from PT, I began work on our old dining table, sanding and washing the surface twice to remove the old finish. After I had given it a few coats of oil and cleaned up, I went upstairs to take a shower. I was feeling fatigued and figured it was probably a good time to stop working. The morning PT was particularly long and grueling. John made sure every session counted. Layers of sawdust and dirt had settled over my clothing and in my hair and under my nails. It felt good to do some work, to have a project.

Ben had come by to chat. We spoke for a short while over coffee, and then he was off to the office. We agreed I would come by the office the following week and say hello to everyone.

I dumped the dirty clothes into the hamper and stepped into the shower stall and turned on the water. Across from me, a tall mirror revealed the scars along my back. I touched them with my fingers and ran my hand along my side. It was not possible to sense anything on the bite marks themselves, which was expected. The skin on either side of the scars, however, was full of sensation. Probing deeper, I could make out the damaged parts of my ribs. As I inhaled, the sharp irregularity where my ribs had broken became more pronounced. It was quite possible I had remnants of shark teeth in my body. As I swept my hands up and down along the scars, I sensed a wave of electricity traveling up and down my torso.

Suddenly, dizziness came over me, and I clutched the shower door for stability. A brief bout of nauseousness followed. Leaning against the shower door, I waited for the feelings to pass. After a few minutes they subsided, and I could steady myself. Standing under a hot shower helped me relax.

Looking up at the ceiling, I noticed that the old shower vent had never been properly repaired. The cover was dangling, exposing several wires outside the wall. Upon closer examination, it was clear that the drywall screws and plugs had lost their traction and were just hanging uselessly. The fan wasn't running, probably stuck from too much dirt or a poor connection. Our house was old, probably early 20th century, and the electrical wiring was not completely up to date. We knew this when we bought the house and had the ground floor wiring replaced.

I reached up and poked the cover, trying to push the exposed wiring back in. Sparks flew out of the vent due to my fiddling, and a surge of electricity ran through my right arm. My arm shook uncontrollably and shooting pain traveled up and down my spine.

At that moment Cecilia walked in and saw me struggling.

"Mark, are…" I heard her say, but her voice trailed off.

"Honey, you better call an ambulance—something's happening!" I yelled after her.

The right side of my face went numb, and I started sliding toward the floor. I could no longer speak.

Cecilia ran toward me. Her mouth was moving but I could no longer hear her.

I slid down the shower wall to the floor. The image in one of my eyes faded, and then it all went dark.

When I woke it was still dark, but I no longer felt any pain and I wasn't shaking. In fact, I was fine. The dizziness was no longer there. It bothered me that I couldn't see anything. There was no sound, at least not initially. It took me a few seconds to grasp that I wasn't actually breathing. Foreboding rose within me. *Where's Cecilia? Where am I?* Something wasn't right at all.

Suddenly, a glimmer of bluish light penetrated the darkness. I had a sense that I was ascending from darkness. The world around me appeared featureless, as if I were floating in an endless pool.

After what seemed like a few minutes, the light grew, and a

scene unfolded before me. I recognized it immediately. I was watching the ocean out of Marci's eyes again.

Fuck! As far as I could see, I was somewhere in the ocean. After all I had been through, I had sent myself thousands of miles offshore, to God knows where, with the shock generated by a useless ceiling fan in my shower.

I was furious with myself. A simple shock from the poorly maintained wiring was all it had taken. *Poor Marci got thrown for a loop, too.* Cecilia was probably tending to her unconscious husband, terrified that he had relapsed to his previous comatose state. *How the hell could I let this happen?*

Thin strands of light penetrated the seawater. Moonlight was refracting through the surface just above me. Thankfully, I was not too deep when I woke inside Marci. It didn't lessen my anger and frustration, yet I desired to find out where I was. Swimming came back to me naturally, as if I had never been away. *So I'm now part shark, part man.*

As my head broke through the surface, I caught sight of a familiar city. I swam in for a closer look. Like slices of upended fruit, the characteristic architecture of the Sydney Opera House was unmistakable. I had managed to teleport myself across the Pacific again.

Still, I had no sense of the time that had passed. Had I been unconscious for any period? My body was clearly still alive back home, since I now inhabited Marci, and I was conscious of my surroundings.

The thought of having to venture out and find another sea storm worried me. *I might not be so lucky next time.*

The shifting, colorful lights of the Sydney Harbor Bridge passed above me. It wasn't exactly how I wanted to visit this charming city. As I surveyed the city from the surface, I began thinking about submarine cables and the sonar array I'd ripped through during my Pacific passage. If I could rip through a sonar array, a submarine cable would be doable. Europe had countless cables connecting various parts of the mainland from different power stations. Would there be any in Australia connecting to nearby islands? I assumed that islands in this region relied on power from Australia.

Partially chewing through one of those cables might do the trick of getting me back, and the voltage levels were considerably lower and therefore less risky than those of lightning strikes. At that time, in my stupidity, I engaged head-on with a cyclone. I'd completely forgotten that submarine power cables connected the Hawaiian Islands. *All's well that ends well, I suppose.*

As I scanned the sea bottom for the telltale sign of a cable, I thought about Cecilia and my recovery. How would I explain my latest departure to her? How would she take it? It was paramount that I find a solution quickly. Time was of the essence. After an hour of fruitlessly searching for cables, I paused and came to the surface. People were milling about the promenade along the opposite shore of the opera house. It all looked quite pretty. *I need to bring Cecilia here.*

If there were cables to be found, it was unlikely I would find them in the bay. In short order, I exited the bay and headed north. I decided to scan the coast both north and south of Sydney. There had to be something electrical I could get my teeth into. Due to the darkness, searching was going to be difficult, so I tried a different approach. Marci's snout was equipped with sensitive electrical receptors called the Ampullae of Lorenzini. Sarah thought these receptors sounded too funny to be real, so she named a pasta dish after them, of her own design. It was actually pretty good.

Once outside the bay, I proceeded in a northerly direction, near the coast. Coasting slowly over the bottom, I closed my eyes and focused on the senses in my snout. Two hours later, I detected the first sign of a signal. Swimming further, I noticed that the signal faded, and I turned around to investigate.

Sweeping back and forth a few times, I was able to narrow down the location of the cable until it was visible directly in front of me. Even in pitch-black darkness, I could see the cable clearly. It was around eight inches in diameter and black, encrusted with coral and mollusks. I did not know which offshore destination it powered, but someone was about to experience a blackout in the name of teleportation. For all I knew, it could be a fiber optic internet cable, but it looked old, and I was desperate.

I prodded it a few times to get the sense of its construction. It was clad in something quite strong and very stiff. The cable was designed to withstand anchors and other marine threats, so successfully chewing through it was not a given. Slowly, I placed my jaws around the thick cable and waited for my courage to build. I hadn't completely closed my mouth when the scene—cable and ocean—vanished.

I heard human voices calling out to me. Opening my eyes, I saw I was resting in a bed in a hospital, and a doctor and a nurse were standing over me. The nurse had her hand on my shoulder. There was an object in my mouth, which tasted like rubber and a metal band tightly wound around my head. I had an excruciating headache.

The doctor and nurse were calling out to me.

"Mark, can you hear us?" the doctor yelled. Their voices were faint at first but gradually grew louder.

I was trying to shout but couldn't with the rubber-tasting object in my mouth. I spat it out.

"Yes, yes. Please stop shouting—my head hurts," I responded weakly.

Reeling from the episode, I Inadvertently said, "I was just about to chew through the cable…"

In front of me a roomful of people stood silent, staring at me with eyes widened and mouths open, surprised by my outburst.

Shit.

The nurse removed the metal band from my head and gave me something to drink to wash out the flavor of rubber in my mouth.

"What the hell is going on!" I yelled at them, aiming to draw their attention away from my previous outburst. Looking down, I could see that my arms and legs were in restraints. "Please release me. I demand an explanation," I insisted.

Cecilia showed up next to the doctor. She put her hand on my shoulder.

"Mark, calm down. You had a seizure in the shower, honey. Do you remember?"

"Barely. I remember fussing with the ceiling vent and getting shocked. Then I was woozy and blacked out. But why am I in restraints?"

The doctor stepped forward and instructed the nurse to unbind my restraints. I tried unsuccessfully to sit up.

"My name is Dr. Rhodes. I'm the resident neurosurgeon here at the hospital. You evidently had a seizure and collapsed at your home. Your family brought you in for treatment and observation. In the hours that followed, you descended into a catatonic state. We applied electroshock treatment to break the spell you were in. It took quite a powerful shock to get you back."

I lay silently on the bed, thinking about what he said. Despite my headache, I had a clear recollection of what I had experienced. *So, it was just a coincidence, then.* I was about to chew through a cable when the doctors here administered their own shock. *Amazing timing.*

The doctor interrupted my thoughts. "You said you were about to chew through a cable. It was the first thing you uttered when you woke. Can you elaborate?"

I tried my best to diminish the importance of my earlier

pronouncement. "Not really. I might have been dreaming."

He did not look convinced. "You were not in REM sleep, Mark. You went from completely catatonic to fully active and aware in short order. We call it catatonia," the doctor said. "There's just one thing: I don't believe you were aware of us during your catatonic state. So I ask you again…"

"Doctor, you wouldn't believe me if I told you. It's just too far out for me to explain to you, or anyone else in the room," I explained sincerely.

Registering my discomfort at answering, he backed off. "Alright. Let's take this up tomorrow. Mark, I recommend taking it easy. I will prescribe some relaxants and ask that you stay in the hospital overnight for observation. Just as a precaution."

Reluctantly, I agreed. From my perspective, the situation was getting out of hand. I had experienced shocks before, mild ones, without any deleterious side effects. So there was a threshold, but how high? Older houses usually only have 110 V wiring installed, but the amperage can be quite high. Shifting my gaze toward my wife, I asked:

"Cecilia, can you do me a favor and reach out to Doctor Holloway? The number is on my desk."

Cecilia nodded. My poor wife looked exhausted, her face flushed, and her eyes reduced to narrow slits from lack of sleep.

"Is he your private physician?" Dr. Rhodes asked.

I couldn't hold back a smile in response. "No, he's my marine biologist."

Dr. Rhodes shook his head and smiled. "And he is significant why?"

"Like I said earlier, you wouldn't believe it if I told you," I replied.

"I'm concerned that you might have a relapse. Do you mind if we lightly restrain you while you sleep?" the doctor asked. "Just in case."

"Is that necessary?" I asked, "As long as I don't get a shock, I should be fine."

In the end, I acquiesced to the doctor's request. In truth, I wanted to rest and think about what I had experienced in solitude. The nurse administered a sedative to me and loosely tied the restraints on my hands. She put a service call button at my fingertips if I needed anything. The doctor informed the nurse to observe me while I rested and then left.

"You're scaring me Mark, I have no idea what is going on and you haven't been exactly forthcoming," Cecilia said, taking a deep breath to try to contain her anxiety.

I tried reaching out with my hands, but the restraints got in the way. She reached over and took my hand.

I tried to reassure her. "Cecilia, I know this all sounds crazy, believe me, I'm the first to agree with you. But you'll get answers soon. Please get in touch with Peter Holloway. It's my best chance in explaining to you what happened."

"I was so hoping you were ready to come home, and now this. How will I explain this to the girls?"

"Just be honest with them. Tell them I had a relapse, and that I dreamt of you all and I'm fine."

"But that's not completely true," she corrected me.

"No, but it's the best we can do for now," I said.

Cecilia left to go home after an hour. She was both confused and upset by the day's events. I hoped she would find Holloway's number and get in touch with him soon. Bound to my bed, I spent the next few hours thinking about how to explain everything. On top of all that, my head was pounding, and I wasn't sure if it was because of the experience of being deep below the sea or getting electrocuted by the hospital staff. Even though I could feel the sedative working, I found it nearly impossible to sleep. I must have gazed at the ceiling for an hour before John showed up with dinner. He brought over the bedside table and helped me sit up.

"You are one interesting dude," he said with a smile. He removed my restraints and then poured some water into a glass.

"How is that?" I asked. "And how are you so comfortable with my restraints removed?"

"They gave you a massive dose of Xanax, enough to knock out an elephant. You're not going anywhere. I dare you to try," he said, and smiled again.

I grinned at him. I was in no shape to take him on, in my present or past form. "Ah, that explains it," I replied.

Then I asked quietly, "John, I got a shock in my shower from the fucking ceiling vent. Did you see me when I came in?"

He looked over his shoulder to see if anyone could overhear us. "They brought you in and at the time you were unconscious. Everybody just thought you had a mishap at home. When you woke up is when the real shit happened."

"What do you mean?" I asked, confused.

John pulled up his phone and played a video he had recorded.

"I have no way to describe to you what happened. Nobody knew what the fuck to do. You tell me." He said as he played the video back.

I saw myself in the video lying on the bed, apparently unconscious. The team in the emergency room were examining me, checking my vitals, when suddenly I appeared to wake. But the look on my face was unrecognizable, and my eyes looked like those of a feral creature. They were wide open, the pupils completely dilated. My body was twitching and rolling. My hands and legs began to spasm uncontrollably. It was as if someone or something else had taken control of my body. The hospital staff called out to me, to no avail. It also appeared as though I was not breathing at all, and my body was noticeably turning blue. Eventually I collapsed, and the neurosurgeon appeared.

I didn't need to see the rest, so I paused the video.

"That was pretty fucked up." I gave John his phone back. "Thanks."

"Don't mention it," he said.

"Did you get in trouble for filming it?" I asked.

"A little, but then the doctors asked for a copy. They figured they might see something they missed. I looked at it a few times myself, and I still can't get my head around it."

"Consider this, John," I said. "What do you think you saw in your video? Have you ever seen a patient react like that?"

"No, never. I've seen patients lose self-control, psychotic shit, but I have never seen that kind of feral behavior. Except with animals, predators, up close."

"Ever had a patient get teleported to somewhere in the Pacific, inside the mind of a large shark? The very beast that once tried to eat him?" I asked straight out, unaware that the medication had reduced my inhibitions. *Oops.*

John grinned. "That Xanax is messing with you, Mark."

"Yeah, probably," I replied.

After I finished my meal, John took my food tray away. "I'll see you in the morning, Mark," he said reassuringly. He left soon after.

I thought long and hard about the feral creature that had inhabited my body. Nowhere in my discussions with the doctors and my family had it been revealed I'd ever exhibited such behavior before. This was becoming a concern. *Did I just swap places?* If this had really happened, how on earth had Marci reacted to all this? And why now?

My concentration was faltering from the sedative, so instead of struggling, I finally gave in and fell asleep.

* * *

I slept until ten o'clock the next morning. Nobody woke me or brought me breakfast. I could hear the staff milling about in the hallways. I was still in restraints. John walked in, followed by Dr. Rhodes and another nurse.

"Hey big guy," John called out to me. "I didn't want to wake you after yesterday's tumble. I figured you could use the rest."

"Thanks. But I'm starving," I said, my stomach grumbling in agreement.

Dr Rhodes stood next to the bed. "Mark, I wanted to discuss something with you, if that's okay."

I turned my attention to him. "Sure thing. What's on your mind?" I asked, interested.

He had one of these portable medical laptops with him and motioned for the nurse to power it up. He turned the display toward me and asked John and the other nurse to leave and close the door. This was a bit unsettling. Once they left, he activated the software and brought up a colored heatmap image of what appeared to be a CT or MRI scan of a human brain.

"When you were first brought in here and treated, we carried out some CT scans of your chest cavity and spine, examining your most severe injuries. Little attention was given to your head and brain. It wasn't until we noticed your coma was unusually deep, almost vegetative in its character, that we carried out further scans of your head, to look for other injuries."

In front of me was a cross-sectional, color-enhanced image of a brain—my brain, I supposed.

"This first image is that of a normally active brain. Note the spread of colors and centers of activity." He pointed at the familiar parts of the brain, the temporal, occipital and parietal lobes, describing their functions.

"The frontal lobe handles self-awareness and expression.

The brain stem controls breathing and other autonomic functions," he continued.

Then he displayed a very different image. This one was much darker and had little contrast.

"This scan represents a brain in an almost total vegetative state. Most deep-coma patients exhibit something like this. Note the lack of activity in all the lobes except the brain stem. This next scan was your brain about one month after we received you."

The image he displayed was quite odd. While much of the parietal and frontal lobe were inactive, there were bright spots in them. Intense ones, actually.

"You have stated that you have no recollection of your time in a coma," he asked.

"Yes and no," I answered. *I chased monsters in the deep and chewed the cable off a Russian sub.* That would not work, so I tried something more delicate, something the doctor could relate to. "While I don't recall a lot, I do remember waking up from time to time in my hospital room. At the time, I didn't understand where I was, and I couldn't move or communicate. But I could smell the room and feel warmth. I remember lying next to my wife, albeit briefly."

"I haven't forgotten the whole 'cable' thing of yours," the doctor commented with a wry smile. "From this image we can see that parts of your mind were quite busy, as if locked in, unable to communicate with the outside world. There is a common misconception that comatose patients are sleeping, but in reality, they are just unconscious. It is a persistent state. No sleep cycles, no dreaming. But in your case, the activity we observed varied over time—cyclic, actually. It was as if you were taking naps during your coma, which makes absolutely no sense, unless..." He paused briefly before continuing, "You were in fact, locked in."

I was quiet, digesting this information. I needed to tread

carefully. My audience, however capable, was not yet ready to hear the truth.

"You might have something there, but it doesn't explain what happened yesterday." I said, deliberately changing the subject.

"I have to admit I'm stumped. Your response in that state was, from my point of view, primitive. Like a wild animal." The doctor's gaze lingered on me; his brow furrowed in concern.

"We're at a loss to explain it. Describing it as catatonic just doesn't do it justice."

"One thing is for certain: I'm staying away from anything remotely electrical," I said.

"Probably a good idea," the doctor responded.

Against my wishes, I was told to stay at the hospital for another three days. Thankfully, Cecilia and Ben and the girls brought food from outside and kept me in regular company. I really wanted to go home. There was no reason to keep me there. Day after day, the doctors checked my vitals and tested my responses. As expected, there were no changes. The doctors removed the restraints the day after my seizure.

"I called the electrician and had him fix the vent in the bathroom and a few other potentially risky spots in the house," Cecilia told me. "Ben also came over to check on things."

"Thanks. What would I do without you?" I replied.

"What are they saying? Can you go home today?" Cecilia asked.

"Not sure yet. Hopefully. They'll let us know."

"Oh, by the way," Cecilia said, "I got in touch with Doctor Holloway. He'd like to meet us."

I perked up. "Really, when?"

"He said he could fly up from San Diego the day after tomorrow. I said that would be fine. We can meet him here or at home, depending on the situation."

"Thank you so much for doing this for me." I reached over and gave her a big kiss. She smiled back at me, clearly satisfied with herself.

As luck would have it, later that day I was given a reprieve and was allowed to go home. I would have run out of the building stark naked if I could. I was so tired of hospitals.

Two days later, the doorbell rang. A familiar, bespectacled, gray-haired man stood at my door. I tried hard to suppress a smile, but I couldn't.

"Please, Dr. Holloway, please come in. This is my wife, Cecilia," I said excitedly.

Cecilia shook his hand, then glanced oddly at me as she invited him into the living room. Undoubtably, she found my excitement disconcerting.

"Please call me Peter," he replied. "I hate formal titles."

"Would you like some coffee?" Cecilia asked.

"Water would be fine. Thank you."

Both Sarah and Amelia sat on the stairs, staring in silence at the older man, clueless about his role in my life.

"I guess you know why we reached out to you," I began.

Cecilia interrupted me. "Actually, before we start, how do you two know each other?"

Suddenly it was very quiet in the room. Peter and I looked at each other.

He then turned his gaze toward Cecilia.

"It's a long story, and it would be best if we all sat down. Cecilia, there are some things I need to show you. I have to caution you that some of it will be difficult to understand, or more precisely, accept. Based on my discussions with Mark, I imagine he has been trying to explain something to you, correct?"

"Are you both serious about this?" Cecilia asked in a mildly irritated tone, "After the events of the past few days, I don't know what to think. But I would like to get a straight answer."

We sat down in the living room. Peter reached down to his briefcase and pulled out a laptop and a thick folder. While his laptop turned on, he opened the folder and pulled out a large color print that brought back memories. It showed a platform, and a sizable chunk of the floorspace was occupied by a large shark. Cecilia picked up the print and gazed at it seriously. I watched her keenly as she studied its contents.

Dr. Holloway was sitting next to the shark, apparently chatting. Josh's mechanical translator was barely visible. I knew it was me in there, but Cecilia did not.

"Is this the shark that attacked my husband?" Cecilia asked.

"Yes, it is," Peter replied cautiously.

"Why would I want to see this?" Cecilia said with some hostility.

I motioned at the picture. "Cecilia, look at what's written on the display."

In front of the shark was a large flatscreen display, and on it were lines of text. Despite having extracted the image from a video feed, the text was easy to read. It began: *My name is Mark Forster. I was born on...*

"Mark, why is your name on the display?" Cecilia asked, her head tilted, clearly bewildered by the contents of the image.

"I was having a conversation with Peter aboard the *Relentless*, about eighteen months after the attack," I explained.

"How?", she uttered incoherently.

"That's me talking to Peter, in that image," I said to her. Peter looked on.

She placed the photograph on the coffee table and put her hands over her mouth. She began gasping for air.

"Before I have a mental breakdown, can one of you please explain everything? I am literally at the end of my rope," Cecilia stated bluntly. She began to sob.

I reached for her hand and held it tightly. Peter was watching both of us intently. This was clearly not quite how he'd intended this to play out.

"Cecilia," I said, "It is imperative that you listen to us for the next thirty minutes or hour that it takes to explain everything. That's all I ask of you. Try to keep an open mind."

She shook her head and wiped her nose.

"Before we start, I need get something," she said, and stepped out of the room. I heard glasses clinking and a bottle being pulled from the liquor cabinet.

When Cecilia returned, she said, "I need a whiskey. How about the two of you?"

Peter and I both nodded. The large bottle of whiskey landed with a hard thud on the coffee table. When Cecilia was angry, everyone knew it. After quickly downing a glassful of the caramel-colored liquor, she appeared to settle down and sat quietly.

Peter watched Cecilia thoughtfully, then took a deep breath. "Look, I've had a sterling career as a marine biologist, much of it based on a lot of hard work and an unrelenting amount of data and God knows how many papers. What I am about to tell you could probably ruin me, if it ever became public. At minimum, it would result in significant embarrassment. And it would put you, Mark, in the media spotlight."

"How so?" Cecilia asked.

"Can we, at the very least, make an agreement between us that nothing leaves this room."

Cecilia nodded.

"A year ago, my assistant Lucy and her team were off the island of Guadalupe, studying and tagging great white sharks.

It's something we do annually to measure the local population of great whites and to better understand seasonal migratory patterns."

Peter stopped to take a sip of his water. "Two cages were down, and Lucy was alone in one of them. On any given day, we typically see between five to ten sharks. The team captures images of the sharks and then catalogs them according to their unique characteristics. In the afternoon, a large female great white approached Lucy. The shark made several passes of her cage. It didn't attack or rush the cage when bait was thrown at it. The shark exhibited curiosity. None of this is highly unusual behavior. We see this in older, more mature sharks."

"This great white approached her and started clenching its jaws on the cage. It repeated this activity several times. We even documented it on video. It didn't dawn on Lucy right away, but this individual was trying to communicate with her."

Peter paused for a moment to catch his breath. Cecilia patiently waited for him to resume. Peter was about to present the great reveal, but he was taking his time.

"Look, the reason I am being careful is that I don't want to add to the trauma that you and your family have already endured."

Cecilia was focused on Peter, hanging on every word coming from him.

"There was a person communicating through this shark. And it was Mark."

Cecilia looked at me in horror.

"What do you mean, it was Mark?" she asked anxiously.

"The shark communicated with Lucy by grating its teeth along the cage bars, using Morse code. It said, and I repeat, 'My name is Mark' several times."

There was an awful silence for several seconds.

Then Cecilia asked, "Even if this was true, how is it possible?"

"I do not have any answers. All I know is that the Mark who was speaking with us wanted desperately to find out why he found himself inside an apex predator after getting attacked off the island of Lanai."

"Are we talking about the same Mark?" Cecilia asked.

"He said he had two girls, and a wife named Cecilia. At this point I had not met the Mark-shark. I was in San Diego at the time. Lucy took the initiative and asked Mark to meet us in Maui, so I could meet him there."

A faint crease appeared on my wife's brows. The pained expression on her features gave me that look of: *Is this guy for real?*

"I know this sounds beyond the pale. But I actually have hard evidence. It's something else when the facts stare you in the face." Peter pulled out his laptop and searched for a video file. Once he found it, he played the video back to us. It showed a large shark parked on a platform, in the ocean off some coastline. Peter sat right next to the shark in knee-deep water, a large screen in front of them. I recognized the scene immediately.

Peter raised the volume so we could hear the conversation between the crew, and see the data being typed on the large display.

"The crew built a clever little gadget they could place in the jaws of the shark so that Mark could communicate in Morse. It worked well for a while. We learned a lot. We also have the full transcript, if you're interested," he explained.

"I would like to read it," Cecilia said.

Peter reached into the folder and extracted a bound report.

Cecilia took the transcript and walked out to the patio to read it. Peter and I sat quietly and drank our whiskeys. After a few minutes, Cecilia came back into the room and sat down.

"So, if I am reading this transcript right, in the discussion you and Mark are discussing entanglement. That somehow during the attack and Marco's collision, Mark became entangled with the shark," she said, shaking her head in disbelief. "What is entanglement, Mark?"

"In quantum physics, there is a theory that particles can interact with one another over great distances. Sometimes it's called 'action at a distance.' When we measure one particle, we get comprehensive information about its paired or entangled particle, regardless of their spatial separation. In the transcript, Peter theorizes that during Marco's collision with the shark and the subsequent ignition of the lithium batteries, my mind and that of the shark got somehow 'entangled'. Essentially, I lived through the shark while in a coma thousands of miles away."

Burying her face in her palms, Cecilia struggled to accept the implications of our discussion. There was no getting around the core tenets of my transition and its subsequent effect on our lives. But like a resilient firewall, Cecilia's mind was only letting a little of the fantastic in at a time. No one could blame her. The entire scientific establishment would be up in arms over this. The universe was teaching us a valuable lesson in hubris and humility.

"You know Cecilia," Peter said, "when Lucy explained to me Mark's situation for the first time, and even with all the physical proof presented, I also found it impossible to believe. It takes a little while to adjust to a shifting reality. Speaking to Mark the first time in person broke that last wall of doubt."

Cecilia nodded while looking down at her whiskey glass.

"Peter," I said, "a few months ago, a fellow diver from the trip came to visit me. Her name is Janet. She described the attack in more detail than anyone else. She was quite close to it, the shark apparently passed right by her. Janet stated that there was a bright flash when the scooter struck the shark. That both the shark and I sank to the seafloor following this event."

"In the police report there was mention of lithium batteries combusting from the collision," Peter remarked, clearly surprised at the new information. "I didn't know that both shark and victim sank after that. The formal accident report only mentions that the shark released the victim following the collision."

I looked over at Cecilia. "How are you doing so far?".

"I'm processing. So, if I am to believe both of you, and all this data and video—which I am not promising—I have a lot of work to do to keep my world from crashing."

"There's more," I said.

She raised her eyebrows. "More?"

"But it can wait," I added.

"So, what do we do?" she asked Peter.

"Nothing," he replied. "Any release of this material would be catastrophic for my career, and the press would hound you. There is no happy ending."

He went on, "We named the shark that Mark inhabited, or rather controlled, Marci. To monitor her whereabouts, we fitted her with a tag."

I'd almost forgotten: the shark was female. Yet another concept for Cecilia to absorb and process, but one that had the least effect on me. Cecilia leaned towards me. "Pity, if I wasn't so upset by all this, I would tease you till your days end."

I lifted my whiskey glass to her.

"There's something else, Peter," I said. "Something from the seizure."

Peter looked up from his glass.

"They showed me a video of my seizure in the hospital. Apparently, I behaved like a wild animal. Makes me wonder if this time around Marci woke up in my body, briefly, at UCSF. As if Marci and I swapped places."

"You have me grabbing at straws here, Mark. But who says that connection should only be one-way? Did you get a sense where Marci was, during that spell?" he asked before getting up.

"Sydney. I recognized the harbor. I even heard voices of people walking along the promenade," I replied.

Cecilia perked up at this admission. Peter looked at an app on his phone and thumbed through some data.

"Marci is currently fifty miles northeast of Sydney, just a few miles offshore from Newcastle, so it fits," he said matter-of-factly.

I'd experienced mind projection, finding myself, my consciousness, six thousand miles away in an instant—and yet I couldn't tell a living soul.

"She's sightseeing," Peter said as he walked to the front door. He looked at Cecilia. "Cecilia, I cannot fathom how this must be for you and your family. Mark, your family needs time to absorb and process this. There's no point in going into further detail. Baby steps, remember?"

Cecilia nodded in agreement.

"I have to catch my flight," Peter went on, "but if you have any questions Cecilia, any at all, please feel free to send them my way."

He held Cecilia's hand. Surprisingly, she gave him a hug. This was a lot for her to take in. As awful as it was to hear, I'm glad she knew the truth.

"Before you go Peter," I asked, "Were there any other anomalies, evidence of odd marine behavior?"

"Now that you mention it, about five months ago an American submarine had to limp back to Guam. Somehow its tow array got shredded. The going theory was that it got tangled on something."

I laughed.

Peter cocked his head. "Would you know anything about that?"

"Apparently, Marci is not taking sides," I quipped, recalling my adventure with the Russian sub.

"Learned behavior?" Peter asked.

"Possibly. But I don't know how."

"Do you recall the orcas off Gibraltar?" Peter asked, his eyebrows furrowed. He was referring to a recent observation of a particular pod of orcas that took to chasing sailboats and destroying their rudders.

"Yes, I do. Should we be concerned?"

Peter shrugged his shoulders. He opened the door behind him.

"Take care, Mark," Peter said. He shook my hand, then he was gone. I shut the door behind him.

Cecilia sat down on the sofa and closed her eyes.

"Mark, this is so insane. I'm finding it so hard to accept," she said in a raised voice.

"I know this is way out there. But what of the evidence, the data? And the fact that I had a seizure?"

"This is madness, and what if you have another seizure? Haven't we been through enough already, Mark?"

Cecilia walked out of the living room into the unlit yard. I could see her standing in the darkness, looking up at the moon, trying to comprehend the impossible. I wondered if she was reaching her limit with all this, with me.

"Can we talk about it?" I asked.

Cecilia shook her head in disbelief. "I don't know if I can handle any more of this. I'm exhausted worrying about you. It's bad enough that I sat at your bedside for two years. I feel this immense weight on my chest, and I'm suffocating."

I desperately wanted to console her, but I couldn't think of what to say or do. We sat quietly on the patio chairs for what felt like an hour. I could hear her breathing deeply as she tried to get her emotions under control. Finally, she got up from the chair and began pacing the backyard slowly. At one point she stopped and stood by our hedge, staring into the foliage. Apparently, tired of brooding, she walked toward me and sat down again.

"So, what was it like?" she asked quietly. She displayed surprising calmness given what had been revealed to her earlier this evening.

"Short version or long version?"

"You decide."

"Terrifying, exhilarating, wondrous, mysterious, but most of all, lonely," I said, using as few words as possible.

"What was a typical day for you—can you describe it?" Cecilia asked.

I considered her question. The answer was elusive.

"Every day was different, but ninety-five percent of the time it was uneventful. Life beneath the waves is surprisingly quiet, tranquil, like a desert in most places," I explained.

"And the other five percent?" she asked.

"Let's just say that there are parts of the ocean I would rather not revisit," I replied with a grin.

"You would think that surviving a shark attack would be enough. If everything you said tonight was true, then you must have experienced something extraordinary."

I started describing some of the highlights, or rather, the challenging situations that I'd found myself during my passage: the fishing boat fiasco, surviving the shark cafe, the orcas chasing me into deep-sea grotto, the whales, and many more. Cecilia looked particularly captivated, her eyes wide like a child, when I went into details of my close calls. Sometimes my storytelling got the better of me. There was much to tell, and most of it sounded ludicrous. I promised her I would write my adventures down while they were fresh. There was, however, one other thing I wanted to share with her.

"Cecilia, those first days on the beach after the attack. Do you recall them?" I asked carefully.

"I try not to—they're painful memories. Why do you ask?"

"You may find this hard to believe, on top of everything else you heard tonight, but I was there. I saw you from the water."

"How? Didn't anyone see you?" she asked incredulously.

"No one did. I was about fifty yards offshore. For a while, I hoped it was all a bad dream. I watched you and the girls sit on that beach for nearly an hour before the police arrived."

Cecilia looked down at the floor, presumably attempting to piece together the bits and pieces of the story. It was all too fantastic and horrifying to take in at one sitting. She sighed.

"I thought I'd died when I woke up inside her," I said. "Then to find out I was still living, my body thousands of miles away. It was a lot to take in, but I saw an opportunity when Peter said I was still alive."

Cecilia sat quietly, deep in thought. I leaned back in my chair and surveyed the dark sky above me. Despite the city lights, I was still able to spot the constellation Orion and the Pleiades cluster. My navigation skills were still fresh.

I wondered where in the world Molly was. *Still prowling the depths between Guadalupe and Hawaii?* I wondered.

From her change in posture, I sensed something stirring in Cecilia.

"Mark, it helped to hear your side of the story, regardless of how crazy and fantastic it sounds. Your telling of it, and Peter's corroboration, and the pictures. I get it. It's too much to deny, and yet still very hard to accept. I need space to process all of this and put it behind me—behind *us*, hopefully. But from what I heard tonight, we're not out of the woods yet. My understanding is that you are still somehow connected to Marci, right?"

"If you're asking me whether this will ever go away, honestly, I can't give you an answer right now. I don't know." I said, knowing full well this was not the answer she had hoped for.

"You know, the irony of all this," I went on, "is that had Marci died in the ocean early on, I might have awakened much sooner. I spent the entire time fighting to survive, learning to survive." I stifled a chuckle as I remembered the ship's captain, who fired multiple shots in my direction.

Cecilia rubbed her nose and wiped her eyes. She nodded and said, "We need to get you an emergency bracelet."

Closure

There it was again. Upon exiting the car, I touched the rooftop and received a mild shock. In itself, it was nothing to write home about. Unlike the surge of electricity I'd experienced in the shower, this shock did not propagate up my arm and it didn't send my mind halfway across the Pacific. It was the side effect of the shock that concerned me. It instilled fear in me. Since my episode in the shower, I had been very careful about touching any object or device that had the capability to discharge electricity, however weak. These lesser shocks were still a concern, though not to my immediate health.

In light of this, Cecilia was making me wear a sensor around my neck to notify medical staff and her of an impending seizure. Who was to say what would happen the next time? I was sure Marci would rather not find herself in a hospital ward again. One look at humanity up close was probably enough, though I doubted her instinctually driven mind could make heads or tails of what she saw.

"Are you OK, Dad?" Sarah asked, cocking her head.

"Yeah, I'm alright. It happened again," I replied, embarrassed.

"You want to go home?"

"Nah, we're here now. I'll be fine."

The windows of the old technology museum were opaque from years of dust accumulation and sun. Cecilia had told me the place was shuttered a year after we last visited. Over the years, the museum had relied on public fundraising to survive, but it was never solvent. Its closure left a swell in my throat. Sarah and I peered through the windows to see if the old relics we were so fond of were still on display.

Sarah and I walked around the building, searching for a better vantage point to view the interior.

"Look, Dad," Sarah said, pointing to an object on the other side of the window. "Over by the door on the left. The old dish we used to send messages to each other."

I peered through the glass and there it was, a grayish-white dish standing near the door to the main exhibit hall. Even from this far away, I could see cobwebs on it. Behind it loomed the dark silhouette of the Caravelle. The urge to break into the now defunct museum and have a closer look was gnawing at me. The place was closed—what could happen? I was doubtful any alarm systems were still active. The entire museum appeared abandoned.

"Do you remember whispering to each other across the room?" I chuckled at the memory, then gazed at Sarah, noting how much she had grown since then. That had been, what, two years ago? Sarah had grown into a young woman in my absence. It was startling to take note of the changes. Her childlike round face had grown slender, more defined. Her hair was also longer and fuller. She was a better version of me, in all respects. I suppose I should have felt pride, a father's pride. Cecilia had done an outstanding job raising her. Instead, I experienced waves of regret for that lost time.

I recalled the argument I had had with Cecilia the day before my fateful dive. How a single poor decision can change the course of your life. Still, I guessed I shouldn't complain. I could be dead. Months of physical therapy had brought me out of the confines of the hospital ward and back to the real world. I still found it hard to accept the reality of what had happened, even though I was reminded daily of my injuries: I still walked with a slight limp and my back was continually sore. The scars itched as well. *But who's complaining?*

The phone in my pocket buzzed. I took it out to see an e-mail from Dr. Holloway. I hadn't heard from him for some time. After reading the e-mail, I sat down to read it again.

"What's up, Dad? Who is it from?" Sarah asked.

I looked up. "It's Dr. Holloway." I shook my head in surprise.

"What does he say?"

I read out, "'Dear Mark, I hope this message finds you well. It's been some time since we last spoke, but I wanted to tell you about something that happened recently that might interest you. We have been tracking Marci on and off, and she popped up in northern Australia, this time near the barrier reef. There was an incident...'"

I paused and looked up at Sarah. She raised her shoulders in a gesture meaning, *And?*

I continued reading. "'Near the town of Agnes Water, a surfer was knocked off his board by what appeared to be a large, possibly thirteen-foot great white shark. The shark circled the surfer several times and then charged the victim, only to be blocked by another, even larger great white. This larger shark repeatedly chased the former one until it broke off its attack. Fortunately, the surfer survived unscathed. A local operating a drone recorded the event. We were able to identify the transponder signal in the immediate vicinity and determine that it was Marci that came to the surfer's aid. I later interviewed the surfer, who described the details of the event and could recall some of the physical scarring on the larger shark, and its sex. This further validates the notion that it was indeed Marci.'"

I sat dumbfounded, absorbing the story. Since my seizure I have often thought of Marci, wondering where she was in the world and what she was she up to. Apparently, she was still hanging out near Australia. As far as I knew, no white shark has ever been documented crossing the Pacific in its entirety. There are multiple groups of these animals around the world, and only one agreed upon species, so at least a few sharks must have made the journey. A single white shark was documented crossing the vast expanse of ocean between South Africa and western Australia twice, covering nearly thirteen thousand miles. One day, a scientist will get lucky and tag the shark that does it.

Could it be that the storm and the lightning strikes had confused Marci? Perhaps throwing her off course. Several months ago, I was getting a brief unplanned tour of Sydney harbor through Marci's eyes, undeniably proving to Peter and myself that she made the crossing, and now she was headed back to the islands, apparently without difficulty. It elicited a chuckle out of me that I might have inadvertently expanded the range of the great white shark.

Within the comfort and safety of my own home, it was easy to reflect on the time I spent with Marci. I had grown fond of that period, nostalgic even. Somehow my mind had managed to subdue the more traumatic experiences. At the same time, I was very pleased to be home with the girls. I so looked forward to getting up in the morning and spending the day with them. Despite the real risk of suddenly finding myself in the middle of the ocean, with each passing day I worried less about it.

During my time in the Pacific, I thought I learned everything about my host. There was a certain predictability in her behavior. But she did surprise me from time to time. It made me wonder sometimes if Marci was adapting to some of my own behavior. When I woke during our transit across the Pacific, Marci rarely veered off course.

She didn't always follow my lead, as exhibited by her hunting and consumption of seals, something I personally refused to do. It was almost as if she was selectively accepting some aspects of my behavior, for example, protecting people from attack or the shredding of underwater cables. This behavior runs so counter to what anyone thinks about regarding sharks.

"Dad," Sarah asked, "Are they talking about your Marci?"

I nodded. "Yeah. Peter and his team are still tracking her."

"Did he say anything else?"

I glanced at my phone. There was a second message after the first one. I read it aloud.

"'Marci is heading due northeast and should, if she holds her present course, make landfall at the Hawaiian Islands in two months' time. If she does indeed approach the islands, there is the possibility of making contact. Would you be interested? We can update you on her progress.'"

My heart jumped. I could feel my pulse quicken. Sarah sat down next to me and read the message off the screen, in part to convince herself this was real.

Getting Cecilia to go along was going to take some convincing on my part. Since our meeting with Peter, Cecilia rarely broached the topic with me about my time *away*. There was never any real closure. My feeling was Cecilia purposefully buried the past to avoid reliving painful memories.

Sarah nudged me and said, "I know you want to do this, but you're worried about Mom."

I nodded. I stared out into space and thought about the implications, and the possibilities.

Even though I had been a part of her for nearly two years, I had always wanted to see Marci from the outside, to view the vessel that had ensnared my mind and fooled me into thinking that I had died and been reborn. I had begun writing down my memories of my time away. A few of those memories were so frightening in their scope that I scarcely attempted to replay them in my head. Over time, I developed a fondness for those experiences and wrote them down. Writing was therapy. Gradually, the number of pages grew and eventually a stack of papers appeared on my desk, a clear reminder of how much I had experienced.

Cecilia had tried reading a few snippets of my writings, to help her understand what happened to me. She was still angry at the world for allowing it to happen. The experience had aged her. Sometimes, though, she would come to me with a page and ask for a more detailed account. Her favorite story by far was the ship on the seamount. She was so enamored by it that it became an independent story all its own. As she explained it, there was something mysterious and adventurous about it. Somehow, she was able to disconnect it from the bigger story. She even began to draw scenes from the text, as a way to express her vision of the story. The giant grouper was spot on.

Sarah and I returned home an hour later. Cecilia was trimming shrubs in the backyard. Spring had arrived, and the detritus of winter needed dealing with. She had her hair tied up in a ponytail and was wearing my oversized work gloves that were covered in topsoil. Her knees were green from squatting in the soil and grass. She looked up and smiled at us. Amelia came around the corner in her own version of a landscaper's outfit, wearing profusely muddied denim overalls and my wife's rubber gloves, and carrying a large, lethal-looking trimmer. I debated taking Cecilia aside and telling her about Peter's offer but thought better of it and decided to wait until the girls had gone to sleep. In the meantime, I reached over and plucked the evil-looking trimmer from Amelia's hand.

After a few hours in the yard, we cleaned up and began making dinner. It was early evening but still quite warm, so we improvised and started the grill. The patio was now clean, and the outdoor furniture had come out of hibernation.

We were all standing around the kitchen island when Sarah

blurted out while chewing on a carrot, "Dad got an interesting message from Dr. Holloway."

Startled, I twisted my face angrily at her for telling Cecilia before I could explain.

"What did he have to say?" Cecilia asked.

I turned toward her. "It's true—I received a message from Peter while we were at the museum. I had hoped to talk to you about that after the girls had gone to sleep. Anyway, Peter mentioned that Marci, *that* Marci, showed up on their radar in Australia."

Cecilia wondered what all the fuss was about. "Is that all it was? An update?"

"Not quite," I replied. "Apparently, a great white shark attacked a surfer, and for reasons unknown, Marci suddenly showed up and chased the other shark away." I watched Cecilia digest this news, and added, "The surfer was not harmed."

Sarah was beaming from cheek to cheek.

Cecilia retorted, "Why are you all smiles, young lady?"

I gazed at Sarah and, with a small hand motion, invited her to explain the rest.

"Marci is heading back to the Hawaiian Islands," she said, "and Dr Holloway wanted to invite us on their research boat."

"Vessel," my wife corrected her. Then she yelled at me, "You gotta be fucking kidding me, Mark! After all we went through, that *you* went through! How can you even consider this?"

Her eyes focused on me in anger even as she kicked the molding on the kitchen island and yelped in pain.

She continued, "Every morning I wake up and see those scars on your back, reminding me how close we came to losing you!"

I tried consoling her, but she was not having any of it.

"I thought you were okay with it all, after all this time," I said. "That we had healed."

"Did you really think I was healed after your attack, on top of you being in a coma for nearly two years?" she yelled.

"I'm so sorry. I thought we were past that."

"You thought wrong," she countered with hostility. "You are such an ass sometimes, Mark."

She pushed me away with outstretched arms. I could see the girls' surprise at their mother's response.

Deep down, I understood her. I could drop it all and forget the whole damn thing. Bury it. But another voice deep inside me wouldn't back down. I waited patiently for Cecilia to calm down. When she suddenly left the kitchen and slammed the bedroom door, I looked at Sarah and gave her a *Thanks, kiddo* look. Her wide smile left the building. I explained to the girls that this was a painful subject for their mother. Adults had a way of complicating things, I explained, but there was no simplifying this.

I asked the girls to finish their homework and go to bed. As I cleaned up the kitchen, I pondered what to do. It would take Marci two months to reach the islands from her current location. There was still time to build a consensus with my wife and get her support. I hoped there was, anyway.

Carefully, I opened the bedroom door after knocking softly to let Cecilia know I was coming in. She lay on her side, facing away from me. Her neck and shoulders were still tense.

I laid down next to her and said sincerely, "I'm so sorry for dropping this on you. I didn't intend to upset you. You're probably wondering why in the world I would want to meet the beast that nearly killed me. I never blamed the shark for doing what comes naturally to it. An instinctual animal has no moral compass. But she changed because of me. I may never get this opportunity again."

I lay my hand gently on her right shoulder, noting the tension in her muscles.

"Look," I went on, "this family means the world to me. Sarah certainly did not intend to upset you. I'll drop it all. I mean it. Just say the word."

Cecilia lay there quietly, though I knew she was listening. I listened to her breathing.

"Honey, I'll send a reply tomorrow and let them deal with it on their own. As far as we are concerned, we're done," I said.

Cecilia turned and looked at me, pressing her face into her pillow, her expression tight with emotion. Eventually her features softened a little, making me wonder if the storm inside her was subsiding. My sense now was that she wanted some kind of closure.

"Don't reply yet, or just let them know you will think about it. I need some time to digest this," she said.

I nodded in agreement. Seeing how this had affected Cecilia had dampened my eagerness.

For a month, we didn't talk at all about Peter, Marci, or the planned boat meeting. I deliberately avoided bringing up the subject. We had never broached the truth about Marci and me to our daughters. To them, I was simply the victim of a shark attack, and Marci was simply a shark we'd tracked with Peter's help.

Quietly, I followed Marci's progress on my own, watching her daily movements on software Peter had supplied me. Sometimes the updates would stop, indicating Marci had gone deep. After several days, she would ascend and break the surface, long enough for the satellites to register her position. The data returned in those instances often revealed tours of the deep. Having once seen the ocean through Marci's eyes, I often spent hours imagining what she was experiencing.

One afternoon, I was sitting in a cafe opposite Cecilia, drinking my coffee and going over some emails Ben had sent me earlier in the day. While I was not technically working, it helped to keep myself abreast of goings-on in the company. I had also promised Ben to make myself available for chats, which I enjoyed. Mostly, though, I spent my days with Cecilia and the girls.

While reading the contents of one of Ben's emails, I heard frantic scribbling coming from Cecilia's side of the table. Looking up, I saw she was sketching a scene on the back of a paper mat. She drew a humorous scene of a man—I assumed it was me—together with a rather bloated shark. The man was apparently *at the controls* inside the shark.

"Fuck it," she said. "Let's do it. I am so tired of looking at all the long faces around the dinner table."

"Are you sure? Cecilia," I asked.

"This family will be the death of me," she said with a hint of frustration. "You are all mad."

I was relieved she finally accepted my wish, but I also acknowledged her pain. We both needed closure to move forward. My feeling was Cecilia wanted to come to terms with the reality of what happened, to confront her fears about meeting Marci and, to some extent, to forgive her. I needed to move on from the trauma, to focus on my family.

Peter kept me regularly updated on Marci's progress, and she was indeed heading for the islands. From the looks of her satellite tracks, she was quite good at navigating. Most shark tracks are all over the place. She actually arrived a few days early and was making steady loops around Maui, almost as if she was waiting.

Our flight arrived in the early morning. One of the ship's crew, Daniel, was there to pick us up. I remembered him from my first meetings with Lucy and Peter. We packed our gear into the Jeep and headed out to Maalaea Harbor. As we pulled into the harbor parking lot, I instantly recognized the profile of the *Relentless*, though it was odd to see the vessel from land.

The ship also appeared larger than how I remembered it. I recognized some of the personnel onboard and waved to them, though they looked confused, as if wondering who I was. Cecilia walked slowly up to the ship. She reached out and touched the hull. The girls greeted Peter, who was walking down the ramp toward us.

"It's so weird to see that ship again," I muttered to myself.

Cecilia turned to look at me. "Did you say something?".

"Nothing important," I replied.

"Good to see both of you again. How was your flight?" Peter asked calmly.

We both nodded to him. "It was fine," I replied.

Peter took Cecilia's hand. "I can't imagine how difficult it was for you to make this decision."

Cecilia replied graciously, "I'm okay. The last year hasn't been easy, with his recovery, and, well, my own. I'm still coming to terms with it."

Peter smiled at Cecilia. "You know, this experience has tested all of us. And still, we can't talk about it in public. This is just between us. But I hope it brings some closure."

Cecilia looked out to sea. "So is Marci here?"

"Yes, she is. She arrived a few days ago and has been running circuits of the island. From the last ping we could see, she was north of the island. We will set sail shortly and make our way to the northwest coast. Let's see if she remembers the boat."

As we came onboard, I recognized the young woman who first made contact with me off Maui. Lucy was leaning back on the gunwale, chatting with a deckhand. I wondered how the shark's vision had affected my memories. Shark's eyes are different from humans: colors are suppressed, the distortion of the optical field more pronounced. Faces look different.

Lucy turned to face me. "Nice to meet you again," she said with a smile. I immediately recognized her voice.

"Yes," I replied with a cheeky grin. We gave each other a big hug.

It took me a second to recognize Josh, who had grown a beard since I last saw him. Looking closely, I saw a small tattoo of a shark near his ankle. Lucy and a few of the others had the same tattoo. Bonded by the memory, it seemed.

"How have you been?" Lucy asked.

"On the whole, I'm doing well," I replied. "I'm nearly recovered. And you?"

"I'm good. Peter has kept us busy. Are you ready to meet Marci?" she asked.

"I don't know. I'm both excited and a little nervous about meeting her," I replied. "Not sure if I'm ready."

Lucy said. "You'll be fine."

"You know, Lucy, I will forever be in your debt for making that connection. I'm not sure what would have happened had I never met either you or Peter when I did."

"That day is permanently engraved in my memory."

Cecilia approached us. "Hi, my name is Cecilia."

"I'm so sorry," I said. "Lucy, this is my wife, Cecilia. And those two rambunctious ladies up by the bridge are our daughters, Sarah and Amelia."

"Lovely to meet you all." Lucy shook Cecilia's hand and then patted her on the shoulder. She waved toward the girls, who smiled back. "This is so exciting!" she called out.

Josh came up from the lower deck with an odd instrument in his hands. It took me a few seconds to recognize the communicator, the tool that was instrumental in getting our communication underway.

"Hey Mark, remember this little gadget?" Josh said as he placed the device in my hands.

"So this was it, the upgraded lab jack?" I asked.

Josh nodded. "This is actually a copy of the original I made on Guadalupe. I didn't get any sleep that night," he added, and laughed.

He then lifted another, larger version and placed it in my hands. "This unit is the one you actually used on Maui, to communicate with us."

I turned the communicator in my hands. With this tool, we created an extraordinary moment in history. The rubber pads had deep teeth marks in them, but it was a robust piece of hardware. I recalled biting into it. The metal hinges were reinforced with carbon steel and the bolts were as thick as my thumb.

"I'm simply overwhelmed by all this," I said emotionally. Of all the memories I had, the boat rendezvous at Maui stood out as the sharpest.

Cecilia leaned into me, sensing my reaction. The kindness, gratitude, and support of these young people was so touching.

The rumble of the large engines of the *R/V Relentless* filled the air. Deckhands and members of the research crew ran up and down the ship, releasing the ropes and pushing the vessel from the dock. Soon we were making ten knots on the open sea. Cecilia and I sat up front, beneath the bridge, and watched the western coast of the island pass by. The seas around the islands were usually calm in the early mornings, and today was no exception. We were about a mile offshore and the captain maintained this course the entire way. Sarah and Amelia sat together in front of us, watching the ship's bow rise and fall as we pushed through the surf.

After a few hours, I heard the engines idling. It was all so familiar. I recalled the sound of the engines underwater when I approached from the sea, years ago.

The ship lurched a little as it slowed. The crane lifted the platform from the rear deck and then lowered it off the starboard side of the ship, coming to rest a few feet underwater. Deckhands were milling about, preparing for Marci's entrance.

Peter stepped down from the bridge. "We don't know what she will do," he told us. "With other sharks, we have to tease them with bait on a line. I'm willing to bet we don't have to, but let's see."

"You are quite the optimist, Peter," I said. "It's not me in there anymore."

He grinned. "Maybe someone else is," he said.

"You know, Peter," I said, "We never asked ourselves the question of why she's returning here, specifically, at this point in time? Why Maui, of all places?"

Peter shrugged his shoulders. "Let's see if we get some answers to our questions today."

There was no precedence for any of this. I shook my head in disbelief at the idea that Marci had become something more than an instinctual beast. I looked back at Cecilia, who was now hanging over the railing alongside our daughters. Everything was so calm. We could just hang for a while, enjoy the scenery. Maybe even catch the sunset and then go home.

Suddenly I felt nervous. Some oncoming anxiety was digging deep into me. I looked over to Peter and asked, "ETA?"

"Josh and Cathy are bringing out the antenna array. This should give a better fix on her position," he replied. "The battery has lost a lot of its original charge, so it's a small miracle we can pick her up at all. Satellites have gotten better over the years at picking up signals from noise."

Cecilia approached us and asked Peter directly, "You said earlier we can never really talk about this in public."

He paused for a moment, then replied, "Yes, that's right. This entire experience is for us only. You can't publish a discovery based on a single data point or observation. It goes against the scientific process. There is another thing: we do not understand the mechanism at work here. Whatever we might publish would be highly speculative. There is also the public reaction to this kind of news. Sensationalism would make all our lives miserable."

I jumped into the conversation, "I'm no longer a part of Marci, so any data that was collected during our first meeting would probably be considered hearsay. There is no way to repeat it to the scientific audience. No validation."

Cecilia frowned, discouraged. She changed tactics. "What about Marci's behavior two months ago? Is that not worth investigating?"

Holloway replied, "I'd be dishonest if I didn't say that it showed something was up. But again, I would be speculating. If Marci has truly evolved, then we will make history in more ways than one. I'm also concerned how this will affect you, Mark."

"I'm already suffering from an existential crisis," I replied, grinning.

I asked Cecilia if she wanted some coffee. It would be some hours before Marci was in range of the ship. She nodded and followed me below deck. Beneath the bridge was a small ship's galley equipped with some basic amenities. While the compartment was clean, the coffee maker had clearly seen better days. Next to the dripper was a large, rusting, much overused Bunn machine. Cecilia peered into the fridge, where to her delight she found a few bottles of coke. She pulled two of them out and began searching for bottle openers.

"Are you sure we aren't stealing from the staff?" I asked.

She replied stoically, "Honey, we're the guests here, and you're the star attraction... well, after Marci, that is." She chuckled.

It was so good to hear her laugh. I leaned back against the wall and sipped my coke.

Peter showed up and said with a smile, "Please, take what you need. There is a pantry behind that door with lots of horrible junk food. Mi casa es su casa," he insisted.

Across from the galley was a small dining table. Peter

grabbed some chips and some coffee and joined us at the table.

Cecilia leaned back on the cushions as he began telling us about his youth.

"My father was a fisherman, you know. He was gone a lot but when he came home, he had these amazing stories. My brother and I would listen to him late into the evening. His imagination and, even more than that, his ability to spin a yarn was quite extraordinary. As boys, we ate it all up. God, I miss him."

I was about to speak when he interjected, "I was thirteen, I suppose, when we got the news that his trawler and crew had gone missing. It devastated my mother. Well, all of us."

I sat quietly and listened.

"My brother and I were forced to work down in the docks. We did whatever we could to keep the family solvent. For years, I didn't know how my future would pan out. My only requirement was that it would have something to do with the sea. I wanted to be close to my father. And so here I am."

He leaned forward. "Pardon me for asking, Mark. I don't mean to pry, but have you had more spells, or anything out of the ordinary?"

"None so far, after the big one I had a while back. But I do relive my time at sea often. I've been writing down my adventures, while they're fresh in my memory."

"I'd love to read them sometime, Mark," Peter said.

"I get nightmares from reading them," Cecilia said. "Goosebumps."

"How are you with all this?" Peter asked her.

Before she could reply, I interrupted her. "Cecilia worries a lot about me, about what this means for us in the long run."

"I am actually looking forward to meeting Marci. For me, this is closure," Cecilia stated emphatically, "I've been so angry with the universe for so long, and this will help me process. At least, that's what I hope will happen. I don't know what I would do if someone or something pulled Mark away again."

An absurd idea popped into my head, which made me grin. "You know, if we had some jumper cables, we could run a test."

Both Peter and Cecilia threw their chips at me.

Despite injections of caffeine and loads of sugar, both Cecilia and I managed to fall asleep in the dining lounge. The din of the crew running on the main deck woke me from my slumber. I gently shook Cecilia's shoulder to wake her.

"Looks like something is happening up on deck," I said. Cecilia looked upwards toward the noise.

Holloway came down the stairs. "She's here, about a mile out."

Suddenly my nerves were on edge, literally queasy at the thought that Marci was nearby. It hadn't dawned on me earlier this would affect me so intensely.

"Come, let's go up," Cecilia insisted.

I was about to go up top when Peter called me aside. I motioned to Cecilia to go up. Peter and I walked into one of the compartments below deck, and Peter closed the door behind him. He pulled a small plastic container from beneath a shelf, then turned and looked at me.

"Mark, I am, like you, fascinated with our little story here. It affects me deeply, both as a scientist and as a human being. But I also understand the immense risk you are taking. You are still connected to Marci. The danger to your health is always there."

I was a little startled by his tone. "What exactly is troubling you?" I asked.

"I would love to continue this relationship, even exploit it for my own selfish reasons. But this is your life. From what I can see, you have more or less recovered. Do we still need this worry over our heads?"

"What are you getting at?"

Peter opened the small box. Within it were two large syringes. I immediately recognized the skull and bones label. Seeing the box made me uneasy.

"Of my concerns, the greatest one is you having a relapse, at the most inopportune moment." Peter said.

"That's why I carry this little thing around my neck," I said while lifting the tag from under my shirt so he could see it.

"Yes, but it still requires someone to administer a heart massage," Peter said. "And a shock powerful enough to bring you back."

"Sure, I get it. But you said it yourself—the science is unknown. Breaking the connection could have consequences."

As Peter looked down at the small box, his brow furrowed. I could see that he was troubled. He tapped the box with his forefinger.

"When we take sharks onboard, we typically carry out blood tests. A needle is placed subcutaneously in the caudal fin and then connected to a delivery plug. You can place the syringe into this plug and the shark will first feel the effects of the drug about twenty minutes after injection. Look, I leave this decision to you. This syringe contains enough ketamine and another agent to put an elephant under. We use it sometimes to euthanize beached whales to ease their suffering. My guess, if we do this, then you'll be free of this connection to her."

"I'm not sure I want this, Peter," I said. The rationale behind his argument was clear, but my heart ached at the thought. I would be sending Marci to her doom. The world would lose something truly unique.

"Look, Peter, I get what you are trying to say, but I am also concerned about the unintended consequences. If the connection were suddenly broken, would there be repercussions? None of us can say with any certainty."

I suddenly felt winded from the conversation.

"Mark, I just wanted to give you the option. This is your life," Peter replied.

I sat down for several minutes to absorb the conversation. The idea of being free of Marci, free of the risk of reconnecting to her, was certainly compelling. My life could go on as before, and Cecilia could relax. But would it work as intended? Perhaps only in theory. The lack of certainty troubled me more than anything.

Oddly enough, I was also content at the idea of being connected to Marci, even if the risk existed of suddenly finding myself deep undersea somewhere in the world. Marci and I had shared an adventure together, spending nearly eighteen months crossing the deepest ocean on the planet, and meeting some unique characters along the way. In all of human existence, I had experienced something truly unique. It didn't matter anymore that she had once tried to make a meal of me.

I walked out of the compartment with heavy thoughts. As I came on deck, I had to shield my eyes from the brightness. As I looked around, I realized it was late afternoon. I looked down at my watch. It was four thirty, almost five hours after we left the harbor. I put the small box containing the syringes aside, walked out to the bow of the ship and looked out over the railing. The chop of the ocean had increased a little. Josh was scanning the horizon with binoculars. Our Sarah was doing the same with a smaller pair loaned to her.

"There she is! Got her. Starboard side, six hundred feet out," Josh hollered.

I scanned the area near the boat, but I still couldn't see Marci.

"There she is!" Sarah cried. "Look, Amelia, look straight there." She pointed off the starboard side of the ship, while handing over the binoculars.

The boat was a frenzy of activity. Both Josh and Lucy

hopped down the ladders to the platform that was swaying in the waves. As I scanned the foreground, I noticed a fin slicing through the water. I could not see the rest of her, but the tall dorsal fin was noteworthy in itself. A familiar, small yellow tracker was attached near the tip. Marci was making a beeline for the platform, just as Peter had predicted. They lowered the platform until it was several feet underwater.

Josh and Lucy waited at the side of the platform. Slowly, the massive bulk of the great white, the very shark whose form I had inhabited, swam onto the platform, with no coercion or bait. This was surprising, considering that I no longer inhabited the beast. If not me, then who?

From his expression, Peter was wondering the same thing. He turned and looked at me with strained eyes. I was feeling unwell from our earlier discussion, but also excited at seeing Marci. She moved her enormous form nimbly onto the platform, as if she was practiced in doing so. *Who do we have here?*

The platform brought Marci's true dimensions to light. She was massive. The smell of fish and saltwater permeated the air. On the platform, Marci made everyone look small. Her dorsal fin towered over everyone. Her tail stood at least five feet tall. She must have been eighteen, maybe nineteen feet in length. Her girth at her widest was close to seven or eight feet. Her width was somewhat exaggerated by the effects of refractive index in water. To think such a large predator had started as something much smaller and survived the gauntlet of threats in the oceans to reach this age—what, fifty or sixty years? Funny to think we were roughly the same age chronologically.

Cecilia was holding her hands over her mouth. I didn't think she had ever imagined that Marci was this large. I wondered what Cecilia was thinking. Was she feeling anger, fear, or hatred toward Marci?

Marci parked herself in the middle of the platform. The

compressors began lifting the platform ever so slowly until Marci was entirely out of the water. She was now pressed onto the platform, her belly spread out because of her weight. When the lifting was complete, Josh placed two hoses into her mouth, pumping fresh seawater through her gills. Her girth was astonishing.

I could no longer wait. I needed to see her up close. Cecilia followed me. Sarah and Amelia stared at Marci with gaping mouths.

I walked around Marci, studying her. Her skin shone iridescently in the sunshine, endless hues of gray and blue along her upper half. It was quite extraordinary. Up close, I saw that smaller, darker patches populated her entire length, like pigmentation in human skin. I recalled memories of being bitten by other male sharks on my right side. Sure enough, the scars were still there. Despite the violence of their creation, they had healed nicely. It was still difficult to reconcile that I had journeyed the breadth of the Pacific Ocean inside of her, *in control* of her. I missed it.

Bending down, I examined her jaws up close, studying the nearly perfect arrangement of triangular teeth. I couldn't help but think of all the teeth I'd lost while cutting through the sonar array. I envied the ability of birds to regenerate auditory hairs, and the shark's ability to heal and regrow a perfect set of teeth. Evolution has not always been kind to humans.

Josh and Lucy began making measurements. Another deckhand replaced the tracker with a new unit. Peter came over to me, staring at the beast in front of us. Marci's mouth was closed, but her eyes were surveying the scene. She was studying us. I crouched close to her face and stared into the black eyes. They were the size of saucers. The iris shone like a bright iridescent blue halo about a dark pupil. Those eyes looked right back at me, focusing on me. For a moment, it seemed as if I was looking back at myself. Perhaps it was some residual memory triggered by my reflection in her eyes. I placed my hand on her smooth skin.

Cecilia walked slowly over to Marci, her gaze full of apprehension. Neither of our daughters dared to come down the ladder. I had never seen them so quiet. Nothing quite beats seeing a large great white in the flesh and up close.

Cecilia kneeled down and placed her hands on Marci's skin. Then she placed her head right up against her. I watched her as she studied Marci. Her eyes widened, flickering between amazement and respect. To be in close company to such a massive animal is humbling.

Water spilling out from Marci's gills was redirected toward the many small holes in the base of the platform. Our clothing became wet from the splashes, but we didn't care. I took a deep breath, closed my eyes and touched her skin. I leaned against Marci for several minutes, soaking in her presence. *This might be the last time I see her*.

Lucy sat down by Marci's tail. I saw her place the needle deep into Marci's skin, near the front edge of the caudal fin. The skin was incredibly tough, and she had to use some force to penetrate the outer layer. With the needle fixed, she took several vials of blood, marking each one for analysis. Once she was finished, she rose and strolled back to the lab below the bridge.

Cecilia was still sitting next to Marci, captivated by her. Looking around, I saw the crew being momentarily distracted, and I used the moment to take out the small box Peter had given me. I stared at it for what seemed an eternity.

Cecilia asked, "Mark, what is that?"

I opened the box, revealing its contents. I looked around to see if anyone was looking.

"What are you doing?" she asked, raising her voice slightly.

"No fucking clue, Cecilia," I answered shakily. "I honestly don't know."

Anxiety built within me. My hands were shaking and sweaty. Cecilia moved closer to me and took my hands to steady them.

I raised my head and saw Marci's eyes looking directly back at me, focused on me. I wondered if she understood what was happening. Did she understand who I was?

"Are you sure about this, Mark?" Cecilia asked, but I wasn't really listening. I lifted the syringe in my hand and gazed at it. I knew Peter meant well, but in the end my conscience would have none of it.

"Yes, now I am," I responded with certainty.

I tossed the syringe back into the box and shut it. I looked back at Cecilia and took her hand. She leaned into me, trying her best to give me some comfort during this ordeal.

I was angry that Peter presented a choice to me, but I was also relieved that I could put a stop to it. I was still bound to Marci, albeit weakly. It didn't concern me I could end up inhabiting her again, and realistically the risk was low. Along with the few thousand great whites with which Marci shared the oceans, she had as much right to exist as I did.

I positioned myself against the wall of the platform as it was slowly lowered into the sea. Water flowed in from both ends of the platform, creating whirlpools on the surface. Cecilia watched me anxiously from the deck of the boat. Her eyes darted regularly at Marci, trying to anticipate her next move. Standing next to her, Sarah and Amelia stood quietly and stared. They probably thought I was barking mad. I thought of the surfer at Alice Waters, and Marci's behavior upon arrival. Did I have anything to fear? It would have been hypocritical of me to deny my unease.

Behind me, Lucy and Josh sat perched atop the barrier, watching for stray lines and other obstructions that could ruin a shark's day. With the platform fully submerged, I looked beneath the surface and could see Marci slowly lifting herself off the platform. I walked alongside her caudal fin and grabbed her tail. Despite being submerged, it felt incredibly heavy and rigid. The power of the creature was not lost on me. It was a power I had once been once intimately familiar with.

Resting my hand on her secondary dorsal fin, I gave her a gentle push and followed her to the edge of the platform. I quickly put on a mask, fins, and a weight belt Lucy had loaned me and plunged into the ocean. With a few, strong kicks I caught up to Marci and swam on the surface above her, the warmth of the sun on my back. Her relaxed pace made it manageable for me to follow her. I reached down and grabbed her dorsal fin and held on to it while she propelled us both near the surface. Watching her drive her tail rhythmically made me nostalgic. *In all that time, did I ever master the beast?* It seemed strange that I'd spent most of my time back then in abject fear of the unknown.

Soon her pace increased, and she began descending. I let go and stopped kicking. Floating idly on the surface, I sensed everyone's gazes on me from the boat. *Is this wise?* A cautious inner voice asked.

Marci continued to move away into the depths. I felt no urgency to return to the boat. She did not exude malevolence either before or after her time on the platform. I was no longer uneasy in her presence.

With barely a ripple on the surface, the crystal-clear and azure colored ocean resembled an infinite pool. I gazed into the depths and came across a shallow reef, some thirty feet below me. Taking a long breath, I tilted my body vertically and, using my weights and gravity, slowly descended to the reef. I leveled off at the bottom and stood upright on the rocky surface of a submerged lava tube. Beams of sunlight lit the seafloor, resulting in a brilliant dance of caustics. It was so peaceful to stand there and marvel at the rich tapestry of life around me.

To my right, a parade of jacks, snappers, and bannerfish swam serpentine along the rugged terrain. Scores of brilliantly colored anthias rose and fell in unison over their coral sanctuary. *I've missed this.*

A short distance away, I spotted a zebra moray eel exit its den. Its long, brown-banded tubelike body swam across the sandy bottom between the coral outcroppings in swift, deliberate strokes. An inner voice cautioned me to turn around, so I did, only to see gently rising terrain and schools of baitfish. Having been underwater for nearly two minutes, I was feeling the first pangs of carbon dioxide enrichment in my bloodstream. The silhouette of the *Relentless* approached slowly above me, its engines running in short pulses. I was about to kick upwards when I saw the telltale shape of a large fish emerging from the gloom and moving up the slope of the reef in my direction. Echoing my first encounter with Marci on Lanai, I found myself captivated. *It was just like this.* This time, however, I did not feel the need to recoil or flee. Despite the desire to ascend, I decided to wait and focused on relaxing. I figured I could hold on for another minute before ascending to the surface, as it was so close.

As my visitor approached, my vision began to experience intermittent blackouts, the scene in front of me would fade in and out, outside of my control. I was not sure if this was due to lack of oxygen or something else physiological, but it was odd. My hearing and other senses, however, were unaffected. My body responses were also getting sluggish. *I need to go up,* I reminded myself. It troubled me I could not stay longer, that my limitations were so egregious. I yearned for the time when I could leisurely hang out in the aquatic world without a care in the world.

My visitor was not far away. *Just a little longer,* I tried to convince myself. When my vision faded again, I raised my arms into the light current. A smooth, solid surface rubbed against my fingers. It seemed endless. I tried pushing my hand into it, but the surface did not yield. I might as well have touched a ship's hull. When my vision returned, I was taken aback to see myself standing on top of a reef, deep in the water. My initial thought was I was dreaming. I was watching myself from the outside. Small bubbles emerged from my snorkel and rose upward. My eyes had a glassy, unfocused look. *Am I drowning? Is Marci right in front of me?* It was so still and very strange to see myself this way. My vision faded.

When my vision returned, I found myself facing Marci. Her massive form filled my vision. Her outstretched pectorals made her appear like a dirigible from a bygone era. She was so close I probably could have touched her.

A hand reached out from behind and gently lifted me upwards. Turning my head, I caught a glimpse of my wife. Cecilia wrapped her arms around my chest and began swimming with slow, confident kicks toward the surface, powered by long fins. She seemed to be avoiding looking at Marci. Was she afraid?

Slowly, Cecilia turned her gaze toward me. She leaned her head softly against mine and pulled me into an embrace as she lifted me toward the approaching surface.

Looking back towards the depths, I saw Marci follow us, a short distance away. I wondered what she thought of us, these ill-adapted beings in her realm, one of whom she had shared a brief existence with. She had become somewhat of an enigma to us, and perhaps an aberration in the eyes of nature, through no fault of her own. We had no way of comprehending what she had become. Yet despite all this, she had evolved into something majestic in my eyes. She reminded me of Molly, one of the few great matriarchs I had come across on my journey. Both Marci and I had grown from this united experience, each in our own ways. It frustrated me no end that her perspective would never be revealed to me.

With slow strokes of her caudal fin, Marci followed us back to the ship. As we neared the ship, I saw Marci drop away into the depths. My last memory before the veil of unconsciousness fell upon me was of caring arms reaching out for me and lifting me upward.

Acknowledgments

Five years ago, *An Ocean Life* began life as a fable, cobbled up in my mind while commuting long hours to work. Unsatisfied with the limitations of the original story, I continually reworked the structure until it eventually filled a full-length novel. I have numerous people to thank for helping me complete this journey. I am grateful to my editors, Kenneth Zink and Tim Major, for their keen advice and sharp eyes. I am also grateful to Dr. Greg Skomal, Senior Fisheries Scientist at the MA Division of Marine Fisheries, for taking the time to read through my draft manuscript and checking it for factual errors. I want to thank the many drone operators whose videos on YouTube gave me a unique introspective on the private lives of great white sharks. I would also like to thank Jedd Wasson, who graciously let me use his photograph for the cover. Lastly, I am eternally grateful to my wife and children for putting up with my late hours and other shenanigans, all in the name of getting this book published.

About the Author

An engineer by vocation, Cotwell began his dive training in Copenhagen, Denmark in 1996, getting his CMAS certification under the tutelage of old school wreck divers. On an early morning dive in the winter of 1997 in freezing waters, the first stage of his regulator froze and free flowed, which marked his transition to diving in tropical waters. Since then, he has dived in the waters off New Guinea, Borneo, Bali, Sulawesi, Hawaii, and the Red Sea.

During his youth, Cotwell often daydreamed about traveling the world and writing about his exploits. Little did he know at the time that some of those "exploits" would seep into the stories he would eventually write. Today, T.R. Cotwell lives with his family near Seattle, WA.

True story:

"While diving a reef in Raja Ampat in 2000, a chain of islands off West Papua, my guide, a curious fellow by the name of Otto, began banging a metal rod against his tank to get my attention. He was about thirty yards upstream from me, and we were about fifty feet down. To get to him, I had to swim against the current, which was quite strong. When I reached the finger of coral he was hanging off, tired from my exertion and somewhat depleted of air, I noticed from the cacophony of bubbles that he was laughing profusely through his regulator. As I raised my head over the coral, I observed a very large shark circling the area. Annoyed with Otto's blase attitude, I hid myself in the coral and watched the shark, spellbound by its presence. The beast was uninterested in us and eventually swam off. Afterward, my guide was silent about the experience, and since none of the other divers saw the shark, it just became a 'fish story'. Through all the excitement, I never made an identification of the type of shark."